HOLDING HANDS WITH AN EXOTIC DANCER

K. Turk Osman

ISBN-13: 979-8-9959485-0-6

Cover design by: Ken Osman
Library of Congress Control Number: 2026911403
Printed in the United States of America

This book is dedicated to all those who have heard the call of the muse...

...but especially to those that answered.

CONTENTS

REGRET

Regret. It's a small word with a big impact, and it is denser and heavier than a collapsed star at the edge of the galaxy. Many people claim not to have any regrets and are proud to boast that if they could live their lives again, that they wouldn't change a single thing. However, if we are honest with ourselves, we realize that for the vast majority of us... this is a lie. It's a lie that we use to justify the choices that we made or didn't make. It's a lie to make us feel better about not taking that risk or risking too much. Most of all, it's a lie that we tell ourselves over and over again to make us feel better about where we are in life. But that doesn't mean that we don't occasionally think about what we could have done differently or what effect different choices would have had on our realities. So, the real question is, if we had the chance to do something over and take another path at a critical life juncture, would we?

This is a story of a man who gets that opportunity. Through a seemingly chance encounter, he gets to see how life could and would be different if he took another direction when making what is probably the greatest decision that anyone can make. This of course, is the choice of a life partner. While this opportunity is welcomed by him, like any great gift, it comes with a price. This price may include being bound to a new reality that did not exist before and in this potential new reality, this new path, there will be more choices to make and new challenges to face. Unfortunately, if this new reality is ultimately chosen, there will be loved ones and experiences that will disappear forever because they are not on the new path and never will be. And yes, that too will come with regrets as each different decision made on the new path will continue to present choices within choices like a Russian nesting doll.

Maybe regrets are inevitable on our human journey, but perhaps they are buffered by a person that completely fits our own narrative. On the other hand, living a new path may be more nightmare than dream. Is avoiding regret impossible? Probably. But could there also be a possibility that a major regret can be reconciled and even eliminated from a life's memory forever by going back in time to change a key decision? If there was, then that would be a story now, wouldn't it?

PROLOGUE

Tuesday, October 10th, 2000

Savannah had finally had enough. Enough promises, enough lies, enough excuses, and most of all, enough bruises on various different body parts. As she made her way to Penn Station from Chad's place in a rather dirty cab, she knew she looked like an absolute wreck with mascara laden tear tracks down her cheeks, and a blooming shiner under her left eye. Although he went to hit her open-handedly as he usually did, this time she flinched and ducked her head a bit when he drew back to slap her, and when the blow landed, the butt of his hand hit her face, and it hit with more impact than usual. She remembered her head exploding with stars that swam in her vision for what seemed like at least a minute, and she almost fell down but was able to recover quickly and fall into one of the two chairs that were in his small kitchen. As usual, Chad immediately tried to fix things by apologizing profusely while simultaneously grabbing a sack of peas out of the refrigerator and giving them to her like some sort of fucked up olive branch. She never told anyone about Chad's abuse, and tonight was just the same horrible nightmare that she had experienced with him for over a year now. But she had finally reached her limit, and it was time to do something about it.

Traffic slowed, which Savannah thought to be unusual this early on a Tuesday morning, but she really didn't care because it was only 4:15 and her train to Washington D.C. left at 7:02. Her best friend Kate lived in an adorable little flat on Q Street in Georgetown, and when Savannah called Kate and told her about the situation with Chad, she insisted that she come down immediately and stay for as long as she needed to so she could clear her head. Kate even paid for her ticket, which was fantastic because Savannah was down to exactly $389, a handful of clothes, and her grandfather's antique gold pocket watch, which was her most prized possession. In the last few months, Chad had maxed all their charge cards and ruined her credit while simultaneously kiboshing what was left of his own rating as well. They had $2.04 left in the checking account and none in savings. So basically, she was flat broke and after the tiny coffee shop that had provided her a job for the last five months went belly up last week, she had little prospect for any additional infusions of cash in the near term, either. Apparently, Washington D.C. was the answer, at least for now.

The driver reached Penn Station, she paid him and then grabbed her duffel bag and small suitcase. Currently, those items held everything she owned. She did have a room full of all her significant childhood possessions at her parents' home, but that home was halfway across the country in Boulder and while she would go there if she had to, she did not want to... at all. It's not that she didn't love her parents, because she did, and she knew that they loved her as well. However, they were never in favor of her move to New York in the first place. They begged her not to drop out of the University of Colorado and admonished her to finish what she had started. They pointed out that she was doing well there and only needed two more years to complete her bachelor's degree so that she could move on to law school as planned. They appealed to her rational side, and they were almost successful in convincing her to stay... until she met Tom. Once that happened, her rational side went into hibernation for a while, but she hoped that tonight was the night that side of her personality finally awakened.

She went into the ladies' room and looked at her reflection in the rather filthy mirror. She put the unwieldy old duffel bag on the counter, unzipped a small compartment, pulled out a plastic soap case, and proceeded to wash her face and reapply some makeup. She wanted to do this before she left the apartment, but as she climbed out of the bed, her plans changed. Chad, who had passed out in a drunken stupor after the make-up sex that she really did not want to have with him, groaned and stirred a bit when she got up so she was worried that he would wake if she tried to clean herself up in the bathroom of the small studio apartment. Because of this, she just grabbed as much as she could as quickly and quietly as possible and got the hell out.

The good news was that she felt much better when her freshening efforts were complete, and when she walked out of the bathroom and headed to the appropriate platform to wait for her train, she felt that she looked much better as well. Savannah always downplayed her beauty, but she was indeed a lovely girl. She was just a skosh above five feet tall with light blonde hair that extended just below her shoulders and had big brown eyes. Her skin still had the remnants of a summer tan that was earned several months ago at the Jersey shore and there were still small freckles on her nose and cheeks as well, but like the tan, those had begun to fade. Her only bad feature at the moment was the shiner on her left cheek, but that was effectively hidden with some makeup as well as the rather large sunglasses that she decided to wear, even though it was still dark outside.

If only Tom had not decided to return to his wife, maybe things would have been different. Maybe she could have had the success that she thought she would have when she left home. Maybe she would have been able to return home triumphant, and not with her tail between her legs. Maybe she would not have to worry about things like filing for bankruptcy, or worse yet, living at home with her parents again for an extended period. While they loved her, she was sure they were still angry at her. Whether or not that was true, one thing that was clear about the relationship was that if she returned, the house would be governed by their rules, and her father was very strict about that. She just didn't know if that would work for her anymore.

Savannah boarded the train at the appointed time, and it pulled out of the station three minutes behind schedule. She took out the cell phone that amazingly, had yet to be shut down by her carrier for non-payment and turned it off. Chad would be up soon, and when he awakened, she would be the first person that he called. She did not want to talk to him now, or ever again for that matter. It was time to put him in her past... forever.

The conductor came by and took her ticket as the train began to pick up speed as it chugged out of the station. She looked out the window as the first rays of sun stretched out to take a swipe at her eyes like a playful kitten who was being especially naughty. Fortunately for her, the sunglasses protected her from these metaphorical cat paws and as she relaxed a bit, she suddenly felt bone tired. She really needed to finish her play, *A Dollar at the Ritz*, but she was hopelessly bogged down in the middle of the third act and had been for two years now. However, finishing this play would not help her immediate problem, as she needed to talk Kate into taking her on as a roommate until she could get on her feet, or she would have to take that trip back to Boulder whether she liked it or not. Unfortunately, she was worried that the latter scenario was likely because although Kate had said, "as long as you need," what she really meant was "for a week or so." Kate was a sweetheart, but she also loved her privacy and even as a freshman in college, she had requested a single in the dorm where they both lived at the time. Savannah knew she would have to come up with another plan quickly if she was going to stay on the East Coast and right now, she didn't see any prospects for a quick way to make money, unless she did something like dancing at a gentlemen's club or even working as an escort. She had never seriously considered either option before, but maybe they would not be such bad ideas if she only had to do those things for a while... just more tests on her road to fame and fortune. She closed her eyes, and as the train began to pick up more speed, the constant dull ache that had been pervasive since the heel of Chad's hand met her cheekbone, intensified. She began to cry softly again, because at that moment, she simply could not see beyond the veil of failure, embarrassment, and hopelessness.

What Savannah didn't know as she sat and wept, was that a change was coming that would put things in perspective and that this change also had the potential to make everything right again. The change that was coming had the power to heal her in every way and make her who she really wanted to be now, and in the future. This change was transformational, and presented an opportunity that would only come once, and never again. When the opportunity came, she would have to trust, and she would also have to be brave, because she did not yet know the sacrifices that would be required to change her stars. This was probably good because if she had known that it was only going to get harder before it got better, Savannah may have disintegrated completely on the spot instead of just slowly falling apart over time. Right now, she just needed to keep it together for a little longer because if she didn't, then there will be no story at all for her. No crowds, no fame, none of the adrenaline that comes with the rush of seeing her work ever come to life on stage. Instead, Savannah Scott would be relegated to a life of anonymous mediocrity and if she was a quitter, she may have been able to swallow that bitter pill and accept her fate. But that was just not going to happen. This was true because Savannah was made of stronger stuff than that, and it was her goal to prove that to everyone.

CHAPTER 1: SURPRISE! YOU'RE A SCHMUCK.

Tuesday, November 25th, 2014

It is said that fortune favors the bold. If you marry that cliché with "nothing ventured, nothing gained," or "seize the day," it is obvious that humanity has placed a high value on taking risks for quite some time. Moreover, these risks have a shelf life and if not taken during their window of relevance, the chance is lost to take them at all. Sadly, there are those unfortunate souls out there who always seem to be a day late to the party which proves another cliché which is, "those who hesitate are lost." Therefore, if fortune smiles at you, or even flirts with you a bit, action is required, even if the price is high, as the important opportunities in this life are rare.

Jake DiVincenzo drove to the airport, listening to *The Frog* Prince by Keane as it was on Pandora, and for the first time in a while good fortune appeared to be grinning his way. For one thing, he had flown to Texas two days ago to meet with Tara Raines, a well-established romance writer, about doing an adaptation of her newest best-seller, *Little Tears*. The meeting had gone well and that was welcome news indeed. It had been a long time since he had done an adaptation of a book, and even longer since he had the opportunity to do one for a best-seller. So, he was really excited about the possibility that this project offered and ready to work on something that diverged from the formula-driven garbage that he usually wrote to pay the bills. He just hoped that his creativity would show up again as it did so easily years ago. Unfortunately, for the last four years or so, this creative side had been dormant and had yet to resurface.

Secondly, although he planned to meet with an author named John Cameron tomorrow about another adaptation, that meeting had now been cancelled. Apparently, the author had decided to dip his toes into screenwriting and now wanted to do it himself. This was good because Mr. Cameron had much less notoriety than Ms. Raines, and his story was trite and unimaginative as well. So, Jake really did not want the job. At all. He would not have even considered this type of project when he was in his prime as a screenwriter, but money was much tighter now, and he couldn't afford to turn up his nose at anything at this point. The cancellation effectively let him off the hook with this dog of a project and the best news was that neither his agent Sybil nor his wife Angela could give him grief about turning down work. That last detail was important, and perhaps more applicable to the latter person than the former.

The most exciting part for Jake was that he now could go home early and surprise his family. Over the last year, he had been on the road more than normal. This was mostly for endless meetings (that should have been held remotely) about feel-good holiday movies that were slated to air sometime in 2016. He always thought that being on the writing team for the Home and Hearth Network would be fantastic because it would offer a stable source of income, and he would not have to rely on the "home runs" that he had received in the past from several high-profile projects. But due to his creativity drought, none of those had come for a while, so the safety of the H&H network offered at least some refuge from the bill collectors. Sadly, his debt continued to grow each year as Angela's spending always outpaced what he brought home, and since she quit her job as a realtor, she didn't make any contributions herself, either. Fortunately, the H&H contract did not prohibit him from taking outside projects. This was very good because he really needed an adaptation job, as the situation was beginning to become very dicey was far as his personal finances were concerned. More than anything, he needed a break... just one.

He arrived at the DFW airport, turned in his rental car, and went through the security checkpoint. Security was always a pain in the ass, but today he needed more Preparation H than normal because it was backed up so far that he began to worry that he would miss his flight. In the end, he got through in the nick of time, and after running through the airport like O.J. Simpson from a commercial in the 70s, he reached the gate and boarded his flight. As he sat in the seat, settled in, and turned his phone to "airplane mode," he thought about O.J. and how his star had fallen after his wife and Ron Goldman were murdered. Although he was acquitted of their murders, it seemed obvious to many people in the world that he was indeed guilty. Although Jake was only 19 at the time, he was still fascinated by the case when it happened as well as the media circus that it ultimately became. As his mind continued to wander about other things that occurred in the Nineties, the plane reached the runway, and the engines howled as the takeoff began. When the Airbus took to the sky, he suddenly realized that he had not told Angela that he was coming home a day early. *Oh well,* he thought and then decided that this may be an opportunity to surprise her. She had been more distant than ever lately, so perhaps some flowers and a nice meal tonight may help her to open up about what has been bothering her. At least he hoped it did.

The plane reached cruising altitude, and he decided that some sleep would be welcome. However, before he closed his eyes, he looked through some pictures on his phone. His wife Angela was the human doppelgänger to the animated main character Princess Merida in the Disney movie *Brave*. Her full head of red hair was curly and long, and she had gorgeous green eyes that were especially apparent due to the fairness of her skin. At about 5 ½ feet tall, she was slender and kept herself very fit although the breast augmentation that she had a few years ago often made her look so top-heavy that sometimes Jake wondered if she would tip over. Nevertheless, she was indeed a beautiful woman, and he often caught his buddies greedily assessing her body whenever there was a gathering of their circle of friends.

While Angela could have been a Scottish princess, their daughter and son almost appeared to be unrelated to her. Since Jake's mother was of Nicaraguan descent, and his father's parents were born in Southern Italy, he had dark hair that was worn short, brown eyes, olive skin, and very strong genes. So, it was not a surprise that his twelve-year-old daughter Kira and his ten-year-old son Jacob Jr., both favored him and not their mother. As he looked at picture after picture of his family on his iPhone, he realized that he missed them quite a bit because he had been gone for two weeks in a row. Because of this, he decided to bring each of them a surprise. Since they all thought that he would return tomorrow, he knew he had enough time to go shopping on the way home from the airport because Angela would not miss him, and the kids were in school. He shut off his phone and closed his eyes because he still needed sleep, and in no time at all, it was upon him.

It seemed like he was only asleep for a few minutes when the flight attendant woke him and asked him to put his seatback in the forward position. The plane landed, and then he made his way off the aircraft and then out to the parking garage where he found his 1968 Jaguar E-Type Fixed Head Coupe which was still in immaculate condition despite its age. He drove to the mall and grabbed his son a few new Xbox games, while getting his daughter the new iPad that she had wanted for some time now. He then went to the grocery store where he picked up a dozen red roses and a bottle of Veuve-Clicquot that he planned to open with Angela later tonight after the kids were asleep. For some reason, she had almost completely turned off the sex faucet for him in the last six months or so and had only allowed him a trickle of marital satisfaction since. He wanted to see if he could figure out how to get his bedroom life back to where it was a year ago and resolved to do so tonight.

He pulled into the underground garage of his Santa Monica condo and parked in the spot next to his wife's BMW. When he did, he also noticed that his neighbor Chuck's new Corvette was in the garage as well. Jake thought this to be very odd primarily because Chuck was a lawyer who was a bona fide workaholic and was almost never home at this time. This would have been especially true this week because with Thanksgiving in two days, Chuck would be burning hours like crazy so he could clear his priorities and actually relax over the long weekend. He was also not one to take the entire holiday week off, and since his wife Lisa's car was not in the garage either, Jake figured that he may have come home sick. If that was the case, it must be bad, because he had never seen Chuck do this before. In fact, Chuck always bragged about not missing work for illness. It was sort of a badge of honor for him. Whatever the reason was for Chuck being home, Jake put it out of his mind as he got in the elevator to go to their unit on the top floor. The kids would not be home for a few hours, so Jake hoped that he may be able to get Angela to turn the faucet back on a little earlier than he had initially planned. It had been over 2 months for him, so he was feeling a bit hornier now than he'd expected.

Since he still wanted to surprise her, Jake opened the front door slowly and quietly and closed it the same way. He then put his bags on the dining room table, removed his tie and blazer, and put his wallet and iPhone on the small table by the door. He saw no sign of Angela, so he figured that she was probably napping. This was perfect, because he could open the champagne, put it on ice, and put the flowers in a vase as well. He went into the kitchen, did all these tasks, removed his shoes, and then walked into the bedroom with two flutes of bubbly in his hands. The good news for him was that when he walked in, she was laying there in the bed already naked, and only partially covered by the bedclothes. The bad news was that she wasn't alone.

Jake froze. Suddenly it felt like he was stuck in thick jelly and would be trapped forever in that moment like a prehistoric insect caught in amber. In that seemingly endless frame of time, he took it all in. Angela was asleep, and her long red hair looked as though it had been tossed by a small tornado. Chuck's meaty right arm was draped over her semi-covered torso, while he snored away beside her, oblivious to Jake's arrival in the doorway. Clothing was strewn everywhere around the base of the bedframe, and the room smelled like sex. So, apparently Chuck was not ill, or at least not in any physical way. Although he tried as hard as he could to quell the anger that was rising in him, as soon as she opened one eye and looked at him, he completely lost his cool.

"WHAT in the actual FUCK is going on, Angela?"

"Jake... you're home," she said while throwing Chuck's arm off her and sitting up. As she did this, she paused for a second while she wrapped the sheet around herself to cover her nakedness as if Jake was a stranger. "I... I don't know what to say."

"Then maybe Mr. Fabulous the lawyer does," said Jake. He was not as loud this time, but he was no less angry, and that was apparent to both Angela and her paramour. "What do you say ol' buddy? Was my wife a good fuck? Is this even the first time?"

"I know it looks bad Jake," said Chuck as gingerly as a cat who had just shit on the bed. "Look, I didn't mean for this to happen... Angela was supposed to have talked to you by now. I promise you Jake, it's not just sex. I didn't mean to hurt you man, but the fact is that we're in love. We just fit perfectly and as you can see; I'll take any risk necessary to be with her. I'm sorry man, but as they say, the heart wants what it wants."

Jake wanted to kick this dude's ass, and he knew that he could if he wanted to. While Chuck was a stout guy who worked out regularly and was into Cross Fit, Jake was a black belt in Jiu-Jitsu who also studied Muay Thai and his 6'2" frame made him about four inches taller than Chuckles as well. He was pretty sure he could put a severe hurting on him, and when he opened his mouth with the "heart wants what it wants line," he just about jumped on his ass. But Jake was 41 now and could neither afford to end up in jail with assault charges nor pay for the lawsuit that would almost certainly come from Chuck afterwards. He choked down his anger, took a deep breath, closed his eyes, and counted to twenty. He suddenly felt like he was in control of his emotions again, which was good. He was no less furious at both of them, but the anger was more distant now and not as sharp and insistent as it was only a hundred seconds ago. He suddenly knew exactly what to do.

"Angela, do you feel the same way?" He inquired to the top of her head because she was just staring at the ground and refused to meet his gaze. What a coward she turned out to be. "Is this why we have only had sex three times in the last six months? Because you were getting boned regularly by the neighbor? I honestly don't think that you could've come up with a more cliché scenario."

Angela raised her eyes to him, and he saw that they were red and puffy and that her cheeks were wet. She was sobbing softly now, and stupid Chuck was gently rubbing her back to show his support. Jake suddenly felt an urge to throw up and nearly did. It would certainly serve them right for being such assholes.

"Jake," said Angela in a thin little voice full of guilt, but not remorse, "I am so, so, sorry." She sobbed some more and then blew her nose on the sheet. Gross.

"Yes, I'm sure you are," he replied. "But you still didn't answer my question. Is he your guy? Do you want to run away with him and fall in love all over again? Are you looking for your fairy tale with him like Julia Roberts in *Pretty Woman*? Please let me know, it may be good material for me."

"Jake, we haven't been a loving couple for a while now, and you know that," she said composing herself a bit. "The good times have been gone for so long, that I barely even remember them, and you hardly even talk to me anymore. All you do is work, but the work is just... hollow because you seem to have lost your self-confidence as a writer. You no longer have any passion for what you do, and it shows. Why do you think that you don't get selected for any big adaptations anymore? Jake, when was the last time that you wrote something creative, really creative, and not the bullshit that you crank out for the Home and Hearth Network? Somewhere along the line you lost yourself, and when that happened, you lost me. I'm sorry Jake, but I can't live with you anymore. I can't see you decay any further, and while part of me will always love you, my heart now belongs to Chuck. He's right, I should've told you earlier, but I didn't want to ruin the holidays. The kids look so forward to them."

Jake's emotions seemed to be in a transformational state as he now found himself feeling quite frustrated with her. After all, she was not inaccurate with her comments because he had buried himself in his own routine to provide for the family and was actually *afraid* to take a chance on a new idea because he did not want to... get stuck... yet again. However, while he acknowledged that he did share some of the blame for the decay of their relationship and possibly even most of it, how she handled the situation was completely fucked up. Worse yet, Chuck did not seem to know that screwing your neighbor's wife was a serious violation of that unwritten set of rules which is commonly known as "Guy Code."

"So, what does Lisa think about this, Chuck? Does she even know?" Jake asked this thinking he knew the answer. As it turned out, he didn't.

"Jake, Lisa filed for divorce four months ago, and she's been seeing another guy on the side for about a year," said Chuck sheepishly. "We wanted to keep it quiet until after the New Year because her parents are visiting us for Christmas. I guess the cat is out of the bag now."

"Angela, you don't need to say another thing, I'll get my shit and go," said Jake turning back to her after a pregnant pause. "For the kids' benefit, let's just say that I had more work come up suddenly but that I'll be back for Thanksgiving. We can fake our way through dinner and come up with a more permanent plan next week."

"OK," said Angela softly with new tears sprouting out of the corners of her eyes. "Jake, again, I'm really sorry, I should've told you earlier. It should've never gotten to this point. I hope you can forgive me for this someday. Maybe we could even be friends?"

"You should have thought of that earlier," said Jake ruefully but also in a matter-of-fact tone. "I'll do whatever I need to do with you to raise our children, but that's it. I don't want a friendship with you or Chuck now or in the future. You both can simply fuck off."

Angela and Chuck just sat like statues as Jake grabbed a large gym bag and stuffed it with clothing and two pairs of shoes. He also packed his two other Rolexes, and a jewelry box that contained several important and valuable items such as his grandmother's engagement ring. In all it took about fifteen minutes, and Angela and Chuck were silent the entire time. The last thing that Jake did as he left the bedroom was remove his wedding band and casually toss it to Angela. She caught it, he glared at her one final time and then left the room.

Jake then exited the condo, took the elevator down to the parking garage, loaded the Jag, and left the complex. His head was swimming with emotions, and he was having a hard time focusing properly, so he decided to go to his buddy Mike's place until Thanksgiving. Mike had a great piece of property in Topanga Canyon that his dad bought cheap in the late Sixties. It was high-rent territory now with several prominent celebrities living in the area and though Mike had been offered some decent cash for his property in the past, he never sold it and was now sitting on a gold mine. His house was hand built by an old hippie in the early Eighties, and while it wasn't large, it was clear that the hippie knew his stuff as it was indeed built very well. As he headed north to Malibu, he turned on the radio and as if some cosmic force was at play, Dashboard Confessional's *I Know About You* was playing. This song, which is all about a guy finding out about his girl's infidelity, could not have fit the situation any better than if he had hand-picked it himself for the occasion. Until that point, he was very angry but as he listened to the song, the anger washed away and was replaced by sadness. Surprisingly, this sadness was not because he would no longer be married to Angela. She had pretty much given up on him years ago, and deep down he knew it, so breaking up was probably only a matter of time. No, this sadness was rooted in the fact that his children would now have to live in a shattered household, and that broke his heart. The next few months would be difficult for them and while he did not want to fast-forward his life, he truly wished that he could do just that until the divorce was finalized. One thing that he knew for sure was that he did not want to jump into another relationship anytime soon. Instead, he would just bury himself in even more work and crank out the predictable made-for-TV dramas like geese crank out turds. He suddenly felt very tired, and as he turned down Mike's rather steep driveway, he just wanted to climb into a bed and fall asleep. The good news was that Mike did not have any houseguests at the moment, so the guestroom was his. He grabbed his stuff, had a quick beer with his host, and then went in and immediately passed out on the queen-sized bed. He did not remember dreaming, but if he had it would have been of nothing but sad things.

CHAPTER 2: AN UNEXPECTED INVITATION

Thursday, September 8th, 2016

It was now time for Jake to move forward with his life and he knew it. The divorce had been final for over a year now, but in truth, he had only seen his ex-wife a total of six times since he found her in bed with Chuck, and two of these times included the very awkward Thanksgiving dinner two days after and Christmas Day a few weeks later. Angela stubbornly tried to have a friendship with him, but he wanted none of it. He was not angry at her any longer for what she did to *him*, but he could never forgive her for Kira's tears on the day he left the condo for good, or Jake's social withdrawal after his dad was gone which kept him in counseling to this day. His kids missed him badly, and since he had moved across the country to live in Northern Virginia, he could not see them as regularly now, either. So, it was a sad situation all around, and he moved through life in a funk much of the time when he didn't have to be cheerful at a social gathering or at work. He learned not to mope early on in his return to single life because there was nothing worse than semi-enthusiastic positivity from someone who wanted to take him on as a personal project where the main objective was "fixing" him. Therefore, he faked a good attitude whenever there was a chance that do-gooders were around, and generally, they would move on to other prey. However, this did not stop the endless tries by amateur yentas to find him a "nice girl." He figured that since this was inevitable, he could at least cope with these wannabe matchmakers because at least they did not have that damn sympathetic look on their face when they spoke of their possible love connections, even if these connections had no potential whatsoever.

The reasons for him relocating were twofold. For one thing, his parents still lived in his childhood home in a neighborhood known as Waynewood, which was just south of Alexandria and accessible via the George Washington Parkway. As a youngster, he and his friends would routinely ride to Mount Vernon on the bike path that ran adjacent to the Parkway and often went fishing on the way home. Due to the level of pollution in the Potomac River at the time, they never ate the fish, but they always caught and released something and had a great time just being kids. His parents were now getting on in age, and since his dad had his first fall last year, he really felt that he needed to be closer to them.

The second reason that he relocated was because of work. The Home and Hearth Network was purchased by a much larger parent company that also purchased several other channels at the same time. Someone at the corporate office must have liked his work ethic so he was hand-picked for a new channel that was known simply as the Swoon Network.

The pay was a good deal better than H&H and since the new headquarters were in Roslyn, right across the Key Bridge from Georgetown, the move made complete sense, even though it meant that he would see his children far more infrequently than he liked.

When the divorce was initially filed, his first inclination was to go for custody. He had a very close relationship with both kids and often thought that their bonds to him were closer and deeper than they were to her. After all, they favored him in looks and for the most part, in personality as well. Tragically for Jake, none of that matters to a judge, and while Angela may have been a cheating slut, she was not a bad mother. In fact, she was and currently remains very active in both of her children's lives. The reality was that she had always supported all their interests enthusiastically. So, whether she had to become the president of the booster club for Jake Jr's little league baseball team or serve as the coordinator of one of Kira's basketball fundraisers, she was always happy to help. Basically, she was a superhero mom and because of this, every lawyer buddy that he knew advised him that there was no way in hell that he would get custody, even if he didn't have the crazy travel schedule that he did at the time.

As for Angela herself, she did not ask Jake for any alimony and married Chuck barely two months after the signatures were dry on the divorce papers. Well before the divorce was final, Jake and Angela sold the condo and split the proceeds. She then moved in with Chuck who had a much easier divorce because his wife Lisa (another, even more successful attorney) did not pursue alimony either and they had no children at all. Jake was required to pay child support, but he did so gladly and also provided each child with spending money each month as well. Additionally, he donated nice chunks of cash to their 529 savings plans so that they would both have more than enough money for college. Not surprisingly, both Jake Jr. and Kira worked hard to involve him with what was going on in their lives and he loved to communicate with them on social media although he was still learning all the arcane rules that the younger generation used when posting. At least he had that, otherwise he would've probably just locked himself at home each night and either drink himself to sleep or let modern pharmaceutical chemistry do that for him instead.

Jake's apartment was in Tyson's Corner, Virginia so it did not take him very long to get to work each day. Of course, this was by design because proximity to work was one of his main requirements when he was on the hunt for a place to live. At only about 1,200 square feet, it was not a big place, but it had a small master with two additional bedrooms that were set up specifically for and by each kid. Jake Jr.'s room had a baseball theme with bunk beds while Kira had a WNBA theme and a nice queen-sized bed which was also just about the largest bed that would fit in the room. The kids had gone with him to pick up every single piece of furniture and had also picked out all the other décor that worked with each theme as well. As for Jake himself, his room was very Spartan with a plain bed and a few sticks of Scandinavian furniture from Ikea. His living and dining rooms were decorated like his bedroom, and only a few wall hangings here and there which made his place look more like the waiting room of a doctor's office than an apartment where someone lives every day.

Jake looked at his Rolex Explorer II and noticed that it was 7:25 p.m. as he continued to awaken from the nap that he had taken immediately upon returning home after a long, unproductive day at work. He was co-writing a script for a particularly cheesy Christmas movie with a young female writer named Jenny who was really into bizzarro plot twists that did nothing but make the story more confusing. She was also a raging control freak who was often overcaffeinated and threw an absolute fit if she didn't get her way. So, Jake had been butting his head with her regularly on what should have been an easy "former small-town girl returns from the big city to save the town on Christmas" theme and so far, the entire project had taken twice as long as it would have if he had done it himself. The saddest fact of all was that out of all her weird ideas for the story, the only one that he had been successful at quashing so far was a weird little plot line where the main character's granddad was reincarnated as a mouse named Ziggy. Like all magical mice, Ziggy whispers in the heroine's ear to tell her about her big-city fiancé's infidelity so she will leave him and marry the former flame from high school instead. As it happens, said flame is now an unemployed lumberjack who is not working due to a fear of heights that manifested itself later in life, and he now had crippling headaches whenever he thought about trees. Since she was a big-city psychologist, she helps him past his phobia, falls in love with him, finally leaves the cheating boyfriend, and somehow saves the town on Christmas as well. And this was all because of Ziggy.

As he climbed out of bed and went to take a piss, he mused that if he told people about her ideas, they would probably think that he was making up the whole thing. Maybe he should just let her have complete control of the story and see where it led? Whatever the answer was, he would not be rid of her anytime soon as she was the daughter of the parent company's CFO. Oh, the horror of a merry holiday season, indeed.

Jake walked into the kitchen, opened the fridge, and realized that all he had was three IPAs, a ubiquitous styrofoam box that contained leftovers from some restaurant that he visited weeks ago, some old milk, and a few condiments. So, unless he wanted to go to the store, he needed to go out for dinner or get take-out to eat in, which was pretty much the norm anyway. Jake groaned, because he was bone tired, and suddenly decided that the three IPAs alone may be enough this evening. Just then, his phone rang.

"Hello," said Jake in his usual bland manner.

"JAKE! Buddy! It's Roger bro! How in the fuck are you?"

"Roger!" Exclaimed Jake excitedly. "Damn good to hear from you, brother! Sadly, I must admit that I've been better. My divorce was final about a year ago and Angela got custody, so I'm missing my kids like crazy, but otherwise I'm good. How are you? How's Elise? You guys ever gonna have any kids?"

"That answer would be a negative, I'm afraid," said Roger. "We split up as well. My fault entirely, too. I let some co-ed that I met at the UVA homecoming game a few years ago talk me into being her sugar daddy for a while. I paid her rent and visited her for some good sex a couple times a month for about three months. Unfortunately, I had to end the entire thing because she was getting a bit... clingy. You know, texting me on my main phone, sending nudes... shit like that. The bad news for me was that she was a bit of a psycho who also e-mailed Elise several pictures of us together after I cut her loose. I think that we're naked in at least half of them. Anyway, that was it for me with Elise, and I also had to change all my phone numbers and stop using social media to escape my sugar baby as well. I know you may judge me for this, but I'm not that upset that it happened. Elise and I were never really in sync after the second year of our marriage. We had almost no common interests or friends, and we pretty much stopped having sex which was why I turned to the college chick in the first place. Don't get me wrong, it was a shitty thing to do to her, and I wish that I just had enough guts to end things with her sooner. But the freedom that I have now is awesome and I get laid more now than I did in college! You used to be quite the stud; I am sure it's the same for you, right?"

"Unfortunately, you mis-remember, my brother," said Jake. "You were always the stud; I was just lucky enough to land a date or two from the bevy of gorgeous girls that you left in your wake of charisma."

"OK, I guess you're right," chuckled Roger. "But my

question is the same, do you have any honeys in your life? If not, I highly recommend a sugar baby... unless she is psycho, of course."

"I'm on my own, Roger," said Jake somewhat dejectedly. "No big deal really. Just haven't found the right girl. As for the sugar babies, I think I'll pass. It doesn't sound like the sex is worth the drama."

"Maybe not," said Roger. "But I'm an idiot, I guess. I've two new sugar babies right now! This time, I had them sign contracts, so I should be good. Anyway, that's not why I am calling. I'm calling because Billy Dee is getting married. Can you believe it? Billy fucking Dee, Lando himself, is finally settling down! I never thought I'd see it happen."

"Billy Dee" Roberts was a fraternity brother in the Kappa Sig house at the University of Virginia. Lawrence or Larry was his real first name, but he became known as Billy Dee due to his resemblance to Billy Dee Williams. Naturally, he was also called Lando because of Billy Dee's most remembered role in the Star Wars franchise, and he was a party animal extraordinaire. Billy Dee had never been close to being engaged in the past, and just like Roger he seemed to prefer an endless stream of girls much younger than he was. The fact that he was getting married was a shock. Jake thought that it may even be a sign of the apocalypse.

"So, how old is she?" Asked Jake.

"I think she's 23 or 24, but that's not important. I've met her, and she's a very old soul. She's also hot as hell; I think she's from New Zealand or something."

"So, are you inviting me to the wedding?"

"Damn, always stealing my thunder, Jake," said Roger, chuckling again. "Yes, he wants you, and me, and Big Dog, and Slug, and even Prop Head to be there for him! We've all sent an RSVP, but we couldn't find you to see if you could be there until now. Of course, *I* was able to figure out where you were! Damn, I'm good! Anyway, can you come? The bachelor party is in Miami Beach and the wedding is at Disney two days later. Fuckin' Billy Dee is pulling out all the stops!"

"When is it?"

"The bachelor party is on December 14th and then there's welcome and rehearsal dinners the next two nights with the wedding itself on the evening of the 17th. Billy Dee's paying for everything and we're all planning on showing up the night of the 13th so we can hang out a bit before it all gets started. Oh, and Billy Dee wants us all to stand with him as groomsmen. Since I'm the best man, I'm in charge of setting this up."

"This year?"

"Of course, this fuckin' year you bozo," said Roger. "So, you in?"

"Sure, sounds good," said Jake. "Fortunately for you assholes, I have nothing going on until my kids come for Christmas, so send me the details by e-mail, and I'll be there. I'll text you my e-mail address. You should know that I wouldn't miss Billy Dee's wedding for anything."

"Awesome, Jake the Snake will be in the house! I'll let Billy Dee and the guys know. Anyway, I gotta go, I have a conference call with our Tokyo office in a few. Take it easy man... and remember what I said about sugar babies. You really should give one a try! Later man!"

With that, Roger hung up. Jake always liked Roger, and he also admired him for his success in the business world. Roger had recently taken over as the CEO of a fairly large IT security firm and over the past two years, the company had increased revenue by 28% and profit by over 40%. But as good as he was with business; he was equally bad in relationships with women. The fact was that Roger was never faithful to any woman that he dated in college, and it looked as if he hadn't changed since. He may have told him that the "sugar baby incident" was the reason for the breakup with his wife, but in all likelihood, it was just the time that he got caught. Elise was a smart girl, and she was damn good-looking, too. In fact, she and Jake dated for a minute or two during their senior year at UVA. They had a decent relationship, and even had sex a few times, but neither felt the magical euphoria that usually accompanies couples who are falling in love. They remained friends after the breakup, and Jake was the one who introduced her to Roger. The weird thing is that Elise knew about Roger's reputation and his tendency to wander from bed to bed but married him anyway. Jake knew this because one afternoon, she met him for lunch and told him that she knew about Roger's cheating nature, but that she loved him despite this and seemed to think that she could change him. If any woman could have made Roger faithful, it would have been Elise because at one time Roger was very much in love with her as well and told Jake as much. The fact that she left him meant that Roger was probably doomed to single life for the rest of his days and apparently, he had opted for a steady diet of sugar babies, parties, and most likely, drugs as well. He just hoped that these metaphorical sweets would not ultimately rot out the teeth of his soul.

For the most part, Billy Dee was just like Roger, if not a bit worse as far as relationships with the opposite sex were concerned. To begin with, Billy Dee was an absolute legend in the Greek world in college. He was a tall guy, about 6'4," and could out chug anyone he faced, do more shots than a Cossack, and talk the panties off just about any girl that he laid his eyes on. Billy Dee was also the total package as he was brilliant and came from an extremely wealthy family in Massachusetts. He literally grew up on a yacht and often threw money around like it was confetti. He was especially fond of "making it rain" at strip joints and strippers flew to him like gnats to a light bulb as soon as he walked in. He usually walked out with a few as well.

The fact that some woman had convinced Billy Dee to give up his amateur status was almost unbelievable. He wondered how long it would last but figured that he would probably cheat on his 23-year-old bride before she turned 25. That was the problem with guys like Roger and Billy Dee. They just could not keep it in their pants, and one woman was never enough. As Jake thought about this, he knew he could never be like them. For one thing, he had a daughter that was becoming a young woman. He certainly would not like someone like Roger or Billy Dee meeting Kira, and if he found out in the future that her boyfriend was cheating on her, he would probably want to kick that dude's ass. However, that was not the only reason that he couldn't be like his fraternity brothers. The thing was that Jake really wanted to be in love. In fact, he originally thought that he and Angela were soulmates, but time had proven differently. If he could find someone of substance... someone like Elise... he thought that perhaps he could give this love thing another chance. Should he give her a call? Would it be worth it to give it another try now that they were both older and had grown as adults? Would it be weird with Roger if he did? He honestly didn't know, but one thing that he knew for sure was that he was not going to try a sugar baby. He had no interest in explaining who Curt Cobain was or who Billy Corrigan is and what famous bands each fronted to some girl who listens to K-Pop. He had even less interest in competing for attention with his sugar baby's cell phone after the sex was over which basically meant, most of the time. No, that was not him and would never be. Ever.

It was now just about 8:00, and Jake was still debating about if he should eat something in addition to the two beers that he had already consumed. He finally decided that he should eat solid food, so he ordered a pizza and when it was delivered, he quickly gobbled it down alone while watching the Carolina Panthers play the Denver Broncos on TV. He could have cared less about either team but watched anyway because it took his mind off the day and let him just zone out a bit. As fate would have it, it turned out to be a good game with Denver coming back from a 17-7 halftime deficit to win 21-20. After the game was over, he took a quick shower, put on a t-shirt and shorts, and laid down on his bed. He thought about Billy Dee's wedding again for the umpteenth time and wondered how it would go. Since all his college buds were going to be there, he knew it would be lots of fun, and that it would probably take him a week to recover from all the drinking that he'd do. He also wondered if there would be anyone that could possibly catch his interest while he was there. After all, weddings were one of the best pick-up scenarios around with lots of young single ladies looking to get caught up in the moment and find someone to spend the evening with. The problem was that the young ladies at this particular wedding were likely to be of the same age as the bride, and this returned Jake to his earlier thought process about sugar babies and why he wanted to avoid them. So, it was likely that he would not find his soulmate, or even an age-appropriate companion at this event, and he certainly did not want a one-night stand with the president of the Justin Bieber Fan Club, either. Basically, he would just have to get nice and toasted and then find his way back to his hotel room each night before he did something that he was certain to regret later.

He stared at the ceiling and then decided to turn on some music. He grabbed his phone, connected it to his Bluetooth clock-radio, and began to stream music from his favorite channel on Pandora. Just then, the song *Iris* by the Goo Goo Dolls began to play. He always loved that song, and tonight, in the mood that he was in, it transported him to a very specific memory with a very specific girl. It was a memory of a moment that could have been more, but while that flame of promise burned as bright as magnesium on fire for an instant, like the magnesium blaze, it went out just as quickly. Right now, he wished that he could go back and make a different decision the night he left her because maybe, just maybe, he could've been happy now. As his mind continued to wander, he thought of other moments, with other girls, that could have all potentially developed into something more and at this second, he regretted not taking more chances, and trusting in where the moments really wanted to take him. When he had these chances, he was afraid. Afraid of making the critical decision with these other girls that would allow him to take the next step with any of them. Instead, he opted to settle for the sure thing when he finally chose his life partner, and he did this because he always wanted the safest option. Of course, safe options are not supposed to eventually sleep with the neighbor, and this thought deepened and fueled his regret fiesta so much that it made him get up to take an Ambien so he could shut off his mind with some chemical brute force.

He laid back down and thought of Kira and Jake Jr. and realized that if he had taken any other path, they would not be with him. He truly loved them, would sacrifice everything for them, and could not contemplate a life without them. Right now, he needed to leave the regret in the past and appreciate his children as a more than adequate reward for the path that he did take. But even as he thought this, he still had a residual image of one face in his mind's eye as he fell asleep, and it was neither his daughter nor his son. His last thought was that if he was presented with another opportunity to take the other path with the owner of that face, that it would be tough not to take it... regardless of the cost.

CHAPTER 3: OFF TO CLOUD CITY

Tuesday, December 13th, 2016

Jake jumped out of the shower, then proceeded to shave, trim his short beard and mustache, and get dressed. He had packed up earlier and his suitcase was already at the door. He just needed to put on his shoes and meet the Uber driver in five minutes. In the past, he would have driven his Jaguar to the airport, but that car was currently in storage as he had no garage at present. In fact, he currently had no other car at all as the lease was up on his Audi A4, and he already turned it back into the dealer two days ago. They tried like hell to get him to lease another car, but he was thinking about getting a pickup truck this time, and that's one vehicle that Audi does not make. In the end, he decided that he'd wait until he got back from Billy Dee's wedding and go truck shopping then.

The Uber arrived at the appointed time, and the trip to Dulles was uneventful. Of course, it was noon on a Tuesday and the holiday traveling had not yet begun, so that was probably the reason for the relatively light traffic. He exited the Uber upon arrival at the airport, went through security (which was not too bad today), and made his way to the gate. His plane was not scheduled to board for thirty more minutes, so he decided to call his daughter because she had texted him earlier and let him know that she was sick in bed at home. He selected her number on his iPhone, dialed, and a picture of her beautiful face filled the screen.

"Hello Daddy," said Kira in a sleepy voice. "I feel like crap, so I was taking a nap. Are you on the way to your wedding?"

"I am sweetie. I was going to ask you how you felt, but your voice pretty much tells the answer. Are you taking your Vitamin C?"

"Yes Daddy, of course! I've a headache too, but I just took some Motrin a few minutes ago, so hopefully it will be better soon. I also took some decongestants."

"Well, I hope you get better fast," said Jake whose eyes were a bit misty. He always missed his kids, but when one of them was sick, he missed them even more because he wanted to be there to provide some extra care. "I wish that I could give you a big hug to make you feel better."

"Me too, Daddy!" she said with discernable sadness in her voice. "But the good news is that we'll be there to see you on the 26th! I am soo excited, and Jake is too! I also have some good news; do you want to hear it?"

"Sure, Sugar Cookie."

"Aww, you used to call me that when I was little! Anyway, I started in the JV game the other day and scored *twelve points*! Can you believe it? The coach said that I might make the varsity team as a freshman! Isn't that awesome?"

"That's my girl!" He said enthusiastically. "Keep up the good work baby, I would say that you are going to be great someday, but the fact is that you already are."

"You're the best daddy ever; you know that don't you?"

"Thanks Kira, I love you and Jake more than anything. Anyway, my flight is boarding soon, and it sounds like you could use some more sleep. Give Jake my love and tell him that I'll call him tomorrow after school. I'll probably be pretty busy tonight."

"Will do Daddy," said Kira with thick sleepiness beginning to overtake the short burst of enthusiasm in her voice. "I love you too, and even though you won't talk to her, Mom cares about you also. Be careful in Miami! I don't want to have to break into my college savings to bail you out!"

"Got it sweetie! I better go. Feel better soon."

With that, Jake hung up and put the phone in the inner pocket of his sport coat. He did not address Kira's comment about Angela because he didn't want to say anything negative about her to their daughter. Even though Angela still tried to resurrect a friendship with him, he had zero interest in doing so. He wondered if that would ever change and knew that she and their children would continue to try to get them back on friendly terms. But right now, all he could think of was her betrayal, and the flame of that memory had not cooled one iota in over two years.

Jake boarded the plane, plugged in his headphones, and promptly fell asleep. He awakened just as the plane was landing, and he was off in short order as he had a seat in the front. Billy Dee had arranged for a driver to pick him up and he made small talk with the driver about South Florida sports on the way to the uber-swanky Fontainebleau Hotel on Miami Beach.

Roger was right, Billy Dee really had pulled out all the stops.

Jake checked in and went to his room. When he opened the door, he was rewarded with a beautiful view of the ocean and a bottle of Dom Perignon chilling on the dresser next to a plate of chocolate-covered strawberries. Wow, this wedding was setting up to be an epic event indeed! He began to unpack his small suitcase when the phone rang. He walked to the phone and answered it.

"Alpha Eps bro!" Roger's voice exclaimed from the receiver. The noise in the background was quite loud, which indicated that he was probably at a bar and was already in full party mode. "Get your ass down here! I am with Slug and Billy Dee, and we are already two mojitos in! Big Dog flew into Lauderdale and is on the way, and Prop Head will be in a bit later. "

"Alpha Eps to you too!" Said Jake. That greeting is unique to the Kappa Sigma fraternity, and he had not used it in years. It was good to be back with his college buddies again. "Let me change into my bathing suit and I'll be down in five. Sounds like you're by the pool, right?"

"Hell yeah, mi bruddah! Oh, and by the way, the honeys here are fucking gorgeous! I've not seen this much floss since my last dental visit."

"Alright, I'll see you soon!" With that Jake hung up the phone, finished unpacking, put on his swimsuit, and headed down to the pool.

He walked out on to the pool deck and realized that Roger wasn't lying. If you're the sort of guy that likes a beautiful girl in her mid-twenties wearing little to no clothing at all, then Miami Beach is your sort of jam. If he was being honest, Jake was a bit overwhelmed by it all. But, as overwhelmed as he was, it certainly did not mean that he didn't notice what was going on. He thought that every sort of debauched fantasy in the last fifty years could have been hatched here, and the excessive display of wealth appeared to be the norm. He moved in a fog, but before long he noticed Roger and Billy Dee waving at him, so he moved that way. He got to where they were and exchanged hugs with all of them.

"Alpha Eps!" Said Slug enthusiastically. Adam "Slug" Bennett was the same age as Jake, but not in nearly as good of shape physically. In fact, at only 5'6", and weighing in at what had to be 225 pounds, Slug did not appear to be in very good shape at all. To make things worse, he had Bozo the Clown hair around the sides of his head (but not on the top) and seemed to favor fashion from when they were all in college together twenty years ago. Basically, he was a short, fat, slob, but his saving grace was his ability to be funny, and funny he always was.

"Good to see you, Slug," said Jake. "You ever going to get married?"

"Like it's worked out so well for you guys?" Inquired Slug while looking at Jake and Roger.

"I guess you got a point there, Slug," said Jake. "But hopefully Billy Dee here will have better luck!"

"Shit, Snake, Layla is one fine woman. There's no way I'm gonna stray from her," said Billy Dee. "She brought a pack of babes with her too my brother, so you should have your pick if you're interested. Rosco tells me that you're single again. 'Bout time to get back in the game!"

"I told him he needs to get a sugar baby, but he doesn't seem interested," said Roger who was also known as Rosco in college. Nicknames are part and parcel of the fraternity experience, and everyone had one. Nothing fit Roger Scoville well except Ken Doll, because he looked like one, but he hated it and made sure that it didn't stick. In the end Rosco (which was formed by smashing the first two letters of his first name with the first three letters of his last name) won out and it was used extensively in the last three years at UVA. "He may change his mind when he sees the bridal party."

"Gents, I'm here to get really drunk and spend some time catching up with you guys, but I've no interest in having sex with a girl who does not know that Pink Floyd is a band and not a person, and who will likely spend most of the time on her phone when we are not actually screwing," said Jake.

"Your choice, Snake," said Billy Dee, turning to a very sexy Hispanic female bartender in a skimpy outfit. "I need a mojito for my friend, senorita! Mas rum in this one por favor, he needs it!" She smiled brightly, nodded, and began to make the concoction. Just then, a booming voice rang out above the din of the music and conversation around the bar.

"Alpha Eps motherfuckers!" Said the voice of Big Dog who was an absolute giant of a man and moving their way. His real name was Antoine Jacobs, and he was an African American gent with striking green eyes who started at right guard for UVA all four years and then played for several teams in the NFL for ten years after school. He was now a motivational speaker and had a pretty good career going in that arena. He had also gained a lot of weight since his playing days which made him even more massive than Jake remembered. He arrived at the spot where the rest of them stood, and on the way, Billy Dee changed his mojito order from one drink to two by looking at the bartender and holding up two fingers as he flashed his million-dollar smile at her. He was getting married in three days and still flirting, but this was classic Billy Dee.

One mojito turned to three for Jake and after about an hour, Alex Yin, otherwise known as Propeller Head or Prop Head for short, showed up to complete their party. Prop Head was of Asian descent and looked like he could be in his late twenties. He was the managing partner in a large consulting firm and was constantly on his phone as the others were recounting college stories while drinking and ogling young ladies. At about 7:30, they all went up and showered and then headed out to Joe's Stone Crab for an awesome dinner. Jake finally got back to his room at about 1:45, full of expensive food and drink and drunk as a skunk. He didn't even get undressed before he passed out.

The next morning, Jake awakened early feeling very rough, but instead of taking a shower, he went down to the pool for a swim. That made him feel better and as he went back to his chaise lounge to dry off, he saw Prop Head at the far end of the pool area and yelled at him. Prop Head waved and came his way. In seconds, he was right there with him.

"Hey there Snake, I was just going for a walk on the beach. You want to go?" Inquired Prop Head.

"Sounds good man, but let's grab some coffees first!"

The two old friends grabbed cups of joe and headed to the beach. They made small talk about the evening before and all the crazy stories that they had recounted, and as they reached the sand, Prop Head turned a bit more serious.

"So, Snake, I heard that you found your wife in bed with the neighbor. That really sucks man. I always thought you guys made a good couple."

"Me too Prop, me too. Sadly, my job took me away too much and sucked the life out of the relationship. She was also disappointed that I wasn't using my talents to their fullest and that the job was sucking the life out of me, as well. She wasn't wrong, but how she left me was pretty fucked up. She keeps trying to forge a friendship, but I've no interest. It just hurts too much."

"What do you mean by that, bro?"

"By what?"

"Not using your talents to their fullest, what does that

mean? Don't you have a good gig as a staff writer for some TV channel? I just don't understand," said Prop Head.

"OK man, here's the story. When Angela and I first got married I was able to land two high-profile adaptations that ended up being very successful movies. I then began to write an original screenplay that two major producers were very excited about when I pitched the concept to them. Money was flowing in by the buckets, and life was generally happy for us as Angela's real-estate business was thriving as well. I really thought we were on our way."

"So, what happened?"

"Basically, the crash of 2008 killed both Angela's real estate business and the potential funding for my original screenplay as well. While both producers were still interested in my original project, everything was put on hold indefinitely. I still had some royalties rolling in and we sold a vacation home in Colorado to make ends meet, but I became worried that if I didn't pick up a steady job fast, that we'd lose the condo in Santa Monica because our spending consistently outpaced our income. For some reason, Angela could never downgrade her lifestyle enough to make ends meet with less." Jake paused for a moment before continuing. The memory of that time was still painful. "Even worse, sometime during 2010 I lost my way on my original project, which was probably about 70% complete, and literally could not move the story towards any resolution at all. So, I finally shelved the entire thing and after blowing two additional adaptation opportunities, I took an offer from my agent to join the writing team for the Home and Hearth Network in 2011. Instead of becoming the next big thing in Hollywood, I settled for steady income writing formula-based feel-good stories that could be cranked out quickly and produced cheaply because they usually involved washed out sitcom stars whose careers had never progressed beyond TV. The job paid the bills, but just barely, and surprisingly it involved a ton of travel as well. Recently, I have taken a job with another network that is slightly more upscale and pays better, but it is the same sort of crap with slightly bigger budgets and marginally better actors. Sadly, my original screenplay is still shelved, and I've done nothing to get it moving again.

"Ahh, now I know what Angela meant about wasting your potential," said Prop Head, beginning to understand.

"Her exact words the last time that I saw her were that I'd lost my passion for living. I was very sad and distant for a while, so I'm sure that's the main reason that she started a relationship with the next-door neighbor. The fact that his marriage was disintegrating as well created a perfect storm, and now I find myself alone, missing my kids like crazy, and no closer to moving forward with my original work than I was in 2010 when I put it in the deep freeze. Honestly man, this wedding is just what I need. Maybe you guys can help me out of my rut?"

"Man, I'm sorry to hear all this. You should've given me a call! I mean, I'm busy as hell and the wife and kids eat up most of my free time, but I always have time for a pledge brother! I agree with the guys that a quick fling with a young lady may help also, although Rosco's sugar baby idea seems morally bankrupt, so I'm not advocating that."

"Believe me, I've tried to find someone to spend time with since I left Angela," said Jake. "But online dating has not panned out, the bar scene sucks, and the setups from friends have not worked, either. I did date a pretty fifth grade teacher for a few weeks who was also recently divorced, but after the fourth date she started hinting at marriage and I'm just not ready for that level of commitment yet, and maybe never again. Plus, she hated football so that wasn't ever going to work."

"No, definitely not," chuckled Prop Head. "How about

someone from the past? I know that you and Rosco's ex used to date in college... what was her name?"

"Elise, Elise was her name."

"Yeah Elise! I know it sounds weird, but Rosco probably wouldn't mind, I mean with his bevy of sugar babies and all... maybe you should call her?"

"I thought about that, Prop, but if you remember we broke up *before* I introduced her to Rosco. We got along great, but there were never any... sparks... you know what I'm saying?"

"Yeah, I remember now," said Prop Head. "But weren't there some other girls in college that you were into? I know it's a longshot, but have you checked to see if any of them are single? Social media is a great tool, if one of them is available, then maybe you could rekindle something."

"There were a few at UVA, and a few after college as well. One night I got really hammered and searched Facebook for a few girls that I used to date. I gave up after only finding three of them, as all were married. Anyway, enough of this shit, let's turn around and walk back for some breakfast. I'm suddenly starved!"

"OK, man that sounds good. But in the future, don't be a stranger! I mean, we agreed to be brothers for life, so anytime you need to talk, just let me know, OK?"

"Will do, brother!"

The two friends turned around and began the walk back down the beach to the hotel. Just as Jake was beginning to tell his friend about the crazy writer named Jenny that he was currently working with, Prop Head's phone rang, and he went from fraternity brother mode to Alex Yin, corporate executive, in an instant. It was clear that this call would take quite a bit of time, so when they got back to the hotel, Prop Head just mouthed "see you later" to Jake and they both headed up to their rooms. Jake figured that the rest of the guys would still be asleep for a while, so he ordered room service which came in fifteen minutes. After he ate, he figured that a shower and perhaps a bit more sleep would not be a bad idea as he was sure that the bachelor party tonight would extend far into the wee hours of tomorrow. He started the shower and let it warm up and then got in and let the water run on him for quite a while before washing himself and getting out. He then threw on a pair of shorts, quickly checked his e-mails, and laid down on the super comfy bed in the room.

As he laid there, he thought about resurrecting his old screenplay for the ten thousandth time. The story was a good one, full of beautiful scenes, and above all, hope that love did indeed have the power to conquer all. He had shit-canned the old working title, which was *A Life Preserver in Oblivion*, because it just seemed too dark for a story as packed full of life and hope as this screenplay was. However, even though his planned ending was beautiful, he lost his direction somewhere along the way and his protagonists were now hopelessly lost in the middle of the story with no way to get to the end. He initially had a plan, but it vanished in to thin air at the same time that he began writing the sort of garbage that he once made fun of. The thing is that he held something back from Prop Head when they were talking on the beach and that was that he had lost his creative voice and couldn't write like he once could. Although he tried to reboot the story a few times over the last several years, he just couldn't figure out a way to move the story to the happily ever after part without inserting such trite devices such as the "missed kiss" or the "mistaken identity theme." So, he just carried on year after year telling himself that he would eventually find his muse and be able to write again so he could get to the finish line. However, he sometimes wondered whether this muse would kiss him when he found her like the stories say or simply punch him in the face because he was just not worthy of her effort. Now, either option seemed better than what he felt currently because a life in limbo is worse than dying a thousand times. Or so they say.

CHAPTER 4: ROCK BOTTOM'S FALSE FLOOR

Monday, October 23rd, 2000

Savannah had been living on Kate's couch for two weeks now and as she anticipated, her welcome was becoming a bit threadbare. However, even though she knew that Kate was less than happy with the fact that she had to share her place, she loved Savannah and was giving a solid effort to make the best of it. But that wasn't the biggest problem. The monster problem that Savannah faced was that Kate's company had decided to transfer her to Europe. Worse yet, Kate had informed her property manager that she'd be leaving prior to Savannah's call from New York three weeks ago, so the unit would have new tenants moving in on December 1st. So, Savannah only had until the end of November to find another place to live as Kate would be moving out right before Thanksgiving. However, considering the state of her credit score, getting a new place in a decent area would be more difficult than ever. So, the trip to Boulder was looking more inevitable all the time. But Savannah was a fighter who didn't want to give in just yet.

At least she was able to find a job waiting tables at a restaurant on M Street that primarily catered to the lunch crowd. This enabled her to buy food for herself and Kate, get a new cell phone, and add a bit to the $389 that she arrived with. If only her credit rating was not ruined by Chad. However, she still thought that she might have a chance to pull out of her tailspin. Because Savannah was a fighter, and she knew that she could get her life back on track.

As far as the future was concerned, Savannah had no idea what the next step was. She worked on her play in the evenings and was making very good progress but was still a long way away from finishing it. She also began focusing on her health a bit more and was running on a regular basis in addition to eating better as well. She had eliminated alcohol for the most part and was only smoking a little weed with Kate from time to time. Best of all, she cut ties with Chad completely and was finally free of him for good. The day after she arrived in D.C., she finally turned on her old cell phone to find her voicemail completely full of messages which were all from him. As expected, they started off angry, then became apologetic, then turned remorseful, and finally they returned to anger again before the space ran out in her voice mailbox. She smashed the phone with a hammer and then threw it in the trash. That part of her life was over, and she wanted to make it final. She did so gladly, and although she was a fighter, that was one battle that she did not want to have anymore.

She was not working today, so after a shower she made some coffee and decided to work on the play for a while. She had to go out in a bit to buy a present for Kate as it was her birthday, but she also had to flesh out a scene that hit her late last night. This was not uncommon, and she always kept a notebook close at hand for when the inclination to write hit her. She was able to get something down on paper which helped her remember the idea that she got from the dream world, although as usual her handwriting was so sloppy that it was difficult for her to discern exactly what she had written when she was barely conscious. However, after a few minutes it came back to her, and she was able to write the scene. Unfortunately, the scene did not work as well as she thought it would when it hit her at 3:30 a.m., so she decided to delete it completely after it was done. The way of the playwright is jagged and full of dead ends that hold promise initially but sometimes fail when inserted into the greater work and Savannah knew this because it had happened many times over the last three years. So, after several hours of effort, she put the entire project away and went shopping. She needed a reboot, and she knew it. Sometimes, putting the fight aside for a moment was necessary.

Savannah walked to M Street and after stopping in several different boutiques, she finally found what she was looking for. Kate wanted a large backpack for hiking when she moved to Europe and hadn't been able to find the right one. Savannah had been out shopping with her several times so she knew exactly what she was looking for and as fate would have it, she found it today. It cost nearly $150, which was a lot for Savannah considering her current financial situation, but Kate had done her a solid by letting her stay, so she happily ponied up the cash. She walked back to the apartment with a big smile on her face knowing that Kate would be thrilled.

That evening, the two friends got dressed up and headed out for Kate's birthday. Besides her waiter's uniform, Savannah had worn nothing but jeans, t-shirts, and sweatpants since she arrived in D.C., so it was nice for her to fix up her hair and makeup, put on a little black cocktail dress and complete the look with dark thigh-high stockings and high heels. She felt sexy for the first time since she left Chad, and that was a good thing because she needed all the self-confidence that she could get right now. If she could see what the rest of the world did, she would brim with more self-confidence than she could imagine. This was true because when Savannah dressed up, she was absolutely stunning. However, for some reason, she had to fight her own self-image as well and that was a fight that she needed to let go.

On the other hand, Kate was not as blessed as Savannah was in the looks department and this was by a pretty wide margin. Kate could best be described as "bookish" or even plain if you caught her on a weekend at her favorite coffee shop on Dupont Circle. However, tonight Savannah helped her with her hair and make-up and convinced her to wear a miniskirt and silk blouse instead of the peasant dress that she had originally chosen for herself. When they left the apartment to head to Kate's favorite Thai restaurant, Savannah thought that she had raised Kate's appearance by several notches and Kate even commented that she felt pretty. That made Savannah happy, and it was good to feel that type of happiness again, even if the rest of her life was a wreck, burned by fights that she could never resolve.

Dinner was fun, and they hit a bar for a quick nightcap afterwards but did not want to stay long because they both had to work the next day. At the bar, two guys even bought their drinks, but both guys were flirting with Savannah, and neither were giving Kate much attention which made the entire situation quite awkward. Savannah decided on taking the "we have to go to the restroom" exit, and the two girls skated out of there without even saying goodbye. They got home quickly, and when Savannah gave Kate her surprise, she hugged her tightly, shedding more than a few tears. They then both retired to bed and Savannah fell asleep immediately.

Over the next several weeks, Kate and Savannah did a lot together. Since Kate's company had paid for her lease termination fees including the last month's rent, she didn't charge Savannah anything and bought groceries for them both. Savannah tried to pay her, but she simply would not take the money. So, Savannah shoved as much as possible into the coffee can in the kitchen pantry and was beginning to amass a decent amount of cash. She owed Kate big-time and vowed to pay her back ten-fold someday. She knew that she could do it and that her fighting spirit would get her through, it was just a matter of time.

Things were also looking up on the apartment front as well. After searching nearly every day for several weeks, she finally found a furnished place in Northern Virginia where the landlord agreed to take her on as a tenant as long as she came up with $1,500 plus $700 for first month's rent. By the time she found the apartment, she already had the $1,500 saved and was working hard on the rest because she was planning on delivering the whole amount to the landlord the day after Thanksgiving weekend. At least she had nothing else but a suitcase and duffel bag of clothing, so she didn't need a moving truck, and getting a car was her priority as soon as she got settled in her new place. She asked Kate if she would consider selling her car, but it was already promised to one of her little brothers, so she hit a dead end there. Fortunately, public transportation is plentiful in the D.C. area, so she figured that she could carry on without a vehicle for a while at least.

During the week of Thanksgiving, Kate packed everything up, and Kate's dad and two brothers came down from their home in rural Delaware to load everything up on the Wednesday before. Her dad was named Bill, and he was a husky farmer who was as "salt-of-the-earth" as it got. Her two brothers, George and Pete, were both a younger than Kate as they were still in high school, and both were miniatures of their father. Kate's family wasn't wealthy, and Savannah thought that they may have even been in financial distress because one day she found a check for $1,000 on the kitchen floor that Kate had written to her mother who was named Anne. When Savannah called Kate to let her know that she must have dropped it, Kate seemed a bit flustered and said something about paying them back money that she had borrowed. While that could have been the case, she didn't believe it. This was because Kate was always very frugal in college, did not ask her parents for cash like virtually everyone else did, and often remarked that there was no way for her to have attended college in Colorado if she hadn't received scholarship money. The reality was that Kate was brilliant and could have gone anywhere, really. It was just that she became enamored with the Centennial State during a high-school debate team trip to Boulder and decided to forgo opportunities at several prestigious Eastern schools for a daily view of the Rockies. She still maintained that she would eventually live there once she made enough money to move her parents with her and buy them a home to retire in. She was always very close with her family, which is why she took a job in D.C. in the first place. Unfortunately, she'd now be stationed in Europe, splitting time between company offices in Paris and Brussels, for at least two years in an advanced management training program that had just been created by her company. The good news was that this program came with a nice increase in salary in addition to an allowance that was more than enough to fund all living expenses. So, even though Savannah knew Kate would miss her loved ones, the money was simply too good to turn down.

To Savannah's mild surprise, Bill invited her to have Thanksgiving with the family in Delaware. Since Kate was flying out of Dulles on Sunday, Savannah would ride back with her and her father after the weekend so they could drop her off at what was now Kate's old place. This is where Savannah would stay until she could move into the new one. She knew that she'd miss Kate dearly, and secretly wanted to go to Europe with her, but if she did, she would burn up most of her saved money on the flight and that would put her in an even worse financial predicament than she was in currently. Plus, Kate would never want a long-term roommate anyway, even if she was in a foreign land.

Thanksgiving dinner was wonderful, and Savannah had lots of fun with Kate's family playing touch football in the back yard, Trivial Pursuit afterwards, and then making smores in the fireplace to cap off the day. After all festivities were over, she took a shower and walked down the hall to Kate's childhood room where the cot that was set up for her was waiting. When she opened the door, Kate was sitting on the bed looking at a photo album. Savannah sat down next to her and noticed that the pictures in the album were from Kate's childhood.

"Wow, look at that outfit," said Savannah pointing to a picture of Kate in a shirt with stripes and pants with polka dots. "I think I have some pictures like that of myself and I remember thinking how pretty I was at the time."

"Savannah let's be honest, you'd still be pretty with a shaved head and wearing a dirty painter's smock," said Kate turning the page. "I'd give anything for your looks."

"Nonsense Kate, you're a beautiful girl," said Savannah. "You just need some new clothes, and I can definitely help with that!"

"Thanks Savannah," said Kate closing the album and turning to look at her. "I was just thinking about those two guys that we met on my birthday. They barely paid attention to me, but both seemed intent on impressing you. I know you noticed because you chose to leave, and I appreciate that but it's still hard for me because I really thought I looked good that night."

"You did Kate, those guys were just immature assholes. Believe me honey, some awesome European guy is going to find you and sweep you off your feet. You're gorgeous inside and out, and you need someone who's worthy of you. The type of guys that were at the bar that night are not in your league. As for me, my life's a train wreck, so who cares that some men find me pretty? Inside I'm an emotional wreck who is terrified of another new relationship with anyone. You've a great career and a bright future. You've also worked hard to get where you are and you deserve it, don't ever forget that."

"Savannah, what are you going to do with your life? I'm worried about you. You've done a great job getting yourself on track, but if I'm being honest, you really should go back home and finish school. I know your parents will welcome you with open arms even if you don't think they will. You've even saved enough money to fly home in style."

"Kate, I've thought about doing that a dozen times since I moved in with you. But if I go home, I'm admitting defeat, and my sense of pride has trouble accepting that. Plus, I found an apartment, and I have steady income now. I can make it... I'm a fighter."

"That may be," said Kate with a very concerned look on her face now, "but you do nothing but work and sometimes you seem so sad... it's hard to watch you go through this. I know you don't want to give up, but you shouldn't look at going home as a defeat. Instead, you should just consider it as a... strategic retreat... so you can regroup. You can still work on your play in your spare time. I really think you should take what I'm saying to heart. I only want the best for you."

"You may be right, "said Savannah after a long pause. "But I just want to try a bit longer before I wave the while flag... or rather, blow the bugle to retreat. I'm *sure* that I can succeed as a playwright and if I go home, my parents will make certain that is not my main focus and that school is. In fact, I'll probably have less freedom than I did in high school. I just don't think I could get used to that again. Don't worry, Kate I'll be fine! Plus, I can always be a stripper if all else fails."

"Well, I guess it shows that we both paid attention to that Civil War class that we took together freshman year with these military analogies," said Kate laughing slightly. "Anyway, I love you and just want the best for you. I know it will be less than... optimal... back in Boulder but I think that if you finish what you started there, you'll finally be able to move forward again. Don't keep fighting for no reason and don't be afraid of another relationship. And don't become a stripper. Like you said to me, the right guy is out there. Maybe he's in Boulder?"

"Kate, just let me focus on tomorrow and worry about men later. Right now, they're just complications. I'll think about what you said, but I must keep trying to make it on my own in the D.C. area just a bit longer. By the way, I love you too. You take care of yourself in Europe, ok?"

The two friends hugged it out after Savannah's last comment. Savannah couldn't fight the feeling that Kate was right about this, but she just could not give up yet. Worse still, she was scared to face her parents as she had not talked to her mother in over a year, and she had not spoken to her father since the day she left over three and a half years ago. She just didn't know what she would do if she had to go back and right now, she didn't want to think about it anymore, either.

"Kate, I think we should get some sleep. Doesn't your dad have plans to take us shopping for antiques tomorrow after we go to that famous breakfast place that he raved about on the drive here?"

"Yes, let's hit the sack. Sleep well Savannah and don't worry, I've confidence that you will find direction in your life eventually. You're too good and too stubborn of a person not to. Just think about what I said before. Whatever constraints that your parents put on you will be better for you than becoming a stripper. Don't be afraid to open yourself up to them again. They love you."

"Thanks, sleep tight, Kate."

The two fell asleep immediately, and the next day was filled with more fun antiquing and sampling local food from several of her dad's favorite places. The breakfast at the first of these places was as good as advertised, and Kate picked up the tab for everyone. On Saturday, Savannah and Kate had a relaxing day, watching old movies and listening to boy band tunes like they did in college. When the song *Words* by the Brit boy band Boyzone came on, Savannah asked to listen to it again because she had always loved it. She knew it was a remake from another famous group but couldn't remember who that was exactly. She went to look it up on Bill's computer, but that old beast was at least six or seven years old and after it took over ten minutes to boot up, she gave up. She'd have to remember to find out who sang that song again later, because she truly wanted to know who wrote it as the lyrics were very special to her for some reason.

On Sunday she said her goodbyes to Kate's family and repeatedly thanked them for their hospitality. She felt recharged from the visit, and for a moment, she even felt happy again. She and Kate then jumped into Bill's pickup truck, and they headed to D.C. just after lunch so that Kate could catch her flight to Paris later that afternoon.

When they got to the airport, they pulled up to the curb for check-in. After grabbing Kate's massive suitcase out of the truck bed, Bill returned to the cab of the truck so that the girls could have a moment together before Kate disappeared into the main terminal. She would've waited for her at the gate (which you could still do at the time) but her flight was still a few hours from departure and Bill needed to get back home tonight as he had an early morning the next day repairing some fences that needed mending back home. Therefore, they only had a few minutes.

"Go do great things across the pond," said Savannah with tears streaming down her cheeks while giving Kate a hug. "You should also know that I have a feeling that you'll find that man that you've been looking for over there, so make sure to keep in touch often!"

"I hope you're right Savannah," said Kate pulling away after the hug. "But whoever he may be, he needs to know that I still plan on moving to Colorado eventually, so he must be flexible as well! Anyway, think about what I said on Thanksgiving. Don't be too stubborn honey, you don't need to struggle like you will on your own. By the time that my management training program is over, you could be out of school and back on track. Please listen to me on this, I only want the best for you."

"I've been thinking about it since we talked, and I'm considering it. But like I said before, I must try for a little longer. I really think I can make it work by myself."

"Just take care of yourself and don't wait too long. Plus, your mom and dad are getting on in years and you'll regret it if something happens to them in the meantime, so reconcile now and make a fresh start. Give me another hug and then I must go."

The two friends hugged again and then Kate checked her bag outside with a Sky Cap and disappeared into the terminal. Savannah climbed back into the truck and was still crying as they pulled away. She didn't fully realize how much closer that she and Kate had become in this relatively short amount of time. She was completely isolated right now, and any decisions that she made were hers and hers alone. At the same time, Savannah had no roadmap for the future, either. Whatever she decided to do would determine her fate, and yet, she really needed someone who could serve as a guide. Someone to help her make the right decisions for her and ensure that she was on the right path. Sadly, with Kate gone, she had no one now and the abrupt realization of that reality hurt probably the most of all.

Bill and Savannah arrived at Kate's old apartment about thirty minutes later and Bill got out to grab her suitcase while Savannah went to the front door of the building. As she walked up the stairs, she felt a bit weird about the fact that she would be staying there alone for the next four days without Kate. Nevertheless, she would have to deal with this uneasiness until the end of the month when she could move out, so she hoped that she could at least get used to it.

When she got to the front door of Kate's apartment, she went to put her key in, and the door pushed open easily. She then noticed that the door had been pried open by something and whatever it was had destroyed the door jamb, thus allowing the door to open easily. It was also apparent that the girls forgot to throw the deadbolt when they left so it did not offer any deterrent. All the hair on her body suddenly seemed to stand on end for a moment as she froze before the front door, frightened to take another step forward. Just then, Bill came up behind her and seemed shocked at what she'd discovered.

"I'll go in and check things out, you wait out here," said Bill grabbing her arm as she began to take a step forward.

"OK," said Savannah in a small, almost imperceptible, voice.

Bill went into the apartment for either several minutes or several hours, Savannah didn't know because she lost track of time. When he came out, his face told her everything. Savannah immediately knew that something was wrong.

"Savannah," said Bill, "someone has obviously broken into this place, because the furniture has been tossed around, and your clothes have been thrown everywhere. I don't know if anything of yours is missing or not, but I'll be happy to help you clean up. We can also knock on the neighbors' doors to see if they saw anyone. I'm so sorry, sweetheart. Let's gather up your things and go back to Delaware for a few days. I don't think you should stay here."

"Did you check the pantry?" asked Savannah with a voice that was now full of terror.

"No, I didn't," said Bill. "But there wasn't anything there anyway because all cabinet doors were open and empty and the only thing on the floor was an old Folger's can."

Savannah's heart hit the floor as she ran past Bill and into the kitchen. The coffee can was there, but her life savings was gone. She searched the kitchen in vain for a panic-filled moment but then resigned herself to the fact that all the hard work that she'd done and all the progress that she'd made was now for naught. She was heartbroken.

Savannah called the police, and this consumed several hours of her time until all evidence was gathered, and the neighbors were questioned. One elderly lady three doors down said that she saw a man in a pair of jeans with a hooded Washington Redskins sweatshirt leaving the apartment, but she was the only one who saw anything. It was late, but Bill still wanted to drive Savannah back home with him as soon as possible. While she appreciated the fact that he was concerned about her, she didn't want to run away from this setback and felt that she needed to face it alone. So, in the end, she was indeed able to convince him to leave and attend to his family. Bill was the kind of person who would do anything for anyone in need and she knew that. However, she also knew he had lots of work to do on the farm and that his family needed him. She hugged him and repeatedly thanked him for his help and then he finally jumped in his truck and drove away.

After three hours everyone was gone, and Savannah finally finished straightening the place up. Fortunately, nothing else of hers was missing, and she still had the pocket watch because she took it with her almost everywhere. With everything back in order, she could now lay down on the bed that used to be Kate's and get some sleep. She was happy that the deadbolt was still usable and even more thankful that the apartment was furnished, or she would've been on the floor. As she laid there she knew now that her situation had changed in the worst possible way. She now had only $257 out of the $300 that she had originally taken to Kate's parents' house for Thanksgiving to her name and no credit. As a result, her options were very slim; and it was now apparent that she would have to make the call that she had never wanted to make. It was a shit sandwich, and she knew it, but that didn't stop her from pulling out her phone and dialing a familiar area code. She prepared to take a bite.

"Hello," said a sleepy voice on the other end. "Savannah, is it you?"

"Yeah Mom, it's me," said Savannah who then paused for several seconds. She finally spoke to break the brutal silence. "Hey, I know that things have not been great between us, but I need a favor."

"Savannah honey? Are you OK?"

"Yes mom, I'm fine. But I need your help... I need to come home."

Savannah was a fighter, but she also knew when to throw in the towel. That time was now.

CHAPTER 5: GENEVA IS BEAUTIFUL THIS TIME OF YEAR

(Or Anytime, Really)

Wednesday, December 14th, 2016

Jake napped until just before noon and then got up, dressed himself in jeans and a nice blue t-shirt that fit well, and threw on some loafers and headed down to the lobby to meet the entire wedding party for brunch. This included the groom and his five groomsmen as well as the bride and her bridesmaids. It seemed a bit unconventional to him that they were all meeting up before the rehearsal dinner, but Billy Dee was never conventional with anything he did. According to him, it would give everyone a chance to get to know each other better before the actual wedding, and Jake was sure that he also wanted to show off his bride-to-be. Conventional or not, when Jake walked off the elevator and saw the group of young ladies wearing sundresses, miniskirts, and short-shorts and talking to Billy Dee and Rosco in the lobby, he tripped on a poinsettia plant that was near the elevator door and then stumbled and fell, tucking and rolling at the last minute to avoid falling on his face. Everyone noticed.

Jake sat up quickly, immediately popped to his feet, and one of the girls ran over to help him. Jake's face must have been as red as the ribbons on the Christmas tree that was in the hotel's lobby as she reached him, and when she smiled, he nearly fell over again. She was almost unbelievably beautiful.

"Are you OK?" Asked the girl who had long brown hair that hung in loosely curled tresses that were progressively lighter until they were almost blonde at the tips. She also had pale blue eyes and was wearing a red sundress with little white flowers on it and some white sandals. She was quite a bit shorter than him, but to him, that was not unusual due to his height, and she smelled as if she had bathed in the flowers that were printed on her dress. "You're Jake, right?"

"Yes, and I'm fine... with the exception of my pride, that is," said Jake trying to regain his composure. She moved closer to him and smiled again.

"That's good, because you are my groomsman, and I need you to be able to escort me properly at the wedding. My name's Geneva, Geneva DeHaan. Nice to meet you, Jake!" As she said this, he noticed a slight accent that he couldn't quite place. Just then, everyone else arrived at the point where they were standing.

"Nice entry, Snake!" Said Billy Dee with a chuckle. "You always were the smooth one! Everyone, meet Jake the Snake."

"Hello everyone," said Jake. "Despite what Billy Dee says, I usually take longer to make a fool of myself. I think I need a drink."

"Me too!" Said Geneva while smiling at him yet again.

"Hello Jake," said another gorgeous girl with long blonde hair and the same pale blue eyes as Geneva. "I'm Layla, Lawrence's bride to be. I see you've met Genny, and this is Emma, Julie, Rose, and Kelley." As she said the names, she indicated each other girl in turn, and they all smiled at him as she said each name. Her accent also sounded like Geneva's, and he still was not quite sure where they were from. "I think I need a drink as well!"

"Very nice to meet you all," said Jake. "I can't place your accent, Layla. Are you from New Zealand?"

"South Africa actually," said Layla. "Genny and I grew up together in Cape Town, Julie and Emma are Brits, and Rose and Kelley are from here in the states. "Genny and I met the rest of the girls in Europe one summer on a trip, and we have been best friends since. Lawrence, we need to go. Our reservations are at 1:30, could you please call your other three friends and get them down here?"

Just then, Big Dog, Prop Head, and Slug strolled up and exchanged handshakes and hugs with everyone. Slug showed up in an old Hawaiian shirt that fit tightly around his midsection with flip-flops and cut-off shorts. When he saw the bevy of lovely young ladies, he started sucking in his stomach to make himself look more fit. Jake thought that was funny, because as far as looks were concerned, Slug had little to no game at all. Fortunately for him, he started cracking jokes almost immediately, and in no time at all, everyone was laughing. In fact, as the party waited for the limo that would take them to brunch, Julie, the short redhead with lots of freckles from London, seemed to be enjoying his humor a lot, and sat next to him on the way to the restaurant.

The place that they were having brunch was on the beach in Ft. Lauderdale, so it took them almost an hour to get there. The good news was that the champagne was flowing, Slug was cracking everyone up, and Geneva was sitting next to him smelling wonderful, so all was more than good. More surprising was how mature and worldly these young women were. Jake expected nearly all of them to be glued to their phones the entire way while he and his buddies relived the glory days yet again. However, that wasn't the case at all, and it became quickly apparent that Billy Dee may have finally found his match with Layla.

To begin with, Rosco was wrong about her age. She was not 23, she was 27 and would be turning 28 in a month. She also had an MBA from Cornell and was currently in line to become a partner with the global consulting firm that she worked for. All the girls were basically the same age and had similar pedigree with advanced degrees and careers that were on the way up. Geneva was the oldest of the group at 29 and had already become a junior partner in a mid-sized law firm in Philadelphia, even though she had only passed the bar just four years ago. So, Jake was more than pleasantly surprised and found himself having a lot of fun.

Brunch was sublime at the little café which was owned by one of Layla's friends who had recently relocated to South Florida. More champagne flowed, but Jake slowed down on the drinking as he knew that the rest of the night would be very booze filled as they embarked upon Billy Dee's last big adventure as a single man. He and Geneva sat next to each other at brunch and then again afterwards on the ride back to the hotel. They talked a lot and found that they had much in common including Jiu-Jitsu. She was easy to talk to, easy to listen to, and of course, amazing to look at. He found himself very attracted to her, even though she mentioned early on that she had a boyfriend back in Philly. They got back to the Fontainebleau at about 4:45 and after more hugs and handshakes, everyone dispersed. Some went back to their rooms to take naps before the evening of craziness at each respective party, bachelor and bachelorette. Others, including Slug and Julie, went out to the pool for another drink. As Jake turned to walk to the elevator, he felt a hand on his arm and then turned to meet Geneva's eyes.

"Hey Jake, do you want to grab one more quick drink with me before you head up?"

"Sure, we can just head out to the pool bar with the rest of the degenerates."

"Actually, Jake," said Geneva as tentatively as a stray cat approaching a new food bowl on the porch, "I would rather have a drink with you alone if you don't mind. Can we just go to the Bleau Bar?"

"Sure Geneva, or should I call you Genny?"

"Layla is my best mate and has earned the right to call me that, but I prefer Geneva. Let's head to the bar!" And with that she hooked his arm with hers and they went to the classic bar that movie stars from yesteryear made famous long ago. They went in, sat at the bar, and both ordered dirty martinis served straight up. Geneva spoke first.

"So, Jake, like I said, Layla and I go way back and share everything. She truly is my ride or die. Lawrence told her what your ex-wife did to you, and she told me. I'm so sorry, that must have been awful. You have kids too, right?"

"It was, and yes, I've a daughter who will be fifteen soon and a son who will be thirteen shortly thereafter. I love them and miss them like crazy. I wish I could see them more, but right now I'm stuck on the East Coast while they're in Cali with their mom. Oh well, maybe at least one of them will choose a college closer to me."

"I'm so sorry to hear that Jake," said Geneva while sipping her ice-cold concoction and giving him the sympathetic eyes that he normally hated from others. But, from her, they were… still just beautiful. "She also told me that you've been living alone for a while and that you pretty much have given up on relationships."

"Wow, I didn't realize that my dormant love life was so interesting," said Jake laughing a bit. "I should've remembered that Rosco has a big mouth. But I'm guilty as charged. I just don't have any interest in a relationship right now. I tried for a while, but whenever I began dating someone, the relationship always fell short for one reason or the other. Why do you think she told you all this? You aren't here to match me with one of the other bridesmaids, are you?"

"The answer is no… and yes," said Geneva. "No, because neither Layla nor I want to set you up with any of the girls here. Rose and Julie are single, so I suppose you could go after one of them although Julie really seems to like your friend. Emma is engaged, and Kelley has just broken up with her girlfriend of three years as she's currently re-thinking her position on men. Turns out that she may like them after all because she just met one that she spends a lot of time with. So, it's anyone's guess what will happen with her."

"OK, that makes sense," said Jake, "but you said that the answer was 'yes' as well. How can that be?"

"Well… it is yes, because Layla has also heard great things about you from both Lawrence and Roger and was hoping that you still may find a love connection… with me."

Jake was floored. He did feel an attraction. Maybe she did too. "But you told me that you had a serious boyfriend in Philly. Is that not true?"

"It's true, but I guess that we're at the point in our relationship where we're trying to decide if we still want to be together or call it quits. We've been together for almost four years and although we get along well most of the time, it seems like all the life in our relationship has been sucked out. Honestly, it could go either way right now."

"Wow, I'm caught at a loss for words, and that almost never happens."

"It's OK, I honestly think that it's quite weird that I'm telling you this at all. I wasn't going to, you know, at least not as of this morning when I got out of bed. Based upon what I heard I figured that you may be looking for a quick lay and nothing more. I didn't want to have cheap sex with you, so I figured that I would just be polite, dance with you at the wedding, and make sure to leave if it looked like you were making any moves. That was my plan at least... until we had lunch this afternoon."

"So, what changed your mind?"

"I saw you as soon as you came out of the elevator before you tripped, and I must be honest... I was immediately attracted to you."

"Were you now?" Said Jake looking directly into those pale blue eyes that were set in that amazing face. Sort of like two sapphires in a perfect platinum setting, just flawless.

"But I liked even better how you handled your fall. You didn't let it bother you at all. Plus, I just enjoyed being with you today. I never expected that your mind and personality would be as handsome as your face, but they are." She paused, downed her drink, and smiled. "Anyway, that's off my chest... I truly hope you don't think I'm weird... I just had to let you know that... that I would be happy to get to know you better... if that's OK."

There was a pause as Jake took all this in. Finally, he spoke. "Geneva, I have a confession as well. When I came to Miami, I made a promise to myself that I'd try to avoid any interaction with any single women for the entire duration of the wedding festivities. Although Rosco would be happy to sleep with pretty much anyone , I don't want to end up in bed with a twenty-something girl that placed her entire value in life on the quality of her Instagram story. Knowing Billy Dee, or at least the Billy Dee from college, I figured that he found some hot young bimbo who he could settle down with for a minute just to say that he'd done it once. I didn't think that there was a chance in hell that the marriage would last more than a year at the most. As it turns out, I've underestimated my friend greatly, because Layla seems to be one special gal, and possibly the only girl that he's ever dated who's allowed to call him Lawrence. So, I really think this could work for him. And it appears that her friends are no less special, either." Jake paused again for a second, but she didn't break eye contact with him as the moment hung in the plasma of time. "To answer your question simply, I'd love to get to know you better as well, Geneva. What do you have in mind?"

Geneva's face lit up when he responded and then she leaned in and gave him a kiss on the cheek. It was obvious to him that she was choosing her words carefully before she spoke. After a period of what seemed like endless silence, she finally responded.

"Jake, there's no way that I can hide this attraction to you, and I think that you feel the same about me or you would've already gone back to your room. Yet at the same time, I am still in a long-term relationship, and you've pretty much stated that you don't want one right now. Also, as I said earlier, I don't want something as meaningless as a one-night stand, either. Since we only have the rest of this week to be together, let's just assume that this is all the time that we'll ever have together. We won't see each other tonight, but from tomorrow until Monday morning, let's drop our barriers and open ourselves up to whatever our time together may teach us. I don't know what will happen, and I may have tons of guilt when it's all said and done. But by doing this, I will have no regrets about not trying to get to know you better and in turn, I'll be learning more about myself as well. What do you say, is it a deal?"

"When you say 'open ourselves up,' what do you mean exactly?" Asked Jake who was now wondering exactly how this beautiful young lawyer had managed to snare him in her web of words. In fact, he'd almost signed on the dotted line without fully reading the contract.

"What I mean is that we just let this relationship flow without barriers. No boyfriends or memories of ex-wives to stand in our way. We just let things flow to a natural conclusion, whatever that may be and when Monday comes, we are free to go our separate ways. Hopefully, we'll have both learned something, but at the very least, I know that we'll have a lot of fun."

"OK, I'm in. No strings, right?"

"None at all," Geneva said as she crossed her perfectly tanned legs to face him. "But nothing cheap, either. We both need to give our best effort. The universe is trying to teach us something, Jake. We need to listen."

"So, should we shake on it?"

"Not a chance," she said and then without warning she moved in and kissed him, but not on the cheek this time, right on the lips. Without even thinking, he kissed her back and enjoyed it immensely. The kiss lasted quite a while.

"Geneva, if you keep doing that in public, your boyfriend is bound to find out about it," said Jake.

"He may, but that's OK because right now we have decided to see other people for a while even though we still live together. Our lease will be up in April, and we'll decide then whether we should stay together or not. So, although it may piss him off, it's the deal that we came up with when I caught him cheating. He's lucky to still have a chance at all, to be honest."

"So, you know how it feels then."

"I do," she said and then gave him a huge hug that he enjoyed almost as much as the kiss. "Jake, I need to go and nap before the bachelorette party. Since I'm the Maid of Honor, I'm in charge of coordinating this craziness, so I need to be at my best. Until tomorrow... cutie?"

"Until tomorrow, Geneva."

She gave him another kiss, but it was much quicker which immediately made him want more. He watched her as she walked out, and she looked back and winked at him as she reached the entrance to the bar. She was then gone and suddenly the world became a little less bright.

He finished his drink and went back to the room. When he got there, he decided to nap as well because his head was still a bit thick after all the champagne and the martini which had only made it worse. He set his alarm for 8:15 as the men were all going out to Shula's Steakhouse for a late dinner at 9:30 before they headed out to what he knew would be more than a few gentlemen's clubs. He knew that Billy Dee would be making it rain tonight.

Jake was awakened by the alarm that he had set earlier, and he called his son Jake as he had promised Kira when he spoke to her yesterday. After a brief conversation, he said goodbye, hung up, and then ambled into the shower to get ready. While he was showering, he thought about Geneva and the deal that they struck earlier. He'd never expected to meet anyone at this wedding, and now he had a date for the entire event. He wondered where things would go with her, and even more than that he wondered what she was looking for as she seemed to be searching for some direction in her own personal life as well. She was gorgeous, smart, and charismatic, but was she someone that he would want to be with? Did he want to be with anyone at all right now? That answer had been a resounding negative for more than two years, but maybe it was time to open his heart. Maybe it was time to finally move on.

After the shower, he went out into the room to turn on some music to listen to while he got ready. When he hit the button on the high-end clock radio in the room, *Love You Inside and Out* by the Bee Gees was on, and he turned it up. Although most known for their music during the disco era of the 70s, the Bee Gees had a vast songbook of their own in addition to the songs that they wrote for other artists like Barbara Streisand, Diana Ross, and several other uber famous musical luminaries. He loved them and preferred their early stuff over the disco music. It had that ethereal Sixties vibe to it, and one of their songs was even Jake's favorite song of all time. Jake thought it was great when Abba was resurrected through the movie *Mamma Mia.* He had always hoped that someone would do something similar with the Bee Gees.

Jake finished getting ready and looked very sharp in his black fitted slacks, black t-shirt, and grey sport coat that was tailored perfectly for his build. He also donned a pair of Florsheim loafers and headed to the lobby at about 8:45. He got there and when he'd arrived, everyone was there but Slug. Apparently, he had several more drinks with Julie before heading to his room and had slept through his alarm. He finally ambled down from his room at 9:05, and then they all jumped in the limo and took it to Shula's.

While at the restaurant, he received plenty of questions about his plans with Geneva as it was obvious to all his fraternity brothers that they liked each other. Of course, Rosco was only focused on the sexual positions that he could try with her, so Jake did not really listen too closely to what he had to say. The food was even better than expected, and Jake made sure to eat well so that he had an adequate base for the alcohol that he would be consuming later. They stayed at dinner until just after 11:30 and then took the limo to the first stop for the night which was an establishment called the *Pink Dolphin*.

They arrived just after midnight, walked towards the door, and on the way there Jake felt a weird feeling overcome him. He consumed several drinks at dinner, but that was not what he felt, this was different. It was more like he was moving in an augmented reality where everything was enhanced. He almost worried for a second that someone had slipped something in his wine earlier, but with these guys, he was sure that didn't happen. What he didn't know at the time was that what he felt was more significant than he could have ever imagined. In the next twenty minutes or so, his life would change forever, and all future plans would be affected by what happened in that very small frame of time.

CHAPTER 6: A SECOND IN TIME

Thursday, December 15th, 2016

Jake had been to many places like this in his life and always found them to be the same. The same smells, the same music, and even the same people or at least the same type of people who all were more than willing to part with their hard-earned money. This "same place" has many names and whether you call it a gentleman's club, a strip club, or just a good old-fashioned titty bar, the objective of seeing part, most, or even all of a girl in her twenties, is easily attainable for anyone with enough cash. Because in this place cash is always king, and this kingdom is almost always open to those who wish to visit the altar of hedonisic indulgence.

This night was no different and as he sat down near the short stage that looked as if brass poles had sprouted directly from its acrylic floor like bamboo shoots, he wondered how many hands had touched them over the years. These poles were well used by the young entrepreneurs of fantasy and lust who had learned how to utilize their youth and sex appeal as well-honed tools to pry as much cash as possible from a clientele mainly comprised of frustrated middle-aged men. In fact, the only thing that was unique about this place was that at present at least, there were no young ladies to keep the poles or the patrons company. All at once, this changed, and through the purple-blue haze of the subdued lighting, he saw a beautiful girl take the stage at the far end and begin to perform her craft. More than he had ever been before, Jake was interested in this girl, and this was weird considering his earlier interaction with Geneva. In fact, for some reason he put her above any dancer that he had seen before while on drunken adventures to similar establishments in the past. He found himself enthralled and couldn't take his eyes off her as she had a lovely face and was quite tall with long beautiful legs that were artfully decorated with ink. He was drawn to her and wanted nothing more than to get closer to her, but the rest of the bachelor party was in his way and Slug was blocking any access that he may have to the dancer at present. After all, she was the only girl in the bar so he would have to wait, but he knew the wait would be worth it. However, he did not yet fully understand why.

As Jake thought about the gorgeous creature that was at the far end of the short stage and who was in the process of being adorned with one-dollar bills, another girl showed up from an unseen door somewhere and plopped down in front of him. While he was certain that she was the fantasy of someone, she was not his girl. As with so many things in life, it always comes down to preference because there will always be choices to make in whatever one does. These choices define us and make us unique, for their sum total is in fact the essence of who we are, who we can become, and who we don't want to be. For Jake, this girl was so out shown by the goddess at the other end, that she didn't even make a blip on his radar screen. He had to do something. He needed to get closer to his objective and he planned to do so as soon as his beer arrived. The best news for him was that the dancer he wanted caught him looking and when she did, she smiled and came his way, parting the sea of dudes like a female Moses. Jake decided that the beer could wait as his cold, jaded, and cynical heart suddenly skipped a beat. That made it twice in one day for two different girls and for him, this was amazing.

As the dancer continued to walk her way across the stage, she now had so many dollar bills in her g-string and halter top that she looked like a smoking hot piñata that was made of money. She was moving slowly as his buddies were still not done tucking bucks as she passed by, and she didn't want to miss any as she came his way. Then, all at once she was there in front of him, and as he reached up to add a few Washingtons of his own, she looked him in the eyes and spoke.

"Would you like a dance from me?" The girl asked in a voice so beautiful that her words took on an almost lyrical quality.

"Absolutely," was his response, but it did not even come close to reflecting the enthusiasm that he felt about being able to spend some time alone with her. He knew immediately that he would want to do this dance with her, even though the dance that they would do barely reflected any sort of dancing at all. He also knew exactly how this worked and had enough cash to extend his time if he wanted to. His ugly divorce was only a year in the rear-view mirror, but in that time, he had not touched anyone of the opposite sex in an intimate way. In fact, he hadn't been with anyone at all since he caught Angela in bed with Chuck. The only exception would be the kiss with Geneva earlier, but that seemed miles away right now. For some reason he needed this moment, and it was now here for him to experience.

She came down from the stage, and as she walked off, it was a majestic sight to behold. Her boots gave her as much lift as a lottery-winning redneck's F150, and she looked him directly in the eyes as she extended her hand to take him to the ubiquitous and semi-private VIP area which was pretty much the same place in all these clubs, everywhere. When he took her hand, she smiled brightly at him, and then she led him to the little vestibule with a couch where this "dance" would occur. There was no one else there, she pointed to a padded bench, and directed him to sit down.

He did as he was told and then she sat down next to him and removed her stilts while still smiling his direction. Jake thought that she was a gorgeous sight to behold. She stood up again right in front of him and looked him directly in the eyes. He knew that the song currently playing was about halfway over when they got to the VIP room and that she would not start her taxicab meter until the next song began, so she was clearly stalling a bit. He decided to break the ice.

"So, what's your name?" He asked.

"Ariel," she replied.

"What's your real name?"

"It's Ariel," she said again, and this time smiled as they locked eyes.

"Why'd you pick me?" He inquired. "There were five of my buddies to choose from, and at least three are better looking than me."

"I picked you because you seemed to be attracted to me," Ariel replied. "I liked how you looked at me. It made me feel... appreciated and not ogled."

Just then, the song was over, and the next one began. Like a cat she removed her halter top and was suddenly there on his lap, facing him. She was so close that he could smell the blend of her perfume and shampoo and the scent was simply clean and beautiful like the sea air at dawn before a day of boating offshore. He looked into her eyes as she gyrated gently on his lap raising the level of his libido and blood pressure at the same time. With almost no conscious effort, his hands began to explore her young body, touching her shoulders and back and then moving to the front of her body and gently caressing her perfect nipples. She did have small breasts, which can be a decided liability for an exotic dancer. To him they were perfect and blended into her form with symmetrical simplicity. Most importantly, her skin was soft and unblemished, and the tips of his fingers deftly glided over her body again and again, yearning to go to yet more unexplored regions as time moved forward. He just could not get enough.

"I think that I may be different than most guys you bring back here," Jake said still lost in the fantasy of the moment.

"Oh, why is that?" She asked.

"Because when I touch you, it's my hope that you will feel as much excitement from my touch as I do from touching you."

"That's sweet," she replied. "I like your touch, it feels good. I'd let you know if it didn't. What do you do for work?"

"Thanks," he replied. "I'm a screenwriter."

"What kinds of movies have you written scripts for?"

"I write rom-com scripts, and most of them are on TV during the Christmas holidays so you may have seen a few. I wish I could say I enjoyed what I did, but the scripts are all based upon a handful of different story formulas so little creativity is required or allowed. On the positive side, I really enjoy writing tales that make people happy. Since these tales are all about love and since most everyone wants to be in love,

I figure that at the very least I can get those who watch them to that happy place for a while."

"I love a good romance," Ariel said with a smile, and then, just as quickly she seemed a bit sad.

She looked at him for a timeless moment and then she wrapped herself completely around him in a warm and wonderful hug. As he squeezed her, she squeezed back just as firmly and then she did something that no other girl at a strip club had ever done to him and it was one of the most brazenly blissful experiences that he had felt in at least the last ten years or more. After she finished the hug, she began to plant many little kisses on the side of his neck. As she did this, each little kiss landed like an exploding butterfly that sent electricity throughout his body. The scent of her hair intoxicated him as she did this and his fingertips continued to move over her back and occasionally around the round part of her butt and along those beautiful thighs. He almost felt as if he was having an out-of-body experience and he didn't want it to end, but the song was now over, and after all, he was still in a gentleman's club.

"Do you want another dance?" She asked, fully knowing the answer.

"Sure," he said.

"I'm glad," she said smiling at him, "but before we begin, I need to hit the pause button."

Just then, the music stopped, and everything was silent. The air seemed to buzz with energy and Ariel seemed to be backlit with light as well, which caused her to glow like a cloud at sunset. The weird feeling that he had when he was walking into the bar had returned and intensified. Jake wondered if he had just passed away.

"Ariel, what just happened?" He asked in a tone that may have been tinged with just a hint of panic. "Did I just die?

Am I dead?"

"No, I just altered the time and space frequency so we could talk. We're moving so fast now that everyone else here appears to be standing still. Jake, what I'm going to tell you is going to shock you a bit. I know this because it's never failed to shock anyone that I've worked with. Jake, I'm not normally an exotic dancer, although I do like playing the role sometimes. I'm what you probably know as a muse, do you know what a muse is, Jake?"

"Are you kidding me?" Said Jake in a shocked tone. Someone had to be fucking with him. "Did those assholes put you up to this? Is there a camera somewhere?"

"Search your soul and ask that question to yourself again. Do you really think I'm kidding you, Jake?" As she said that, Ariel got off his lap and magically transformed out of her G-string and into a long, silvery-white dress that was cut very low in both the front and back. As she moved to the door, the fabric seemed to glow and shimmer which looked like moonlight hitting the surface of a pond while a gentle breeze blew. She now had bright green eyes, silver hair that was just slightly darker than the dress, and a delicate wreath of laurel leaves made of crystal around her head. Most importantly, she seemed to have an energy about her that was indescribable. The only thing about her that resembled the exotic dancer that he came into the VIP area with was her face, and it was even more lovely than it was before if that was even possible. Jake didn't know if what he saw was a hallucination or something real, but he didn't feel buzzed with alcohol in the least, so he was leaning towards the latter even though he couldn't explain it at all.

"No, I guess not," said Jake as his head was still swimming in a lake of incredulity.

"OK, so I ask you again; do you know what a muse is?"

"Of course I do, I studied Greek mythology in both high school and college. There were nine of you, right? Is this really happening?"

"Yes, there are nine of us, and yes, this is really happening, although it will take some time to adjust. Come with me." As she said this, she held out her hand which he took immediately and then she led him out of the VIP area and out into the main bar. What he saw there was astounding.

His friends were still in the main area of the club, some sitting and some tucking dollar bills into the smallclothes of the dancers on the stage, while waitresses were busy taking orders or delivering drinks as the bartender manned her position at the bar. All of this would have been completely normal except for the fact that everyone and everything was completely frozen as if was all part of a bawdy diorama in some future alien's museum of human life. Jake now knew that he was part of a supernatural experience and although his primary emotion trended to terror, it was mixed with a good dollop of intrigue as well.

"Wow, I guess that *this*, whatever *this* is, is actually happening," said Jake resigning himself to his fate, whatever that may be. "What do you want with me? If it's to help me with my writing, you should know that's a lost cause before you waste your time. I've lost my creative voice."

"Jake, I didn't find you, you found me. In fact, you needed me so badly that I couldn't stay away. I had to meet the man who may be on the verge of a possible re-birth and who's called out so loudly with his heart that I could hear almost no one else. When I saw you tonight, I was more than intrigued and when you took my hand, I was sure I'd made the right choice. Jake, I'm here to fix you and make you an artist again. And I don't work with lost causes."

"I appreciate that, but I don't remember asking for help

at all. My writing is not what it used to be, but it's good enough to make a living, and I've learned to accept that."

"You sound just like Winston," said the muse. "He was once ready to give up before he had his chance to shine, and if it wasn't for me, all of Europe may be speaking German right now. You may not remember calling to me, but your heart does. Your creative spirit is dormant, Jake but it's not yet dead. You need inspiration, but to get it you first need to clear a lot of regrets. You need to make peace with some decisions that you made in the past to be able to move forward and truly believe in yourself again. I'm going to give you that opportunity."

"I'm guessing that you were talking about Churchill, right?" He asked and she nodded. "Not going to lie, it's nice to be compared to that dude. I don't disagree with you about my creative spirit, Ariel, even though I really want to. I'd love to find my voice again, what do I have to do?"

"Nothing," she laughed, "or at least nothing yet as I'll make the first move. Jake, your biggest issue has always been finding a life partner, and I know that. I also know that there were a few decisions that you made in past relationships that you think of often and sometimes wish that you had handled differently. Those regrets are suffocating you, Jake, so it's now time to let them go. And the way to do that is to re-live them again because sometimes the only way to move forward is to go back."

"So, what's going to happen?"

"Jake, I'm going to give you the chance to re-live up to three different past relationships from the point you that decided to leave them. You'll be transported back to the first of these relationships sometime before daylight tomorrow morning. When you get there, it will be at what's known as a *critical juncture,* and you'll have the opportunity to make a different decision this time than you did before. It will be the choice that you have often wished you made the first time and when you get there, you'll know exactly what that is. Once you do that, you'll then have three days to live with that decision and try the life that you could've had. If you don't like the results you can leave at any time after the first twenty-four hours by simply saying, 'I confirm that I am ready to return to my original reality, please take me there now.' However, if you feel that the alternate path is the right direction for you, you simply have to say, 'I know now that this was the right decision, and I confirm that I want to adopt this reality forever.' Please understand that staying has a huge cost, as everything that you have done or created between that point and now will cease to exist... and that includes your children."

"Well, I love my kids more than anything, so I don't think I'd stay, but it may be interesting to get a glimpse of what could have been. Three days is not long, either. I do have a question though. What happens at the end? Will I be stuck there if I don't say that I want to return before my time runs out?"

"This is your anchor point, or home reality, so you'll always come back here if you fail to act when your time expires in another alternate reality. There will also be a signal when you begin your time there, when you have twenty-four hours left, and when the three days are at an end. You must act before the final signal is complete, or you'll return home. So, Jake, what would you like this signal to be?"

"How about a song by the Bee Gees?" Jake replied. "I love them, know almost all their songs, and they aren't played very often these days. When I hear their music, I'll know it's you."

"Perfect. The Gibb brothers are such dears, such beautiful minds with kind souls as well. I helped each one of them and they rewarded the world with amazing music. When you're in the other realities and 'randomly' hear a Bee Gees song, it will be a signal. Do you have any other questions?"

"If I leave the first alternate reality and return, how long will it be until I have to go to the next one? You said there were potentially three, right? Will it happen right away?"

"Yes, it will happen within twenty-four hours of returning from the first alternate reality, and it will be the same for the third alternate reality as well if you make it that far. Jake don't underestimate the power of the moment once you return to these former places in your life. You'll feel all the emotions that you had then with the same power that they had at that moment. They'll not be dulled by the passage of time as they are now. It can be very seductive."

"I understand," he said now completely intrigued by her offer. "I guess that I don't have any choice about doing this either, right?"

"No, you don't," she said with a slight smile. "If I gave choices, Shakespeare would have been a beggar and Mary Shelley would have never submitted a book about a monster when no horror genre existed. There would have been no Odyssey, no Iliad, and no Gettysburg Address. If I gave choices, we would all be deprived of some of the most beautiful words ever written, or spoken, or sung. You get no choice, Jake because I believe in you and cannot wait for you to finally realize your potential. Remember, you can decide to leave as early as one day after you get to each alternate reality, but you still must go and stay for that time at least."

"OK Ariel let's do this. I don't know how this will solve my writing problem, but I'm going to trust that you know what you're doing. But now I should get back to my friends. I'm sure that they don't want to be stuck in time anymore."

"Don't worry Jake they won't notice, because our entire conversation has taken just a second of time, and you'll be placed right back in the same spot you were in when I altered the time frequency. I'll be gone, however, to finalize the preparations for your... adventure. Don't worry, you'll be able to find me if you need me, and I'll likely find you and check in first. Bye for now Jake, and if you like, you can call be by my real name. I don't let many do that anymore. Can you guess what it is? Do you remember any of our names?

"I'm sorry, I really don't know my muses that well anymore so I can't even make a guess," said Jake a bit embarrassed. However, he also decided that since he did not have time to prep for meeting a mythical creature in the flesh today, that he probably needed to cut himself some slack, and maybe she would too. "What is it?"

"Calliope."

All went black.

Jake was suddenly back in the VIP area, by himself. He got up and rejoined the party which was in full swing. Besides the high fives from Rosco because he got a lap dance, no one seemed to have noticed that he was even gone. Everyone was carrying on like nothing at all had happened, and he wondered several times if the meeting with Calliope had taken place at all. He figured that he would know for sure soon enough.

They went to several more clubs that were exactly like the first one, and even though Jake had a lot of fun, he did not want another lap dance at any of them. Everyone kept drinking throughout the night, and they all became sloppy drunk. Except Jake. For one thing, he wanted to make sure than no one ended up in jail, and that was a tall order towards the end of the evening, so it was good that he at least was almost completely sober. But the real reason was the meeting with Calliope, or whoever she was. If what she said was true, he didn't want to be hammered, even if the effects of drinking didn't extend to his former reality if he was indeed transported there later.

The party finally returned to the hotel at about 3:30, after a slight detour to Denny's for some late-night grub. Rosco brought a dancer back with him and took her back to his room as soon as they arrived. Surprisingly, Billy Dee returned alone and did not "make it rain" once all night. Jake went to his room, showered to wash the smoke smell out of his hair, and then brushed his teeth and climbed into bed at about 4:30.

As he laid there trying to fall asleep, he couldn't stop thinking about both women that he met over the last twelve hours or so and wondered what tomorrow would bring. He finally let sleep overtake him and when it did, his dreams were an intense flurry of images without a coherent story. It was as if he was watching events from his life swirl around in a huge cosmic blender and the entire effect was dizzying, even though he was asleep. He finally awakened in a cold sweat and noticed that the sunlight was streaming in past curtains that he had forgotten to close the evening before. In the next second, his mind awakened fully and when it did, he knew what was happening in an instant. Calliope had told him the truth.

CHAPTER 7: ELSA ERIKSSON

Saturday, July 10th, 1993.

Jake was astounded. He had awakened in the duplex that he lived in during the summer that he was in Indianapolis, Indiana between his junior and senior years at UVA. Suddenly, the events of that time in his life came rushing back all at once and a tsunami of memories, feelings, and emotions hit him like a shockwave. For a second, he lost his breath. Once he recovered, he realized that Calliope was right, because he felt all the sharpness of the emotions that he had at the time, and the events leading up to this moment were suddenly crystal clear to him again.

How he got to Indy that summer was typical because he followed a girl. Her name was Amy and they met at UVA about a month before the end of the spring semester. Amy graduated because she was a year ahead of him, and since she was from Indianapolis, she moved back home. They were in that magical beginning phase of their relationship, so she convinced him to move back with her for the summer so they could see if the relationship had any promise. When he got to Indy, they found a place to live together and then he landed a summer job waiting tables at Bazbeaux Pizza which is a community fixture in the part of the city that's known as Broad Ripple. For about three weeks, everything was lovely. Then at the beginning of week four, the old high school boyfriend came out of the woodwork, proposed to Amy a week later, and to Jake's surprise, she accepted. She immediately moved out of their summer rental, which was half of a duplex on Kessler Avenue, but agreed to pay her portion of the rent until the three-month sublease of the unit was over. Since Jake was making decent money and had a nice place to live, he decided to stay.

After the Amy debacle, he met a girl named Laura who had mousey brown hair, average looks and worked with him at Bazbeaux's. Although they did go out on a few dates right after Amy left him, there was no chemistry between them so they both decided that they were better as friends, and they did a lot together. Last night, he went with her to see a band that she was really into at a local club in Broad Ripple called the Patio. When he got to the bar, Laura was already there and told him that a friend of hers would be meeting them before the band started. Apparently, this mystery girl was a student with Laura at nearby Butler University, and during the school year, they had worked together at the university's library.

While Jake was happy to be out seeing a band, and always had a good time with Laura, he was not initially excited about hanging out with a uber-geeky librarian chick. Since he also figured that it was Laura's way of setting them up, that made things even worse. He had never imagined himself with a girl who owned six cats, read romance novels by the dozen, and had glasses as thick as Coke bottles. And he didn't want to hurt her feelings by saying "thanks but no thanks," either. Before long, a girl with a bad complexion, sloppily braided pigtails, worn jeans that were way too large, and a t-shirt with a picture of Chairman Mao on it, appeared in the doorway. Jake figured that was who they were waiting for and expected Laura to wave her over at any second. Except she didn't.

In fact, in the next minute or so, a nerdy guy who appeared to be the male equivalent to the nerdy girl in almost every way, walked in the door and gave the girl a hug. They then walked to a table together and sat down, so whoever Laura was meeting, it wasn't her. It wasn't the next three girls that walked in the door either, although all of them were better in the looks department than the first girl. Ten minutes went by, several more women came in the door and each time, Jake wondered if each woman was Laura's friend. However, none of them were, and Jake could see that Laura was beginning to get concerned as her friend was now twenty minutes late.

Jake was trying to take her mind off the situation by talking with her as she continued to look at the doorway intently, but it wasn't working well because her face was showing more worry with each passing moment. After all, Laura was always the nervous, excitable type. Suddenly her face lit up, and she jumped up waving her arms in the air and yelling "Elsa, over here!" When she did this Jake turned to look at the door and almost fell out of his chair. The girl that waived back was like no librarian that he had ever seen.

As Elsa walked over, he quickly realized just how gorgeous she was. She had long, full blonde hair, blue eyes, and a killer body. She was wearing cut-off jeans that fit her perfectly with a Nirvana concert t-shirt and some sandals that used a rather elaborate system of straps to fasten them to her feet. She walked over, gave Laura a hug, and introduced herself to Jake. The moment she smiled at him, he was hooked, and he resolved to get to know her better. The good news was that as soon as they started talking, it was obvious that she wanted to get to know him better as well and as the night unfolded, they both seemed to be pursuing that goal on a regular basis.

They stayed at the Patio for two hours listening to an awesome band called Lazy Dazy. The band was primarily a cover band, but they played a wide variety of really good music and were excellent musicians as well. All three of them loved the show, and Jake found himself dancing with both girls several times while the band was on stage. They had several drinks as well, and as the night moved on, Elsa began to flirt with him more and more.

While at the concert, Elsa introduced both Jake and Laura to her friend Lee who was a bartender there. After the band finished their last set, Jake, Elsa, and Lee, all went down the street to another nightclub called the Vogue. Laura didn't go because she had to drive to Vincennes the next morning as she had promised to visit her parents for church service and then spend the day with them. So, after hugs by all she went home, but before she left, she whispered "good luck" in Jake's ear while hugging him and then winked at him as she walked away.

Elsa, Jake, and Lee ended up shutting the Vogue down, and afterwards they all decided to take a cab to his place to have one or two more beers and perhaps smoke a little weed. When they got there, Jake grabbed the beers from the fridge while Elsa went to the bathroom and Lee rolled a doobie. They all got baked, and each had two more beers as well while they listened to music and talked about a variety of topics from favorite foods to the most shots of booze that each had taken in a single evening. Everyone was beginning to get very tired at about five minutes until four, and Lee looked like he may pass out at any moment. Suddenly, he spoke.

"I need to get a cab home," Lee said while standing up. I gotta drive to Bloomington tomorrow morning to help a friend move out of his apartment and will have to be up extra early so I can walk to the bar and retrieve my car first. Since I need to be down there about noon, if I don't crash soon, I will be useless to him. Elsa, would you like to share the cab?"

Elsa paused and did not respond right away. She then looked at Jake, then at Lee, and then back at Jake again. Jake picked up her hint.

"Elsa, if you want to stay here, you can have my bed if you like," said Jake. "I've some extra pillows and blankets, so it's no problem for me to make a comfy place to sleep for myself on the couch."

"Really? That'd be great, Jake," she said looking at him. "Lee, I really don't live that close to you, and I don't want to ride by myself in a cab at this time of night from your place to mine. I think I'm going to stay."

"Are you sure?" Asked Lee, with a semi-concerned look on his face. It was clear that he wanted to make sure that she was comfortable staying with someone that she didn't know very well. Jake appreciated this because Lee was just being a good friend to her. "I could always have the cab drop you off first."

"I'm sure Lee," she said smiling first at him and then at Jake. "I'll be fine. I know that Jake will be a complete gentleman, won't you Jake?"

"I certainly will, m'lady," said Jake standing and bowing to her. She smiled again. "Lee, the phone's in the kitchen."

"Thanks," said Lee and then he walked into the kitchen and called his ride.

The cab showed up in about ten minutes and once it arrived, Lee admonished Jake to be a gentleman for the third or fourth time, and then after hugs and handshakes, he was gone. All at once, Jake was alone with Elsa. He decided to break the somewhat heavy silence that they both found themselves in.

"OK my dear, let me change the sheets for you so you can go to bed. I promise, I'll be the complete gentleman that I said I would... although I must admit, I really don't want to."

Elsa walked over to him, stood very close, and looked him in the eyes for another long moment with a mischievous half-grin on her face. "I don't want you to act like a gentleman either, unless being a gentleman means that you will kiss me right now."

There are days where almost everything goes well and other days where nearly everything goes wrong. There are even days where nothing seems to happen at all. Each type of day will repeat itself many times during a normal human lifetime and by the time we've lived enough years to get gray hair, we learn how to deal with all of them. However, there are also days when something happens that is so special, that you know that moment will last forever in your mind and never be forgotten. When the fantasy of kissing someone you are attracted to for the first time goes from possibility to probability to certainty, the day moves to the good category automatically. However, when this level of attraction was as off the charts as Jake's was with Elsa, it becomes one of those special times and last night, Jake found himself in the midst of one of these moments. All he needed to do was kiss her. So, he did.

Once the kiss began, things progressed quickly from there. They both kissed each other with vigor and probably looked as if they were trying to eat each other's face like malfunctioning zombies. They were both drunk and stoned, so they stumbled their way from the living room to his bedroom, trying to remove each other's shirts as they went. Once her shirt was off, he then removed her bra to reveal a pair of perfectly shaped breasts which Jake caressed as he kissed her. They finally fell on the bed with pants and cutoffs still on, and even though he was unbelievably horny, he was also unbelievably fucked up and tired as well. So, after making out with her for a few minutes, he passed out.

As he finished remembering every detail of the night before with Elsa, he found himself lying in the same place where he was many years ago. After the memory of last evening and how he got to where he was now came flooding back, Jake suddenly remembered that he wasn't alone. He rolled over in bed to find the girl that he knew he would find, right there and at that moment. Elsa Eriksson looked every bit as Nordic as one would expect with that last name and his excitement about her hit the same peak as it did the first time he was with her, which was either last night or over twenty years ago depending upon the perspective. He realized that his heart was pounding, and he could feel the adrenaline surge through his body. It was euphoric to suddenly be young again, and at the moment, Jake was reveling in it.

He laid there next to her, both still half naked, and he knew he had a choice to make. He also knew that this choice may change everything for him, because as crazy as it was to admit, Calliope was not wrong about his burden of regret. Suddenly, he was back at the time and place of one of his greatest regrets and he could change everything right now if he chose to do so. This must be one of the critical junctures that Calliope spoke of, so he could do what he did before and experience an identical outcome, or he could do what he had beat himself up about not doing for several years now. He finally decided in a world where most people only get to live once, he got a "do-over," so it was time to take the next step and do what he wished that he had done before. And he knew exactly what this next step was.

As she laid there sleeping, he made his move. Elsa had her naked back to him, so he curled up behind her in a "spoons" arrangement and pulled her close to him. She was still mostly asleep but returned his snuggle by pushing herself into him, which was nice. Her hair smelled wonderful (albeit a little smoky), and after a minute or two, he began to rub his hands all over her butt, down and up her leg, and then up to her torso where he eventually found her left breast. She protested a bit, but did not stop him, so he decided to move forward by pushing aside her long hair and planting kisses on her neck while continuing to pay the breast attention as well. Again, she protested slightly, but after a few minutes, her breathing began to change. He figured she was now awake, and judging by her breathing, she seemed to be enjoying this. This is about as far as he remembered going with her the first time in his main reality, but she appeared to be still giving him the green light, so he moved on. It was now time to change the past. It was now time to move past regret.

After several minutes kissing her neck and fondling her breast, Jake moved his hand back down her torso and over her abdomen to her waistline, where his fingers found the button to her cutoffs. He deftly unbuttoned them while continuing to kiss the back of her neck. She was breathing harder now, and this only increased as he pulled down the zipper so he could continue his exploration of her body under her panties. In the next moment he moved his fingers into position, and as he touched her secret areas, she began to moan softly. Jake had no idea how long this lasted, but she was now grinding into him as his fingers explored, making him quite aroused as well. In the next instant, she turned around and began to kiss him while tearing at his belt and shorts to pull them off him as soon as possible. As this was happening, he began to pull her cutoffs and panties off as well and then all at once he was on top of her with his shorts still around the bottom of his ankles. However, at that moment, neither person seemed to care about that in the least, and as they moved together on the sea of passion, he was amazed how good it felt, and surprised how long it lasted. As he released his energy, they both screamed and then he rolled off her slick with both of their sweat. It was a transcendental sexual experience, and he didn't think he would ever forget it, even if he returned to the present and didn't live in this reality for good. After that moment, much of him wanted to stay. But even though the sex was as good as he'd hoped, he still didn't know if there was enough there yet to justify staying permanently. Right now, it was not enough to say goodbye to his children forever, and the memory of his love for them still burned bright although exact details about them were fuzzy and distant. But this had just begun, and he was curious to see where it went. Apparently, she was too.

"Jake," said Elsa, still out of breath and staring at the ceiling. "That was amazing, I had no idea you were so talented!"

"Right back at you, Elsa," said Jake still breathing a bit hard himself. "I wanted to do that last night, but the cumulative alcohol consumption in addition to the weed made that impossible. When I woke up and saw you laying there with your shirt off, I thought I'd see if we were on the same page. Turns out we were."

"I'm so glad you did, Jake. I mean I basically threw myself at you all night," said Elsa and then she rolled over and kissed him. The kiss was warm and wonderful and reminded him of how it tasted to be young. She laughed gently and playfully after the kiss and then kissed him again. "Don't worry honey, I passed out right after you did. You know what? I'm really hungry. Do you want to get some food?"

"Sounds great, Elsa. My car it still over by the Patio, but I have a motorcycle if you don't mind going that way."

"Are you kidding me, you are a great lover AND you have a motorcycle? This just keeps getting better!" She smiled brightly to punctuate the last comment further.

"OK great," said Jake. "We can grab some food and then get my car, and you can drive it home while I ride the bike.

Then, I can give you a ride back to your apartment afterwards. Can you drive stick? I have a 72' Datsun 240Z, so this plan won't work unless you can."

"Jake, I have a better plan," she said with her eyes sparkling. "Why don't we get some food and then go to my place before we get the car? We can take a shower there, and I can then make myself up and put on clean clothes. I can also grab some clothing for tonight and tomorrow. If you take me out to a nice dinner, I may even let you take me to bed again later. Oh, and manual transmissions are no issue at all." She smiled again.

Just then, his clock radio alarm went off. He remembered setting it for 10:30 the night before last as he worked the lunch and early evening shifts yesterday. He always preferred waking to music rather than a buzzer so when the alarm went off music played, and the song that was playing was *I Started a Joke* by the Bee Gees. Jake suddenly knew that he was now past the critical decision and that his time in this alternate reality had officially begun. So far, everything that Calliope had said had come to fruition. It was the same girl, the same moment, the same everything. Except this time, he made the move that resulted in their remarkable sexual encounter just a few moments ago. The last time, he didn't do that, and Jake had always believed that if he had tried to have sex with her and things went well, that they may have had a relationship. The first time around, she only stayed with him that evening, part of the next day and afterwards, they never saw each other again. This was always disappointing to him and had created the regret that he continued to harbor until just a few minutes ago. Now, that regret was cleared, and he was in uncharted territory. What he didn't know was that Elsa would continue to make his decision to leave this alternate reality even more difficult. For one thing, she seemed to enjoy the sex as much as he did and seemed to want more. He hit the snooze button, and the music stopped playing.

"Jake!" Exclaimed Elsa. "What are you doing? I love that song, turn it back on!" Jake complied, and the music began again. "Who sings this? I heard it on the oldies channel the other day and really wanted to know who did it. One of those awesome British Invasion groups, I'm sure. Do you know?"

"It's the Bee Gees, Elsa. They're one of my favorite groups."

"Wow! They sound so different than they did when they were in their disco phase. I think I need to listen to them more. So, you OK with my plan?"

"Heck yeah!" He said and then kissed her and jumped out of bed. "Let's get out of here, I'm starving!"

She got out of bed and caught him looking at her naked body as she got up. She smiled and he smiled back.

"It looks like you like what you see," said Elsa. "For the record, I like what I see as well."

He smiled at her again and then threw on some clothes. Since he knew that a shower was planned at her place, he just put on what he wore last night, and packed a new shirt, underwear, and another pair of shorts and put it all in a small backpack. She only had a cross-body purse, so she agreed to wear his backpack to "snuggle him closer" on the ride. They left the duplex and took his bike out of the small garage. It was only a little Honda 450, which looked a lot like Fonzie's motorcycle on the TV show, *Happy Days*, and it started right away. They both put on their helmets, he jumped on, and she climbed on behind, wrapping herself around him with both her arms and legs.

They took a five-minute ride to a little greasy spoon nearby called the Hoosier Grill. They sat at the counter because the place was packed and then they both devoured a breakfast of sausage links, eggs, toast, and sliced tomatoes along with several cups of decent diner coffee. They were both sufficiently full after their early feast, so Jake got the check, paid it, and they left.

On the ride to her apartment, she snuggled herself even closer to him, and he remembered the last time that this happened. While he did give her a ride back to her apartment the first time that he was with her in the other reality, they had not had sex, so she was not quite as enthusiastic about holding him as she was now and did not really snuggle him at all. But that was different now and the sun was shining bright as they motored down the road. He began to think that his feelings were more intense for her now than they were before as well. He had no way of quantifying this, but the intensity of those feelings was beginning to make his old reality, the one with his children in it, more blurry and less tangible than before. If things continued like this, he honestly did not know what he would do when the time came to make a decision about staying or going back.

They reached Elsa's apartment, went in, and put their helmets and his backpack on the kitchen table. Without warning she grabbed him and kissed him aggressively. He didn't mind in the least.

"Jake," said Elsa after kissing him for at least a good minute or so, "Let's take that shower. The motorcycle made me super horny again, I don't think I can wait."

"Works for me!" Said Jake enthusiastically as he suddenly became very aroused himself. "I was feeling a bit dirty anyway so that's a great idea."

"That's what I was hoping you'd say," said Elsa and then she walked towards what Jake figured was her bedroom, taking off her clothes as she went. He followed suit.

The shower lasted the better part of a half-hour, and during that time, they both enjoyed each other's body again for the second time in the last couple of hours. He could not believe how toned she was, and her enthusiasm for sex was amazing to him. She was very vocal as well and at one point he was certain that the neighbor would knock on the door at any second to make sure that everything was OK. In the end, they both stepped out of her shower fully cleaned and fully spent. His head felt like it was floating, and his emotions were on overload. He suddenly felt very thankful to be here and silently thanked Calliope for the opportunity. Although it may have been residual adrenaline or some other neurotransmitter, he couldn't remember being so happy.

Jake and Elsa dressed, but she took quite a while with her hair and makeup, so he watched TV in her living room. The apartment was small, and she lived there with a roommate named Suzy who was out of town for the weekend and would not return until tomorrow morning. When Elsa finished making herself up, she came out and Jake was floored by how lovely she looked when she did. She was wearing a pair of white shorts and a blue tank top with white high-top Reeboks, her long hair was in a ponytail, and her makeup was perfect. She also had some additional clothing with her and a small makeup bag that she stuffed into Jake's backpack which now held the clothing that he had worn on the way over. His heart began to beat faster yet again as she packed her clothes, because he noticed a bit of lace that looked like lingerie. This night had the potential to be epic.

They rode back to the parking lot where he had parked his car last night and she jumped off the bike, got in the car, and fired it up. She followed him back to the duplex, they dropped off the car, and then she put her helmet back on and jumped back on the bike behind him again like she did earlier.

"Take me on an adventure today, Jake," she said. "Wherever you want, let's just enjoy the moment."

Jake didn't reply, he just put the bike into gear and headed out. He knew exactly where to take her, but it would take some time to get there. She wanted adventure, so he figured that the least he could do was give it to her. Somewhere in the back of his mind, he still could hear his children's laughter, but the sound was getting fainter all the time. His past led to his future and his future had returned him to the past. And now, he had no idea where he would end up.

CHAPTER 8: FOOL'S GOLD

Saturday, July 10th, 1993

They rode out of Indy on I-465 and then hit I-74 West towards Illinois. The little motorcycle purred along as Elsa continued to hug him tightly. He was not very familiar with Indiana as he only spent one summer in his life there, but he did remember taking a canoe trip down Sugar Creek in Crawfordsville with another waiter from Bazbeaux's earlier that summer. It was too late in the day for the canoe trip, but he also remembered that it ended by a nature preserve. What was even weirder was that he was pretty sure that he still knew how to get back there. As it happens, he did.

They arrived at Pine Hills Nature Preserve at 3:10 according to his watch. They spent about two hours there exploring, and Elsa seemed to be enjoying every moment. It was all very romantic, although it was a bit hot as well, so after about an hour of hiking and stopping to make out a few times at one picturesque spot or another, they decided that they had enough adventure for the day and rode back to Indy.

The couple got back to his place at 6:15, and they went in to get ready as they had decided to go somewhere nice for dinner. He wanted to shower with her again, but this time, she told him that she wanted to wait for later because she had something special planned. So, he just got ready instead although he really wanted to skip dinner that night and go straight to dessert.

Jake decided that this would be a good day to dress up a bit, so he put on a blue blazer with a white Oxford shirt, khaki pants, and penny loafers. Elsa dressed in an ankle-length skirt that was gray with diagonal black stripes and wore a black top with short sleeves that was very short and exposed a tantalizing view of her belly button. Her hair was down like last night and she topped the entire look off with four-inch heels. In other words, she looked as good as two blackjacks after splitting aces. They got in the old sports car and headed downtown.

Jake and Elsa arrived at St. Elmo's Steakhouse which is a fixture in Indianapolis and has been in business since 1902. In his main reality, Jake knew that he probably wouldn't have worried about the expense associated with this type of place because he assumed that he made a lot more money there (and then). However, he didn't know that for certain because he really could not recall exactly what his career was later in life. In fact, he couldn't even remember the exact year he came from except that he felt that it wasn't too far in the future, maybe fifteen or twenty years. Basically, he remembered almost nothing about the future at all. The only things that he did remember was that he was here because of Calliope the Muse and had to abide by the rules that she had set for the visit, that he had taken the other path at the critical junction with Elsa, and that he had two beautiful children in his main reality. Somehow, their memory was tied so intrinsically to him that he knew that they were there and that he loved them as they loved him. Unfortunately, he really couldn't remember exactly how they looked anymore or even their names at this point, and as things progressed with Elsa, he remembered less all the time.

They both ordered St. Elmo's famous shrimp cocktails, which were followed by excellent filets, both served medium rare. They sat, talked, and had a nice bottle of wine. They then split a piece of New York cheesecake, and he had some coffee to clear his head while she finished the remainder of the wine. They left the restaurant shortly after they finished dessert and decided to take a stroll around Indy's famous circle downtown which gives the city its nickname. In the center of the circle is the Soldiers' and Sailors' monument which sits in the middle of a large, tiered circular fountain and they stopped there to kiss for a while before they moved on. It was a nice walk, but after a while, she started dropping hints about going back to Jake's place for a night cap and some more dessert, just not the kind that included the consumption of additional late-night calories... at least not most of the time. So, they found the car, jumped in, and drove home. The drive was not easy for Jake, because Elsa was all over him the entire way. She kept kissing him on the neck repeatedly, while her hand wandered down his chest where it found his belt buckle, then the top button to his slacks, and finally, his zipper. Like a bank robber she disabled all these defenses easily and deftly and then began to touch him in the way that he had wanted her to for several hours now. He drove as fast as he could, swerved left and right several times and had one hell of a time shifting the gears, but somehow, they were able to make it back to his place without crashing or getting busted.

They stumbled in, removing each other's clothing as

they went and were finally able to navigate their way to the bedroom where they both fell into the bed in various stages of being undressed. He barely was able to get his pants off from around his ankles before she took the initiative, pushed him down on the bed, and moved to the top position with her skirt still on, but her top and panties off. After climbing aboard, she spent quite a while there and soon her ride went from a slow canter to the Kentucky Derby. She began to move faster and faster with each passing second and as she increased the intensity of her lovemaking, this made her even more vocal than she was earlier. Suddenly, after what could have been an hour or a few minutes, she screamed and shuddered and five seconds later he followed suit. It was a magnificent moment for Jake, and even though this was the third time that he had been with her that day, that moment was probably the best. They both collapsed afterwards, and in minutes, Jake was asleep.

Jake awakened to the smell of coffee as a ray of sunlight assaulted his retinas. The smell of bacon and eggs cooking was also present, and it wafted in like a siren's song as his olfactory system took over and compelled the rest of his body to get out of bed. He still wore nothing at all, and his clothing had been neatly folded and placed on the chair in the room with the blazer hung on the back. So, it was obvious that Elsa had cleaned up and had apparently made breakfast as well. Jake was beginning to think that she may be a keeper and was struggling more and more to remember any details at all about his children. Jake thought that if the relationship kept going like this, it would be hard not to stay here in this alternate reality.

He got out of bed, put on a pair of gym shorts and a t-shirt, and walked out into his small kitchen where Elsa was finalizing breakfast preparations by serving bacon and scrambled eggs to the two place settings at the table and then pouring each of them a cup of coffee. She was wearing an oversized t-shirt with a big picture of a bottle of Little Kings Cream Ale on it, and her hair was in a loose ponytail.

"Hello there, sleepyhead," said Elsa cheerfully. "Ready for some breakfast?"

"You bet," was Jake's reply. "Everything smells wonderful, and you even cleaned up our trail of clothing from last night. I could get used to this." As he uttered the last remark, he saw what looked like a flash of sadness cross her face and then, just as quickly, the bright smile returned as if it had never gone.

"After the good time that you showed me last night, and all day yesterday, making breakfast was the least that I could do. I must admit that I lost count of the orgasms that I had yesterday and... I really enjoyed every other moment we had also, Jake," she said as she paused awkwardly. Then she burst out, "Let's eat!"

With that she gave him a quick kiss and then sat down to breakfast. He dug in as well and found the food and coffee to be completely delicious. The eggs were fluffy and buttery, but not undercooked, and the bacon was crispy just like Jake liked it. Last, the coffee was the perfect strength, and even though the ingredients were simple, everything blended as well as it might in a Michelin Star restaurant. Or maybe that was just due to the company.

"So, I'm supposed to work this afternoon, but we could do something fun in the meantime," said Jake. "What do you think? How about another shower at the very least?"

"Ooh, I like that idea," said Elsa. "One more for the road, and then we can both return to reality. I can't wait."

That hit Jake like a Louisville Slugger swung by Sammy Sosa. "What do you mean? This *is* reality, or at least I was hoping that it was, I thought we could get together again after I get off work. You must admit, we're off to a great start." Her comment had caught him completely off guard. In his mind, they were compatible in every way with their sexual synergy at the head of the hit parade. What was he missing? The frown on her face reappeared but this time, it didn't go away. He would soon find out the answer to that question.

"Jake... I should've told you something earlier, but I was having so much fun, and you were so amazing to be with that I just couldn't bring myself to do it. Please know that I never intended for things to go this far."

"What are you saying... that this was just a two-night stand?" Asked Jake, suddenly sick to his stomach.

"Yes Jake, I'm saying exactly that, I'm afraid," she said while looking at him with sad, glassy, eyes that truly looked sincere. She grabbed his hand, and he barely felt it.

"Wow, I wasn't expecting that... I just don't understand... Why?"

"Jake, I've been dating the same guy since I was a freshman in college. His name is James. We broke up about six months ago, after I found my roommate's panties in the glovebox of his car. He swore nothing happened and made up some bullshit story about how the panties got there which was completely unbelievable. The bad news for him was that Kathy, my roommate, couldn't handle the guilt and eventually told me the truth. So not only was he a cheater, but he was also a liar, and since I was pretty pissed off, I left, and we agreed to see other people."

"If that's the case, then why can't you take a shot with me? Let's see where this thing goes!" Said Jake, who also found this story very familiar for some reason. He could not place why exactly so he figured that that feeling came from something in the future.

"Because... because even though my boyfriend wasn't faithful and has even dated two more women since I was with him last, I still love him, and I want to work things out. I know

I may be a sucker, and I may regret it but... we have history, Jake."

"I honestly don't know what to say," said Jake feeling more than a bit hurt. "Was I just used for revenge sex then? Please be honest, I think I deserve that much at least."

"Jake, meeting you was unexpected. You should know I've not dated or been with anyone since I left James... until you," said Elsa, looking sadder by the minute. "At first, I thought that you'd be a perfect person to have a fling with because I was instantly attracted to you. Then, after you passed out while we were making out the first night, I figured that maybe sex with you wasn't the right thing and was planning on slipping out before you woke up. Of course, I fell asleep as well, you woke me up in the wonderful way that you did, and the rest is history." Elsa paused and looked him in the eyes. "You turned out to be way better than revenge sex, Jake. You also need to know that I really like you and for a few moments yesterday, I almost changed my mind. But... like I said before, I just have too much invested with James, so I must try again. I'm so sorry that I can't give you more, and I really hope that you'll at least try to understand... but I get it if you don't."

"So, when I take you home later, that's it, right?"

"Yes, Jake, I suppose it is," said Elsa even more sadly. "I'd love to be friends with you, but considering what happened yesterday, I think it would always be awkward. Jake, you're a gorgeous guy who really knows how to treat a woman, and if I wasn't hung up on James, I'd be the first in line to be with you. But sadly, I know what I want now, and that's a life with another man. Once again, I should've been honest with you earlier. I didn't realize that both of us would develop feelings for each other and know that I may live to regret not giving a relationship with you a chance. But you really don't want me if I can't give myself completely to you, and I don't think that either of us would be happy in the long run. All I can say is that

I'm sorry, but I know that's not nearly good enough."

Jake just sat there and looked at her. All this time, he had two main regrets from his first interaction with her that happened in his main reality before he traveled back to this moment. The first regret, which was the basest of the two, was that he didn't have sex with her. That regret had now been cleared, and he was able to live out one of his oldest "what if" fantasies.

The second regret was that he never had the opportunity to have a relationship with her. However, after traveling back to this place in time, he now knew that he never had that opportunity at all. All she wanted was a release; partially because she felt the need to get back at her boyfriend for what he did with her roommate, and partially because she hadn't been with anyone for six months, and their attraction was palpable. Alas, this relationship wasn't to be, and the sooner that he returned to his main reality, the better. He knew exactly how to handle it from here.

"Elsa, you're right, I *am* sad about this," said Jake. "I really wanted to get to know you better and thought that we had a lot of potential together. But I also know that you've probably done a lot of soul searching and your heart has led you to where it really wants to go. So, I must let you go, and I know it. Just know that I'll never forget these two days and that I don't know if I'll ever find a better lover. I hope you're happy with James, Elsa. I also hope he appreciates how lucky he is to have you."

"Thanks," she said and then gave him a hug that turned into a long embrace. After a time, she pulled back to look at him again. "I still wouldn't mind another shower with you. After all, if things go the way I want them to, you'll be the last person that I'll ever be with before I'm with James for the rest of my life."

Jake disengaged from their embrace, extended his hand to Elsa, and led her into the bathroom where he turned on the water in the shower stall. He then undressed her while she did the same for him and then they both stepped in. For the last time ever, they explored each other's body to the fullest. It was one of the weirdest moments in his entire existence, and he hoped that it was one that he'd never forget. However, once he left this alternate reality and returned to his own primary timeline, this would have never happened, so he knew he may not remember anything at all. He just hoped that what he did remember would be enough to clear his regrets about Elsa completely. For some reason, he was sure that it would be.

After their shower, Elsa gathered her things and then he drove her home. When they got there, no words were exchanged, only a long hug and a kiss on the cheek, and she was gone. At least he had made an impression. Unfortunately, it would not be one that she would ever remember once he returned to his main reality because that version of Elsa never had sex with him at all. What a concept.

After he dropped her off, his first inclination was to return to his own reality immediately by speaking the words that Calliope had taught him and surprisingly, the memory of those words was very clear. However, he rather enjoyed being in his college years again and loved how it felt to be in a body that did not have a bad shoulder and a worse knee, and for some reason he remembered his future injuries very well, just not how he was injured. So, although he should be going to work, he figured that he would head to a local watering hole in Broad Ripple known as the Pawn Shop Pub instead. After all, it didn't matter if he went to work as he didn't plan on staying in this reality. This place wasn't flashy at all, and was pretty much exactly what most people would have expected when they went in. The décor included lots of dark wood, and several taps lined the wall behind the massive walnut bar. He pulled up a chair, ordered a Guinness, closed his eyes, and just sat for a second to collect his thoughts. Just then, he felt someone sit down next to him, and then the bartender said, "what'll it be lady?" When he heard her voice, it was instantly recognizable and when he opened his eyes, there sat Calliope looking very dapper in a gray business suit, round glasses, and her hair (which was now jet black) pulled back into a long ponytail.

"Hello Jake," said this very polished version of Calliope. "If the look on your face wasn't enough to let me know that things didn't go well with Elsa, the fact that you're in a bar by yourself in the afternoon drinking removes all doubt. Do you want to talk about it?"

"She just wanted a fling. That's it," said Jake turning to look at her. "Did you know this would happen?"

"Well, let me just say this. While I wasn't certain what the outcome would be exactly, a future reality that had you and her together as a couple was a very low probability even if the conditions were perfect. I'm not quite sure what would have made them perfect, but nevertheless, I'm also guessing that you'll be returning to your main reality now, right?"

"I really could've seen myself with her, Calliope," said Jake in a faraway voice. "The sex was better than I could have imagined that it would've been, and for some reason I know that I've imagined what sex with her would be like many times. What I didn't expect was that I would fall for her a little bit. I mean, I wasn't exactly in love or anything like that, but I really did enjoy our time together and could easily have seen a life with her... so I guess that I'm a little sad. But your guess is right, I'll be returning. And as good as it was with Elsa, I'm more than a little ashamed of myself that I almost gave my children up for what was just a physical relationship. Wow."

"Don't beat yourself up Jake," said the muse. "Like I told you before, your feelings are as intense right now as they were the first time you had them. You know what to do to get home, you can go back anytime."

"I gotta admit, I like being in this younger body again," said Jake. "Plus, I wanted to wait until tomorrow morning to see what Bee Gees song you selected for the one-day warning signal."

"All right, stay a little longer if you like, this is all for you anyway," said Calliope. "I do have one question, however. Did you learn anything about yourself?"

"Well, besides what I've told you already, the main thing is that I'm not always in control of everything that happens to me. Somehow, I remember that after the original night with Elsa I thought that all I had to do was to change one thing and that would have resulted in a relationship that could have led to a lifetime partnership. What I found out was that the only thing that I had control of that night was whether we had sex and that as far as she was concerned, a relationship was never even on the table for consideration. I was so much in my own head, that I failed to see that she drove the agenda, and I just merely played my part."

Calliope stepped off the barstool, downed her drink which was a shot of Ouzo, and threw a $10 bill on the bar. She smiled at him in that winning way that only she could, and after looking into his eyes for a while in silence, she finally spoke.

"Jake, from my perspective this has been a success," she said still smiling. "But you still have at least one more journey back in time to make, and the lessons will get harder."

"And I still can't opt out, either. Right?"

"Not a chance," said Calliope. She turned and walked to the door of the bar and then paused to turn around and look at him one more time. "I'll see you again soon and take care of yourself until then. You'll be disoriented a bit when you return, but it will pass in a few minutes and the good news is that you'll still remember everything that happened here as the memory of this reality is now a part of your soul. Oh, and here's the song that would have played tomorrow morning because there's no reason for you to stay until then. Bye for now, Jake."

Calliope walked out and as soon as she left, the late 70s classic *Night Fever* began to play on the jukebox. That song was not one of his favorites by the Bee Gees, but it was one of their most famous tunes, so several of the bar patrons began to nod their heads or tap the bar to the beat. However, whether he liked that song wasn't important. The moments with Elsa were nothing more than night fever itself and that fever doesn't always include love or even the promise of affection from the other person and he needed to remember that. Sometimes time spent with a lover is constrained to a moment that needs to stand on its own. Sometimes, it just needs to be appreciated and remembered. And sometimes, all you get is a glimpse of the full dream of a relationship and nothing more is promised or even intended. He downed his beer, went to take a piss, and while standing at the urinal, he said the words that Calliope had taught him. All went black as he moved forward in time to where he began this journey. Unfortunately, this "long strange trip" had just begun, and the lessons would only get weirder, and more difficult, from here.

CHAPTER 9: AN UNWELCOME GUEST

Monday, November 27th, 2000

Savannah awakened just after 10:00 a.m., showered and then got ready for a shift that began at noon. She didn't sleep well the night before because she was still worried that someone would try to break in again. This was a somewhat irrational fear because the police had assigned an officer to keep an eye on her building and a police car was parked out in front of the building until morning. However, she just didn't feel safe there anymore and with Kate gone, this was doubly true.

She was also upset that she was forced to move home and had booked herself on a Greyhound tomorrow at noon. The conversation with her mother went better than she expected, and her father even said hello and was surprisingly nice to her considering that it had been years since they had spoken. They even bought the bus ticket for her and that was extremely helpful considering her current lack of funds. However, as good as the reconnection with her parents was, she still felt like a failure and since she had housing for only four more days at the most, she had no other choice; she figured that her time as a vagabond playwright was over.

Savannah worked her shift at the restaurant and then turned in her notice to the manager on duty who was a guy named Dave. When Savannah told him the story about the robbery, he offered her a place on his couch which she might have considered if he was not the slimeball that he was. Dave was in his early forties, lived alone, and was constantly making sexual innuendos around the young females on the wait staff which made all of them feel uncomfortable. Apparently, he was married until a few years ago when his wife caught him smoking pot in their living room with a girl who had just started as a hostess. The fact that they were smoking pot was not the issue, but the fact that they were both sitting in bathrobes and nothing else was, so she kicked him out the next day. Nope, life with a creeper like Dave was not an option, even for a short period of time.

She also made the painful call to the gentleman that was going to rent her the apartment and told him what happened. He was not unkind to her when she gave him this information, however it was also clear that he was frustrated with this turn of events and refused to refund any of the $500 that she had given him to hold the unit. So, she was still very low on funds although she was able to add about $50 to her coffers from the tips she received from her final shift at the restaurant.

After the shift was over, Savannah went to an Army-Navy store in Northern Virginia to buy a military-style green backpack. Her duffel bag had developed a large hole and was basically falling apart so she threw it away. Additionally, her old suitcase was unwieldy to carry around and looked like it had seen its best days two decades ago. She just wanted something big that she could stuff everything into which was easy to carry around on her back and fortunately, that store had just what she needed for a very reasonable price. While there, she was also talked into buying a small can of pepper spray from the owner who had many tattoos on his body including one that ran the length of his forearm and said "Semper Fidelis" in huge script letters. He seemed very concerned that she wouldn't be able to defend herself if she was attacked. Considering that he also was prepping for what he called the "imminent implosion of society," it seemed clear that he wanted to help her prepare for this apocalypse as well which, according to his sources, could occur any day. Even though he was a bit extreme in his beliefs, he was a big teddy bear of a man who reminded her of her grandfather and really did seem to have her best interests at heart. He even threw in an old Vietnam-Era field jacket that looked very good on her and was very warm as well. Savannah thanked him and then left his store feeling a bit better about her life even though she still had to take the trip that she never wanted to take back home to Boulder the next day. Even if she had wanted to go, a two-day trip on a Greyhound was brutal in and of itself and she hoped that the number of weirdos on the bus would not be too high. If only her parents had booked a flight for her instead... but she couldn't wallow in that thought, she just needed to get home and fix the relationship as Kate advised.

After grabbing a quick meal of bean burritos at Taco Bell, Savannah headed back to Kate's place to pack up. Kate's dad Bill called her right as she walked into the apartment. He wanted to make sure that she was OK, and when she told him what she was going to do next, he told her that she was making the right decision and that he knew that Kate would think so also. Savannah knew for a fact that Kate would approve of her decision to go home because she had told her as much, and she let him know about their conversation. At the end of the call,

Bill wished her well and while she appreciated his concern and knew that he and Kate only wanted the best for her, that didn't make her feel any better about going westward tomorrow. She just wished that she could look at the situation as anything but a defeat.

She walked in the door, put her new backpack on the kitchen table, and put her purse down next to it. She then turned to walk back and throw the deadbolt as the doorframe was still broken, and anyone could walk in by simply pushing the door. Just then, her cell phone rang, and it was one of the other waitresses from work. This girl, named Megan, was always very friendly to Savannah and the two had drinks together after work a few times. She was not at work today and had just found out that Savannah was leaving town.

"Savvy, I just heard the news," said Megan. "Why do you have to leave? What happened?

"I went away with my roommate Kate for Thanksgiving and when I got back, it was clear that someone had broken into the apartment. Unfortunately, whoever it was found all the money that I had saved for a deposit on a place of my own. Losing the money is bad enough, but even worse for me is that I'll be homeless in just over three days because Kate was transferred with her job and someone else has already put a deposit down on her unit. So, I must go back home to Colorado on a Greyhound Bus tomorrow to regroup. That's unless I want to move in with Dave. He did offer, you know."

"Eww," said Megan who sounded like she had just taken a bite of something rotten. "That wouldn't be an option for me at all! It's too bad that I can't offer you a place, but I'm sleeping on my brother and sister-in-law's couch myself. I'm so sorry to hear it Savvy, if I had any extra money, I'd pay the deposit for you, but saving has never really been my strong point. Is there anyone else who could put you up for a while?"

"There's no one, Megan," said Savannah sadly. "Or at least no one that I'd feel comfortable staying with. Oh, and thanks for your concern, I appreciate it. I guess that I'm not very good at saving, either, or at least at keeping my savings safe. I really wish I could stay but I must now retreat to my childhood home and figure out how to get back on track with some sort of career. I think it may be time to come to terms with the fact that a career as a successful playwright is nothing more than a pipe dream for me."

"Whatever you do Savvy, don't give up on that dream. When you let me read the first act of the play you're working on, I thought it was amazing. It would be so sad if you didn't finish it so you can share it with the rest of the world."

"You're so sweet, Megan. Thanks for the support. I really did enjoy working with you and I hope that we can keep in touch. I'd hate to lose you as a friend."

"Don't worry about that at all, honey," said Megan, "you are my girl! Anyway, I must go, my brother needs my help cleaning the cat box. I guess that is part of the price that I must pay to stay on his couch."

"Thanks for calling, Megan. I look forward to hearing from you soon."

"You will, Savvy, I promise. Be careful out there and call me when you get to Colorado, so I know you're OK. Bye sweetie!"

Savannah put down the phone and noticed that it was now 8:38 p.m. She packed most of her clothing in the backpack and left in on the kitchen table. She also figured that a shower would be nice, so she turned on the water and undressed while it was heating up. When she stepped in, the water felt great, and she decided that she would just let it run on her for a while before she even started washing herself. After what must have been at least 20 minutes, she finally turned off the water, put her hair in a towel, and then wrapped another towel around her body. Kate left her these two towels because they were older and had begun to fray at the edges. She figured that she would just throw them away when she left. Just as she opened the door to the bathroom, she heard something click in the front room; it was the deadbolt that she had forgotten to throw. Terror suddenly filled her as she looked across the small apartment to the door where very familiar eyes then met hers. Somehow, Chad had found her.

"I always loved looking at you in a towel, Savvy. Of course, I liked it even better with the towel removed," said Chad who was sitting there wearing Levi's jeans and cowboy boots. He also wore an expensive looking green turtleneck sweater, a gorgeous tan cashmere overcoat, and a Burberry scarf. It was a unique look, but Chad managed to make it look extremely dashing and fresh at the same time. Certainly, his ruggedly symmetrical face, jet-black hair and grey eyes did not hurt in augmenting this look, and it would likely fail completely for other, lesser mortals in the looks department. What she didn't understand was how he could afford such righteous duds in the first place. The coat alone had to be at least $500.

"How did you find me?" She asked with shock and anger apparent in her voice.

"Good question," he said still leering at her in her almost-naked state. He then pulled a small notebook out of the pocket of his overcoat, and she knew immediately what he was going to say. "It seems as if you left a bit too quickly and forgot something. Amazingly, this address was written in here at the back with train times written under it. While it took me some time to find this little notebook, once I did, it was all I needed."

"OK, so you found me, good for you," said Savannah in a voice that was tinged with both annoyance and fear. "What do you want? If it's another chance with me, just know that you're wasting your time."

"A month ago, I would have begged you to come back to me, but that's over now. I've found that two aspiring actresses are way more fun than one pathetic wannabe playwright, and the best thing is that they're both my roommates now, so I really don't need you at all anymore. The problem is that you owe me, Savannah, and now it's time to collect."

"Owe you? What the hell are you talking about? You ruined my credit, had me pawn virtually all my jewelry to pay the rent, and then decided to treat me like a punching bag whenever you were having a bad day! What in the world could I possibly owe *you*?"

"The problem is, Savannah, that my services come with a price. Remember the three off-Broadway acting gigs that I got you? They may not have been the roles that you were looking for, but you did make about twenty-five grand from them. Since we were living together at the time, I waived my agent's fee for you... as a courtesy, you know. However, now that you and I are no longer... affiliated... that bill has come due, and I am here to collect my 20 percent."

Savannah fought to quell the rising terror and was instead trying to focus on the anger that she felt as well. What a bastard! While it was true that he got her those acting roles to help her out, two of them were bit parts that barely yielded $3,000. The third part was much better because the play ran much longer, but still $25,000 was not enough to survive on in New York for very long. The worst part was that none of them led to the people that she really needed to meet, and he had not helped her get any other work for several months now. Moreover, he was slurring his speech which meant that he had likely had several single malts prior to his arrival at Kate's apartment. This was bad indeed.

"Chad, I was robbed over the weekend. I have nothing to give you because I am flat broke."

"Yes, I know," he said looking even more smug if that was possible. "Do you have anything to drink? I could really use another belt."

"No Chad, there's nothing here but the expired OJ in the fridge. What do you mean *you know*? How in the world would you know that I was robbed?"

"I was at a seedy little bar not far from here recently when this skinny homeless looking dude in an old Redskins hoodie comes in and buys a round for the five people sitting at the bar because he just had come into some money. I then talked to him for a while and found out that he had robbed an apartment where two girls lived over the Thanksgiving holiday. Apparently, he was a pizza delivery guy who had been casing the place out for a while, and while he was disappointed that most of the valuable things in the apartment were gone when he got there, he did find a fat wad of cash in a coffee can and took it. So, I fed him more drinks and after he passed out on the bar, I liberated him of the cash he had left and took my leave. By the look on your face, I'm guessing that you know who these two girls are."

"You asshole!!!" Screamed Savannah. "That's my money!!! Give it back or I'll call the cops!!!"

"Pipe down there, sweety," said Chad in an even keeled voice that infuriated her even more. "The money is pretty much gone at this point, so even if I wanted to give it back to you, I couldn't. More importantly, like I said, you owe me. The good news is that being the nice guy that I am, I have already applied it to your balance. The problem is that by my accounting, you still owe me about 3000 bucks, so if we could just settle up, I'll be on my way. Oh, and about calling the cops, good luck proving that anything that I told you is true. That's the problem with cash, Savvy. Once it's in someone else's hands, it's theirs."

Savannah was furious. She wanted nothing else at that moment but to jump on him and pound his stupid face to a pulp. But he was much larger than her and if she tried it was likely that he would injure her badly. After all, he had hurt her in the past and she remembered exactly how hard he could hit her all too well. To make matters worse, she was still wearing nothing but a towel, and her phone was in the new backpack on the kitchen table... along with the pepper spray that the old Marine had convinced her to purchase. Unfortunately, Chad was now between her and the backpack. If there was any chance for her to get out with any money at all, she would have to somehow get to the kitchen without him stopping her first. She also needed to force down her anger because she knew that was the only way that she'd be able to achieve her objective. She had to think clearly.

"So, what else do you want Chad? I have literally nothing left but about $200 and the clothes on my back. How can I work off this debt that you think I owe you? Should I just expect you to force yourself on me like you did several nights when you were good and drunk? Is that what you want?"

"Don't flatter yourself, Savvy, you just aren't that valuable," said Chad coldly. "Although I wouldn't mind banging you again for old time's sake, I don't plan on getting sent to jail after you make a police report with my DNA all over you. The juice is just not worth the squeeze. But I'm also pretty sure that you aren't telling me the complete truth anyway because the reality is that you do have something that would settle our debt. Savannah, I want the watch."

"Fuck you, Chad! That was my grandfather's, you're not getting it unless you take it by force!"

"Which I'm completely willing to do," he said while putting on black leather gloves that he had just removed from the overcoat's pockets. "And then I'll knock you out, tie you up naked, gag you and leave you here to be found later. Although, since it appears that you no longer seem to have a roommate, that'll be a while and I'll be long gone by then, so good luck. Oh, and just to make things interesting, I plan on turning off the heat and opening the windows as well. I heard that hypothermia can be pretty brutal for a while... at least until you lose feeling. Who knows? You just might make it if someone decides to check in."

"Wow, I had no idea that you could be this cruel, Chad," said Savannah with tears now streaming down her cheeks. "I mean you're a horrible abuser of women, but guys like you seem to prefer excuses and apologies after your temper tantrums to things like this. How far have you sunk into this new world of violence that you seem to be in now? Is there any good left in you? I used to think there was, but maybe I was wrong all along."

"You hurt me, Savannah!" Chad said forcefully. "I loved you, but you burned everything down. You MADE me hit you, you pushed my buttons and caused that side of me to come out. It was NOT my fault and if you'd just had some more patience, and gave me the respect that I deserved, everything would've been fine. Now it's come to this, and I don't even want you anymore. But I do want to see you suffer, so the choice is yours. Give me the watch, and I'll be gone. I'll even let you keep the 200 bucks so you can run back to mommy. Or you can take Door #2 where things will get even worse for you. Think about it for a few minutes, I have time. What's it going to be?"

Savannah felt like she was in a bad dream where she couldn't wake up. It seemed that whenever life seemed to be getting better, something would happen to slap her in the face yet again, and these slaps seemed to be getting progressively harder as well. She would rather die than let him have the watch, but she would rather figure out another option if possible. If she could only come up with a Door #3 that would allow her to escape Chad with her watch, her money, and most importantly, her life, that would be great. She suddenly had an idea, but she would have to pull herself together to pull it off.

"OK, Chad, you win. You're right, I really have no choice, and all I want to do right now is see you go. Trust me, giving you my grandfather's watch hurts me more than you will ever know. If you wanted me to suffer, then you should know that you've hit your mark. Nothing hurts me more than to let it go."

"Good girl!" He said with a sort of self-satisfied look on his face. "I always knew that you were a survivor but also thought that you clung a bit too hard to sentimentality. Consider giving up the watch to be a liberating experience for you. I've freed you from the moldy old guilt that your grandaddy saddled you with on his deathbed. When you think about it, I've helped your career yet again and you know what? This one's on the house."

"It's in the kitchen. You can stand by the door to make sure that I don't run out. Please let me take one last look at the watch before I give it to you, ok?"

"I think that'll be fine, Savvy," he said somewhat gleefully as he got up and stood by the door. "If you let the towel drop, I will give you an extra minute or two."

"Thanks." With that she walked gingerly to the kitchen and grabbed the backpack. For once today, something was working in her favor as the bottle of pepper spray was sitting at the top of the backpack, ready to go. She needed to get close enough to him to make sure that she got a full shot into both his eyes, so she walked towards him while simultaneously digging in the backpack for the watch. Of course, she really didn't intend to grab the watch at all, as she was buying time until she was just beyond arm's reach. She took a breath to steel her resolve and all at once, she acted.

She looked up and met his eyes, and then, like a flash

she pulled the pepper spray from the backpack, leveled it at his head, and pulled the trigger as hard as she could. In that instant, time froze, and Savannah was able to see the stream of pepper spray hit his face right between his eyes which caused a massive amount of the irritant to pool in both eye sockets and fill the entirety of each before he could react fast enough to close them. Chad immediately howled with pain and doubled over grabbing his face with both hands. At that moment, Savannah ran into him knocking him over and this allowed her enough time to throw the deadbolt, open the door, and run out into the hall.

"HELP!!! THE BURGLAR CAME BACK AND HE TRIED TO RAPE ME!!! HELP!!!

Doors opened in the hallway of the apartment building, and a kind looking, older woman at the end of the hall motioned her to her apartment.

"Come over here, honey," she said. "Cecil, call the cops. The thief's come back!!!"

Savannah ran to her door, still wearing her towels and clutching her backpack which held her most prized possession and most of her clothing as well. She made it to the door, went inside, and when she did, she could still hear Chad screaming as well as other commotion as if several men were in the process of securing him for the police when they arrived. The noise was close enough that he must have made it out into the hallway before he was subdued. Savannah broke into tears at that moment and the old lady had her sit on the couch and gave her a blanket. She couldn't believe that she did it, that she got away from him, but she did. Savannah was a fighter, always, but suddenly going back home didn't seem like the worst idea in the world anymore and at this point, she wanted to start over with everything. The two-day rumble down I-70 was something that she was now looking forward to and after her years of misadventure on the East Coast, she didn't know if she ever wanted to return in the future. What she still didn't know is that that she would meet someone soon and that meeting would be a transformational event in her life. The reality was that in less than a day's time, her perspective on life would be very different. She just needed to make it to that juncture.

CHAPTER 10: RETURN TO (A) REALITY

Thursday, December 15th, 2016

Jake woke suddenly in a cold sweat again, just like he had done a few days ago in his past reality. It took him a moment, but after a brief period of disorientation, he finally realized that he was lying in his bed in the Fontainebleau, and he could see faint rays of light peeking in at the bottom and side edges of the curtains. He looked at the clock radio and it said 6:31 and he then grabbed his iPhone from the nightstand to validate the time as well as the date and most importantly, the year. When he did this, he quickly realized that he may have only been gone for hours or even minutes rather than days, and this fascinated him. Irrespective of the timeframe, one thing was clear and that was that he was not the person that he was when he left earlier.

For one thing, his memory of the evening with Elsa was now completely different and he no longer counted that moment as a missed opportunity. He also now knew that there was no future with her even if he had wanted one. Most importantly, he finally realized that not everything was or is under his control so regret in many circumstances is rather silly because it makes no sense to regret something that you can't control. However, there was still a small bit of sadness because Elsa was and likely still is a great girl. In the end, he would not have minded a life with her, but that decision was never his and that chapter was now closed forever.

Jake decided to stay in bed and fell asleep for another hour before finally getting up and going to the bathroom where he started the shower and stepped inside. As he stood there under the running water, he wondered if what happened to him was either a very lucid dream, or a hallucination from some substance that may have been slipped to him last night at the bachelor party. However, deep down he knew that what happened to him was neither of these things and that he had experienced something supernatural. If that was indeed the truth of it, and what Calliope had done to him was real, then he had potentially two more of these alternate realities to visit before this adventure was over. As he stood there with the soothing hot water pelting his back, that thought was almost overwhelming.

What Jake really needed was someone to talk to about his... situation. The only issue was that he had no idea who that could be. There was no one from work that he knew or trusted well enough and his only fraternity brother at the wedding that was likely to listen and possibly offer useful advice was Prop Head, but he had some big work issue to deal with right now, so it may be difficult to carve out time with him when they were not involved with some event that Billy Dee has set up for the wedding party. Today would be particularly challenging because a limo was leaving at noon to take the entire wedding party to Disneyworld where they would "drink their way around the world" at Epcot before meeting at the California Grill on top of the Contemporary Hotel for the official welcome dinner later in the evening.

Due to the schedule of events, it was clear that there would be no time at all to talk to Prop Head today unless he called him right away which in this case meant right after he finished his shower. So, he decided to give that a try, but the whole thing made his head hurt and he was also now reminded of his lower back and knee injuries that all seemed to throb at the same time this morning. Normally he would have attributed these aches and pains to a hangover and considering that he had attended a bachelor party last night, it would seem logical that was probably the cause of his discomfort. But he stopped drinking after he had his first interaction with Calliope, so he didn't think that a hangover was the cause of his woes. Instead, he had another theory about why things felt worse today. He developed this theory because yesterday, or twenty years ago depending upon the temporal context, he didn't feel these aches and pains and the reason that he didn't feel them was because they didn't yet exist when he was in the past reality. So now that he was back, all the old aches and pains had returned as well, and he noticed them more than ever. He thought to himself that it was truly amazing what humans get used to as they age.

Jake got out of the shower and realized that he had spent nearly twenty minutes there. He then shaved, got dressed, and then packed his bag so that he'd be ready to go when Billy Dee's limo arrived. After he was finished, he went over to the in-room coffee maker and started brewing a cup of coffee for himself. He then called Prop Head's room to see if they could talk, but all he got was voicemail. He decided that he'd try again in fifteen minutes or so.

It was just after 9:30, and he didn't know exactly what to do for the next two and a half hours, so he figured that he would start with his cup of coffee and then see where things went from there. If all else failed, he could always try to edit yet another poorly written scene by Jenny, but he was really hoping that he didn't have to resort to that. Just as his coffee finished brewing, the hotel room phone rang. He suspected that Prop Head must have gotten his message, so he picked up the receiver and gave the usual Kappa Sig greeting.

"Alpha Eps Bro! Thanks for calling me back," said Jake enthusiastically. However, it wasn't Prop head at all.

"Hello, Jake? It's Geneva, do I have the right room?"

"Geneva," Jake said brightly. "You do indeed. It's so good to hear your voice! How are you this morning? Did you guys have fun last night?"

"I'm actually great, and yes, we had a blast," said Geneva. "I mean, I did stay up until about four, but I stopped drinking early to make sure that we didn't lose any bridesmaids along the way. The bride was also hammered, so I was forced to play mum to her as well."

"That's hilarious because I did the same thing. They're lucky to have us, aren't they?"

"They are indeed. But that isn't my reason for calling. The reason that I called is because tomorrow has now become today, and since that's the case, I'd like to meet you for a mimosa and a walk on the beach before we head to Disney. Are you in?"

The conversation that he had with her before suddenly came rushing back to him. Today was to be the day that they were to have what was essentially an extended date with each other. While they both agreed to no strings or complications, it appeared that Geneva wanted to give this... whatever it was... life. Although he didn't remember her at all when he was in the alternate reality with Elsa, he remembered who she was now, and all the excitement that he felt when he met her the first time flooded back the moment that he heard her voice.

"I'm most definitely in, Geneva," said Jake with the excitement that he felt evident in his voice. "I'm also ready to go whenever you are, and I'm packed and ready to take the adventure to the land of the mouse. So, let me know where and when you'd like to meet."

"How about the pool bar in fifteen? I still need to finish making myself beautiful, so a few extra minutes would help."

"By my recollection, you'd look good even if you had bed head, but fifteen works for me. See you then."

"You're too kind, sir," she said with lots of flirty undertone. "See you soon. Oh, and remember our agreement, OK? Don't smack me if I grab your hand."

"I wouldn't dream of it," said Jake with his head now in a bit of a fog.

Jake was dressed in the Hawaiian shirt that Billy Dee had selected for all the groomsmen to wear today along with some new khaki shorts and light brown topsiders. He had also purchased a Cuban-style straw fedora and pulled the whole look together with some Maui Jim sunglasses and the Rolex Explorer II on his wrist. He called his daughter to see how she was feeling, and she told him that she felt much better, which was good news. He then went down to the lobby ten minutes after he got off the phone with Geneva, and he headed to the pool bar and ordered two mimosas. Ten minutes later she showed up and she looked even more gorgeous than she did the first time that they met yesterday. Instead of the sundress, she was now wearing a tan miniskirt that looked to be designed for golf and a pink, tightly fitting golf shirt with the word "Maid of Honor" written in script above her left breast. She also wore a matching pink visor and had artfully crafted it into her hairstyle which did nothing but accentuate her beauty.

"You look like you're ready to hit the first tee," said Jake when he saw her. He knew he was being a bit of a smart ass. He also knew that she'd likely appreciate that.

"Yes, I know. It was Julie's idea. She plays a lot of golf and thought it would fit with the overall Florida theme and be comfortable at Epcot as well. I must admit, I do look sexy, don't you think?"

"Let's just say that I would probably be your caddie for free," said Jake and with that she hugged him and then, without warning, she gave him a kiss that was far more than a simple peck and lasted for longer than he would have expected. It was clear that Geneva was going to give her all to whatever relationship that they would have over the next few days. He was unexpectedly ecstatic about this.

"Let's go for that walk," said Geneva as she grabbed her mimosa off the bar. "I just got a text from Layla, and I guess they want us at eleven to pre-game for the limo ride. I've a feeling that this will be a long day of partying. Hope you are up to it!"

Jake and Geneva walked out of the pool bar area and down to the shore, mimosas in hand. At first, the conversation was somewhat superficial, and both recounted stories about certain members of the wedding party and their escapades while they were inebriated last night. Everything was flowing well and was a lot of fun but at some point, Geneva stopped rather suddenly and looked Jake squarely in the eyes.

"So, I have a question for you, and I want you to be honest," she said quite unexpectedly. "I don't care what the answer is, I just want the truth, OK?"

"That sounds like a bear trap to me, Geneva," said Jake with a slight smile on his face. He found himself feeling a bit uncomfortable, but even so, he was no less attracted to her. "I mean, if the question is significant, and I couldn't imagine it not being significant coming from you, then my answer is critical. I may be one bad answer away from you punting me to the curb completely! That's a lot of pressure!"

"No pressure at all Jake, I just want to see if we're on the same page. If we're going to do this... micro romance... then I need to at least know your level of attraction to me. Does that sound fair enough?"

"Sure Geneva, I'll bite. After all, what do I have to lose?"

"That's the spirit Jake," she said with enthusiasm. "Don't worry, I won't hold your answers against you, and you need to give me the same courtesy, OK?"

"You got it. You go first."

"Jake, have you already fantasized about having sex with me and if so, how many times?"

That question was to the point and completely unexpected. Jake felt like he was knocked off-balance, and it was a second before he could recover. The fact was that right after he met Geneva, he did almost nothing but think about her. Several of these thoughts were about how pretty and personable she was but many more were about what she would look like naked and how things may play out if they found themselves naked together. The bear trap was still set, but now Jake had willingly agreed to step right in. Damned lawyers, always the same!

"Geneva, I've thought of that many times, but there's no way that I could've kept count. Since I only met you last night, let me estimate that I have thought of probably ten different scenarios where we had sex. Some were impulsive and passionate while others were intimate and steamy. But in all of them, we both went to sleep happy."

"Wow, both flavors seem great to me," she laughed and then gave him an unexpected kiss. It didn't last long but was no less heavenly. "I have you beat. I've imagined at least twenty-three different ways that we hook up and in almost each one, the end result was that both of us were thoroughly satisfied."

"So which ones fell short? You did say 'almost'."

"Well, there was one that involved my father catching us and there was another at a rugby game under the stands, but even in those situations, it was still pretty damn hot."

"Wow Geneva," said Jake. "I think that you have an amazing imagination. Sadly, you may find that I'd probably let you down."

"Now why in the world would you say a thing like that?"

"I don't know Geneva, and I'm sorry to ruin this game. I want you to know that my answer was sincere, and I think that you may be one of the most beautiful girls that I've ever met. I'd love to live out a fantasy with you, but I just don't want to let you down. I may write romance scripts, but what I currently write is all done according to formulas and guidelines. Really telling someone how you feel is dangerous because it allows someone else access to your wounds, and some of those wounds have only recently stopped bleeding. I hope you can understand."

Geneva looked at him through her Tom Ford sunglasses and then grabbed his hand and smiled as if what he said was exactly what she wanted to hear. "Jake you beautiful broken man, you need to wake up because there's a whole world out there for you to explore. If you don't take a big enough bite of the world in your first try, you must try again and again until you get results that you can live with. Getting those results may be messy, and when you get them, they still may be less than what you hoped for, but who the fuck cares? At least you tried! Jake, you promised last night to let our relationship go where it wanted to, but I knew that it wouldn't go anywhere until I cleared the air about our attraction to each other. So, as I see it, the bottom line is that we both want to 'do' each other, but we also want to be enlightened about it and do the right thing. Why don't we just drop all this baggage where it is and let things flow. We know where we want to go, let's just let the river take us."

With that, Jake grabbed Geneva and kissed her hard. He just couldn't resist anymore. For some reason, he had initially thought that getting involved with a girl as young as Geneva was a bad thing and would make him look completely superficial and even a bit desperate to his kids. However, after spending what was really a few moments in the grand scheme of time with this wonderful woman, he had re-evaluated his thinking completely. Kissing her felt good, plain and simple, and as he got to know her better, he only wanted to know her more and that was not just because she had a lovely face, either.

"Wow honey, that must've lit the fuse, said Geneva, smiling at him. "I think that I might've finally gotten you to the correct headspace. Shall we finish our walk, or should we just run back to the room now and do what we both want to do with each other anyway?"

"I sort of like the tension that is built through waiting myself," said Jake. "But that's just me."

"OK, let's go with that Jake, this 'tension' sounds like fun… for now at least."

"It'll be worth it, I promise," said Jake. "I do have one more question about our arrangement, however. How should we act around the wedding party? My fraternity brothers have already noticed and are gleefully waiting to see what happens with us next. Frankly, I could care less if they give me a hard time if I was to show you affection, but I'm concerned about you... especially because you still have a boyfriend."

"Like I said yesterday, Jake, he's lucky that I haven't left already and frankly, even if you hadn't come along, that's what I'm planning to do very soon and probably even before the lease is up. Most importantly, I know now that I'll keep those plans, irrespective of what happens with us over the next few days and have even drafted some notes of what I want to say to him when I get back to Philly. So please, don't worry about him. As for the girls, they all think you're adorable so if you show me any affection at all, it will be smiles all around from the bridal party. Jake, I love your attention to detail, but you still need to lighten up and just let things flow. I promise, it will be way more fun that way... but I also know that will be hard for you, so I'll help where I can, OK?"

"OK, Geneva, you got it. Let it flow."

With that, and since he was still holding her, he gave her another huge kiss and she returned it with even more enthusiasm than before. After they finished kissing, they disengaged from their embrace, she grabbed his hand, and as requested, he didn't smack her for doing so. They walked slowly back to the hotel stopping to throw a frisbee with some kids along the way. They also talked about other things of importance like their favorite foods, what types of cars they liked, and where they liked to vacation. As it turned out, they seemed to be compatible in all these areas, and Geneva even had a new Jaguar SUV on order that was to be delivered in a month or so. They laughed and kissed a few more times and got to know each other and Jake felt feelings that he had not felt since... about fifteen years ago before he got engaged to Angela. However, the feelings that he remembered feeling then were not for his ex-wife but for someone else entirely. He silently wondered if he would see that particular girl again soon and that thought simultaneously confused and amazed him because seeing her again had the potential to put a monkey wrench in the gears that seemed to be turning very nicely with Geneva.

Jake and Geneva made it back to the lobby at about 10:45 and the entire wedding party was there except for Rosco, Julie and Slug. When they saw them walk up hand-in-hand, smiles abounded from everywhere, and Billy Dee's was possibly the brightest smile of all.

"Well look at you Snake, you must be pretty good to have charmed Ms. Geneva here, she's a tough one," said Billy Dee.

"Maybe it's Jake who's the tough one, Lawrence," said Geneva with a smile.

"Hey, we're just enjoying each other's company," said Jake. "But Billy Dee is right, I'm punching way above my weight class with Geneva. Where's Rosco? Still with the stripper from last night?"

"Haven't seen him," said Big Dog. "But I did call him to make sure he was still alive. Dude sounded rough, but I'm sure we'll see him in a few minutes."

"Sounds about right," said Jake who paused and looked around. "Apparently I'm not the only one who's getting on well with members of the bridal party as I don't see Slug and Julie, either."

"They're doing shots in the Bleau Bar," said Layla. "We may have to watch those two or they won't make it to the welcome dinner tonight!"

"Agreed," said Jake. "Hey, I need to go upstairs and get my bag. See you all in a few minutes."

"Don't be long," said Geneva right before she kissed him in front of everyone. More smiles and happy looks appeared on everyone's face and then he headed upstairs. He found himself wanting to be back as quick as possible so he could spend more time with his new South African beauty. He was shocked how good it felt to be excited about someone again.

Jake returned just as Billy Dee was cracking a magnum of Dom Perignon, and everyone was in the process of filling their glasses including Slug and Julie who had returned from the bar. After the magnum, he popped two more regular sized bottles and then several toasts were held before they made their way to the door and headed out to the "limo" which turned out to be a Prevost bus that included food, booze, and every possible amenity for the three-and-a-half-hour drive to Orlando. The driver was in the process of loading all bags underneath when Rosco finally arrived, and by his scent, he was wearing "Essence of Hangover" this morning and smelled like the runoff from a distillery. Jake just hoped that Rosco's liver would last until Monday.

The drive to Orlando took just over 4 hours with traffic, so it was good that the bus left about fifteen minutes early. The ride was a blast and in addition to good music and good conversation about virtually everything, there was also the re-telling of several college stories by several of the Kappa Sigs including a rather embarrassing one about some legendary chic that Jake almost had sex with one night while he was living in Indianapolis between his junior and senior year at UVA. No one knew how that story had changed in his own mind, and this he found to be very interesting. He remembered his time with Elsa far differently now than he did only a few hours ago but in the minds of his friends, everything was the same as it was before. He figured that memory was his alone and that it was given to him by Calliope to ensure that he would harbor no more regrets about that situation in the future.

The bus pulled into Epcot just after four, and they all walked into the park and went back to the World Showcase to drink their ways around the world. To make things more fun, each pair (bride and groom, groomsmen and their respective bridesmaids) was a team in what would also be a competitive event, and they needed to work together to consume at least one drink in each country that they visited. To make it even more fun, this was a challenge that had a prize of $1,000 from the groom for each successful team, so completion had a decent incentive. Geneva had known this was coming and had warned Jake in advance to make sure to pace himself on the bus ride up so that he'd be able to drink when they arrived. He had taken that advice, and with Geneva showing some competitive enthusiasm, he decided that they were going to complete this challenge and take a grand off Billy Dee. Jake thought that it would be interesting to see what happened with everyone else.

After a short walk from the main park gate, they arrived at what is known as The World Showcase which contains several miniature versions of eleven different countries from around the globe. Since this part of Epcot is arranged in a circle, once you visit all countries on the loop, you can simply start over again if you so choose. Since it is a tradition to start with Mexico, the group went left and headed to the margarita stand. Geneva decided to be the member of the team to drink here so Jake had nothing except for a bottle of water. He knew hydration would be key today.

They then went to Norway where he had an Einstock White Ale, and then the group proceeded to China where she had a Tsing Tao. Julie, Slug, Rosco, and Kelley dropped out of the challenge at this point, as they all had consumed quite a bit of booze on the bus. Additionally, Rosco was probably still a bit drunk from the night before when this new round of drinking began, so he was sort of a mess from the beginning. Jake figured that he would miss the welcome dinner tonight and since he was Billy Dee's best man, he didn't know who would end up doing the toast that Rosco was supposed to make when the time came. He figured that the groom's party would have to deal with that later.

The trip around the world continued, and Jake and Geneva continued to alternate drinks as they moved from country to country until they finally got to Canada, which was the last one on the loop. They were careful in their planning and chose to mostly drink beers with lower alcohol so that they'd be able to finish the challenge. Geneva also grabbed some snacks for them along the way, like a big pretzel in Germany for example, and these snacks were designed to soak up drinks while they moved along. It turned out to be a good strategy because at the end, only Big Dog and Emma and Jake and Geneva got the $1,000. Even Billy Dee and Layla opted out after France, so he felt pretty good about that and while he was not sober, he only felt mildly impaired which put him in a very festive and happy mood. Geneva fed off his mood and was the life of the party who also acted like a cruise director. Of course, she never missed an opportunity to grab his hand, or hug him, or give him a kiss whenever she wanted to, and Jake started to feel very good about the fact that she'd come into his life. For the first time in quite some time, he had some hope that there was maybe someone out there that fit with him perfectly. The problem was that if he accepted what happened last night as being real and not just a dream or hallucination, then he still had two more trips to make to the past before his life settled down again, and he knew that at least one of them could be a gamechanger. If that gamechanger included the girl that he thought it would, he honestly did not know if he could let her go again, regardless of the cost. But that was a thought for later, and right now he was going to continue having fun. He figured that he deserved at least that much before everything was turned upside down yet again.

CHAPTER 11: A WELCOME DIVERSION

Thursday, December 15th, 2016

Geneva finished with her makeup and was now putting the last touches on her hair. Although she was always good at getting ready quickly, she kicked it into an even higher gear tonight because she was very short on time. The drinking around the world at Epcot ended at about 6:45 but they didn't make it to the Grand Floridian to check in until 7:30 and she didn't make it to her room until 7:45 so she only really had about 40 minutes before leaving to meet Jake at 8:30. Honestly, she was actually very proud of her efforts because she thought that she looked great. For one thing, she was having a great hair day, and her makeup was pretty damn flawless as well. As she donned her newest "little black cocktail dress" and matching black four-inch heels she felt beautiful, and every woman wants to feel that way, especially if there is someone that she wants to impress. Tonight, that is exactly what she wanted to do.

When she came to Florida for the wedding, Geneva had no desire to meet anyone that she could become involved with romantically. After all, she was still living with Joe, her boyfriend of just over five years, but after she found out that he had cheated on her with a Philly-based flight attendant, she really didn't trust him any more even though he had tried his best over the last six months to get back into her good graces. To Geneva, breaking trust was like ringing a bell, and once sounded, there was no way to "unring" it. Plus, if she was really being honest with herself, the relationship had been over for at least two years as they had fallen into a rut where they were basically roommates anyway. So, his infidelity was a way out for her, and she'd planned on taking her leave from him as soon as their lease was up, irrespective of what she'd told him already.

On the other hand, from the moment that she first saw Jake, her frame of mind had changed completely. While it didn't hurt at all that he was exactly her "type" physically, the fact that he was as brilliant, sensitive, and vulnerable as he was, sealed the deal as far as attraction was concerned. So, Geneva now found herself in the beginning stages of falling for him, and the more that she tried to deny this was happening, the more that she found herself doing things to embed herself deeper in his reality. It was like he was a magnet who kept pulling her in and instead of fighting the pull she was embracing it. The thing was, that there was no good reason for her not to fall for him because he was unmarried and available. He was about fourteen years older than her, but that made no difference as far as she was concerned. She wanted to take the next step with him, but she had no idea what that next step was or even if that could lead to something that would exist longer than the short timeframe that she set up with him yesterday.

Geneva finished getting ready, grabbed her clutch purse, and headed out the door to walk to Jake's room so that they could take the monorail to the Contemporary Hotel together. Walking to his room took longer than expected due to the size of the hotel and the distance from her room to his, but she made it only two minutes later than planned and knocked on his door. She found herself almost buzzing with anticipation as she heard the door unlock and, in a moment, she was looking into his eyes which seemed to get lovelier each time she saw him. By the look on his face, he was impressed by her appearance also.

"Hello there, drinking buddy," she said. "You ready for this dinner?"

"Damn Geneva, to say you looked like a million bucks would undervalue your appearance significantly," he said, standing there in nice black pants, matching shoes and a pressed white shirt with a red tie. "Let me get my jacket and we can go. It might take a bit to get there so let's head down now."

"Sounds good to me, lover," Geneva said playfully. She liked to see him off guard.

"Lover, is it?"

"You never know, the night is young," she said and then gave him a quick kiss. "But you're correct, we do need to go. Oh, and you look sharp yourself... lover."

Jake smirked at her in a good-natured fashion and then donned a very nice camel colored blazer and grabbed his hotel key and wallet. They then walked out of his room and headed to the monorail station at the hotel where they met Julie, Slug, Big Dog, and Emma. They all rode together to the Contemporary, passing by the Magic Kingdom on the way, and finally arriving in the iconic hotel that has the monorail trains running directly through it. They were all talking and having fun the entire way there, and when they finally made their way up to the California Grill at the top of the hotel, they realized that they were ten minutes late. Fortunately, it didn't matter because, Billy Dee, Layla, and the rest of the wedding party were just sitting down at the table that had been set for them. As she sat down between Layla and Jake, Geneva suddenly realized that everyone wasn't there. Roger, or Rosco as the guys called him, was nowhere to be found. Considering his drinking over the last two days, she wasn't surprised.

Unfortunately, since Roger was the best man, she knew that he'd written a toast for this dinner, as she had spoken to him over the phone last week about how they would do toasts at the welcome dinner, rehearsal dinner, and wedding reception. The plan for tonight was to eat first, then Roger would give a short toast, and then she would follow him with a short toast of her own. These were not supposed to be as elaborate as the longer toasts that they'd make at the reception Saturday night, and they were definitely not appropriate for the audience mix that would undoubtedly attend the actual reception or even the rehearsal dinner. Tonight, they were designed to be fun and a bit dirty. Geneva really hoped that she wouldn't be the only one to make such a toast, because hers was a bit bawdy to say the least. It would be much easier if someone stepped in for Roger, if only to share a bit of the mild embarrassment that she would undoubtedly feel if she had to do this on her own. As if she somehow called out to him with her mind, Jake was there to help her out.

"Geneva, since Rosco is passed out in his room, I've been chosen by Billy Dee to do his toast for him. He also made some smartass remark about choosing me because of my experience writing soft-core porn scripts for housewives and I sort of resemble that remark. Nevertheless, I agreed to do it so you wouldn't have to make a toast alone. I hope that's OK."

"Jake, you sure know how to make a girl warm up to you," said Geneva who then gave him a huge hug and a peck on the cheek afterwards. "Was the panic evident on my face? My toast is a bit… inappropriate for some audiences."

"OK, well Billy Dee gave me Rosco's notes, and there's no way that yours could be worse," laughed Jake. "I have the rest of the meal to figure out what I should use and what I shouldn't. I don't want to go very long, what are you doing?"

"I wrote a dirty limerick," said Geneva a bit sheepishly. "It's very silly, and I really would appreciate you going first."

"Well, I suck at limericks, but if we both do one, that will make the toasts quick. I think I can come up with something that will work well enough tonight."

Geneva found herself smiling at him again. This wedding was turning out to be a very fun event and she was especially enjoying her time with him. She wondered if he would be interested in a roommate tonight. If so, she had no idea where things would go, and mostly just wanted to get to know him better. But if sex was to become an option… well maybe. At this point, she figured that "maybe" would likely be contingent on how much alcohol they both consumed.

The food was wonderful, the wine was sublime, and Lawrence, a.k.a. Billy Dee, continued to impress Geneva with the events that he and Layla set up for this wedding. The conversation during the meal was always interesting and fun, and she continued to flirt with Jake openly the entire night, which seemed to make him a bit nervous a few times. The dessert finally came, and when it did, Jake, who had been scribbling furiously on a cocktail napkin for the last five minutes on what she guessed was his limerick, stood up and clanked his knife against his wine glass until everyone was quiet. Of course, the bride and groom used it as a signal to kiss each other and did so while Jake paused and seemed to be gathering his courage to do the limerick.

"Since Brother Rosco has decided to pass out for the evening, the groom asked me to step in and do the toast that he planned for tonight," Jake announced. "Although I agreed to do it, after I saw Rosco's notes, he had enough material for at least an hour of speaking and while I'm sure that all of you'd love to hear every last detail about Billy Dee and Rosco's adventures twenty years ago, I know that everyone would also like to get some sleep tonight and it's getting a bit late. So, the lovely Geneva and I have come up with something perfect that will only take a few minutes of time."

Jake cleared his throat, took a drink of wine, and then held out the cocktail napkin in front of him. He then read his limerick.

"There once was a man named Billy Dee,

The size of his penis was something to see.

But now the girls are all sad,

Because Layla wants him bad,

And said, 'His monster is all for me!'"

Everyone laughed, glasses clinked all around, and then Jake and Lawrence embraced each other. Geneva then stood up and hit her glass with a knife as Jake had done, and Lawrence and Layla kissed again. Everyone got quiet once more, Jake kissed her on the cheek and sat down, and she unfolded the paper with her limerick on it.

"OK everyone, that was certainly memorable, and mine's at least as silly," said Geneva. "So here goes". She thought that it seemed obvious to everyone that she was nervous, and she really didn't understand why, because she did plenty of public speaking as an attorney. Maybe it was because Jake was there, which was also sort of irrational on her part because he had just embarrassed himself first. It was her time to follow his lead.

"There once was a man named Larry,

Who found pubic hair particularly scary,

So, imagine his surprise,

When he opened Layla's thighs,

To find her cooter was bald and not hairy!"

Laughter once again filled the room with more cheersing and clinking and then hugging as Layla and Lawrence, both gave her one, followed by Jake who then kissed her as well. She decided that part was her favorite.

The party went on for about thirty more minutes until the bride and groom informed everyone that they were retiring for the evening. When that happened, everyone else except the groomsman known as Prop Head decided to get an Uber to Disney Springs so they could get a nightcap or two. Geneva initially agreed to go, but really didn't want to as she really wanted to spend time alone with Jake. She had already consumed many drinks, so her inhibitions were completely gone now, and this meant that all Jake needed to do was to throw off one spark to start the inferno. She just didn't know if he was on the same page. Nevertheless, she needed to find out and decided to make a move. *Nothing ventured, nothing gained, right?* Fortunately for her, she didn't have to do a thing.

"Geneva," began Jake quietly in her ear as they stood next to each other in the elevator that was packed with the remainder of the wedding party as well. "I don't know about you, but I think that I would rather go back to my room and relax than have more drinks with the group. I've had plenty. If you want... no pressure at all... but if you want, we could put on an old movie and maybe get to know each other better back in my room. You did say you wanted to see where things might go with me so..."

"Jake shut up," she said in his ear, and then gave him a long passionate kiss which was followed by hoots and hollers from everyone in the elevator. "Of course, I'll go to your room. Let's just stop by my room first to get a toothbrush and some jammies for me. I want to be comfy, lover."

"OK, that works. But just know that you are under no obligation to stay, and I'll be happy to walk you back to your room if you want me to at any time."

"Sounds good, Lancelot," said Geneva with a small giggle. "I'm going to break away from the group with the 'I need to change shoes' line. You can come with me to make sure I don't get lost."

"I think I'm probably more likely to get lost than you, but that plan will get the job done," said Jake. "After all, they probably expect us to sleep together tonight anyway."

The elevator reached the floor of teh monorail platform and when she let everyone know what she and Jake were planning to do, she got quite the lurid set of looks and gestures from nearly all of them. After that, she, Jake, and Prop Head took the monorail back to the Grand Floridian while the rest of them went down to meet their Uber. She found out that Prop Head's real name was Alex and thought him to be a very nice guy after they talked briefly during the ride back. Lawrence and Layla were nowhere to be seen, as they were probably already back at the hotel because they left about ten minutes before the rest of the party.

Alex said goodnight to them when they got to the hotel and went to his room, and then Geneva and Jake visited her room to get her toothbrush and pajamas. She also grabbed a lacy black negligée which she shoved into her bag just in case the need arose for its use. Right now, she was hoping that she may have the opportunity to put it on, just to be taken off by Jake a few minutes later. However, as they were walking back to his room, he seemed tense to her, like there was something that he wanted to say but for some reason the words were stuck in his mouth. The entire day had gone too well for it to end with him being uncomfortable with her now. For Geneva, Jake had started out as nothing more than a welcome diversion from reality, but now he seemed to becoming something more. If this, whatever-it-was, was going to progress, she needed to figure out what was going on with him, and she planned to do exactly that as soon as they got back to his room.

CHAPTER 12: VANISHING IN THE LIGHT

Friday, December 16th, 2016

Geneva and Jake got to his room and went inside. Just then, she decided to ask him what was wrong, so they could clear the air. She was not prepared for the answer that she'd get, and she had no idea that the night ahead would change her perception of the world forever.

"Jake, since we left my room, you've gotten very quiet. Are you OK? Are you sure you want me to stay with you to-night? If not, I understand I guess, but I want to know why because everything else has gone so well today. Or at least *I* thought it had. Could you tell me what's going on?"

He paused a moment before speaking. "Geneva, you're right, there's something bothering me, but it has nothing to do with you. I've enjoyed our time very much so far and can't wait to get to know you better. But if you want to stay here with me tonight... I need to tell you about what's on my mind before we go any further. This is difficult for me because after I tell you, you might think that I've truly gone off the deep end and since I don't want to freak you out, you must have an open mind, OK?"

"Sure," said Geneva who was now feeling a bit worried about what Jake wanted to tell her. "You don't have some dark secret that keeps you on the run from the law or something do you?"

"No, nothing like that," he said plopping down on the bed. "It's just that I've had the most bizarre things happen to me over the last couple of days... and I can't explain any of them. Although I could've been dreaming or hallucinating, please just listen and know that in my mind, everything that I'll tell you really happened, OK?"

"Jake," said Geneva sitting down next to him. "I'm all ears. Don't worry I won't judge. I've been known to have an unbelievable thing or two happen to me, as well."

"OK, so, as you know I've recently finalized the divorce with Angela, my ex-wife. Although she cheated on me, there were many reasons that the relationship died, and I must admit that I was probably the main reason that the relationship started going to hell in the first place. You see Geneva, right out of college, I wanted nothing more than to explore a career as a writer. Since I had some money saved up, and got a nice graduation gift from my grandfather, I decided to tour Europe for a while to get inspiration. I was there six months, and, in that time, I visited lots of beautiful places and met many incredible people. My six months of wandering abroad turned into six more months of wandering domestically before I finally ended up in Southern California where I worked as a bartender while getting my Master of Fine Arts in Screenwriting at Pepperdine University. It took me about three years to finish the degree and during that time I also did a few internships at some smaller studios around L.A. Although I was able to publish a few decent short stories and write screen plays for three short films for some of my fellow students at Pepperdine, I still couldn't break in as a screenwriter anywhere. So, as fate would have it, my dad had a good friend in Virginia who owned an advertising firm and needed a copywriter. The pay was good, and I was starving, so I went back across the country to Northern Virginia and moved back in with my parents. By doing that, I figured I could save some cash and plan my next move since I still really wanted a career as a screenwriter, but I had no idea how long that would take. Little did I know at the time that fate would step in and change everything yet again."

Jake paused to take a sip from the bottle of water that was sitting there. Geneva really didn't expect this much detail, but she really liked Jake, so she didn't mind listening. While nothing that he'd said so far was out of the ordinary, he was taking so much time with the backstory that she figured he was setting up for something... big. "So, what happened?" She asked.

"It was early November in 2000, I was still working as a copywriter, and making decent money, but also bored as hell. Out of the blue, my boss decides to send me to a copywriting seminar in Chicago, and while I was there, I met my future wife Angela at a bar. Although we had a great time the night we met, it was just a one-night thing, and neither of us thought that we'd end up together. That all changed at the end of the month, when I took a trip back to Chicago to see her after several weeks of long phone calls and e-mails with Angela. I must have really liked her then because I endured a bus ride from Washington D.C. to Chicago in late November as my car broke down in Pennsylvania, and I was forced to 'Go Greyhound.' Nonetheless, when I finally made it to Chicago, we had a great time, got engaged by the end of January, and were married by the end of June. Then, things got even better as one of my profs from Pepperdine found a huge novel adaptation opportunity for me. The author loved my ideas, so I got the job, and I was able to knock it out of the park with the screenplay. You remember the movie *Remember the Rain?* That was me!"

"I loved that movie," said Geneva honestly as it was one of her favorite romantic movies. Everything that she found out about Jake impressed her, but this was a doozie.

"Thanks, it was fun to write the screenplay, and the author even thought that my proposed ending was better than hers, so we used it. Shortly after that, we moved to Santa Monica and Angela began selling real estate while I was kept busy with several other screenwriting projects. I did my second adaptation which was made into the movie *Delight and Jealousy* the following year, and two producers were very interested in the original screenplay that I was working on at the time when my agent pitched the concept to them. We had two young kids, and everything seemed idyllic, but we began to spend a lot of money by living a fabulous SoCal life. Then, three things happened to change my life, and not for the better. First, the economic crisis in 2008 resulted in Angela's real estate agency going belly-up because of the collapse in the housing market. Second, this crisis also caused funding issues for the producers that were interested in my original project, and it was put on hold by both. Last and most importantly, for no reason, I simply lost my creative voice, couldn't write anything decent at all, and lost my way with the original screenplay just as one of the two producers had re-engaged me about possibly moving forward in 2010. It was amazing how quickly it happened too, because one day, I was full of ideas and creativity and the day after, I couldn't finish a scene. This issue ultimately cost me two huge adaptation projects as well because every time I tried to adapt a scene; it turned to garbage. Fortunately, I still had no problem with trite, formula-based story creation and was lucky enough to grab a job at the Home and Hearth Network to at least make a living by writing stories that someone else developed. Oh, and I was a good proofreader as well. However, the reality is that I haven't written anything original or done any good writing since 2010 and while I can still write a sentence, I no longer can enhance a story with a better ending or add additional plotlines that make a movie pop off the screen. I'm effectively stuck."

"I'm sorry to hear that Jake," said Geneva. "Is this what you needed to tell me? That your career has stalled? If you're worried about how I'll look at you, please don't. I don't value those in my life by their success in the working world, I value them by the quality of their character."

"Thanks again Geneva. But the reality is that when I lost my creative voice, I also changed and one of those changes was to basically immerse myself in my work, cranking out lots of paint-by-numbers scripts, proofreading others, and in doing so, I ignored my marriage, and it died. How she left me was cruel, but in the end, I was ultimately responsible for everything going to crap. The bad part is that I feel even more miserable now than I did before she left me. Since I'm completely on my own most of the time, I've had plenty of time to wonder if I should've done something different with her or followed a different path in life with one of the women I dated before her and to some extent, these thoughts have dominated my mind. The crazy thing is that somehow, I now have the ability for a 'do-over' if I want to take it."

"I agree, you do indeed have a 'do-over' and this do-over just might be sitting with you right now," said Geneva excitedly. It was a bit aggressive on her part, but she was still feeling tipsy, and she thought that she knew where he was going. It turns out that she didn't have a clue.

"While I agree that you and I may have something together Geneva, that's unfortunately not what I was talking about," said Jake as he looked her in the eyes. "This is also where it gets really weird, and like I said before, I promise that I didn't make up what I'm going to tell you. Unless it was a dream... or a hallucination... that is. Are you ready?"

"Sure Jake," said Geneva who was still stuck on 'I agree that you and I may have something together.' "Tell me whatever you want to, I'll keep an open mind, I promise."

"OK, you need to remember that! Anyway, the other night at the bachelor party, we went to a gentleman's club after dinner, and I was coerced into a lap dance by a beautiful young dancer." He paused as if mustering his courage to utter the next words. "The thing is that she wasn't a dancer at all; she was Calliope, as in Calliope the Muse from Greek mythology. When she revealed that rather unbelievable piece of information to me, she changed from a stripper in a g-string to a beautiful woman with silver hair, wearing a gown that shimmered like a lake in the moonlight, and a crystal laurel leaf on her head. Oh, and she stopped time, too. Pretty crazy, right?"

"You're sure that Rosco didn't slip you something while you were there?" Geneva now knew why he kept insisting on an open mind. Maybe he was drugged? She didn't know Rosco well, but she had seen *The Hangover*, so she just wanted to rule it out.

"I actually thought the same thing at first," said Jake. "But everything from that night is so clear and I can remember every detail like it happened five minutes ago. If I was on drugs, I don't think that would happen. You see, Calliope said that she needed to help me find my creative voice again and for me to do so, I need to clear some major regrets from my mind that are still holding me back. And, since these major regrets all concern relationships that I wished I had pursued, I needed to go back in time to revisit each situation at what she called a critical juncture, or a place where a different choice would have potentially changed the outcome of the relationship. Once I got to each juncture, all I needed to do is make the other choice and do what I failed to do to first time in each situation, and she said that I would know what that choice would be each time. Of course, I thought the entire thing to be ludicrous and I was still sure that it was some elaborate mindfuck by Billy Dee all night long. In fact, I thought this right up to the point that I awakened in my old duplex in 1993, and then my feelings changed dramatically."

"Wait, are you telling me that you have actually time-traveled to your own past?" Asked Geneva, who was still trying to keep an open mind.

"Well, basically yes, but according to Calliope, it's not the past in this reality, but a trip to an alternate reality that looks the same to me when I'm there. I also need to go back again twice more unless I decide to stay in the next alternate reality which is a part of this... gift or test or whatever it is, that I've been given by Calliope. While there, I only have three days before I must decide to either return here or live in that alternate reality for the rest of my days. Of course, if I stay there, many things that I know here will also be gone from my life forever and sadly this includes my kids."

"So, you said that you already went back, and since you're here now, you obviously didn't decide to stay. I'm not surprised, considering the way you've spoken about your kids. In fact, I couldn't imagine you ever wanting to stay in an alternate past reality at all."

"I agree, Geneva, and I tried to get out of the next two trips when Calliope showed up again after I had decided to exit the first past reality and return. It was a very emotional experience, and I just don't want to do it again two more times. Unfortunately, she's adamant that I need to re-live these critical decisions to clear my regrets and in doing so, learn more about myself as well. Or I can just stay in the past reality on one of the remaining trips back and start over." Jake paused and put his hand to his face, rubbed his eyes, and let out a long breath. He looked so tired, and Geneva found herself feeling worse for him all the time. "I'm sorry, my head is absolutely swimming with thoughts right now and I'm exhausted. I really appreciate you listening and trying to understand."

"Anytime Jake, that's what friends are for. Did you learn anything from the first trip back?" Geneva asked, getting more intrigued by the moment. Whether this all was true or not, *he* certainly thought it was, which meant that he was either telling her something remarkable or possibly needed significant emotional counselling and treatment. "More importantly, have you reconciled your... regrets associated with that situation?"

"What I learned is that things aren't always under my control and that I shouldn't regret not having a relationship that the other person involved never wanted to have in the first place. I also learned that sometimes I need to take things at face value. While I don't want to get into specifics about what happened, I will say that I've indeed resolved any regrets that I harbored about that situation. It's been sort of a weird relief, and I do feel a bit... lighter... in a way."

"So, where do we go from here?" She asked, grabbing his hand, and giving it a squeeze.

"If this is real, then in a few hours, I'll be sent back to a reality that looks like my past again," said Jake with tears in the corners of his eyes. "Even though I agree with you that I'd never want to be without Kira and Jake, when I went back the first time, things were different for me; I felt all the emotions exactly as I felt them the first time I was in the situation, and they were rather intense. But the bigger challenge that I faced on the journey was that I barely remembered anything about this present reality at all. I could barely remember that I had children and didn't even remember their names, just that I loved them and that they were important to me. So, what I'm, saying is that I may not return, and you need to know that's a possibility."

Geneva nodded feeling unexpectedly worried, and then asked, "Do you really think that's a likely possibility, Jake?"

"All I can say Geneva is that I sure hope not. But maybe everything I told you about just now was just a lucid dream, and if that's the case, then I may just need a new shrink, and some time off work. Anyway, I think there's a way to find out for sure. Can you help me out?"

"Sure Jake, I'll be happy to. I'm not sure how I can help and have no idea if what you said is true, but I'll give it a shot because I'm very intrigued, fairly drunk, and I sort of like you a little. Just tell me what you need."

"It's late so I think that we should get ready for bed and hit the rack," said Jake smiling at her. "Then, when you're ready, all I need you to do is to snuggle up next to me. That way, you'll know if I vanish to another time and place. I'm pretty sure that my body will have to go with me if this is real, but I don't think I'll be gone long because time works differently there. That is of course, unless I decide to stay."

"Tell you what Jake, I'll do you one better. Why don't I just stay up and watch you for a while when you're sleeping," she said. "That way, if you're having troubled dreams, I can wake you up. And we can still snuggle."

"That sounds perfect, Geneva, I really appreciate it. I know I hit you with a lot tonight, and I appreciate your understanding. I also want you to know again that I really enjoy spending time with you. In fact, I enjoy my time with you more than I have with anyone in many years, and that timeframe predates Angela."

"Let's get ready for bed," she said, and then kissed him.

Afterwards they shared a brief smile, and this melted her heart even more.

Geneva then got up, grabbed her stuff, and went into the bathroom to change. She thought about the lingerie for a hot minute but realized that tonight was not the night for that sort of thing and threw on boxer shorts and a Phillies t-shirt which was old and comfy instead. She washed her face, brushed her teeth and hair, put on some skin moisturizer, and exited the bathroom. When she went out, Jake went in to do his own sleep preparations and she laid down in the bed and propped herself up with several pillows against the headboard and one on her lap. She grabbed her phone and cued up a song on it to play for Jake, and when he came out in a t-shirt and loose shorts of his own, she was ready for him.

"Come lay your head on my lap, lover," she said. "I've just the thing to calm your nerves."

Jake turned off the lights, climbed into bed, and put his head in her lap as she instructed. She ran her fingers through his hair and massaged his scalp and then kissed him gently on his head. "I really do want to get to know you Jake, so thanks for telling me what you told me tonight. For the record, I don't think you're crazy, just stressed out. Here's a song that may help you relax, and it sorta describes how I feel about you." With that, *Closer* by Travis began playing and Jake closed his eyes, smiling as it played, and she kissed him on the forehead again. Before it was over, Jake was asleep.

It was just after 1:00 and Geneva laid there, listening to a few more songs while her mind began to wander. Jake was the first guy in years that she felt really excited about, but his story simultaneously fascinated and bothered her at the same time. In truth, she didn't think that he really traveled to a past reality last night and was almost certain that he wouldn't do so again tonight. Instead, she felt that whatever caused him to lose what he called his "creative voice" several years ago was at the root of all this, and if she was serious about pursuing him as a love interest, she needed to figure out what that was. As she had these thoughts, she gently stroked his head and then she closed her eyes for a moment because her fatigue coupled with the alcohol was beginning to win the battle for her consciousness. It felt like she had only closed her eyes for a minute, but when she opened them, she noticed that the clock now showed 5:02. So, she must have drifted off for quite a bit longer. However, Jake was still there as expected, so she began to push him off her and on to the pillows on the other side of the bed so that she could get up and use the restroom. And then it happened. Without warning, Jake's body began to glow, which was probably the strangest and coolest thing that she had ever seen. She opened her eyes wider to make sure that they were not playing tricks on her and as she did the glow got even brighter until the entire room was filled with light. Then, as she thought that this brightness would blind her, the light was gone and with its departure, Jake was as well. Suddenly, her perspective on what he had just told her changed dramatically along with her perspective on reality in general, but although she should've been in shock that she had seen something supernatural take place in real time, only one thought lingered in her mind, and it obliterated all others. More than anything else in the world she just wanted him to return and unfortunately, she didn't know if that would happen. So, all she could do now was wait, and hope, and in this optimism find the courage to expect a return that may never take place.

CHAPTER 13: PENELOPE COLLINGWOOD

Thursday, May 25th, 1995

Jake awakened disoriented as he had done several times recently, and as he opened his eyes, he realized that he was in a bed in another hotel room. He knew immediately that he had traveled back to the past again by the presence of the large CRT-based TV, and as the fog lifted, he once again experienced the sensation of no longer feeling injuries that would occur later in his life. All at once it hit him where he was. There was no one there with him in bed, but when he heard the shower running in the bathroom, he knew exactly who would be there, and when the critical juncture for this relationship would occur.

When Jake was traveling around Europe after he finished at UVA, he met a girl named Penny in a bar in Amsterdam. This happened in late November of 1994 and took place a week or so before he was to return to the United States. They'd both graduated from college that year and were doing the same thing by traveling for a while before beginning careers that would probably not allow for that type of adventure again. When they met, there was chemistry from the start. She was taller than any girl that he had dated before at 5'10", had jet-black hair with stunning blue eyes, and a dancer's body with long, beautiful legs. They met in a bar one night while they were both out with their respective sets of European traveling companions and they slept together for the first time later that same evening. After that, they were virtually inseparable until he flew back home at the end of that week. She still had almost three months left on her visa, so they did not see each other again until February of 1995, when Penny flew home from Europe to join Jake for Mardi Gras in New Orleans. They then traveled the United States together for the next few months as Penny had access to lots of money, and Jake still had not yet decided what his next step in life would be at that point in time. For a second, he pondered that if he had stayed with her, he may have never had to worry about money again. This was because Penny's blood ran dark blue, and money had never been in short supply for her at any time in her life so far and likely never would be in the future.

Penelope Anne Collingwood was born in Greenwich, Connecticut to Lloyd and Rebecca Collingwood who were from an old New England family that could supposedly trace its ancestors to the Mayflower. Lloyd was a famous architect who had designed some of the most innovative and iconic office buildings in major cities around the globe. His reputation had grown to such a level that his firm was now one of the most sought-after design firms in the world. However, while he was indeed successful, he was not a self-made man, as his family was one of the most respected names in New England. So, although he was undoubtedly talented, it certainly did not hurt to have his father's financial backing when he first stepped out on his own. After all, how many college graduates get to begin their professional lives with over $100 million in the bank? Lloyd did, and the best part was that instead of being a spoiled brat and squandering his inheritance as so many with old money do, he made the most of his opportunity. Unfortunately, he now expected the same level of greatness that he was able to achieve from Penny who was the oldest of three girls that he and his wife Rebecca produced together. That was very hard on her and there were many times that she broke down in front of Jake over the pressure that she felt from her father to conquer yet another universe as he had done.

Jake suddenly recalled how close that they had gotten to each other, and how much chemistry that they had together. This was true because she was highly intelligent, adventurous, silly, and passionate about everything that she put her heart into. As he sat up naked in the bed, he also remembered that this moment was from late May in 1995, right before Memorial Day, and the digital clock radio told him that it was 9:15 a.m. They had travelled together from New Orleans to the West Coast and then back east, visiting several places in between as they worked their way to the coast on the opposite side of the country. However, their travels were now at an end, and he realized that the hotel room that he now occupied was at the Ritz-Carlton in Boston. This meant that it was the last day that he would be able to spend with her before she went to her parents' summer home on Nantucket Island where she was planning on staying for the summer.

The first time that he was in this situation in his main reality, she emerged from the shower and invited him to spend the long holiday weekend at her summer home on the island so that she could introduce him to her parents. Jake always thought that it was probably her way of taking the next step with him. Considering that she let him know that she had not brought another man home to meet the Collingwoods during her four years at college, he was more than a bit nervous that the meeting would not go well and that they may not like him. He was also reticent about going with her for a few additional reasons as well.

For one thing, it seemed increasingly clear that she had plans to settle down with him for good, and although he liked her very much and was also incredibly attracted to her, he remembered not knowing if he was ready for that kind of commitment. At least not at that time. Additionally, he was very intimidated by her father, and although he had never met or even spoken to the man, his list of accomplishments in addition to his wealth and influence cast a long shadow over Jake's confidence level. Last, Rosco had set up an "ultimate guys weekend" for Memorial Day in Vegas that he really wanted to be a part of because it sounded like a blast.

In the end, or the first end at least, he chose Rosco and the boys over Penny with the rationale that she would still be there when he got back. Unfortunately, the message to her was that he prioritized his friends above her, and this upset her more than Jake could have ever imagined. So much so that when she went back to Nantucket without him that weekend, she rekindled a romance with an old flame and dumped Jake a week later telling him that he needed to re-orient his priorities and jump into the adult world. He never spoke to her again and figured that she eventually settled down with that dude on somewhere in New England. He couldn't remember his name, but for some reason the names "Chip" and "Skip" came to mind. Suddenly he thought that it was very odd that he remembered that as his memory of the future was essentially non-existent for the most part. Perhaps Calliope forgot to wipe that bit from is mind.

As he heard the shower shut off, he knew that another

one of Calliope's critical junctures was nearly upon him. Although he didn't know for sure, he felt there were many times over the years when he had thought about what his life would have been like with Penny as a wife. They were compatible in so many ways, and they could have likely had a great partnership together. Moreover, in addition to his romantic goals with her, marriage could have also furthered whatever his career ambitions were much quicker by becoming part of a family with nearly unlimited means. He knew that the decision to not go to Nantucket with her that weekend haunted him and that this was indeed a missed opportunity to be with a great girl. He knew that this was why Calliope had sent him back to this moment as the regret of this decision, at this particular critical juncture, had to be weighing him down in the future. But now he had the power to change it and as a towel clad Penny came out of the bathroom smiling at him, he planned to do just that.

"Jake, I have the most fabulous idea," said Penny as she sat down on the bed. She looked beautiful, even with wet hair and no makeup. "I know you have your 'guys weekend' planned, but why don't you just come with me instead? I'd absolutely love to introduce you to Mom and Dad, and my sister Valerie will be there, too. It'll be a blast, and once they get to know you, they'll probably ask you back to visit again later in the summer. I'll even buy your plane ticket! What do you say?"

This was the moment. He could either see what would have happened if he went to Nantucket or turn her down and return to his main reality sooner which a small part of him really wanted to do for some reason, but he just couldn't remember why. Ultimately, with Penny sitting right there in front of him, he couldn't think of much else and as expected his feelings burned as bright for her now as they did the first time that she asked him that question. He made his decision.

"Penny, I think that'd be great," said Jake. "I'm sure my

buddies will give me crap for cancelling out, but one less person will mean that someone won't have to sleep on the floor, and they'll undoubtedly do this again at some point. I'd love to meet your family, and most of all, I want to spend more time with you."

Penny's blue eyes flashed with excitement for a moment, and then she kissed him hard on the mouth. In the next moment, he was frantically removing her towel, as she was exploring his body below the waistline. Since he was already naked, it was easy for her to find what she wanted quickly, and then all at once he rolled on top of her and merged with her very willing body. As they moved together on the hotel bed, breathing heavily, and working up a sweat, the clock radio went off again just as it had the last time he went back to the past, but this time the song *To Love Somebody* was playing on the radio. He knew this was his signal and as he listened to what was one of his favorite Bee Gees songs, he moved back and forth with even more enthusiasm while she wrapped her long legs around his body. As the song continued, the sex became even more intense and as it ended, they both screamed with delight and as he collapsed on top of her still breathing hard, happy about choosing a different path with her this time around. Just as he had that thought, the clock radio then played *Afternoon Delight* by the Starland Vocal Band. *Nice touch, Calliope,* he thought.

"Well, that was fun," said Penny whose naked body glistened with sweat and residual moisture from the shower. "I'd say that we should do it again in a few minutes, but we both have a plane to catch to the island."

"Yep, I need to call and get a ticket. Do you have the phone number handy?"

"I do, but that's not necessary. I took the liberty of buying a ticket for you yesterday. I figured that you wouldn't come and that I was probably wasting my money. But I've lots of that, so I decided to buy you one anyway on the chance that you'd come along, and I'm so happy I did! Thanks Jake, this means the world to me."

"No problem, Penny," said Jake smiling as she smiled brightly back at him. "I can't wait to meet the family, although I must admit that I'm more than a bit intimidated by your dad."

"Don't worry honey, he's just one big teddy bear hidden in the body of a seemingly stuck-up New England preppie. He'll love you, I'm sure! And I've never been wrong about my dad."

"For my sake, I certainly hope so," said Jake, still not feeling much less intimidated.

"It'll be fine, let's get ready and get out of here. The flight leaves at five!"

With that, both got out of bed and jumped into the shower to rinse off before they got ready. They then got dressed in shorts, t-shirts, and athletic shoes, and finally, packed up. In about an hour, they were finished packing and decided to do a little sightseeing in Boston before heading to the airport. It was a lovely spring day, the sun was warm on both faces as they walked the Freedom Trail, and when they were done walking, they grabbed lunch in a pub.

At about two, they took a cab for Logan International Airport so that they could take the short flight from Boston to Nantucket and on the way there, he used Penny's cell phone to call Rosco and leave him the message that he wouldn't make it to Vegas for the weekend. He couldn't afford a cell phone at that point in his life, as cell service was rather expensive in 1995. Of course, Penny had one, because she pretty much had everything.

The small plane took off on-time, and both fell asleep for the short flight of just under an hour. This was probably due to the cocktails that both had consumed prior to boarding, and when they landed and got off the plane, Jake still felt a bit tipsy. They walked through the small airport and while walking, Penny called her father to let him know that she'd arrived and would need a ride to the house. As soon as they went out the front door of the airport, a beautiful Silver Rolls-Royce pulled up, stopped right in front of them, and put on its flashers. He always loved cars, so he recognized it as a brand-new Silver Spur and when they climbed in and he smelled the leather seats, he was astounded by the luxury. *Wow* was the only word that made sense.

Penny snuggled close to him on the ride, and the driver had the *Spring* portion of Vivaldi's *The Four Seasons* playing as they drove away from the airport. He could not have envisioned a situation where he felt more high-class, and he was so happy that he had made the decision to see if the relationship with Penny had legs. As time moved on, he was increasingly confident that perhaps it did.

After a short but blissful drive, they arrived at the Collingwood estate in the part of the island known as Siasconset and better known to those that live there all the time as 'Sconset. Siasconset is the most exclusive part of the island, and some of the most beautiful estates that can be imagined have been erected there. Since Lloyd Collingwood was an architect, this was no less true with his place, and the sheer size of the home caused Jake to freeze in place and take notice. Most surprisingly for Jake was the fact that the house was not the traditional wood-framed coastal house that most would have expected. Instead, it was more of an homage to the Mid-Century Modern style of Frank Lloyd Wright. It was truly brilliant.

"I must admit, she is beautiful," said Penny.

"You can say that again. Do we have our own wing or something?"

"Well, more or less. Right now, they'll probably be having cocktails on the back porch. Let's join them!"

Her eyes flashed with excitement again as she made the invitation, and he suddenly wanted to follow her anywhere. They walked into the front door of the spacious estate, and as soon as they opened the door, a short, stout, red-headed woman in a starched maid uniform came running out of seemingly nowhere like a bullet from a gun. Or, perhaps more accurately, like a cannon ball from a mortar cannon.

"OH MY STARS, AS I LIVE AND BREATHE!" The old woman shrieked. "MY LUCKY PENNY HAS COME HOME!"

"It's good to see you too Vivian," said Penny as the woman collided with her and squeezed her in a death grip like a human-sized stress ball. "How in the world have you been? How are John and the girls?"

"John's out choppin' wood for a fire tonight. Still been a little chilly of an evening on the island. Adel just had her second daughter and Sarah is still out wandering the world, just like you!"

"Are either of them coming this weekend? I'd love to see both," said Penny as she turned to Jake. "By the way Vivian, this handsome devil is Jake. Jake this is Vivian, the woman who probably spent as least as much time as Mother did raising me. Her family has worked for my family for many generations and her daughters Adel and Sarah were like sisters to me and my sisters when we were all growing up."

"Nice to meet you Jake," said the rotund little rosy-cheeked woman. "I would love to spend more time talking, but dinner is in fifteen minutes so you two should get ready fast. I think your father is pulling out a few special bottles from the cellar tonight. You won't want to miss it! They're already done with cocktails, but I can make a few gin and tonics and have them at the table when you come down. Now scoot!"

"Very nice to meet you as well," said Jake. "Penny, sounds like we better scoot!"

"Daddy can be such a brat," said Penny chuckling. "He can wait five minutes extra for us, it won't kill him."

With that they went up to a large bedroom with a large adjoining bathroom. Everything in the room seemed to recount a significant achievement of Penny's life on the island. From the impressive collection of equestrian ribbons to the equally impressive array of sailing trophies, to the group of several rods and reels that were leaning together in a corner. Jake suddenly remembered that Penny was always the outdoorsy, adventurous type, and the room provided evidence that this behavior was not new.

The room had a massive king-sized bed with a nightstand on each side, a huge wardrobe against one wall, and a lovely antique writing desk against another. As he admired her room in what had always served as their *summer* home, he shuddered to think about how big her room must be in the Collingwoods' main residence. It was clear that she certainly lived life at a different level that he was accustomed to... or even could imagine most of the time. And it was damn cool.

Jake and Penny changed into appropriate dinner attire which was nothing fancier than khaki slacks and a white button-down shirt for him, and a white sundress with pale yellow flowers on it for her. He finished his look with penny loafers, and she simply wore white Keds. She also threw her long black hair into a ponytail and ditched the contact lenses for stylish glasses that were somewhat large and round as the fashions of the time dictated. She had no makeup, but her blue eyes glowed with the fire of youth and happiness as she grabbed his hand and walked down to the dinner table where her father sat at one end and was flanked by a middle aged, but no less attractive copy of Penny on one side, and a younger copy of her with no glasses on the other. They all stood, and everyone hugged each other as Lloyd, Rebecca, and Valerie Collingwood introduced themselves to Jake. Everyone was very warm and there were smiles all around which made Jake suddenly feel very welcome.

Jake was also surprised how unbelievably... normal they were. Lloyd was a tall guy, about Jake's height if not a bit taller, in good physical condition, and had a full head of gray hair which was parted on the side like a Kennedy. He wore simple gray slacks with a light blue golf shirt and Sperrys on his feet. Jake also noted that the only jewelry he wore included a gold Rolex Daytona, his wedding band, and what he assumed was his college ring on his right hand. In like fashion, his wife Rebecca was also in great shape and only had small streaks of gray in her long black hair. She wore a khaki miniskirt and a green sleeveless blouse that was also probably golf apparel. Last was Valerie, and when she stood up Jake noticed that like Penny, she was very pretty, but about four inches shorter than her sister, with short hair that was cut about an inch below her chin. She was dressed in a sundress as well, but hers was a pale blue with a faint pattern of zig-zagged lines to give it texture. Both women wore Jack Rodgers sandals, and all three newly met Collingwoods had the same blue eyes as Penny. They sat down to eat, and in a few minutes, Vivian came in with the drinks that she promised to Jake and Penny earlier.

"Here you are, my dears," said Vivian. "Enjoy!"

"Thank you, Vivian," said Lloyd. "I know you're busy with the final preparations for dinner, but when you get a chance, I'll take another scotch."

"Would you like a double, sir?" Inquired Vivian with a wry smile on her round face.

"Naturally," replied Lloyd with a small chuckle. "So, Jake, I'm so happy to finally get to meet the guy that Penny has been going on about for months now. Glad you're here, welcome to the place that the Collingwood family calls *The Beach-side Nirvana*. Cheers!"

He raised his glass and everyone else followed suit. Jake felt like he had to say something but was temporarily frozen. That shadow on his self-confidence was particularly dark at the moment. Fortunately, Penny bailed him out.

"Daddy, I'm *very* excited that Jake is here so don't be too hard on him tonight, OK?" Said Penny in a tone that only a favorite daughter could use with Lloyd. Not rude exactly, but with a certain firmness that likely lived next door to rude and had an extra key to visit any time. She wanted her father to know that she meant business.

"Oh, come on Penny, I'm not that bad," he chuckled again. "But I'll try to be on my best behavior. So, Jake, what do you plan to do with your life?"

"Dad!" Screamed Penny. "That's what I'm talking about!"

"Penny, it's no problem," said Jake, "Actually, Mr. Collingwood, I'm trying to figure that out right now. I was an English major at UVA, so I'd like to do some sort of writing, but I may just go back to grad school and go the teaching route instead. I really wouldn't mind being a professor."

Jake answered as he would have at that time because he still believed it. He couldn't remember that he'd lost his ability to write or that he had success in the future as a writer. Otherwise, the answer would've been different.

"He really is a wonderful writer," Penny piped in. "He even wrote me a short story while we were traveling together. You should read it!"

"I'd love to!" Said Lloyd with more enthusiasm than Jake would have expected. "Do you have a copy handy?"

Jake remembered this story well. While he and Penny

were on their travels together, they had discussed what they wanted to do with their lives and Jake had mentioned writing. She challenged him to write a story for her and gave him a notebook and pen that she bought at a drugstore so he would have no excuse not to do so. What he produced was a little tale about a blind girl that falls in love with a boy that teaches her how to "see" him with her heart. In the end, he has an accident that unfortunately costs him his life, but after his death, doctors use his corneas to enable her to see. While she no longer has him, his gift to her was the ability to see the world as he saw it for the rest of her life. Jake remembered that from the moment he finished the story, that he thought the plot was a bit thin, and didn't consider it to be that great of a tale. It certainly didn't take him long to write because he finished it in two days, and he also often thought that it would have likely been better if he had taken a few additional days. Nevertheless, Penny was a big fan and thought it was wonderful.

"Well, it's hand-written in a notebook, but if you have access to a copier, I'd be happy to copy it for you," said Jake, suddenly feeling very encouraged about the relationship with Penny.

"Great, after dinner give the notebook to Vivian and she'll use the copier in my office. I look forward to reading it!" Said Lloyd. "Have you looked at any schools yet?"

"Not yet," replied Jake. "However, since my parents are on this side of the country, I'm hoping that I can find one on the East Coast."

"That sounds great, Jake," said Lloyd. "I've got lots of connections with schools in New England, so let me know if you need any help."

Once past that initial interaction, the conversation flowed well for the rest of the evening. Lloyd proved to be a very gracious host and as they ate a delicious meal of Cornish game hens, mashed potatoes, and asparagus, Lloyd cracked a few bottles of Pinot Noir from a vineyard in Napa called St. Supery. Lloyd loved to talk, and he lavished praise over Penny and Valerie's academic accomplishments in addition to bragging about both girls' prowess as sailors and equestrians. Valerie, or Val as they called her, was four years younger than Penny and had just completed her freshman year at Vassar. She seemed to like Jake from the beginning and was quite flirtatious with him as well. Penny also had another sister named Jane who was a year younger than her and had just graduated from Amherst. However, that sister couldn't come back home for the weekend because she had just left for a post-graduation trip around Europe with her college friends as Penny had done the prior year.

Last, but certainly not least, was Rebecca. Rebecca, went by her full name rather than a shortened version like Becca, or Becky, and had also attended Vassar like her youngest while Penny and Jane had both attended Amherst. The best part was that Rebecca was witty and even a bit foul mouthed at times as she was quite good at telling dirty jokes. Jake found himself having a great time, and Penny's face glowed as it appeared as if her family really liked him.

After a wonderful apple tart with French vanilla ice cream, coupled with a snifter of fine Cognac, everyone retired to their respective bedrooms as the plan was to get up early and go sailing. Penny and Jake were exhausted, and since Penny also felt uncomfortable about having sex in her parent's house they both got ready for bed and just laid down together while she snuggled close to him. As they were falling asleep, Penny had only one thing to say.

"Jake, I think I might just be falling for you."

"Me too," was all he could think to say before she kissed him. As he fell asleep, he vaguely remembered his children back in his main reality. The memory was faint, like two weak points of light in the night sky, and while he still thought there was another important reason for him to return, he had no idea who or what that was, or why it was even important. He decided to put it out of his mind completely, and in no time at all, he was out like a light.

CHAPTER 14: MODERN FEUDALISM

Friday, May 26th, 1995

Jake awakened to the ring of an old-school alarm clock that seemed to rattle his brain as the annoying little bells at the top were repeatedly struck by the tiny hammer bouncing back and forth between them in rapid succession. He took a blind swipe at the infernal noisemaker and hit home on the first try which killed the cacophony immediately. It was 7:30 a.m., and as his head cleared a bit, Penny walked out of the bathroom dressed and ready to go in white shorts, a blue Izod polo shirt, and white Jack Rodgers sandals that were identical to the ones worn by the other female Collingwoods last evening. Her hair was done up in one long, thick, braid and her makeup was impeccably applied. She looked radiant.

"Time to get up, *sleepyhead*!" Said Penny in a manner

that emphasized the cliché in that particular phrase.

"OK, but why so early?" Replied Jake groggily.

"It's a beautiful day to sail, so we must make the most of it! Get ready, Jake, and meet me downstairs in 30 minutes."

With that, she gave him a peck on the cheek and left the room. Jake got up, took a quick shower, shaved, and then donned some khaki shorts and a dark blue polo shirt with an orange "V" on the right front breast pocket for his alma mater. He threw on topsiders, grabbed his wallet, and headed out the door to find Penny.

Jake arrived in the kitchen where the entire family was having coffee. They then left the residence and drove to the marina nearby and boarded a boat called the *Stella Cadente*, which was a 65-foot ketch that Lloyd had recently purchased from an Italian couple on the Amalfi Coast. Since it was a ketch, this meant that it was a two-masted vessel with a large mast in the front, and a smaller one (called the mizzen mast) in the rear. Jake thought it was gorgeous.

The boat moved out under the power of its diesel engine and as they motored, the Collingwoods all sprang into action with Lloyd at the helm barking orders like a modern-day Captain Bligh, while the three ladies began the process of raising the sails. Jake asked if he could help, and the reply from Lloyd was that he needed to head below deck so he could open the champagne and Beluga caviar and pour a glass of bubbly for everyone. Jake laughed because he knew that he was put on bar duty so he wouldn't screw anything up on deck. Since him screwing up had a high probability, he headed below without protest.

They began to sail, and as they picked up speed, the boat began to heel over (or lean) to the port (or left) side. It took a few seconds for Jake to adjust to the new angle of the boat, but he figured it out quickly. He then opened two bottles of Dom

Perignon, placed them in two built in ice buckets in the galley's counter, and then covered them with ice from the cooler. Penny came down, smiled at him, gave him a kiss, and then grabbed stemless wine glasses from the cabinet above. Jake was amazed at how easily she moved around the boat with it heeled over, and in the next few minutes they were able to fill all glasses and distribute them to the captain and the rest of his crew. Last, Jake opened the tin of caviar and spooned it into a stainless-steel bowl that was one of two bowls placed side-by-side in the center of a cutting board with stubby wooden legs. He then spooned sour cream in the other bowl and placed Carr's Table Water Crackers around the bowls. The cutting board had a stainless-steel ring around the top to keep the crackers on the board and he finished the whole thing by shoving smalls silver spoons into the center of both the sour cream and the pile of fish eggs as well.

Penny went topside with the hors d'oeuvres and Jake grabbed a bottle for top-offs and followed her up to enjoy what was turning out to be a beautiful day with great wind. The *Stella Cadente* was a portly girl with a broad beam and as such, she was built more for comfort than for speed. However, the wind was strong enough to propel her along at about ten knots, and that was not too shabby at all. Jake found the entire experience intoxicating and was beginning to fall in love with the whole package that Penny could potentially offer him. She, of course was the crown jewel of that package, but having Lloyd and Rebecca as in-laws would be pretty darn cool as well. Disturbingly, his children were now only wisps on the edge of his perception now, and he remembered almost nothing about his main reality at this point other than the fact that he made a different choice with Penny the first time around. Fortunately, he also remembered the rules that Calliope informed him about on the night he met her and how to get back if he wanted to do so. However, he had no idea when that meeting with her took place, or where he even was at the time. He was moving closer and closer to choosing to stay here and had less reservations about doing so with each passing moment.

They sailed for hours that day and drank expensive bubbly the entire time. There was much laughter to accompany the libations as amusing stories were told by everyone. Some of these were told by parents about funny things that the girls did as children. Some were told by Jake, to help everyone get to know him better. And some were told by the sisters Val and Penny with at least one of them told by the elder girl making Jake's face red as a beet. Jake even got to take the helm for a bit as Lloyd taught him things like what the tell-tales were on the sail and how to tie a bowline knot. It was a memorable experience, to say the least.

They pulled into the marina at about 3:00 and then took a short ride back to the house where everyone decided to take a nap. After a snoozy afternoon, everyone awakened and went to dinner at 8:30 and there were drinks followed by Trivial Pursuit afterwards. Jake impressed everyone with his knowledge of trivia as he prided himself on being the "gatekeeper of useless information." He and Penny won the game, much to the chagrin of everyone else and after a nightcap, the evening was over. Everyone departed for bed at that point, and although Jake tried to get Penny to be as frisky as he was when they climbed into bed, she rebuked his efforts like a goalie on the former Soviet Union's hockey team. After three shots on goal, he gave up.

The next day, Jake awakened early while Penny continued to sleep. He dressed in a UVA hoodie and jeans and then slipped out and went downstairs where he found a smiling Vivian who offered him a toasted croissant with butter and a cup of coffee. He heartily accepted both and then sat down at the large breakfast bar where she handed him the steaming cup.

"How do ya take it?" She inquired.

"Black will do," replied Jake. "Extra caffeine, please."

She chuckled and then proceeded to prepare his croissant. They made small talk about the weather, Penny, and other things as she prepared his buttery treat, and then made more small talk while he was eating it. About that time, Lloyd walked into the kitchen.

"Well, hello there, Jake," said Lloyd. "I hope you had a good time sailing yesterday, it was a beautiful day."

"It was indeed, sir, and I enjoyed it very much," said Jake honestly.

"That's great to hear," said Lloyd before pausing for a few seconds. "Jake, do you have a few minutes? There's something that I need to talk to you about. I don't mean to sound ominous, but it's important."

"No problem, sir," replied Jake. I'm sure Penny won't be up for a while!"

"Follow me," said Lloyd.

Lloyd led Jake into his office, which was everything that one might expect from a well-educated aristocrat in the Northeast. It was a large space with bookcases full of books lining three of the four walls with the wall not covered by books having an enormous window that looked out on the ocean. Jake noticed that many of the books were of military history with a large portion of them about either the Civil War or World War II. All the bookshelves were made of cherry wood, and matched Lloyd's massive desk that was topped with several items including a blotter, a green-shaded brass desk lamp, and a brass nameplate with Lloyd's name on it. There was also a beautiful green rug on the even darker hardwood floor. This rug had ornate patterns on it that could have only been woven by the finest artisans somewhere in Asia. Last, there were two chairs that were also made of cherry in front of the desk, and as Lloyd entered the room and closed the door, he motioned Jake to sit in the one on the right while he went behind the desk and sat down in a padded chair covered with burgundy leather. Jake had no idea what was going to happen next and found himself very uncomfortable in the silence while Lloyd read a message that had been left on the blotter for him. Mercifully, Lloyd finally broke this silence.

"Jake, I've a question for you," began Lloyd. "It may sound a bit strange, but I promise that I'm going somewhere with this, OK?"

"Sure, no problem, Mr. Collingwood," said Jake even more bewildered now than he was a few minutes ago if that was even possible.

"Alright then, Jake, answer me this: how are empires built?"

"Well, I wasn't a history major, but I'd say off the top of my head that empires are built by conquest."

"A good answer," said Lloyd with a look on his face that said he knew Jake would say exactly that. "And not inaccurate because there have been many times where conquest has been required to build an empire. Perhaps a better question for you is this: how do you maintain an empire once it's built?"

"There are many things I suppose, are you looking for just one thing?"

"Yes. What's the most important tool in maintaining an empire?"

"Well, I could go with maintaining a strong army, or even being a man of the people and making them love you, but in my opinion, there's even a stronger way to make a bond, and this can even make an enemy become a friend," said Jake, who paused for a beat, surprised at his own answer which until that moment had remained dormant in the back of his mind since college. However, he was a lot closer to his college years in this reality, so there's that. "That way, Mr. Collingwood, is through marriage."

"Jake, I must admit that I'm as impressed with your answer just now as I have been with your ability to fit in with our eccentric family since we met the other night," said Lloyd with a look on his face that may have been disappointment or even sadness. "That'll make it easier for me to explain my situation, but even with that said, I'm pretty sure you'll hate my guts as soon as I tell you what I'm going to tell you... and I must do it right now, I'm afraid. Before I do, I've one more question for you. Has Penny ever told you about Kip?"

"No, she never has," said Jake who began to feel a massive knot in his stomach. *Kip, why was that name familiar?* Wherever this was going, it wasn't good... at least not for him.

"I feared as much," said Lloyd who removed the reading glasses that he had donned when he sat down to read the message on the blotter. He then rubbed his eyes and leaned back into his huge leather chair and exhaled loudly. "Jake, fasten your seatbelts, it's going to get a bit bumpy. Kip and Penny have been friends since they were both three years old. The reason for this is that Kip's dad, Sam Carlson, is a very wealthy real estate developer here in New England, and an old friend of mine. Even though I've plenty of money and a rich family myself, the combined wealth of my entire family, including me, my father and two brothers, is only about a third of Sam's wealth. He literally is the richest guy in town nearly everywhere he goes. Anyway, Penny and Kip spent so much time together that a romance bloomed between them when they were both about thirteen. This puppy love turned into more and by the time they were in boarding school, the two were virtually inseparable. It was that way for them until the end of their senior years, and that's where the problem that I'm going to tell you about was created. This problem was that at that time, Kip told his dad that he didn't want to marry anyone else but

Penny and as soon as Sam heard that from is son, he called me immediately and insisted that they needed to be together. Most importantly, he told me he would be willing to give me a prime parcel of land that I could use for a passion project that I had wanted to build for several years if Penny was to marry Kip. Since it appeared that the two were on a collision course anyway, I agreed. The only fly in my ointment was that less than a year later, Kip cheated on Penny, and she left him. Based upon the fact that you've never heard of him means that she is probably still quite angry with him." He paused again. This was obviously difficult. "Anyway, for the last four and a half years, I've let Penny roam the world and sow her wild oats, so to speak. Unfortunately, Sam has been very insistent that Penny give Kip another chance and had also made several... overtures... that indicate that he'll feel as if I've breached the marriage contract that I agreed to when I took his land for that project years ago if she doesn't marry him. That would not be good for me, considering his wealth and influence and I while didn't fully realize it at the time, it was in essence, a dowry. So now I've the unenviable task of informing you that irrespective of how much I like you or how much Penny cares about you, there's absolutely no way that you can be with her, because she must marry Kip. And that pretty much brings us both to this moment."

"Wow, " was all Jake could say as he was still trying to process what he just heard. Like some feudal vassal, Lloyd had promised a first-born daughter to the first-born son of his liege lord and in terms of good strategic moves, that one was solid. However, in the end the entire situation was absolutely fucked up, and Jake couldn't believe that Penny would want to go back to a guy that cheated on her. Plus, Jake was also pretty sure that Penny still was at the very least, partial to him.

"So, if I understand you correctly Mr. Collingwood, what you're saying is that since you agreed to marry Penny to Kip, that you now need me to step aside so that this can happen.

Right?"

"Well basically, yes," said Lloyd in an emotionless manner. "Jake, you're a wonderful young man, and it's too bad that you didn't show up with Val or Jane. I would've welcomed you into the family wholeheartedly. I really am sorry."

"What if Penny doesn't want to marry Kip anymore, and what if I just convince her to run away with me? She's a free spirit, you know."

"She is indeed Jake and if she did that, I suppose that I'd have to suspend her funding until she followed through with the plan to marry Kip. While that might make me sound like the worst father in the world, let me tell you something about my daughter. That something is that she knows that she couldn't live in any other way than as she's been raised. She's used to the good life, and she'll always choose it above anything; even what she may construe as love. Plus, she and Kip have deep ties to each other, and he'll be here at about one this afternoon. I really think that the best plan is for you to leave the island, and I'll be happy to buy a first-class ticket for you to anywhere you'd like to go. I know you think that I'm an absolute bastard right now, but the union of Penny and Kip must and will happen. Once again, I'm truly sorry."

Jake was frozen in silence and couldn't believe what was happening or what he was being asked to do. Plus, he wondered if he should believe Lloyd about Penny and Kip and their relationship. He had absolutely no idea what to do. Just then the answer to his problems would be at hand and it would come from yet another unexpected source. At that moment, Lloyd hit the power button on the Bose Acoustic Wave stereo system on the sideboard behind his desk and the Bee Gees song *Massachusetts* began to play. It was his one-day warning signal and suddenly Jake remembered Calliope, his kids, and something or someone else that was important in his main reality. He now knew exactly what he needed to do.

"Sorry, I've never liked silence in stressful situations," said Lloyd.

"It's no problem, Mr. Collingwood, I was leaving anyway," said Jake and with that he stood up and walked towards the door while the music continued to play. He then stopped and turned around because he had one more thing to say. "You know, I understand everything that you're telling me and get the entire nobility on the left side of the Atlantic thing, but that doesn't mean that I don't still think it's pretty fucked up. That said, I'll be happy to get out of here and I don't need you to buy me a ticket. Just distract Penny for a bit, and I'll be gone before noon. And sir, if you don't mind me saying, you should be ashamed of yourself."

"Jake, I honestly can't say that I disagree with you," said Lloyd. "Good luck young man. I really mean that."

With that, Jake turned and walked out of the room, down the hall, and finally into the bathroom at the end of the corridor. All the while, he could still hear the music playing in Lloyd's office. Although a part of him wanted to, Jake couldn't bring himself to see Penny again, because he knew that they had no good path to any future together at all. While he may have been able to convince her to run away with him, that would be cool and fun right up to the point where Penny doesn't get seven-star service for a week or two. Then everything would likely degrade rapidly. 'Twas a shame because they did have chemistry, and this chemistry may have been on the edge of becoming something more. But it was now time to return to his main reality and he knew it. And then, without any further ado, he said the words that the muse had taught him so he could return. All went black again.

CHAPTER 15: THE RE-ENTRY BLUES

Friday, December 16th, 2016

Jake awakened again in his main reality, but this time, his disorientation was a bit less, so that was good at least. However, he really didn't have time to be disoriented anyway, because a very concerned Geneva rushed over to him as soon as he opened his eyes and sat up. In fact, she nearly tackled him with her embrace.

"I thought I'd lost you," she began, "you were lying there sleeping and suddenly, you began to glow with light that was so bright that it blinded me. The light only lasted a second or two, then it was gone, and you were gone with it. Jake, I believe everything you told me now. I really thought I'd never see you again!"

"Geneva, I can't tell you how good it is to see you," said Jake who was feeling a bit exhausted from two trips back in time on consecutive evenings in his main reality. Technically, he slept last night... but that was in the other reality, so he had no idea if it counted here or how his body was even holding up at this point. He also felt all those old aches and pains again as well, and they hit harder than ever right now for some reason. He needed to find Calliope and end this madness... and he needed to do so now. "How long was I gone here? It was two days for me."

"Just about two hours, so an hour here must equal a day where you were," said Geneva pulling back to look at him. Her eyes were wet, and tears escaped from the corner of each eye and raced each other down her cheeks on the way to the bottom of her beautiful chin. "I'm so glad you're back."

Jake had no choice but to kiss her, and she kissed him back enthusiastically. Jake couldn't believe that he didn't remember her at all in the other reality. After all, how could any mortal man forget a face like hers?

"Geneva, what just happened to me started out great, and finished in an incredibly bizarre fashion that was horrible. I really don't want to do this again."

"Want to talk about it?"

Initially, Jake hesitated in responding to her. He suddenly felt a wave of guilt hit him for what happened with Penny in the alternate reality. The thing was that he didn't even remember Geneva at all when he was there, so it's not like he knowingly cheated on her. Plus, at the point where he returned to the relationship with Penny, he was in a monogamous relationship with her, so having sex would be a pretty normal part of that, right? Nevertheless, the guilt persisted, and in addition to that, he was worried that Geneva may not be so understanding if he came clean to her about what happened.

This may have also been why he was reluctant to tell her about his first trip back and his lusty weekend with Elsa when he told her about the entire adventure that Calliope had set up for him. However, his first trip back was before he and Geneva had begun anything together, and his feelings for her then were certainly not what they had become now, even though in real time it had only been about a day that they had been involved with each other. In the end, he concluded that he needed to tell her everything and just let the chips fall where they may. This was a weird situation to be sure, but even alternate realities and mythical creatures shouldn't be used to justify dishonest behavior with someone that could potentially be a life partner. He felt amazingly close to Geneva already and for that reason, he owed her the truth.

"It's OK," she said after a rather uncomfortable moment of silence from Jake who was lost in his own head. "We don't have to talk about it. I just wanted to let you know that I'm here for you.

"Geneva, the truth is, that I *do* want to tell you about it, *all* of it," said Jake. "I just don't know where to begin."

"How about the trip that you just returned from? You said it was horrible, and I think that's where we should start," said Geneva as she disengaged with him and moved to a more comfortable position sitting cross-legged on the bed in front of him. He then pulled himself up and leaned against the headboard.

"Yeah, that sounds good," said Jake. "Remember when I told you that I traveled through Europe for six months and then domestically for six more before I started grad school?"

"Yes, I do."

"Well, at the end of my six months in Europe I met a girl named Penny in Amsterdam, and we had an intense little relationship for about a week until I had to return to the U.S.

She still had two months remaining on her visa, and when it expired, she returned to the U.S. and met me in New Orleans. We then traveled the country together for about three months. I must admit, it was a great time in my life because Penny and I were compatible in just about every way, and it didn't hurt that she was from old money in Connecticut, either. So, we had plenty of cash to roam, and we always had the nicest places to stay and the best food to eat. It was a first-class lifestyle to be sure."

"So, what happened?"

"One decision changed everything, and as with the theme of this little torture test that Calliope is putting me through, that decision had long been a large regret of mine. You see Geneva, at the end of May in 1995, Penny had planned to return to Nantucket Island so she could spend the summer with her parents there before beginning her first 'real' career. As I pondered my next step in life, she invited me to her father's massive estate on the island for Memorial Day weekend. I think she hoped that her parents would like me and ask me to stay all summer. The first time around, in this reality, I turned down her invitation so I could spend the weekend with Rosco and a few of his friends at work as they were having a guys' weekend in Vegas. As it turns out, that decision really pissed her off, she reconciled with her ex two days later, and that basically was the end of our story together."

"I think I understand," said Geneva grabbing his hand. "But this time, tonight actually, you decided to take that trip to Nantucket. But since you're here now, something obviously happened to make you want to return, right?"

"Yes, and this is the bizarre part, because this break up had nothing to do with Penny or our attraction to each other, that was fine or at least seemed to be. The family was great also, and we had a great day sailing together on her dad's beautiful sailboat and playing Trivial Pursuit afterwards. Everything was idyllic for me and as time went on with her family, I remembered less and less about anything in this reality, including my children... and you, sadly, I remembered nothing of you. Unfortunately, things got derailed when her father called me in to his office the next morning and basically said that he had promised her hand in marriage several years ago to an even more wealthy business partner's son named Kip in exchange for some real estate. Apparently, Penny and Kip had been a thing in boarding school, and they broke up before she went to college. I guess her father was getting heavy pressure from the dude who traded him real estate to honor the marriage contract. I was the fly in the ointment, and he needed me out of her picture. The weirdest thing was that she never mentioned Kip to me at all."

"Wow, so like some medieval lord, he promised his daughter to his liege lord in exchange for land... that's crazy. I didn't think that stuff happened anymore. Was he nasty about it when he told you?"

"No, and that's the funny part because he seemed to like me a lot," said Jake. "In feudal lord fashion, he even said that had I shown up with either of Penny's younger sisters instead, he would've welcomed me to the family. Her youngest sister Val was there and very flirtatious with me, so I probably could've negotiated a decent dowry for her had I asked."

"Wow," said Geneva, "and all this happened in the two-hour period you were gone. Fascinating. So, you obviously told him to pound sand and returned. Did you talk to... Penny... before you left?"

"No," said Jake flatly. "As soon as the conversation with him was over, I decided that a life with her would never work, and I left. Maybe I'm a coward but seeing her would've only made matters worse and not better, so I really don't think it was a good idea. Plus, the fact that she never told me about Kip and their relationship, sort of shattered my trust with her anyway. It was very upsetting. Geneva, when I'm in the alternate realities, my feelings are as intense as they were the first time that I experienced them. I know I told you this before, but it can't be understated. It's almost like the version of me that's talking to you now has never existed when I'm there, and in the context of the alternate reality, that's essentially true. So that's why what I must tell you next is very difficult."

"Let me guess, you slept with Penny... am I right?" Said Geneva with a look that was somewhat unreadable but did not really portray anger or disappointment. Jake was blown away by this.

"Umm, yeah," said Jake. "I'm so sorry, Geneva. I don't know what to say."

"Then don't say anything, Jake," said Geneva taking and squeezing his hand. "It's safe to say we're in uncharted territory here, and while I hate the idea of you being wasted on another woman far less desirable than myself, I also have no idea how I can be angry at you for sleeping with a girl in 1995. The whole thing blows my mind, really."

"Geneva, I appreciate your understanding. I don't know how I would've reacted in your situation. I just had to tell you... for some reason, you're already very important to me."

Geneva leaned in and kissed him, it started as a simple peck and turned into a much bigger affair than Jake would've expected. Geneva was special, he felt a real connection with her and couldn't believe that she hadn't run away screaming earlier. He also was amazed how quickly she processed the entire situation. For those things and a thousand other reasons, she was a brilliant girl, indeed.

"Jake," said Geneva looking at him seriously, "with me you passed the test. First of all, you came back from wherever you were, and that alone says a lot. Second, I figured that if you were back in your own past at a critical juncture in a relationship, that sex would likely play a part in the story. The thing is that you were honest about it and that means the world to me. Jake, you get one more pass on the last trip back in time that you told me you must make. After that, if we're to be a thing, you've got to promise me that there will never be anyone else. Otherwise, I simply need to move on now."

"Geneva, I'll make that promise without reservation. More importantly, I don't want to go back to the past again. I need to find Calliope and sort this out. I've found you, and I feel confident that if we continue to get to know each other, that all past regrets will fade away. Thanks again for being... amazing."

"It'll be OK, honey, I promise," said Geneva taking his hand and kissing it. "We'll get through this thing together. But right now, I'm really beat and it's nearly half past seven in the morning. Let's get a few hours sleep. There aren't any group activities until five when we need to be at the rehearsal. A little sleep will be an answered prayer for both of us."

"You're right Geneva, let's crash," said Jake sliding down and readjusting the pillows so he could lay more horizontally as Geneva spooned into him after hitting the light by the bed. They laid together silently as she interlocked her fingers with him as her left arm was draped over his. "Geneva, thanks for being here. Sleep well."

"You too, lover."

Jake awakened and looked at the clock which now showed 12:15 p.m. He then realized that he was alone, and that Geneva was no longer there. Just as that realization hit, he sat up and when he did, he noticed the piece of paper on Geneva's pillow that explained that she had gone back to her room to freshen up and then meet Layla for lunch. That message mellowed him out immediately, and just as he was thinking about going back to sleep for a bit longer, there was a knock on the door.

"Hello, it's housekeeping. Do you require service today?"

"Um, sure, just a second," said Jake as he got out of bed, put on the hotel supplied robe, and answered the door. As soon as he opened it, he was greeted by a familiar, if no less beautiful face.

"Hello Jake," said Calliope who was now dressed as a maid. "Rumor has it that you need to talk to me."

"Yes, I'm so glad you're here," said Jake. "Please come in."

Calliope walked in the room and the door shut behind her. She then sat in a chair at the small table in the room and he plopped down on the bed. "So, Jake, I'm sorry that the last trip back was so brutal. I had no idea that would turn out the way it did. Honestly, I haven't seen that sort of thing... a marriage contract in exchange for land, that is... for quite some time."

"I got to admit, Calliope, it sure shocked the hell out of me."

"Jake, I don't control how these trips to your past will go and this is because you're essentially creating a new reality for yourself. Please understand that there are an infinite number of influences that all have the potential to change any given reality, so only so much can be controlled. For the record, the chance that you and Penny would end up together was below twenty percent."

"Based on the trip back, that sounds about right. For that exact reason, I've had enough," said Jake flatly. "I can't go back again, Calliope. I'm exhausted. Please let me out of this... test... or whatever it is. I really think I can move on. After all, I've met the first woman since..."

"Since you were with the girl that you're pretty sure you'll see on your next trip back, right? You know, the largest regret that you've ever had. Do you really want to quit before you see *her* again?"

That was a tough one for Jake. On one hand, he was exhausted with these trips to his past. While each had more than their fair share of good moments, the end of both were emotionally draining for Jake. This was especially true with the last trip because he had a relationship with Penny for several months while the two-night stand with Elsa was just that, a two-night stand. Plus, he really liked where things were going with Geneva. He didn't want to muddy the waters with her further by taking yet another journey back in time that was likely to be as successful as the first two had been.

On the other hand, a large part of him really wanted those feelings with the girl Calliope was referring to again, and he also really wanted to spend time with her again because she was truly one of the most beautiful, intelligent, and wonderful creatures that he had ever met. However, since they collided and spent time in November of 2000, he hadn't seen her at all as she was nowhere to be found on social media, and all other computer searches proved to be fruitless as well. He hadn't looked for her in the last seven or eight years, so maybe things had changed. He decided to check this out on his laptop after Calliope left.

"Is that an option?" Asked Jake with mixed emotions still on hyperdrive.

"Well, no, but I still think it's a valid question," replied Calliope. "And I really believe that this entire exercise will ultimately be a huge waste of time for both of us if you don't take the final trip. I know it will be painful at the end, irrespective of your final decision. But it must happen."

"But Calliope, like I told you, I'm exhausted. And I really

like where things are going with Geneva, who's the woman I mentioned earlier. I really think I can move on now. This relationship will kill the last regret forever. I'm certain of that."

"OK Jake, this is what I can do to help you out a bit," said Calliope after pausing to consider what he just said. "I can delay the final trip back for a day. This means that you'll stay put tonight and if you want to, you can continue to explore the relationship with Geneva without worrying that you'll head back to the past. Unfortunately, that's the best I can do. Once it's set in motion, the sequence must be completed, and I can only slow it down for a day. You must either decide to stay in one of the alternate realities or visit all three and return from all three. That's the only way to get out of this, I'm afraid."

"Well, I'll take it if it's the best you can do. But on the last trip I may just make the same decision that I did the first time and come back early instead of taking the other path."

"That's your choice and if you can do that, then I'll be impressed. But remember how your feelings are when you're back there. I think you'll find that to be a Herculean effort indeed. Jake, I must go. I know it's hard for you but as the young people in this time are prone to advise; you must trust the process. Bye Jake, see you soon."

Calliope left the room and Jake just sat there on the bed, still very nervous about the forthcoming trip back in time. He was happy that it was delayed, but very disappointed that it couldn't be cancelled altogether. At least he and Geneva would get some real alone time tonight after the rehearsal dinner, and that made him happy. He kept telling himself that it was almost over.

Jake got up, took his MacBook Pro out of his backpack, and set it on the small table in the room. He then sat down in the chair that Calliope had just vacated, put some music on his iPhone via Pandora, and began to surf the web on his laptop. For shits and giggles, Jake went to Facebook and did a search for both Elsa and Penny and was able to find both easily, by searching with their maiden names. Elsa was the mother of four teenage girls who were all as blonde as she was. Her husband was blonde-haired and blue-eyed as well, and from the pictures that were posted, he appeared to be massive in both height and girth. Elsa looked the same as he remembered in the face, but she also seemed to have added about thirty pounds, if not a bit more. Jake didn't know if he was the boyfriend that she told him about during his visit with her, but they at least looked like they were happy together, and they had settled down in the Chicago suburbs.

The years appeared to be much kinder to Penny and she was now the spitting image of her mother when he met her in the past. She had two college aged children (one son and one daughter), was still married to Kip Carlson, and still lived in Connecticut. Her pictures depicted a very happy and comfortable life, and there were even a few pictures of Lloyd and Rebecca who seemed to be in good health and had aged gracefully as well. He found himself happy for her, and a few pangs of jealousy hit him as he stared at a shot of Penny and Kip together in evening wear at a gala black-tie event somewhere.

After he was done with this research, he knew he needed to check one more name. He then took a deep breath and typed the name Savannah Scott in the Facebook search box. This was the girl that he knew would be waiting for him on his last trip back in time, and for some reason, he needed to know where she was now. While several women with that name did pop up in the search results, none of them was his girl and most of them seemed to be in their late teens or early twenties. Apparently, Savannah had become a very popular name. After spending several minutes looking for her, he figured that she still had no social media, so he did a search for Savannah Scott in Boulder Colorado on Google instead. When the results came up in the search engine, the first one that popped up made is breath catch in his throat and his heart sink to his toes. He followed the link which took him to a picture of Savannah wearing shorts with a tank top and outfitted in mountain climbing gear and a helmet. She looked as gorgeous as he remembered, and a tear fell from his left eye as he read what was below the picture.

> *Savannah Scott of Boulder, aged 36 years, passed away while vacationing in Austria on May 12th, 2010. Savannah was an aspiring playwright and a fast friend to everyone she met. As a Colorado native, she was an avid mountain and rock climber and had a true love of life that is rarely replicated. She died far before her time, but in her short years on this planet she touched many hearts. She is survived by her mother, Sandy and father, Joe. She will be greatly missed by all.*

Jake was floored by this. Basically, he would be going back in time to see someone who was now dead. His brain was on fire, as he pondered this trip and the impact that it may have. If he went back and made the other choice at that critical juncture, would that save her life? If he did that and stayed, maybe she would live, but then again, she may die anyway if one subscribes to the theory that everything is predestined. Plus, if he saved her there, he'd have to stay as well, and he really didn't want to do that anymore after all that he had been through on the first two trips back. Worse yet, when he got there, he knew there was no way that he would remember that Savannah dies in 2010. His memory of the future was useless when he had traveled back before, and he was certain it would be again.

Jake was still exhausted and thought that a few more hours of rest would help, so he decided to lay down. As he rested in the hotel bed, he put on some music and the song *A Bad Dream* by Keene came on. When it did, he thought that nothing better could have fit how he felt at that moment. This was a very bad dream indeed, and he had no idea how he would survive it mentally and emotionally, and possibly physically as well. All he could do now was sleep, and it finally came to him after much longer than normal. His body was finally able to rest, but not so his mind because the bad dreams just continued in his sleep as they did when he was awake. He truly hoped that his sanity would last a few more days, but right now, that didn't seem to be a good bet at all.

CHAPTER 16: LEAVING D.C.

Tuesday, November 28th, 2000

"Cecil, boil some water," said the kindly lady who rescued Savannah just a few minutes ago. "I need to make some tea for our guest."

"Sure thing Alpharetta," said Cecil as he got up from his chair and walked to the small kitchen. "Coming right up!"

"What's your name, child?" Inquired Alpharetta. "As you just heard, I'm Alpharetta and my husband's name is Cecil."

"My name's Savannah, thanks so much for helping me, I was really scared."

"Well, isn't that exciting, we're both named after places in my beautiful home state of Georgia," said Alpharetta. "You see Cecil, I told you she was good people. Dear, you have been through a fright tonight, what happened?"

"I came home from work and forgot to lock the deadbolt which is currently the only latch on the door. When I got out of the shower, the burglar was sitting on the couch waiting for me. Fortunately, I had some pepper spray that I just bought today in my backpack on the kitchen table and was able to trick him into letting me grab it. I then hit him between the eyes with a full spray, so I'm pretty sure he'll be hurting for a while." As Savannah said this, she could still hear Chad screaming in agony in the hallway, and it made her feel oddly better to hear his suffering. After all, he'd certainly put *her* through enough.

"Well, you're safe now," said Cecil from the kitchen. "You must've done a good job with that spray young lady. That boy's been wailing for a while now. Police should be here soon."

"Yes honey, they will," said Alpharetta. "They always get here within about ten minutes. That's how long it took when the woman in 4B was robbed last April, do you remember that?"

"No ma'am, I don't," said Savannah. "I came to stay with my friend Kate in October. She's the girl who used to live there. I was only staying with her until I'd saved enough money to get my own place and I'd just about saved what I needed until it was taken last week."

"Savannah, why do you say Kate *used* to live there? Did she move?" Asked Alpharetta.

"Yes, she was transferred to Europe by her company," said Savannah. "I would've loved to have taken her place but by the time that I came to visit, the transfer was already in the works and the apartment was already rented. It will be occupied by another tenant effective December 1st. I had another place lined up now that I've lost my money, that's no longer going to happen. Since I have nowhere to live, I'm leaving too. I'm taking a bus back home to Colorado. Thanks again for helping, I really needed it tonight." As she finished saying this, she realized that Chad's screams had finally stopped. She still hoped that someone was at least holding him in an uncomfortable position outside.

"Oh, child, you *have* been through the ringer, haven't you? Said Alpharetta taking Savannah's hand. "I'm sad to hear that Kate's gone, she's such a nice girl and she even helped me with my groceries a few times. But you seem like a nice girl too, and I'm sorry that I didn't take the time to introduce myself earlier, because I did see you coming and going from time to time. For some reason, it just seems like you've been here longer than a month and a half. I must be gettin' old." With that she cackled a little laugh, smiled, and squeezed Savannah's hand.

"I told you to take them some biscuits," said Cecil from the kitchen again. "You know everybody loves them biscuits Alfie."

"Cecil, I don't need no comments from the Peanut Gallery, OK? Just be a good husband, and finish making the tea," said Alpharetta. "I tell you honey, training a man is about as impossible as training a snapping turtle. It just can't be done."

"I heard that," said Cecil. "She still makes some damn fine biscuits, though. I tell ya Savannah..."

"CECIL!" said Alpharetta in a sharp tone cutting him off. "You swear again, and I'm gonna wash that mouth out with soap!"

"Sorry dear, it was the biscuits, they're so good they mess up my thoughts," said Cecil with a big grin on his face as he popped his head out the kitchen door.

Just then, they heard the police arrive outside and begin the process of arresting Chad and reading him his rights.

"Alpharetta," began Savannah, "there's more to tell. That man out there is my ex-boyfriend and this was personal. He hunted me down after I was sure I'd escaped him in New York, and when he found me, he wanted me to suffer. He's a horrible person who's capable of anything."

"Don't you worry at all, child. I'll sit here with you when the police come in and you can tell them your story. Oh, and when they leave, you can stay here tonight, and Cecil will take you to the bus stop tomorrow."

"That means a lot, Alpharetta. I can't thank you enough."

Savannah got up and then went into the bathroom to throw on some sweatpants and a t-shirt. As expected, a few minutes later the police knocked at the door, and asked if they could speak to her. For the better part of an hour, they asked questions about what happened. Savannah told them that her attacker's name was Chad Forrester and that he was her ex-boyfriend. She didn't spare a detail about the threats that he made to her and even told them about how he followed her to Washington, and they took lots of notes. In the end, he was taken downtown and booked for a nice stay in the pokey. What Savannah didn't know at the time was that was the last time she would ever see or hear from him again. In fact, she never knew that Chad got out of jail, went to rehab, and eventually got his life back on track with a decent job and an endless stream of new girlfriends. Sadly, he had the misfortune to be taken out of this world in 2005 when a bolt of lightning hit him as he finished his best round of golf ever. A massive price for a 79.

Cecil and Alpharetta made sure that she was comfortable in their guest room, and Savannah suddenly found herself bone tired. She had a horrible day, and nothing had gone positively for her since she returned from the trip to Delaware with Kate to meet her family for Thanksgiving. At least Cecil and

Alpharetta had been there for her, two angels amid the brutal indifference that comprises the vast majority of human interactions on this planet. She would never forget them.

The next morning, Savannah awakened to the scent of breakfast, and she jumped out of bed and got dressed immediately. When she exited the guest room, Cecil was already sitting at the kitchen table while Alpharetta was setting a large basket on the table. Apparently, she'd made her famous biscuits after all, and Savannah couldn't wait to try them. When she did, she realized that Cecil was right, and when she looked at him after her first bite, he just said, "I told you so!"

After breakfast, Savannah went back to Kate's apartment to grab the few things that she had left, and when she returned, Cecil was ready to leave. After goodbyes that took longer than she expected, Cecil took her to the bus station where he dropped her off at 11:00 a.m. Savannah boarded her bus at about 11:45, and then sat, waited, and watched as everyone else stepped aboard and claimed a seat. The man in the very front seat sat down and then took a blanket from his backpack and put it over his seat and the seat next to him to form a tent of sorts. He then popped his face out occasionally as people boarded sort of like Gollum hiding from Orcs in Mordor. He was a bit weird, to say the least.

After a few minutes, the bus was nearly full, and the seat next to Savannah was still unoccupied. She was suddenly optimistic that she may have an empty seat next to her for a while at least, and this was definitely a good thing. She didn't want another Gollum next to her. Unfortunately, she ended up getting an even more annoying ride companion, and after only a few minutes, the thought of Gollum next to her wasn't really that bad anymore.

"Hello," said the girl that sat down next to her. "I'm Sylvia, although my friends usually just call me Syl, so you can too, if you want to. Before we go, would you like some tinfoil?

I always find that it's good to be protected on a trip."

"I'm Savannah, nice to meet you. How exactly does tinfoil protect me?"

"Well, for one thing, there's the stray gamma rays that are still around from the nuclear testing in the fifties, then there's also the government's RF signals which are always dangerous, but the real threat is from the... aliens," said Syl as she leaned in close and whispered the last word. "They are by far the biggest danger and the good news is that the foil does a good job of blocking everything! Platinum would be even better, but that type of foil would be too expensive for me, I think."

It was immediately obvious to Savannah, that Syl was not in a normal state of mind. She wore what appeared to be many layers of clothing with an old blue hoodie on top that was quite filthy. She also wore a wool skirt that went almost to the floor and finished the look with combat boots that probably saw their best years several tours ago. She smelled of pachouli and body odor and wore what appeared to be gardening gloves with the tips of the fingers cut off. She was way out there for sure, and Savannah decided to use that to her advantage.

"I would normally take you up on your offer, but I actually have something better," said Savannah as if she was talking to a perfectly rational and sane person. She then pulled the portable CD player out of her backpack. "This looks like a regular, everyday CD player, but it's much more. If I put these earphones in both ears and turn it on, it protects me from all those nasty things you mentioned, and I can safely monitor frequencies as well. So, if the device is on and working, I'm safe."

"Wow really? I've never heard of that. Where can I get one of those things? I'll still wear foil to be safe, but that would be awesome!"

"Oh, these aren't for sale. It was given to me by... well let's just say he wasn't from our world."

"Wow, OK then, you better get those earphones in your ears then," said Syl. "The transmissions are really getting bad this close to the holidays!"

"Yes, definitely. I'll monitor the transmissions and let you know if anything weird comes up!"

"Thanks! What did you say your name was again?"

"It's Savannah. Very nice to meet you, Syl. How far are you going on this bus?"

"Oh, I'm just going to Somerset Pennsylvania, which is a few hours away. My boyfriend lives there. You should get off with me there and stay with us for a few days. I'm sure Mark would love to see that... CD player."

"I'd love to Syl," said Savannah. "But I have important business in Colorado... if you know what I mean."

"Oh yes, I understand," said Syl. "Get those headphones in and I'll leave you be. Tell me anything that you think might be important!"

"Will do, Syl!"

With that, Savannah put the earphones in and pressed play. As soon as she did, the song *Why Does it Always Rain on Me*, by the band known as Travis began to play, and she closed her eyes while the bus pulled out of the station to begin its journey westward. While she was able to get out of a protracted conversation with Syl, she couldn't get away from her smell and it was beginning to make her ill. At the next stop, she needed to figure out another solution. The bus was mostly full, but there were still a few open seats so maybe she could just move to one of those. In any event, Pennsylvania wasn't that far so she figured she could survive until Syl's stop if she had to. She also hoped another weirdo didn't follow right after her. Considering the clientele on this Greyhound bus, Savannah figured that was likely to happen unless she could recruit some new and much saner person to sit by her at one of the stops. For now, at least, that was her plan.

As it happened, Savannah was able to fall asleep, and for the next two hours, she crashed out, although she was occasionally awakened when the bus stopped or hit a big bump that bounced her head off the glass. Syl also fell asleep and snored like crazy which woke Savannah a few times as well. Even worse, she would sometimes lean her head on Savannah's shoulder, which prompted her to readjust immediately each time it happened. The bus stopped several times before they reached Pennsylvania, a few people left at each stop and sometimes a few got on this chariot from hell, but no one that was traveling alone looked to be any saner than Syl, so Savannah did no recruiting. She just hoped that some miracle might occur at Somerset to give her a traveling companion that at least smelled a bit better. She decided that even a kindly old grandmother who incessantly complained about her diverticulitis and smelled like old-lady perfume would be a huge upgrade. She opened her CD player, removed the disk that was in there and popped in REM's *Out of Time* CD as it was always a favorite. She hit random play, and the familiar strains of *Shiny Happy People* burst through her headphones. She smiled as the tune began, and because it was also effective at silencing Syl's snoring, she was again able to drift off to sleep.

The bus stopped and Syl jumped up out of her seat as soon as the lights went on which woke Savannah immediately. "Well, Savannah, this is my stop! You sure you don't want to meet Mark? He's got real recordings of... certain beings... talking to him. Like I said before, he'd love you!"

"That's very sweet of you to offer, but like I said, I need to be in Boulder. BIG things going on there, you know!"

"Oh yes, I forgot," said Syl. "Glad you're on our side! See

ya!"

"Bye Syl, take care," said Savannah and with that Syl left her in peace and perhaps a bit more stinky than she was when she boarded the bus in D.C. After Syl disappeared into the bus stop with a man who she assumed was Mark, Savannah decided to stretch her legs and use the bus stop bathroom as she had held her pee for the last hour. She got up, grabbed her stuff because she still didn't trust anyone remaining on the bus, and headed to the land-based facilities. She figured that she should go quickly so she'd be able to get the same seat that she was in before as it was a safe distance away from Gollum.

She went into the bus stop, used the restroom, freshened up a bit, and then bought some potato chips and a Diet Coke. She then walked back to the bus, where a few new people were boarding. One was an old man who seemed normal at first until he turned around and gave her a lecherous leer that sent shivers down her spine. She decided that she'd rather stay here with Syl and Mark than sit next to that guy. The other person boarding was a woman in her mid-to-late forties wearing a Pittsburgh Steelers jacket with a large bag that held what looked to be knitting supplies. If her seat was still available and that woman sat in it, Savannah decided that she would ask to occupy the seat next to her. However, as soon as she got on the bus those plans changed immediately because the knitting Steelers fan sat down in the seat right across from Gollum. She then looked down the aisle and saw that her old seat had now been occupied. However, it wasn't occupied by the creepy old man as she'd feared. Instead, the person who sat there seemed to be an answer to her prayers as he was young, clean-cut, and gorgeous. Her heart was suddenly in her throat as she approached him, and as she met his eyes to ask if she could sit in the seat next to him, his smile made her weak in the knees. She thought herself to be quite the cliché.

"Hello," said Savannah meekly. "Is this seat taken?"

"No, by all means, please sit down," said the young Greek god who was still smiling at her.

"Thanks," said Savannah as she thought that he really needed to stop that... or on second thought, maybe he didn't because it was a beautiful smile. She stowed her backpack and sat down next to him and then she noticed that he smelled very good although she couldn't place his cologne. This was much better for sure.

"So how far you going?" Asked the handsome stranger.

"Sadly, all the way to Boulder."

"As in Colorado?"

"Yep, and so far, it's been a bit brutal as my last traveling companion believed that she needed to wear tinfoil to protect herself from alien signals. She also smelled really bad, so you are a decided upgrade." As she uttered the last word, she smiled as sweetly as possible at him only to meet that beautiful smile of his yet again as she met his eyes.

"Well, I think I'm pretty boring and normal myself, and sadly, I'm only going as far as Indy," he said. "Then I catch a bus to Chicago from there. But I'll be happy to keep you away from weirdos for at least that long. I'll tell ya, I have my eyes on that dude up front who is under the blanket. Goodness knows what he is doing up there... and I really don't want to know."

"You mean Gollum?" Asked Savannah with a flirty little giggle that she really didn't consciously intend. "He pops his head in and out occasionally and sometimes makes grunting noises. I really don't want to know what he's doing, either."

Just then the driver started the bus, and they pulled out of the Somerset bus stop. Savannah was happier that she could have ever expected with this turn of events. The streak of bad luck that she'd had since returning from Thanksgiving with Kate's family had been rough, but really, her bad luck extended far beyond that to the day when the guy that she followed to New York told her that he was going back to his wife. That was almost two years ago now. Who knows, maybe this new guy sitting next to her could be someone special? In any event, the fact that he smelled good and had an amazing smile was probably enough, and for that she was eternally grateful.

"By the way, my name is Savannah, Savannah Scott" she said and offered him her hand.

"I'm Jake DiVincenzo," he said, taking her hand and giving it a brief shake. "It looks like we have several hours together, so I look forward to getting to know you better."

"Me too," she said as the bus got back on the Pennsylvania Turnpike. What she didn't know at the time was that the ray of sunshine that she had waited for so long had finally arrived and he was sitting close enough to her that she could feel his body heat. She suddenly felt like a schoolgirl again, and even if this newfound friend turned out to be a footnote in what would become her future it was good to feel that way again. She smiled and he smiled back again. Yes, it was good to feel this way... even if it was only temporary.

CHAPTER 17: ONE PRISTINE EVENING

Friday, December 16th, 2016

Geneva opened the door to her room at the Grand Floridian, walked into the room and started the shower. Her watch told her that it was 11:15, so she figured that she'd take a shower and then lay down for a few hours afterwards because she was truly exhausted from the night before. She would've stayed in the room with Jake, but she didn't have any of her makeup there and figured that he may need some space to process everything that he had been through over the last few evenings. She needed some time to process things as well, and a shower and rest would help with that processing.

She stepped into the shower, closed her eyes, and let the water run on her face which also thoroughly saturated her hair. After a minute or so, she turned to let the hot water run on her back which felt great, and the steady massage of the shower jets set her mind to wandering. It seemed that the processing had begun.

The whole thing with Jake was so weird and for a second, she still doubted that it even happened at all. To begin with, she was falling for him and every time she thought of his face, she felt the excitement that accompanies strong attraction surge through her body. While this unexpected romance seemed to be straight-forward yesterday, it had become more complicated than she could've ever imagined. For one thing, he had apparently traveled back in time and although she wanted to doubt that was even possible, she couldn't deny the fact that he just... disappeared in the room last night. If that wasn't weird enough, the fact that he had sex with his old girlfriend while he was back in time, made Geneva feel very odd and even a little upset. However, she expected something like this would happen, and like she told him earlier that day, she really couldn't be angry at him for sleeping with a girl in 1995. Plus, he gained a lot of trust when he came clean about it immediately, and he genuinely seemed to feel bad about it even though the relationship with her was only a little over a day old. So, she figured that he probably did have real feelings for her, and because of those feelings, it was important for him to be honest with her. That made her feel good, and, in the end, she let him off the hook for anything he had done so far on his first two visits back in time. She also told him that she would forgive him for anything he did on his final visit, and that visit was what worried her most at the moment. As with the other trip back, she expected that he would have sex with the girl that would be there. While Geneva wasn't happy about it, she figured that it was inevitable considering that he told her that he didn't remember her at all when he was back in time. However, that wasn't her main concern. What really worried her was what would happen if he didn't come back at all and decided to stay in the past. If that happened, would she even remember him or would the memories of him and the last two days simply evaporate from her memory once he's gone? She really had no idea, and the supernatural adventure that she was now on with Jake became more complicated all the time. Her head began to throb.

Geneva finally got out of the shower after 30 minutes or so and then did a quick dry of her hair before putting on pajamas, closing the curtains, and laying down in bed. More than anything right now she needed rest, even if it would only be for a few hours. She had initially planned on meeting Layla for lunch and had told Jake as much, but Layla texted her before noon that she and Lawrence needed a last-minute meeting with the wedding planner so they could go over final details. In truth, Geneva was thankful for the opportunity to get some additional rest and figured that she would be with Layla most of the day tomorrow anyway. She was also a bit hungry, but her fatigue trumped her hunger at that point, and in minutes, she was out like a light.

The alarm went off at 3:01, and Geneva was suddenly rocketed out of a very deep slumber. She groggily hit the snooze button, and in what seemed like a second of time (that was actually over ten minutes), a text came through from Jake asking if he could come to her room. As she shook off the cobwebs, she told him to come over and then jumped out of bed, brushed her teeth, and put on a robe. Within seven minutes there was a knock on the door, and her heart jumped again as it did whenever she saw Jake as she opened the door to see his face. Any upset feelings about old girlfriends suddenly evaporated as instinct took over and she kissed him.

"It's good to see you too Geneva," said Jake smiling at her as they finished the kiss. "I've got news for you, can I come in?"

"Sure, lover," said Geneva as he walked into the door and sat down on the bed. She sat down beside him. "What's up?"

"Well, I saw Calliope earlier. She was posing as a hotel maid this time."

"Wow... what did she say? Did you get out of the last trip to... your past?"

"Sadly, no," he replied with a somewhat forlorn look on his face. "Trust me, it wasn't due to a lack of trying. But she did do one thing to help me out, and I think you'll be happy about it. I certainly am."

"Really? Please tell me then."

"She saw how worn out I was, so she delayed my final trip back by a day. For tonight at least, I'm all yours and I'll stay put in this reality. That is... if you still want me after all the weirdness that I've put you through."

"What a development," said Geneva coyly while smiling as brightly as possible at him. "Whatever shall I do?"

"I think you should stay with me again tonight after the rehearsal dinner. I'd love to focus on you instead of this last trip back in time that I must make. I promise to make it worth your while."

With that comment, Geneva kissed him again, and then the kiss began to turn into something much more. She wanted to pull his t-shirt off and let him undress her as well, but she also wanted to wait and not have to rush things. After all, the rehearsal began in about an hour and a half, and she needed to get a bite to eat before getting ready as she was now famished. As much as she wanted to let this kiss turn into a moment of passion right now, there just wasn't enough time... or at least not enough for the first time with him. She wanted it to be special.

"OK, whoa, tiger," said Geneva as she reluctantly pushed him away. "Let's save that for later. Let's also make it my room this time, OK?"

"Agreed," said a red-faced Jake. "Thanks for putting on the brakes before things got too out-of-hand. Are you hungry? Would you like to get a quick snack?"

"You must've read my mind, lover. Let's go!"

They walked down to the Gasparilla Island Grill which is the quick service restaurant at the Grand Floridian. There they were able to get a small salad for her and a Reuben for him, along with a few cups of coffee. They then headed back up to the room, ate their food, and then Jake returned to his room to get ready. They needed to be at the rehearsal in the Wedding Pavilion at 5:00, so they both needed time to make themselves presentable.

As Geneva put on her makeup after wetting her hair, she thought of all the possibilities that a relationship with Jake may hold. She didn't want to get ahead of herself as they were barely two days in, but she liked where things were going. If only he didn't have to go back in time again to see another girl. If only she had met him a year earlier, maybe she could have stirred his creativity and been his muse instead of Calliope? Maybe she could've been enough to inspire him alone? While the answers to these questions may never be known, what she did have was tonight. And she was determined to make the most of it.

Geneva dried and styled her hair which involved some straightening due to its natural waviness. She then put on a short blue party dress that was lacy and adorned with sequins. Geneva particularly like its sheer "flutter sleeves" and as she looked at herself in the mirror, she was very pleased with the appearance of the girl who looked back. It was ten minutes to five, and right on cue, there was a knock on the door.

"Hello beautiful, this is for you," said Jake as he handed her one long-stemmed red rose. He was dressed in what appeared to be a very high-quality gray suit that was double-breasted and wore a shirt that was nearly the same color as her dress with no tie. She couldn't have coordinated their look as a couple any better, and it happened completely by chance because neither of them told the other one what his or her attire would be. To top it all off, he smelled great as well. In short, he was stunning.

"Yes, I'll accept your rose and maybe let you into the Fantasy Suite with me later," said Geneva with a crooked smile as she referenced a well-known TV show.

"Oh, so you feel like you're on the *Bachelor*, huh? Said Jake chuckling. "Well, considering my trips back in time, I can certainly understand why."

"Yes, I do. But do you know what? I also plan to be the girl at the end," said Geneva before giving him a quick kiss. "Let's go so we're not too late."

With that the two walked out of the room and made their way to the Disney Wedding Pavilion which is directly adjacent to the hotel. They got there about five minutes late but weren't the last to arrive as Roger arrived last. Apparently, he was doing shots at the pool bar with a group of young ladies that were on a "girls' weekend." What a dog.

The rehearsal went off without a hitch, and at the end, Lawrence told everyone that he had a big surprise for his bride tomorrow during the last five minutes of the wedding before the recessional. Layla poked, prodded, and tried, to pry the surprise out of him all night but was never successful. Geneva couldn't wait to see what it was, and based upon everything so far, she knew it would be huge.

After the rehearsal was done, the wedding party matriculated to Albert and Victoria's. This restaurant is also at the Grand Floridian and is not only one of the swankiest restaurants at Disney World, but also in the Southeast United States as well. When they got there, they were seated at a table in a prime location where they dined on culinary delights that most people only read about or see on the Food Network. As expected, the wine pairings were completely on-point, and the entire eating experience was one of the best that Geneva had ever had.

During the dinner there were more toasts, not the dirty limerick type, but of the more heartfelt and impromptu variety instead. Of course, these were made with the understanding that the toasts at the reception tomorrow evening would be more formal and planned with specific persons having to make them in a set order. There were also more stories as Roger was in attendance tonight and in rare form. By the end of the evening, every one of Jake's fraternity brothers was basically roasted as Roger told tales involving each of them with his main objective being maximum embarrassment. He was able to achieve his objective with all of them except Alex and Jake as they always seemed to be the guys that made sure that the rest of them stayed out of jail. However, he did mention that Jake was a part of one of their milder shenanigans in Las Vegas one night during a guys trip the year after they all graduated from UVA. To her, the funniest part was when he told everyone that Jake had blown off some rich girl from Nantucket to join him on that trip, and that the rich girl never forgave him for doing so. When that story was told, Jake glanced at her with a face that was perhaps a bit crimson, and this gave her a smile. If the rest of them only knew what happened to him last night.

The whole thing ended at just after nine, and while most of the wedding party (which now included parents of the bride and groom as well) went to The Enchanted Rose for a few nightcaps, Geneva and Jake opted out, and broke away from the group as catcalls from nearly all of them followed them out. It seemed like the entire wedding party now considered them to be a "thing" at this point. She did too, and still liked the path they were on together, despite the situation with his time travel.

It was a balmy night in Central Florida, but there were no stars in the sky because of some rather dense cloud cover. It was also apparent that it rained hard just a short while ago as there was still quite a bit of standing water on the paved portions of the ground. The good news was that the forecast called for clearing skies and included no additional rain. As the Epcot fireworks show began in the distance, Geneva thought that it would be nice to have some fresh air before they moved to the next part of their evening together.

"Jake, let's take a walk."

"You must've read my mind," he said and then took her hand in his. "It looks like it may shape up to be a beautiful evening."

"I'm really happy we have this moment, Jake," she said as they strolled along with the percussion of the booming fireworks from Epcot made the scene seem vaguely like they were in a French village close to the Western Front during the First World War.

"Me too, and I'm glad that we got a few moments away from everyone else because something happened that I need to tell you about. It's been bothering me all night."

"Jake, you should know by now that you can tell me whatever you want," said Geneva as they walked along. His last comment suddenly made her very uneasy. "I haven't done anything to upset you, have I?"

"No, nothing like that at all. It's about the third trip back tomorrow night," said Jake. His voice betrayed nervousness. "The fact is that I know exactly who I'll find when I go back there and if we're gonna move forward, I need to tell you about her."

"No problem, Jake, I'm all ears."

"So, remember when I told you about enduring a bus trip from Pennsylvania to Chicago in the winter to meet up with Angela, my future ex-wife?"

Geneva nodded.

"Well, there's more to the story," said Jake who then paused for a few seconds. "I got on the bus at a station in a small town called Somerset and sat down. After a few minutes, this beautiful girl about my age got on and asked if she could sit next to me. I was immediately attracted to her, so it was an easy 'yes' from me. We talked almost non-stop all the way to just outside Columbus, where the engine on our bus decided to die. Fortunately, the next exit had a Holiday Inn and was only about a quarter mile away. Since Greyhound couldn't get us a new bus until the next day, she and I walked with a bunch of passengers to the exit where most of us got rooms. Due to the circumstances, the hotel opened one of its meeting rooms to bus passengers if they wanted to sleep on the floor for free. I didn't want to do this, so I got a room, and Savannah stayed with me. On that night, and for most of the next day, we got to know each other very well... probably as well as I have gotten to know you now. Oh, and we never had sex although it was apparent that we both wanted to. Sound familiar?"

Geneva smiled at him and was suddenly hit by some rather sharp feelings of jealousy. This obviously was an important story for him, so she listened intently. However, she had no idea where it was going but wanted to hear more even though these feelings grew by the moment. He continued.

"We left the next afternoon and when we finally got to Indy at about eight in the evening, I had a choice to make. I could've either driven back to Chicago with Angela and her friend as they came to pick me up, or I could've taken the other path and stayed on the bus with Savannah all the way to her hometown of Boulder, Colorado. I obviously chose the Angela path all those years ago, so I'm pretty sure I'll go the other way and continue the ride with Savannah instead when I go tomorrow night."

"Jake," cut in Geneva, "Can you choose to do the same thing? I mean, could you just go to Chicago and not chase after... her."

"Well, yes, I can. But remember, I'll have all the same feelings and emotions that I did at the time. And the worst thing is that I won't remember you. It really sucks. If I'm honest with myself, I did have significant feelings for Savannah at that time, and they were intense. The reality is that I may not want to come back, and sadly, my current self can't do anything about it."

"That's a lot for you, Jake, I'm sure. Obviously, I don't want you to disappear from my life, but I can't worry about that now. Jake, I think there's something more. You need to tell me what's really bugging you. This girl Savannah seems like a keen example of young love for you, and my guess is that you'd probably expected to find her on one of these trips back anyway considering the significance that this relationship seems to have for you. I can see it in your eyes, what else is wrong?"

"You're so perceptive, Geneva. It's amazing," said Jake to her sincerely. "You're right, the relationship was very significant to me... but there's one more wrinkle: in this reality, right now, Savannah is no longer living. Here, look for yourself."

He handed her his phone and on it was an obituary for a Savannah Scott from 2010. When she saw the picture, Geneva admitted to herself that Savannah was a beautiful girl. After she read it, she was convinced that this entire situation couldn't get any weirder. Unfortunately for her, it would, she just didn't know it yet.

"Jake, I don't know what to say. Do you think you can save her by traveling back?"

"I don't know… I just don't know," he said shaking his head. "Once again, I won't even remember that she died in this reality when I get there, so I probably won't even realize that she needs saving. Geneva, my head is swimming, and I can't stop the thoughts that I have bombarding the inside of my skull. What if I *can* save her by staying? On the other hand, what if I stay and she dies anyway? If I don't return to this reality, will you remember me? Will Kira and Jake cease to exist? I just can't take it anymore."

Geneva embraced Jake and then pulled back to look him directly in the eyes. "Jake, you can only change what you can control, so don't feel guilty about something that you have no influence over at all. Most importantly, stop worrying about what may happen next and just appreciate the 'now.' Live in the moment. Lover, I don't know what will happen with you tomorrow and have even less insight into the future beyond that if you do return. But what I know right now is that we have tonight and that this may be our only time together. Don't create yet another regret by letting *this* opportunity pass by. Because all we have is this moment… this one pristine evening. Let's make the most of it and deal with the rest later, OK?"

Jake kissed her in the way that a girl always wants to be kissed. He then looked at her once again and said, "you're right, I need to appreciate what I have in front of me, and Geneva, you're a better prize than I deserve… in every way. Shall we go back to your place?"

"Jake, let's make a memory."

Jake and Geneva kissed once more and then walked back to the hotel hand in hand, with fingers interlocked tightly. They took their time and even joined the wedding party for a drink at the Enchanted Rose before proceeding to her room. When they got there, Geneva pulled off Jake's jacket and then hung it in the closet. He then went to kiss her, and she put her index finger to his lips instead and simply said "Not yet."

Geneva went into the bathroom and slipped out of her dress, and then out of her bra and panties as well. She brushed her teeth, freshened her makeup, and put on the hotel robe with nothing else. There was no need to make this more complicated than necessary.

As Geneva entered the room, Jake met her as naked as the day he was born. He looked her in the eyes as he grabbed her and pulled her close. What she didn't see was his other hand which held his i-Phone. He then pressed play on his music app and *(You Want To) Make a Memory* by Bon Jovi began to play on his phone.

"The words don't quite fit this situation, but you inspired me with what you said earlier," said Jake in the mostly dark room that was subtly illuminated by a sliver of moonlight that sneaked between the curtains currently covering the doors to the balcony. "I put it on random play after the song is done."

"You're such a geek, Jake," said Geneva as she pushed away from him gently, untied the cloth belt on the robe and let it slide off her shoulders to the ground. "Sorry, I needed to get even with you. Now, let's see if you can live up to your pet name... lover."

In one move, Jake picked her up off the ground and then carried her to the bed where he laid her down as gently as one would a piece of fine china. The whole move was rather grandiose and surprised the hell out of her, but the feel of his toned body and the ease in which he literally swept her off her feet, did nothing but make her more turned on. In the next moment he was next to her and kissing her... not just her mouth but her nipples as well and as he did so, his hands greedily explored the area below her waistline and between her legs. Geneva was in heaven and her passion was building by the second.

All at once, she couldn't take it anymore. She had to have him now, as the foreplay had done its job sufficiently and it was time for the main event. She reached down to find him at least as ready as she was to start this party, and when she touched him, he gently rolled on top of her as she guided him to their mutual objective. As they joined in that way that humans can't seem to get enough of, it did not feel the least bit dirty or hedonistic as it did with a few other men she had been with in her life. Instead, it was gentle and forceful, plush and firm, light and heavy, and as exciting as the day you take your first ride on a roller coaster. As Jake moved, she moved with him and as this dance that they were now engaged in continued, her excitement moved like mercury in an old thermometer on a hot July day in the South. Suddenly, the teakettle whistled and as the fireworks exploded in the Magic Kingdom next door, so did Geneva who was followed by Jake just seconds later. Tears had made two shimmering tracks from the corner of each eye to pool in both ears. She didn't even remember crying.

"I'm not even sure I have words for what just happened, Geneva," said Jake who had just rolled off her, far more winded that she would've expected.

"Don't worry lover, it seems that we do just fine without words," she said smiling at him with the glow of pure satisfaction. "In fact, we really only need four words for the rest of the evening."

"And those are?"

"Let's do it again."

CHAPTER 18: COME TO ME

Saturday, December 17th, 2016

Geneva didn't even remember falling asleep after the evening with Jake, and it certainly was something that she would never forget, even if he ceased to exist in this reality and chose to stay with... her. When they made love the first time, she felt as if it was one of the best experiences of her life, but it was also only the beginning. The second time was at least as good but longer, and on the third time around she fulfilled her cardio requirement for the week. She did remember them turning the TV at about 3:30, but she was completely out minutes after turning it on and the next thing she knew, the alarm on her iPhone was chiming like mad, which told her it was 8:00 a.m. Although she would much rather stay in bed all day with Jake, she knew that Layla wanted her in an hour to begin the bridal party's wedding day festivities. So, she had to get up.

She climbed out of bed as Jake rolled over and groaned. "Is it that time already?" He asked, appearing to be at least as tired as she was.

"Sadly, yes," said Geneva. "But on the positive side, this should be a very fun day... although I don't think anything could match last night. Thanks for more than living up to your nickname, lover."

"The pleasure was all mine, babe. I'll never forget it... well at least not in this reality," said Jake with a wry smile. "I know you have Maid of Honor stuff to do, so I'll take my mangy ass back to my room to sleep for a bit. Billy Dee said he doesn't need us till noon."

"Lucky you," she said and then kissed him. "I'm sure I'll be fine after a mimosa or two. See you at 3:30."

With that Geneva jumped out of the bed and put on the robe that was still lying on the ground from the night before. Jake got up as well and dressed in the clothes that he had worn last night. She mused to herself that it was about time that the guy did the walk of shame for a change and smiled as she had that thought. Jake noticed.

"What are you smiling about?" Said Jake as he finished dressing. "Do you think it's funny that I have to do the walk of shame this time?"

"As a matter of fact, I do," she said brightly as he read her mind and then she kissed him once more. As he opened the door to leave, she grabbed his arm and pulled him in for a huge hug. "Jake, I loved last night, but I also know that it may be our only moment together. I... just wanted you to know how much it meant to me... and that I have no regrets. I mean that."

"Geneva let's just take it one step at a time. For the

record, last night was uniquely wonderful for me also. I've never felt that way with anyone. See you at the wedding, gorgeous."

Jake winked at her and walked out, and Geneva flopped down on the bed with her mind full of emotions. First and foremost, after last night, she was certain that she was falling in love with Jake, and that made her pulsate with energy like she used to when she was a teenager and was first learning what human attraction was all about. That energy made her happy and excited at the same time and normally she would be on the phone telling all her friends about everything and speculating about the future and what that might look like as Jake's "significant other." And then there was the dark cloud that tempered this excitement. This, of course, was Jake's final trip back in time. She'd already given him a hall pass for what will probably happen there, but she truly hoped that he wouldn't use it. She also wished that they were just a normal couple, two people who found each other at a wedding as so many have done before. Unfortunately, this... magic... that has intruded upon Jake's life was far more malevolent than she would've ever expected, and it had the ability to completely undo everything that had been done to get them both to where they were now. She felt as helpless as a young child lost in a department store.

Geneva finally got up, took a very hot shower, and donned the purple sundress that she'd brought for the occasion. Purple was Layla's thing, so everyone in the bridal party would be wearing something purple for the brunch and then afterwards they would change into the lovely lavender bridesmaids' dresses that she helped Layla pick out. She grabbed her dress out of the closet after putting on her shoes and then headed out of the room to meet everyone at the front to take a limo to the Animal Kingdom Lodge where they would have brunch at Jiko, which is one of the restaurants there. Since both Geneva and Layla were from South Africa, and the food at that hotel was based on African recipes, it seemed like the perfect place for the girls to start the wedding day festivities. Everyone was on time (although Julie seemed a bit worse for the wear), and they piled in the limo for the short ride to the other hotel.

The food turned out to be wonderful, the mimosas flowed like water, and everyone wanted details about her night with Jake. She tried to deflect at first by saying things like they just really got on well together, or that she greatly enjoyed his company, but these girls were not satisfied... they wanted the dirt. She finally broke down and admitted that he did spend the night in her room and that he may or may not have had his clothes on, but that's all she would give most of them. The one exception was Layla, and privately, she told her everything, including all the sordid details which Layla appeared to thoroughly enjoy. Mostly, she really seemed happy for Geneva. If only Layla knew what was going to happen with Jake tonight.

After brunch, everyone went back to the Grand Floridian for massages and facials, although Layla cut off the booze because everyone was beginning to get a bit tipsy from the mimosas. Geneva thought that was an excellent idea, especially for a few of them as they were beginning to round the corner into Drunktown. She was pretty sure that Julie wouldn't even make it to the wedding at all if Layla didn't do this, and the reality was that there would be plenty more to drink at the reception later.

All spa treatments were done just after 1:00, and then a small army of makeup artists and hairstylists arrived to make all of them look even more beautiful than they normally did, and to make the bride look her absolute best on her special day. The stylists all turned out to be incredible, especially a small, flamboyant, gent named Oscar who was amazingly talented and began the beauty session by announcing to everyone that Layla's hair and makeup was his and his alone. As he said repeatedly, "it takes a queen to make a queen!"

Everyone was ready by 3:00, and they all looked amazing. As soon as the last girl's hair and makeup was finished, Layla turned the mimosa faucet back on as everyone had sobered up from brunch and she was feeling a bit nervous. As with most brides on their wedding day, she was stunning. Her dress was a simple, "mermaid" gown that was sleeveless, low cut in the back, and made of the finest quality satin. It had a relatively short train and fit Layla's beautiful shape perfectly. She topped the look off with a veil that was so sheer that it seemed to be made of mist. Geneva thought that her groom may get weak in the knees when he saw her and hoped that Jake would be there to catch him if he did. As she had this thought, her mind wandered to last night with Jake, and the butterflies in her stomach became active again.

Christian weddings in the U.S. are all rather similar and many of them share the same characteristics. For example, the processional is often *Canon in D* by Pachelbel or the *Bridal Chorus* by Wagner, the readings often come from First Corinthians 13 or Ecclesiastes 4, and the vows are fairly standard with the *Wedding March* by Mendelssohn being played on the way out. This however was not the case with this ceremony, and many of the selections that were made were a departure from the norm. Geneva had a hand in everything except the vows as she and Layla had talked about this day many times over the last several months. The vows were written by the bride and groom separately, and while she did not know what Lawrence had written, Geneva thought what Layla came up with was perfect. They both really wanted this day to be something unique and wonderful, and Geneva sincerely hoped that everyone would be happy with their choices.

At 3:30, the bridal party prepared to walk out of the dressing rooms at the Wedding Pavilion and march into the sanctuary where the ceremony would take place. All of them gave Layla a careful hug (to not smudge her makeup) and then they prepared to march in individually by taking their places in a row that was led by Geneva. As soon as they were lined up and ready to go, *Only Time* by Enya began to play and the doors to the sanctuary were opened by the ushers who were standing next to them. As soon as they were opened, the first thing that Geneva saw was Jake's beautiful eyes and warm smile, and as she began her walk down the aisle, he mouthed to her the words "you look beautiful" which not only widened her own smile but also intensified the electrical storm that was happening inside her neurons. She made it to her appointed spot and stood as the rest of the bridesmaids filed in, one at a time. Then, Layla appeared with her father, and everyone stood up as she walked down the aisle and took her place in front of Lawrence who wore a white dinner jacket with his tux while the other groomsmen wore traditional black jackets. The music stopped and for a few seconds, all was silent. Then the wedding began, and while Geneva and Jake should have been paying attention to the bride and groom, for much of the ceremony, all they did was look at each other.

The wedding itself was great, with unique passages being read at two different intervals in the ceremony. The first passage was *A Time to Laugh* by Sister Joan Chittister and was read by a girl named Ellie who is Layla's closest cousin. The second passage was read by Lawrence's sister Natalie and was from an anthology called *Bread for the Journey* by Henri Nouwen. While Geneva had never heard of either of these before, she thought them both to be excellent selections. The wedding moved on quickly from there and before she knew it, they had read their vows to each other. While she knew what Layla would say, it sounded even better to hear her say the words out loud to him and she was impressed that she had memorized every syllable and didn't miss a word. Lawrence did not memorize his and instead read from a small black notebook. Geneva didn't know him well, but his vows revealed a very gentle and loving side to his personality and most importantly, the depth of the love for his bride. It was wonderful to watch and like most single bridesmaids and maids of honor, she secretly wished that she was standing in Layla's place and today at least, she saw herself there with Jake.

After the vows, the ceremony stopped, and the groom addressed his wife and everyone else in attendance.

"My beautiful Layla, I wanted to give you a gift that you'd never forget, so here it is. I think everyone here will like it as well."

Just then, the door opened, and a man entered the sanctuary with a guitar. Geneva recognized him immediately as John Rzeznik from The Goo Goo Dolls because that was one of her favorite bands. He walked down the aisle, gave both the bride and groom a hug, and sat down on a stool that had been suddenly and magically placed up front by Disney staff. He then put his guitar on his knee, and said, "Lawrence, thanks for having me. This is for you and your bride."

After he said this, he played the song *Come to Me.* This song is tailor made for a wedding and would have been perfect even if a recording of it was played. However, hearing it live was different, and in all ways, far superior. Each note held a special weight and value, and each second was gold. Geneva couldn't believe that Lawrence was able to get a celebrity like this to play his wedding yet, there he was. As the words rolled off his lips and floated into the air, she looked at Jake and as expected, he returned her gaze. They were transfixed in this eternal moment, and in that moment, Geneva found herself loving Jake even more. The music ended and the groom and bride just stared at each other with tears streaming down their cheeks. They then kissed and were pronounced man and wife to a thunderous applause from everyone in attendance. After that and almost without warning, the recessional began. Layla was always a huge fan of the movie *Love Actually*, so the recessional had to be *All You Need is Love* by the Beatles. However, this time it was played by the Goo Goo Dolls' front man, and it was done perfectly. The music played, the bride and groom strolled out, and Geneva took her leave after they moved down the aisle a bit and smiled when she took Jake's arm and followed the bride and groom out of the sanctuary along with the remainder of the wedding party. Everything went perfectly, and Geneva knew that Layla would be very happy with how well it all came together. Geneva hoped to have a wedding day half as nice as today was so far and somehow knew that she would someday. However, at that moment, this feeling was probably overly optimistic and fueled by the vortex of emotions that were produced by the wedding itself as well as the experience with Jake last night.

They did the traditional receiving line before proceeding to the reception. At the reception, the cavalcade of toasts took place, Geneva's went better than expected and made Layla cry yet again, and for a change, Roger's toast was heartfelt and sincere. Dinner came next and after a wonderful meal of Chateaubriand and winter vegetables, the dances began. It was all great and certainly a wonderful experience for Layla and Lawrence, but all she really wanted to do was be alone with Jake. Because of how the head table was arranged, she couldn't sit next to him, and this drove her mad because she really needed to get one more moment with him before he went back to... Savannah. She needed just a little more time, just one more second really, in the grand scheme of the universe. Just one. She had no idea when it would happen, but she knew it would; it just couldn't come soon enough.

Fortunately, relief was on the way in the form of a dance, or rather, several dances. Of course, there are always the obligatory dances that are prescribed by wedding tradition, and those had to come first. One of these was a dance with Roger, which couldn't have thrilled her less. To her surprise, he was the consummate gentleman, and in truth it wasn't horrible dancing with him. Another was a dance with Lawrence, who she was really beginning to like a lot. Finally, after all these dances were complete, the music went from slow to fast and everyone hit the dance floor. Of course, this included Jake and when she saw him out there, she made a beeline for him before anyone else could claim him as a dance partner. This was easy because it appeared that he had exactly the same intentions and when they met, together they became a five-alarm dance inferno.

Geneva couldn't believe how good a dancer that Jake was. He flowed in and out of each dance move like a snake and happily took her with him. She had no idea that he could dance, and not just adequately, but with virtuosity and flair. So, she just let him take her along for the ride and she happily followed where he led. She didn't know how many songs had been played or how long they were dancing, but they were both having a magnificent time when suddenly, the music stopped. Then, right after the DJ announced that it was time to slow things down a bit, *Is this Love* by Bob Marley and the Wailers began to play and when it did Jake took her into his arms.

"I didn't know you could dance," said Geneva.

"My mom was a dance teacher. I spent much of my life until age fourteen or so in a dance studio. I like to dance and even did it competitively for a while. But the reality is that I liked sports better," said Jake.

"Well, thanks for the lessons, because to be honest, it was hard to keep up. I was super impressed!"

"Thanks, I appreciate that. I took a lot of flak as a kid for being a dancer when I was young, but it looks like it's finally paid off," said Jake with a slight chuckle.

Without warning, Geneva kissed him. She didn't know why and really didn't care. Most importantly, she didn't care who saw her because there were probably fifty people in close proximity. To her, it really didn't matter, she liked to kiss Jake and couldn't give a shit about what the world thought about it. It was wonderful, and when it ended, she had only one thing on her mind.

"Jake, are you listening to this song?"

"Sure, it's Marley, he's the best! A classic!"

"Jake, for a smart guy, occasionally you're so thick," said Geneva. Sometimes, she just didn't get men at all. "What I want to know is if what we're feeling together *is* love like the song asks... you know... between you and me."

"What is it for you?" Inquired Jake, as he looked at her with an unreadable expression.

"Love..." said Geneva after a small pause in an almost normal, everyday tone even though she wanted to scream. At this moment, she wondered what he would do.

"Well... I think it may be love for me, too," said Jake. "I just wish.."

"Shush, don't say anything else. It'll make me too sad."

"Don't be sad... at least not yet," said Jake. "I mean, the first two trips back have been disasters."

"Yes, but this time you will be with the 'girl that got away' and not a spoiled rich girl from New England," said Geneva.

"I know it'll be tough, but I can get through this one too," said Jake. "Geneva, I wish that you didn't have to deal with this, but at the same time, I've thoroughly enjoyed the ride with you. It's impossible not to love you, and I have succumbed like everyone else in the world. I know I will come back and when I do, let's see what we can make of this thing, ok?"

Geneva kissed him again. "You can't promise that, so

right now, I can't either. But my love for you will never waiver, irrespective of the outcome. That said, that is 'then' and we still have a bit of 'now.' So, why don't we break off and go to your room so we can have at least one more moment before you disappear into your past yet again. You up for that, lover?"

"I am, and I do love you."

"I know, I feel it."

Geneva and Jake did not say goodbye to everyone else at the wedding that night because they knew that it would take at least 45 minutes to get out of the reception area if they did. The toasts and dances were over and the only thing remaining was the bouquet and garter tosses, and neither of them cared about those events. They knew they were on borrowed time together and that what would happen later to Jake would change whatever existed between them, forever. She needed just one more second of time where she could be intimate with him, one more fantasy where she could surrender herself completely to him before the entire thing was corrupted by his final trip to what was certainly her version of hell. Maybe it was the mimosas followed by the wine, or maybe it was indeed true love, but the intensity of her feelings drove her, and she wasn't about to let up until she got what she was after.

They went back to his room this time and before the door had fully closed, they were undressing each other. They moved towards the bed as they did this and when they finally got there, they both pulled off any garments that remained on their bodies before literally jumping into bed with each other and making love in a frenzy that shook the pillars of her world yet again. Afterwards, they both dozed off for a bit, and Geneva awakened when Jake got up to use the restroom. It was just after 5:00 a.m., and just as she thought that maybe he would not be going back in time again, that maybe Calliope had decided to spare her the possibility of losing him forever, it happened.

Light poured forth from under the door of the bathroom and then, just as suddenly as it began, it was gone. Geneva got up, walked to the bathroom door, and opened it to confirm that Jake was no longer in the room. When she saw that he was gone, she was suddenly overwhelmed with the situation and broke down as she felt as if she may never see him again. She went back to the bed, had a good cry, and then after about ten minutes, she was finally able to compose herself and make a cup of coffee with the small coffeemaker in the room. She then decided to turn on the TV because the entire situation was eating at her, and she flipped channels until she found the version of *A Christmas Carol* where George C. Scott plays Ebenezer Scrooge. The movie had just begun, and Scrooge hadn't yet met the ghost of his old partner, Jacob Marley, so she decided to watch it. As she watched, she began to draw parallels between Scrooge and Jake as both were forced to learn lessons in a supernatural way, and it was obviously an emotional journey for both as each visit to their respective alternate realities revealed unexpected truths. In fact, the only real difference between the two (besides the fact that Scrooge was a miserable old bastard) was that Jake always went backwards while Scrooge explored realities (and potential realities) in the past, present, and future. Although she knew the ending to the story well, when Scrooge was finally transformed to the good man that he became at the end, she couldn't help but wonder what Jake's transformation would look like when the credits on his adventure began to roll across the screen, and if she'd still be a part of his reality or not.

No sooner had the movie ended that something unexplainable happened. From out of nowhere and everywhere simultaneously, she felt what could only be described as a shockwave hit her, and for a second it seemed as if time stopped and then restarted again. When this "shockwave" hit, it didn't knock anything down like a normal shockwave would, and it made no sound at all. In fact, whatever this was seemed to have a leading edge that looked to be vaguely liquid that approached quickly and washed over her like jelly that was completely dry. It was almost like for a moment she existed in limbo, and when it was gone, she'd no idea what had taken place, only that for some reason she felt very different, but not in any way she could put her finger on. It bothered her so much that she went into Jake's mini fridge and grabbed one of the beers he'd purchased yesterday. It was very early, but she needed a drink more than ever because Jake had now been gone over two hours. If their assumption about how time worked between this reality and where Jake was now was correct and one hour here equaled one day there, then he had less than one hour (or one day) left.

Geneva went to the restroom and then came out and decided to surf the web on her phone. The clock kept moving and still no Jake. Soon he had been gone two and one-half hours and then two hours and forty-five minutes, and she was beginning to wonder if he had decided to stay. She also wondered if that decision had triggered the weird wave of energy that passed through her earlier. She began to panic, and this panic made her do what she promised herself she wouldn't do before Jake left and did a search for Savannah Scott's obituary. She had to see this girl, her rival from another time and place, one more time. However, when she did this, she didn't see what she thought she would and what she saw caused her to drop her phone in her lap. What she saw was a gamechanger and she suddenly realized that she may never see him again. The tears began to fall as the hope that she held for a future with him began to fail. She had no idea how this Greek tragedy would end and right now she didn't want to know, because she was already sad enough for one day... or maybe even for one lifetime.

CHAPTER 19: THE BUS IS BUSTED

Wednesday, November 28th, 2000

"So, I don't mean to pry," said Jake, "but you don't seem like the type of person who'd normally ride a Greyhound Bus, Savannah."

"Really? Why's that?" She replied.

"Well, I've taken a few bus trips in the past and it seems that most people that use this mode of transport exude a certain aura of desperation. I was a little desperate because my car broke down and I need to get to Chicago. Others are running to something or running from something... or someone. Although I just met you, I see strength, rather than desperation in your eyes. I'm guessing this trip wasn't one that you wanted to make. Am I right?"

"Is it that transparent?" Asked Savannah with a little laugh. "You're right, two weeks ago, this trip wasn't on my radar screen. And yes, I wish I wasn't here at all."

"Do you want to talk about it? Sometimes complete strangers are the best listeners."

Savannah was unsure what to do at that moment. On one hand, he was very attractive to her on several levels, and she felt a certain sense of ease being near him although they'd just met. On the other hand, Chad was a handsome devil himself, and at first had been extremely charming and kind. She wanted to proceed cautiously, but in the end decided that telling Jake at least the main parts of her story would do no harm. Especially since they only had a few hours together.

"Well, Jake, I'll give you my tale of woe, but to do so, I need to go back in time a little, ok?"

"Fair enough Savannah," he said with that damned smile again. "It's not like I've anywhere to go. Tell me what you need to, I'll listen."

"So, I was always a good student and had lots of options for college right out of high school. My father wanted me to study law and because of this he had me apply to schools that had strong law programs. He was happy because I got into almost all of them except Yale and Georgetown but was wait-listed at both. It was exhausting for me because in the end, I sent out over twenty applications. Absolutely brutal. Anyway, when it came time to decide, I chose to stay close to home because my high school boyfriend convinced me that he loved me and couldn't stand the thought of me being so far away. Since he'd decided to take a job selling Chevys like his big brother, he wasn't going anywhere, and like the doe-eyed idiot I was, I stayed."

"There's no shame in that Savannah, I moved to Indiana one summer with a girl I met in college at the University of Virginia," said Jake. "She was from Indianapolis, had just graduated, and was moving back to be close to her family. I had a year left, but she thought we could 'play house' for a few months to see if the relationship had any legs and asked me to spend the summer with her there. It turns out it didn't have any legs at all because she ran off with her high school boyfriend three weeks after we sublet a duplex together for the summer and that left me alone. As it turns out, it wasn't too bad because she paid her portion of the rent even though she didn't live there, and I had a lot of fun living alone for a while. But I could've lived in Florida with a few buddies for the summer instead, and for me that would've been a better option overall. Sometimes, you get sucked up in someone else's vortex and just go along."

"Thanks Jake, that makes me feel better," said Savannah. "But you only lost a summer, while I gave up the opportunity to go away for school and that's why I made an even worse decision after my sophomore year. Basically, my relationship with my boyfriend Paul ended about six months into my freshman year. I was doing college things and had college friends, while he was hanging with his big brother and several guys from the dealership. I tried to make it work, but his friends were all assholes with his brother being the biggest one of all. He didn't like my friends either, so one St. Paddy's Day, we broke up in a rather ugly and public way at a bar after far too much green beer. After that I never saw him again because he decided that Colorado wasn't big enough for him anymore and moved to California."

"Sounds like a complete moron. You're better without him."

"I agree completely Jake, and I didn't even date anyone for quite some time afterwards because of it. After all we'd been together since the beginning of our sophomore year, and when I realized that relationship was just a remnant of my high school experience, I was able to finally move on. When I did, I felt free, excited, and willing to try new things. Regretfully one of these new things was going to a lecture on writing plays that was taught by a handsome young playwright in his early forties named Tom Martin. Tom was visiting from New York and had already written several plays that had successful runs. So, when the Theater Department at CU found out that he was in town, they invited him to prepare a lecture, and he accepted. I met him at the meet and greet afterwards, gave him my phone number, and before long, I was spending the night at his house on a regular basis."

Savannah paused for a moment and hoped that Jake wasn't appalled by what she just told him. However, she was also surprised with herself that she was worried about what he was thinking. After all, she figured that she'd probably never see him again after tonight anyway. So, since he continued to be listening intently, she decided to move on.

"He originally said that he was in Colorado because he was working on a new play that was set in Boulder, and wanted to live here a while so he could learn as much as possible about the people and lifestyle. Later, he also admitted to me he was going through a divorce and wanted to be away from his soon-to-be-ex because their relationship had gotten very sour. Initially, I freaked out and didn't want to see him anymore when I learned that he was married, but he eventually wore me down and convinced me that it was over with his spouse, and I continued to see him although we kept our meetings secret at his request. He told me that he was worried about Paparazzi finding him and making his divorce even more difficult by taking pictures of him cavorting with a 20-year-old co-ed. I agreed to keep the secret because the whole thing was very exciting to me, but I was also learning from him as well and found that I rather liked creative writing and loved writing plays. In fact, as it turns out, I guess I'm pretty good at it because every time he got stuck when he was writing, I came up with a way out for him and when he couldn't figure out the ending of the play he was working on when I met him, I wrote that as well. Basically, I deserve partial credit at least, but I've yet to ever see a royalty check, so I don't think that's ever going to be a reality."

"So, what happened with him?"

"At the end of the school year, he said that I was his muse and asked me to put school on hold and move to New York with him so we could collaborate on another play. Looking back, he probably assumed that we would sleep together regularly as well. So, like the dumbass I am, I left college, created a massive rift with my parents, and followed him out to the East Coast where he promptly reconciled with his wife and left me high and dry two weeks after we arrived. I should've gone back home then, but since I was able to move in with a girl that I'd met through Tom, I decided to stay because I still had quite a bit of money in my savings account and wanted to try to make it in the big city. Sadly, I also love to get into bad situations and in classic Savannah Scott fashion I did just that by immediately getting involved with a charming actor/talent agent just a few years older than me named Chad. Chad promised me the world and claimed that he could help me be famous and at first everything went well. Unfortunately, after I moved in with him, he turned into the asshole that he really was and basically used my savings to support his rather hedonistic lifestyle. When the money ran out, he convinced me to get credit cards as his credit rating was crap and then we maxed those quickly also as the limits weren't very high. So, about six weeks ago, I decided that I'd had enough of him and left to live with my friend Kate for a while in Georgetown. Unfortunately, that was only a temporary solution because Kate was in the process of being transferred to Europe with her company, was heading there after Thanksgiving, and the apartment had already been rented to someone else. So, I got a job and had just about saved enough money to get my own place and start over, and then someone broke into Kate's apartment while we were both away at her family's house in Delaware celebrating Thanksgiving. Sadly, all the money I'd saved was in a coffee can in her kitchen cabinet and it was now gone. So, since I had nowhere to live and no money, I called my parents and begged them to let me come home, and this pretty much brings us current."

"Wow," said Jake. "That's quite a tale. So, what will you do now? Go back to college?"

"At this point, that's the plan, but my dad will undoubtedly want me to look at law school again, and I want to do something different," said Savannah. "To be honest, I really want to write. I even have a play that's nearly done, and I think it could be a hit. That is if I ever finished it."

"Savannah, we've something in common," said Jake. "I actually have a Master's degree in screenwriting. I like to write scripts just like you do, but for some reason I just haven't been able to break through with that big project yet. So, I'm now working as an advertising copywriter for a friend of my dad's. Completely unfulfilling, but it does pay the bills."

"I knew I picked the right person to sit by, and while I feel bad that you haven't had any screenwriting success, it does make me feel a bit better that I'm not alone in failure in the field that I desperately want to be my future."

"First off Savannah, you're not alone and never will be. Millions of writers are at work every day on their craft, and most of them will never be able to earn a living from it. Only the fortunate few get that opportunity. Second, and most importantly, the game's not over yet. You must keep trying if you ever want to get to where you want to be. I don't know a lot about theater, but if you were able to come up with an ending for a playwright that has already had significant commercial success, then I think that you certainly have the chops to live your dream. That is, if you don't give up on it and become a copywriter first, like me."

As Jake said these words to her, Savannah's attraction for Jake intensified. Not only was he nice to look at and a good listener, but he also said things that made sense and made her feel better. Most importantly, he was a writer like her and because he was a writer, he understood her only as a fellow writer could. He understood that to bring a character to life, at bit of your soul is invested in the process and that you lived and died with each of them on their paths through the world you create. While they behave like lost children at times, each child is filled with a portion of your lifeforce and each dream that they have is really a secret goal or desire of your own. For Savannah, to connect with a man like Jake would be wonderful even if he was as ugly as a troll. The fact that he was the opposite of ugly and had that beautiful smile, made the rest of her attraction to him even deeper, and the reality was that she'd only known him for minutes. She decided that if she only had hours left with Jake, she wanted to make the most of that time.

"Jake, thanks for being so kind," said Savannah. "It's much appreciated. I won't give up; I'll follow my dream. My father will just have to get used to it."

"That's the spirit!"

"OK Jake, so what's your story? Why aren't you in Cali writing movie scripts? And why in the world are you going to Chicago in late November?"

"Well, since you told me your story, I suppose I have to tell you mine," said Jake. "To be fair, you know."

"Naturally," said Savannah with a smile.

"OK, here goes," he said. "I graduated from the University of Virginia and didn't know what to do with my life, so I went to Europe. Near the end of my time there, I met a girl named Penny and we travelled together for a while in Europe until I had to leave and come back home when my visa expired. Since she had two months left on hers, she stayed, but we decided to meet up when she came home to America. Once I got back stateside, I decided to travel the U.S. for a bit, and Penny eventually met me in New Orleans and then we traveled together again for a while in the states. We really liked each other, had lots of common interests, and had loads of fun together. Oh, and it also didn't hurt that she was filthy rich, either. Anyway, I fucked everything up because instead of going home with her to meet her family on Memorial Day that year, I decided to go to Vegas with my friends instead. She never forgave me and married some other dude within a year or so after dumping me. I was pretty bummed out about it, so I went to California to get my master's degree which I did indeed receive. Unfortunately, after many tries at selling a screenplay, I bagged the whole idea of working as a screenwriter and took a job that paid the bills. Pretty sad story, really but not tragic, at least not in the literal sense."

"Well, I suppose that explains part of the story, but what about Chicago?"

Jake paused for a moment and then continued. "Since Penny, I've not had any significant relationships. I've had a few dates here and there, and as much as I hate to admit it, a few one-night stands were in the mix as well. But nothing else that was even remotely significant. About a month ago, I met a girl named Angela at a bar in Chicago while I was at a conference for copywriters. She and I had a great time and ended up sleeping together but neither of us really thought that we would have any sort of relationship beyond that night. However, after a few long e-mails that were followed by even longer phone calls, she invited me to spend the weekend with her in Chicago before she leaves for a vacation with her family for two weeks. That's why I'm on a bus there now."

Savannah's heart sunk. Until he told her that he was going to see a girl, her night was full of promise. Now, it was decidedly gloomier on the bus for her at that moment and hope of anything with the man sitting next to her suddenly felt slim. However, Savannah's fighting spirit didn't want to give up just yet because she still felt that there was something about him that was special. So, she decided to probe him further to see how he really felt about this Chicago girl. After all, she'd nothing to lose.

"So, if you don't mind me asking, are you serious about this girl?"

"Honestly, I'm not sure Savannah," he said. "I mean, we had a lot of fun when we were together and the physical attraction is definitely there, but I don't have much else to go on except for e-mails and phone conversations. I must admit, I've been alone for a long time, and it'd be nice to have someone special in my life, but I'm still not fully convinced it's her. In fact, the main reason that I'm going is to see if there was enough there to take the next step with her… but I really don't even know what that next step is right now."

"So, I still have a chance then?" Asked Savannah whose mood was lifted significantly by what he just told her. The relationship with this Angela chick was in its infancy and even though Savannah barely knew him, she wanted to know him better. She figured that she might as well ask if he wanted to know her better as well.

"Are you saying you're interested in me?"

"Yes, I guess I am."

He looked at her for a moment as if he was trying to find the best words to say to her. It was clear that she'd caught him completely off guard. He finally spoke.

"Before I answer that question, let's get to know each other better, OK? I'll admit, I do think that you're beautiful. In fact, I'm surprised that you might be interested in me."

"Don't sell yourself short, Jake, maybe I'm the one that's surprised," said Savannah with a slight grin. "Anyway, I think that's a fair way to proceed. So, I'll begin. What's your favorite movie?"

For the next four hours, Savannah talked with Jake about a wide variety of subjects. She found out that his favorite movie was *The Shawshank Redemption* and that his favorite musical genre was alternative. She learned that he loved his parents and had no siblings and she also learned about what types of movie scripts that he wanted to write. Of course, she shared much about herself during this time as well and the more that she revealed to him, the more that he revealed to her. The hours melted away as they spoke and she found herself not wanting this ride to end, and she didn't want him to take that trip to Chicago, either. If only there was some way to change his mind. If only there was a way to spend more time with him alone. Just as she had that last thought, her wish was granted by the universe. Suddenly there was a very loud noise from the rear of the bus where the engine was and after a few choice words that everyone on the bus heard, the driver pulled the bus off the road and parked.

"Sorry folks, the bus is busted," said the driver as he stood up and faced the passengers. I'm gonna try to see if they can get another bus to us tonight but I'm not optimistic about it. I'm really sorry about this but we may be stuck here. The good news is that if that's the case, there's a Holiday Inn at the next exit which is only about a quarter mile away. Hold tight and I'll call the station in Columbus. We're only about 35 miles away."

The bus driver then took out his cell phone and made the call. After a conversation that was very short, he made the announcement that no other busses were available and that they'd have to walk to the hotel as there wouldn't be one until tomorrow. He also asked everyone to give him their cell phone number if possible so he could contact them with updates about the situation.

"Well, that sucks for me because I'm low on cash and still must make it all the way to Boulder. I may have to sleep in the lobby tonight," said Savannah.

"Savannah, you won't have to do that, not if you don't want to at least," said Jake somewhat sheepishly.

"Why do you say that?"

"Because if you don't feel too uncomfortable about it, I'd like you to stay with me. I plan on getting a room."

Savannah just stared at him, smiling as usual as he said this. He was going to meet a girl that could be someone special to him and yet, he wanted to spend more time with her, and more importantly, this time would be with her alone. Maybe things were looking up for her, but either way, she still had nothing to lose and really didn't want to sleep in the hotel lobby.

"Jake, I think that'd be awesome. Let's go so we can get there before everyone else," said Savannah. And with that they grabbed their stuff and headed out into the night, giving the driver Jake's cell number on the way out. For once in her life, she thought that fate may finally be on her side. Only time would tell.

CHAPTER 20: A HOLIDAY AT THE INN

Tuesday, November 28th, 2000

Savannah stepped off the bus with Jake and was very glad he was there. It didn't look far to the next exit, but it was cold and dark, and cars were whooshing by them as they walked along the shoulder with everyone else from the bus. Jake seemed to sense her uneasiness and grabbed her hand. His touch was reassuring and wonderful, and just what she needed at that moment. She was just so grateful not to be alone.

"Jake, thanks for helping me, I really appreciate it," said Savannah.

"It's my pleasure, Savannah," was his reply and then they walked on, hand in hand as if they were a real couple. She felt herself falling for him. Not too much yet, but still the feeling was certainly there. If she wasn't careful, she might find herself in love, and the problem was that falling in love right now was the last thing she needed.

They finally reached the hotel and got in line for a room. Unfortunately, there were four people in front of them and because the parking lot looked mostly full when they walked up, Savannah suddenly became worried that there may not be any rooms available by the time they reached the desk.

"Savannah," began Jake, "I'll make sure to get a room with two beds. I'm not the kind of guy that takes advantage of women. I promise, you'll be completely safe with me."

"And you also may have a girlfriend... so thanks for saying that. But you did grab my hand..."

"Ok, let me be completely honest. I'm very attracted to you Savannah and I'm telling you this because I just want you to know where my head is at. At the same time, I don't want you to think that I'm an opportunist, either. I've had a moment or two with Angela, and I don't know if there will be more with her or not. I mean, she and I seem to get along very well but we've only spent one night together so calling her my girlfriend is a bit premature. I do know that I want to get to know *you* better."

"So, you're saying that there's a chance," said a smiling Savannah who was now feeling very excited, "Jake, I really appreciate your honesty, and for some reason, I feel like I can trust you. I'm obviously attracted to you, too. But even as I say this, I'm worried that I may get hurt if I let my guard down completely. After all, you're on the way to see someone that's important enough to endure a bus ride across the Midwest in late November to see."

"So, should we just be friends then? If that's what you want, then I'll respect it," said Jake who now wore an obvious look of disappointment on his face.

"It doesn't seem like that's what you want, Jake. And yet, you're still on your way to see a girl."

"Savannah, for me it's like this. Since I'm not in a committed relationship, I'd rather not put you in the 'friend zone' just yet. Can we just see where things go and let fate be our compass?"

This was quite the interesting turn of events, and Savannah's spirits were lifted yet again with his question. Her rational self, the same side of her personality that was responsible for her being on a bus back home, urged her to say "thanks but no thanks" to Jake and insist on a platonic arrangement. But even as she had that thought, her mouth had other ideas and was already uttering a response.

"OK, Jake, that's fair. I guess we have until the bus reaches Indy for us to decide what to do. Right now, I just hope we get a room. I guess we're up next."

Jake and Savannah reached the check-in desk and when they got there, there was one room left. As fate would have it, it only had one king-sized bed and even though Jake hesitated when the clerk told him that, Savannah immediately said that one bed would be fine. There was no way in hell that she was going to sleep in the lobby; it just wasn't going to happen. In the end they not only got the room, but it was also the biggest room in the entire hotel and Jake happily forked over way more money than she would've been able to afford at that moment to pay for it. Once again, she felt thankful to have crossed his path.

The couple reached the room to find some rather spacious accommodations. Apparently, they were put in a room that also doubled as a hospitality suite. These types of rooms are common in places where conferences are held like big cities or resort towns. She was surprised to find a room like this in a run-of-the-mill Holiday Inn thirty-something miles from Columbus, Ohio. Nevertheless, she was glad to be there and was thrilled to be there with Jake. She couldn't wait to spend more time with him and couldn't believe that she'd be able to spend this time with him alone.

"Savannah, this room is huge and there's a couch that almost certainly has a pull-out bed. You can have the bed if you want, I'll take the bed in the couch," said Jake.

"Once again, I appreciate your chivalrous gesture, Jake, but why don't we leave the sleeping arrangement decisions until later. I'm hungry and thought that maybe we could get some food. I don't have much money but would be happy to take you out tonight if we could go somewhere... reasonable."

"I'm hungry, too, Savannah, and I appreciate your offer, but this one's on me. As you know, I sort of like you and want to do nice things for you as well. More importantly, I think you need to be reminded that there are still good men in the world because it sounds like you've met some shitty representatives of the Y chromosome. Let's just go to the restaurant downstairs, OK? We can have a few drinks and talk about whatever you want to."

"Sounds good, Jake," said Savannah and then they went downstairs for dinner.

With all the additional people from the stranded bus, the relatively small restaurant was packed, but there were two chairs open at the bar, so they sat there instead of a table.

"So, how about a drink? I know I can use one," said Jake.

"Why not?" Replied Savannah. "But at least let me get this round, OK?'

"Sounds good, thanks Savannah. And thanks for your company, also. Meeting you has made what has begun as a sort of disastrous trip much, much better. I'll take a house Cab."

"Yes, red wine would be great. Bartender, two house Cabs please."

The bartender nodded to her and then brought over two menus, set them down, and then poured their glasses of wine. He was a short, portly balding gent with blue eyes, a gray mustache, and wearing a white shirt with a bowtie. He looked to be of Mediterranean decent and was probably in his late fifties or early sixties. He also had a friendly face, a jovial nature, and a big smile appeared on his rather large face as he delivered the wine and took their orders. Since the menu was rather limited, they both ordered French Dip sandwiches with fries and quite unexpectedly, the food was pretty darned tasty. This was good because Savannah was very hungry as she had only eaten the biscuits that Alpharetta had given her for the ride, and she'd finished the last one before she met Jake, which was hours ago. So, she was happy that her stomach was now full, and three glasses of wine did a pretty good job of relaxing her further. She was beginning to enjoy herself and after more great conversation with Jake about sports, she liked him more all the time. In fact, the only negative from the whole interaction with him was the fact that he didn't like the Denver Broncos or their legendary QB, John Elway. Although Elway retired in 1998, he was still her favorite player, and retired or not, this would never change in her mind. While she could live with his Bronco hatred tonight, if this relationship was to progress any further than tomorrow, she'd have to make him see the error of his ways.

Jake did let her pay for the first round, but he got everything else. They walked out of the restaurant and up to the room and this time, she grabbed his hand, and he gave her a squeeze when she did this. She smiled at him as they got on the elevator and on the way up, she almost decided to give him a kiss. Apparently, the wine had done its job with her inhibitions.

"I'm going to get a shower, I feel scuzzy," said Jake as they walked into the room. "Please make yourself comfy and you can jump in after me if you like."

"Sounds good, Jake."

Jake went in and showered, and Savannah turned on the TV. She was watching a documentary about ancient Egypt when Jake came out dressed in sweatpants and a t-shirt and then let her know that the shower was now all hers. She then went in and took a quick shower herself, dried off, and put on her pajamas before she left the bathroom. She went in and Jake was sitting on the bed watching the same documentary.

"It's fascinating, isn't it?" Asked Savannah.

"It is," said Jake. "I still think the pyramids were built by aliens though."

"I'm sure the girl that sat next to me before you got on the bus would agree with you," laughed Savannah.

"So, I don't want to keep you awake, I'm sure you're tired. "I'll just get my pull-out couch set up and we can crash."

"Jake..."

"Yes?"

"Can we talk for a little while longer?" She said to him as she was sitting down in front of him cross-legged on the bed while she finished drying her hair with the towel. "I have a good buzz from that wine and don't want to go to sleep just yet."

"OK Savannah, what's on your mind?" Asked Jake with a look on his face that betrayed his curiosity."

"Jake, have you ever seen a movie called *Before Sunrise*?" She paused for his answer, and when he shook his head, she moved on. "Well, you should as it's awesome and about two young people who meet on a train while traveling in Europe.

They decide to spend a romantic day and night together in Vienna and fall in love before they must part in the morning and go their separate ways."

"So, I guess you think that's like us then, right? What happens? Do they eventually end up together?"

"I'm not going to spoil it for you, you need to watch it yourself. But there are a few scenes that come to mind that may be fun to re-live tonight. You up for it?"

"Why not?" Said Jake. "Let's do it!"

"Just a second then," said Savannah and then she got up, grabbed the CD player from her backpack, sat down again even closer to him, and put one earbud in Jake's ear and one in hers as well. "OK, in one scene, the main characters, Jesse and Celine, go to a record store, and listen to an album together in a listening room. It's a cool scene because in that moment you know that there's a strong attraction between them as the music plays. However, both Jesse and Celine are afraid to reveal that attraction to each other as they are both worried about how the other one would react. So, let's do that scene now and see if we can channel their emotions. I've already picked a song."

She pressed play and the classic Goo Goo Dolls tune *Iris* filled one of each of their ears with the haunting melody that song is known for. As they listened to it, she closed her eyes, Jake grabbed her hand, and they interlocked fingers as their feelings were becoming interlocked as well. She felt the same sort of sexual tension in that moment with Jake as she did for the two lovers in the movie, even though she and Jake had already revealed their attraction to each other. She wondered if he felt it also. All at once the music was over but in truth, she barely remembered hearing it and only recalled the feeling of her fingers interlocked with his.

"I love that song," said Jake. "And I loved the moment

with you also. I can't imagine it being better in the movie. What's the next scene."

"In the next scene, they go on the famous Ferris wheel in Vienna and get in one of the little enclosed cars together. They are the only people in that car, and they are so close to each other that you find yourself just wanting them to kiss each other. Celine finally breaks the silence by asking Jesse if he wants to kiss her... just like I'm asking you right now."

"I'm not sure what Jesse's answer was in the movie," said Jake. But mine is... yes."

"Then what are you waiting for?"

All at once, he took her into his arms and kissed her, and what a lovely kiss it was. Images of fireworks and other metaphorical clichés filled her mind as serotonin rushed through her body on a jet-powered motorcycle, while its buddy adrenaline sat in the sidecar, screaming all the way. It was a very nice kiss that was not awkward or weird in any way. Rather, it was tender and warm, and as comforting as a cup of chicken soup, but also exciting as if someone had added several drops of tabasco with a shot of tequila on the side to wash it all down. When it was over, they just looked at each other smiling. Jake spoke first.

"So, Savannah, how'd we do? From where I'm sitting, I bet we're at least on par with the movie, right?"

"No, we're better, definitely better, I think," said Savannah who suddenly felt very warm. "I think maybe we should go to bed now before this gets too out of hand, but I'd really like to sleep with you in this bed as long as that's all we do tonight, OK?"

"Sounds good, I think that's probably best for tonight anyway," said Jake who may have sounded slightly disappointed.

"So, are you saying that there may be another night?"

"Anything's possible," he said smiling at her for the umpteenth time.

Savannah moved from her cross-legged position, they both got under the covers, and she snuggled against his side with her head on his chest as he laid on his back. He put his arm around her, and she could hear his heartbeat.

"Jake, can I ask you one more question about Angela?" Asked Savannah.

"Sure, what's up."

"Well, since we've been together, you haven't called her, and she hasn't called you, I think that's a bit odd."

"She did try to call once," said Jake evenly, "but I put my phone on vibrate before I got on the bus and when I felt it vibrate two hours or so later, you and I were in a very deep discussion about acting methods, so I decided not to answer. She left a message that she was going out drinking with a friend who was celebrating her 30th birthday. I called her back while you were in the shower and left a message that the bus broke down and that I didn't know when I'd be in tomorrow. I was going to tell you sooner but got a bit side-tracked. I'm sorry about that oversight, and I turned off the phone in case she tries to call later. After all, if I only have tonight and part of tomorrow to get to know you Savannah, I'd rather focus on you full-time and not anyone else."

Savannah was flattered, but this whole situation was almost too unreal to believe. She laid there, snuggled up to a man that she could easily fall in love with and yet, she couldn't let herself go any further with him until she knew if he wanted to pursue a relationship with her. On one hand, he said the nicest things to her, and these things really made her feel special. He also made comments that made her believe that he wanted to be with her, and this made her feel hopeful as well. On the other hand, he was still communicating with Angela, and he still wasn't sure if he would keep his commitment to spend the weekend with her as he originally planned. Sleep would help, and for now at least she decided that she'd just be happy with the moment.

"Jake, thanks for letting me know. I really hope that we have more time together after tomorrow, but for now, let's just get some sleep. Oh, and I'm very glad to be here with you now, whatever happens. Goodnight, Jake." With that, she gave him another long kiss and then put her head back on his chest.

"Goodnight Savannah, I'm happy to be with you as well." said Jake, and then almost immediately, she was asleep.

The next morning, Jake got a call at 8:30 from the bus driver informing them that a temporary bus would be leaving for Columbus at 10:30 and that they'd have to transfer to another bus once they got there. They left as planned and got to the bus station about 45 minutes later. Fate seemed to still be working in her favor because they were then delayed for almost five hours as the replacement bus took far longer than expected to arrive. During that time, they talked more and had a late lunch that she insisted on paying for. They kissed a few more times, and there seemed to be sparks each time. In fact, the only awkward moments of the entire day came when he spoke to Angela. He did this two times with a very quick update call in the morning and then another quick call when the bus finally left Columbus. In fact, all was better than good for her until his phone rang about 30 minutes outside of Indianapolis. As she feared it was Angela, and although she couldn't hear what she was saying to him, whatever it was seemed to trouble him greatly. He hung up and delivered the news, and as expected, it was shitty for her indeed.

"Savannah, that was Angela," said Jake in an unreadable tone. "Apparently, she and a friend are driving to Indy to pick me up, so I don't have to take the next bus to Chicago. I guess they are two hours away right now. To be honest, I want to stay on this bus with you, but at the same time, I feel bad for Angela and now that she's coming to pick me up, I feel even worse. Savannah, I don't know what to do."

"Jake, I can't answer that for you," said Savannah trying to mask how heartbroken she really was at that moment. "I'd love for you to stay with me because I think we click in a way that's unique and wonderful. But Jake, I'm not going to beg you to stay, either. You must do what you think is best and while I'll be bummed if you don't pick me, I'll understand if you don't. Unfortunately, this is a path that you must walk alone."

"Savannah, you're right about everything," said Jake now looking very sad himself. "We do click, and we are also very attracted to each other as well. I can honestly say that in this very short period of time together, I've never had so many good discussions with anyone." He then paused, which of course spelled doom to Savannah immediately. The bad news was coming, and she knew it. "Savannah, I must make good on my promise to visit Angela. I just feel that to break that commitment with her wouldn't be fair as she hasn't done anything wrong, and she was looking so forward to it when we talked last week. Also, I don't like breaking promises. I hope you understand, and I also know that I may be making a huge mistake."

"Jake, I understand, but I don't have to like it," she was fighting hard to stave off the tears as she spoke. "I'll never forget you Jake, and I hope that everything works out with Angela. I'm sure she's a great girl."

There was nothing more to say, and for the rest of the trip, they rode together in silence. She was able to regain her composure and fight off most of the tears and finally quell them completely, but that didn't mean that she was any less disappointed with this outcome. She had met the most wonderful man she could imagine, and yet, they had only spent a little over a day together which was sad because she wanted so much more.

The bus finally rolled into the station at 8:20 by her grandfather's pocket watch and stopped when it reached its correct location in the station. Jake stood up, gathered his things, and seemed to be searching for the right words to say. He finally spoke.

"Savannah, I loved our time together. Finish that play and take the world by storm. Maybe we will meet again."

With that he took his leave and walked off the bus. There was no sun shining, and a cold wind blew in as the bus door was opened. Savannah thought that maybe she'd escaped it this time but right on schedule, her black cloud showed up yet again. Somewhere in the distance she could almost hear Chad's sarcastic laughter and at that moment she wondered if her destiny was to never be happy again.

CHAPTER 21: SAVANNAH SCOTT

Wednesday, November 29th, 2000

Jake's eyes were struggling to recover from the blinding light that had just assaulted them, and he once again felt the disorientation that he knew he felt before, but really didn't remember very well at all. As his head stopped swimming, his memory of Calliope and their deal returned to him like the only old friend that he had now and then he realized that he had once again traveled to a past reality. He still could remember his children and even their names, and that was one memory that he knew was also part of the deal, because it was the one thing that he was sure he remembered from his other trip or trips back as well. However, for some reason he wasn't sure whether he had gone back once or twice and which timeframe (or timeframes) of his life he had visited. He just knew that he had done it before.

His vision was clear now and he found himself sitting on a toilet in a rather filthy grafitti-covered stall somewhere. Most of the graffiti was run-of-the-mill and included several phone numbers that promised a good time, ten or more juvenile depictions of male genitals, a few religious symbols, and a paragraph written about the impending world's end. Just as Jake grabbed some toilet paper to finish his business, he realized that he was in the bathroom at the Greyhound station in Indianapolis and that he had just left the girl that he really wanted to be with to honor a commitment with another girl who was enroute to pick him up at that moment. But he also knew that this was his second chance, and this was his opportunity to make the other choice at a critical juncture. Most importantly, this was also the opportunity to see Savannah again, although he still had the weird sensation that he just left her which in this reality was indeed the case.

He pulled up his pants, buttoned them, and suddenly realized that if he wanted to see her and take the alternate path this time that he better get a move on. She was on the bus and as soon as they completed a mandatory driver change, it would be on its way and his chance would expire. So, he flushed the toilet, washed his hands, and then walked towards the part of the station where her bus was parked. He wasn't going to miss the opportunity to be with her this time, and as expected his feelings for her were as sharp and intense as they were when he was here before. Although he didn't realize it back then, Jake was falling in love with her, and now the feeling felt more pristine than any emotion that he had experienced in the past. He couldn't remember for sure, but he thought that it was perhaps more pristine than anything he had experienced in the future as well.

Jake found the area of the station where the bus was parked, and to his relief, it was still there. His heart leapt into his throat in anticipation of seeing Savannah again and looking into her big, beautiful brown eyes once more. In fact, he found himself wanting to see her more than anything else in the world. And then, as if the universe had decided to fuck with him a little first, his trusty Nokia phone rang and it was Angela, the redhead that he was on his way to see in the first place. He figured that he must've chosen her the first time, and that this was the critical juncture. While he had no idea if the relationship with Angela was successful the first time around, he had a nagging feeling that it wasn't. Either way, this was the juncture, and he was going to leave here tonight with Savannah. Unfortunately, that couldn't happen until he took what was certain to be a very awkward phone call.

"Hello, Angela?" Asked Jake as he answered the phone. "Are you almost to the bus station?"

"JAKE!" screamed Angela over the phone. "Yes, we're only about an hour away! I can't wait to see you, you big, beautiful hunk of man. But... I am a little drunky, and maybe a little horny too."

Before he spoke, he had to gather his composure a bit. It was obvious that she was a bit hammered and figured that when he did this the first time around, they probably had a wild time together this evening, unless of course, she got sick and passed out first. Unfortunately, her state of sobriety (or lack thereof) tonight made what he had to do next more difficult. He was sure that her drunk mind would have a hard time processing what he had to tell her, so he decided to make what he told her tonight as simple as possible.

"Wow, I'm shocked that you came down here, Angela and I'm also very flattered and appreciate the effort. But it also sounds like you may be more than a little drunky. How long have you been drinking, Angela?"

"Not too long, silly willy, I only started when we left

Chicago, and I'm perfectly happy and ready to party with you... you know what? You know what?" There was a pause, and Jake was just about to answer her when she continued. "You're gonna get laid tonight, Jakey! And you know how I know that? 'Cause I'm gonna be the one that lays you." She began to laugh like drunks all laugh when they are good and plastered, and Jake realized that she was even drunker than he initially thought.

"Angela, could you put Cindy on the phone?" Asked Jake.

"No silly, she's driving. I can't drive because I'm drunky... and horny... don't tell anyone but... what was I saying?"

"Angela, I need to talk to Cindy." Jake heard some rustling around and then another voice came to him over the phone.

"Hello Jake, sorry about Angela, she's had more to drink than I realized. You may need to hold her head tonight later, I'm afraid," said Cindy.

"Cindy, I won't be able to do that," began Jake. This was the tough part, but he had to get through it. "I'm sorry that you've driven all the way down here with Angela, but I'm afraid it's a wasted trip because I won't be here when you arrive. The thing is that I'm not waiting at the station for you guys tonight, I'm leaving on a bus with another girl that I met on the trip here. I'm sorry."

There was silence for a few seconds and Jake could hear Angela in the background asking Cindy what he was saying. Jake knew that this wouldn't go well, and when Cindy finally spoke, it was worse than he thought it would be. After all, she had driven quite a way for her friend, and she didn't want to see her get hurt.

"Jake, I don't know what's gotten into you, but you can't do that to her," said Cindy almost pleading with him. "She's done nothing but talk about you since you two met. Please don't break your promise to her."

"Cindy, I hear you and feel like a total asshole for doing this, but sadly, I must. I don't expect you to understand, but I may've met my soulmate and there's nothing you can do to change my mind. Once again, I'm very sorry and will call Angela to tell her in person when she's sober tomorrow."

"Jake, don't bother," said Cindy with contempt dripping off every word after another uncomfortable pause. "Both she and I thought you were different, but unfortunately, you're just another asshole looking for another woman to add to his conquest log. Fuck you and don't call back. Don't worry, I'll pick up the pieces tomorrow. Someone must." With that she hung up.

That was a very tough interaction, and Jake felt bad that he had to do it. However, this was an alternate reality for him now and unless he decided to stay here after the three days are over, Angela wouldn't remember it and they will have the same relationship that they had the first time around, whatever that was. He couldn't shake the feeling that he may have married her and that she may indeed be the mother of his children. One thing that made him feel that way was the fact that as soon as Cindy hung up, he could no longer remember their names, even though he knew he could before the phone call. Nevertheless, he was so excited to see Savannah, that he put that thought out of his mind, turned off his phone and put it away, and walked to the bus where he knew she'd be waiting.

Jake got on the bus, and as he did, their eyes met. Her brown eyes were red and puffy but no less beautiful than he remembered, and her face was even more gorgeous. In fact, he couldn't believe that he left her there in the first place. Her expression showed confusion, but she did manage a hint of a smile as he walked up to her with his suitcase in tow.

"Hello Savannah," he said still taking in her beauty. "I just wanted to let you know that I changed my mind. If you'll still have me, I'd love to ride to Boulder with you."

"Jake, I've been sitting here since you left hoping that you'd come back, and was just about to give up hope," she said. "I would absolutely love it if you would go to Boulder with me."

"I was hoping you'd say that. Unfortunately, I need a ticket, do I have time to get one? There's no driver on the bus right now so maybe I can run in quickly and ask."

Just as Jake said this, a Greyhound employee stepped on the bus and announced that the new driver that was assigned to the bus was ill, so the trip would be delayed for 30 minutes or so until a replacement driver could get there. This was great news for him, and he couldn't believe his good fortune. Fate seemed to be on his side today and that was nice for a change.

"OK, that's good news," said Jake. "I'll go in and get a ticket. You sit tight."

"No way," said Savannah who now wore a very bright smile that made her look angelic to him, "I'm not taking the chance that you won't make it back. I thought I'd lost you forever. I'll go with you."

"Sounds great, let's go. Fortunately, the bus is a lot emptier than it was on the way from Columbus so we should find seats together easily when we return."

Jake and Savannah stepped off the bus and walked into the station. There was a fairly long line at the ticket counter, so Jake was glad she came with him. As they got into line and put down their bags, Savannah suddenly threw her arms around Jake's neck and kissed him. When she did this, he knew that he'd made the right choice this time and as they were kissing, *How Deep is Your Love* began to play over the somewhat crappy stereo system in the station. He knew that his three days had begun.

"Wow Savannah, that was wonderful, I'm speechless," said Jake.

"I've been wanting to kiss you again since we kissed in Columbus earlier today, and I held back because I wanted to distance myself from you. But things have changed. I do have one question, however. Jake, why'd you change your mind? "

"Savannah, I changed my mind because I couldn't get you out of my head. I've never met someone that I feel so compatible with. I'm at a crossroads and felt that my connection to you is stronger than it is to Angela, and I want to explore it to the fullest."

"Have you called her to let her know?"

"I didn't have to, she called me. I tried to speak to her on the phone but couldn't get anywhere with her because she was blotto drunk. So, I spoke to Cindy, the girl that was driving her to Indy, instead. Naturally Cindy was pretty pissed when I told her that I met someone else and that I wouldn't be at the station."

"You told her that you met someone?"

"I did, and I also said that I'd call Angela back tomorrow to tell her myself when she's sober. Cindy told me not to bother, but I'm sure Angela will probably call me tomorrow anyway. Unfortunately for her, I've changed my mind about talking to her and have already turned off my phone. I've made my decision Savannah. I want to spend time with you."

"Jake, I'm all-in with you too," said Savannah right before she kissed him again. Jake found that he enjoyed kissing her quite a bit. "Please try not to hurt me."

"Believe me Savannah, hurting you is one of the worst things that I can imagine," said Jake truthfully. Unfortunately, if he didn't stay after the three days were up, that's exactly what he'd probably do to her, and the thought of that made him quite sad. He would just have to enjoy the next three days with her to the fullest.

They stood in line together holding hands and talking the entire time about Colorado and everything that she loved to do there. She also talked about her parents, and Jake told her about his dad and mom as well. He suddenly felt very happy that he was here. They finally got to the ticket counter and when they got there, they were informed that the bus had just departed and that there wasn't another one until tomorrow morning. He had no other choice, so Jake went ahead and bought tickets for the morning bus, however the simple fact was that they were now stuck in Indianapolis for the evening.

"I'm so sorry Savannah; I wasn't paying attention to the time. Looks like you're stuck here with me," said Jake.

"And what's wrong with that?" Said Savannah with a smile and a peck on his cheek.

"Alright, I've got an idea," said Jake. "Remember, I used to live here. I've a buddy named Lee that I think still lives here with his wife Kathy. I'm sure that he'd be fine if we stayed with him tonight. Let me give him a call."

Jake turned on his phone, and to his surprise, there were no messages from Angela. Then again, she was currently hammered. He then dialed Lee's number (which was saved on his old phone) and Lee was not only there, but he was also insistent that he and Savannah stay with him and his wife tonight. Even better, when Jake asked for his address, Lee even said he would come and pick them up. Jake thanked him, hung up the phone, and turned it off again.

"OK, Savannah, I've got a place for us to stay tonight. My old buddy Lee lives in Broad Ripple which is the cool little part of Indy where I used to live. Anyway, he's on his way to pick us up right now and will be here in about thirty minutes. I think you'll like Lee and his wife Kathy a lot. I don't get to see them much lately, but they remain dear friends."

"Jake, that sounds perfect," said Savannah. "So, how are you going to introduce me?"

Jake was always the cautious, rational type and normally would have hesitated to answer that question by deflecting to some other topic. He always liked to carefully weigh each option and make his decisions based upon lots of reflection and thought. Except this time. This time, he was sure immediately.

"I'm going to say you're my girlfriend," said Jake looking into her deep brown eyes once again. "Is that OK with you?"

"So, are you just telling him that, or do you actually want me as your girlfriend?"

"Savannah, I know we just met, but I want to live for the now and not for what may happen in the future. I want no more regrets. So, I could either wait to ask you to be my girlfriend for two weeks or two months or even two years, but I know that my feelings about you won't change. In my mind, you're my girlfriend already and I really hope that you feel the same... but I think you do."

"I was hoping that you'd say that. Sure, I'll be your girlfriend," said Savannah with a somewhat unreadable look on her face that turned into a bright smile. "After all we've known each other a day and a handful of hours. It's time for a commitment."

Jake kissed her again and then they talked more, this time about Europe because Savannah had never been before but always wanted to go. They held hands the entire time as they waited on a bench outside the bus station. To all that saw them, they were indeed a couple. This happened way faster than it did for Jake with anyone else he'd ever gone out with, but Jake really had no choice. He now had less than three days, and the clock was ticking. He needed to confirm that they were on the same page.

After about 20 more minutes, Lee and Kathy showed up in their Honda Passport SUV, and Jake and Savannah piled in. Following some quick introductions, they all decided to head to Bazbeaux's for some pizza. They walked in and sat down, and when the waiter came over, Lee ordered a pitcher of beer. They decided to get a large pie with sausage, black olives, bell peppers, and mushrooms and when the waiter came over to deliver the beer, they placed the order. Everyone was hungry, but the beer went down as easy as the conversation flowed between the couples, so it seemed like the pizza arrived in no time at all and when it did, they all feasted.

Jake did indeed tell them that Savannah was his girlfriend but neither Lee nor Kathy could believe it when he said that they had just met and were both visibly shocked when he told them. Kathy even made the comment that she thought that they had been together for months at least, and maybe even more than a year. She also said that Jake and Savannah looked "right" together, and this comment yielded an impromptu kiss from his new girlfriend which made him happy once again.

The best news of the evening came when Lee asked why they took a bus instead of some other means of travel. Jake told him it was because he had car problems and when he told him this, Lee announced that he would be happy to give him his Great Aunt Sally's 1972 Oldsmobile Delta 88 that had been taking up space in his garage if Jake wanted it. Apparently, the car had been there since she passed away last year, and although it ran well and had a current tag, it was just too much of a land yacht for either of them to drive around regularly, and it got poor mileage as well. Lee said that he was planning on selling it anyway but felt like giving it to a friend in need was what Aunt Sally would've wanted. Of course, Jake graciously accepted, although he also told him that he'd pay him back someday.

The foursome had two more pitchers before leaving and heading back to Lee's house which was just north of 49th Street on Rosslyn Avenue. When they got to the house, both Lee and Kathy worked to get Jake and Savannah settled into the guest room. Once they had finished replacing the bed clothes and left them towels to use when they showered, they bid their goodnights and went into their bedroom as both had to work tomorrow.

Jake and Savannah took their turns in the bathroom before meeting back in the bedroom for bed. Savannah went first this time, so when Jake came back into the bedroom after his shower, he found her sitting on the bed winding what appeared to be a lovely gold pocket watch.

"That watch is beautiful, Savannah," said Jake as he sat down next to her.

"It was my grandfather's. It's probably my most important possession in the world. Would you like to see it?"

Jake nodded and she handed the watch to him. It looked to be quite old, at least 19th Century he thought, and was very heavy. Its face had Roman numerals, and an ornate moon phase dial at the bottom. It was something that anyone would want to own, and given that it was her grandfather's, he figured that it was priceless to her.

"Thanks for showing it to me," said Jake handing her back the watch. "I can understand why you love it so much."

She then kissed him, and then the kiss began to evolve into something more. Jake was suddenly very turned on and Savannah seemed to be following suit. They fell back onto the bed together and as soon as that happened, Savannah put on the brakes by disengaging with him and sitting up.

"Jake, I'm sorry but I just can't... at least not yet. I

know that you care for me already, and I love that you said that you've committed to me as your girlfriend, but my last relationship was so incredibly awful, that I've not sought out any other relationships since. I'm sorry but I still just need to get my head straight and that might take a minute as I process my feelings for you. Please don't think that this means that I don't want to be with you, because I do. But there's a lot that I haven't told you about Chad, and right now, he's the ghost in the back of my conscience," said Savannah who looked at him and grabbed his hand. "I hope you can be patient with me."

Jake sat up and gave her a huge hug that lasted for several minutes. He then pulled back to look her in the eyes. "Take your time Savannah. I certainly don't want to make you feel uncomfortable in any way. If you want to talk about Chad let me know, but I will wait for you on this."

"Thanks Jake, that means a lot. I really am falling for you, you know."

With that, they shared one more long, passionate kiss and then turned off the lights and laid down in the ever-popular spoons arrangement, with her on the inside. As he held her, he felt even closer to her than he did a few moments before and was thinking that he really might be her soulmate as he told Angela's friend Cindy earlier. He also began to think that at the end of three days that he just might stay this time. After all, he barely remembered that he had ever had children at all at this point, and didn't even know anymore whether they were boys, girls, or both. This trip back was different, and he knew it. As he fell asleep, he was certain that Calliope probably knew that as well.

CHAPTER 22: ST. LOUIS SERENADE

Thursday, November 30, 2000

Jake awakened before Savannah and when he did, he laid there for a moment and watched her sleep. She had beautiful skin with faint freckles across her small, but perfectly proportioned nose. He also looked at her hair and noticed that it had blonde roots which indicated to him that she was a natural blonde. That wasn't really that important to him except for the fact that it was unusual for true blondes to have brown eyes like Savannah did. As he had that thought, she opened those eyes, looked at him, and smiled.

"You're staring at me," she said while still smiling. "That's a bit creepy, don't you think?"

"No, not at all. Not when I'm staring at something as

beautiful as your face."

Savannah kissed him, and although they both had morning breath that would stop her grandfather's pocket watch, the kiss was just as warm and wonderful as all the other kisses with her. He loved just being with her but also knew that he had a ticking clock that was counting down the minutes until he had to make the decision to stay or leave. He thought that unless something weird happened to mess up the relationship over the next two days, it would be hard not to stay.

"You're so sweet," said Savannah after the kiss was over. "You even kissed me with morning breath. So, when are we heading west?"

"I dunno, let's get some coffee and figure that out," said Jake. "Maybe Lee left some for us in the kitchen."

Jake and Savannah both got out of bed and walked into the kitchen of Lee and Kathy's small one-story house. It was only 8:30, so the coffee was still warm, and Lee and Kathy had left them half a pot so they both poured a big cup in the oversized mugs they found in the kitchen. Next to the coffee machine was a note from Lee. Jake read it out loud and it said:

Jake,

I hope that you and Savannah slept well. We left some coffee for you guys but if you sleep too long, you'll have to turn on the burner again to warm it up. Also, there's English muffins in the breadbox and butter, eggs, and bacon in the fridge if you're hungry, just help yourself.

I don't know what your plans are or when you have to be in Boulder, but my office is closed tomorrow so Kathy is taking the day off tomorrow as well, and she and I are both leaving work for the rest of the day today after lunch. We've both been working long hours, so it's much needed time off.

We'd love to meet you two for lunch before you hit the road.

If that sounds good, meet us at the Corner Wine Bar in Broad Ripple at noon. If not, travel safe and take care of Aunt Sally's beast. The keys are hanging on the wall by the back door and the signed title is in the glovebox, just pull the garage door up as it isn't locked. Last, please remember to lock the back door when you leave and pull down the garage door after you back the car out.

Laters!

Lee

"What do you think we should do?" Asked Jake.

"I'm fine with meeting them for lunch, I really like those two," replied Savannah. "But right now, let's make some bacon and eggs, I'm starving!"

Savannah and Jake worked together to make a breakfast of eggs (cooked over medium), bacon, and English muffins. When Jake was done cooking the bacon and she was done making the eggs, they plated everything, and he put on an additional pot of coffee while Savannah buttered the muffins. They then sat down to eat, and everything was delicious, but the conversation was even better. As usual, the words never ran dry with her, and as he got to know her better, he fell harder for her all the time.

The couple cleaned the kitchen after they finished eating, and then they both showered individually before making the bed and packing up their things. They then walked out the back door and into the garage as instructed and jumped into the massive white vehicle that did appear to be in excellent shape for its age. Its bright white exterior was nicely counterpointed by a light blue cloth interior and accented by an equally white vinyl top because they were all the rage in the early Seventies. It was snazzy to be sure. The most unusual thing about the car was that it only had two doors, and these doors may have been the longest doors that Jake had ever seen on any car. When he fired it up, it came to life immediately and seemed to be running very smoothly. As Jake went to put the land yacht into gear, he noticed that it only had just over 63,000 miles. It was a very nice gift from Lee, and he knew that the car would have no trouble getting them to Boulder, so Jake was very happy about the entire situation. Then, after he pulled the car out, he exited, shut the garage door, and got back in the vehicle. Savannah then snuggled up next to him on the massive bench seat and then he backed out of the driveway and hit the road. He knew this drive would be a fun one for them and he couldn't wait to spend more time with Savannah. In fact, all things Savannah currently dominated his mental space, and he wondered if he'd be able to survive without her if he decided not to stay in this reality.

The couple took a drive around Broad Ripple and he showed her some of the highlights, with one being the duplex where he used to live. Jake parked at about 11:30 and both had a drink before Lee and Kathy arrived. When the couple showed up ten minutes late, Jake ordered another round and included drinks for the new arrivals when he did. Both he and Savannah were happy to see them, and just like last night, they all got along famously.

The lunch lasted far longer than Jake expected, and Lee, Kathy, and Savannah all had several drinks over the two plus hours that they were there, while Jake stopped at two. In the end, Lee tried to talk them into staying one more evening because there was another good local band playing at the Vogue. Jake really wanted to stay, but also really wanted to get Savannah back home before his three days in this reality were up, and the only way to ensure that would happen was to hit the road today. So, he politely turned Lee down but promised to make another visit to Indy with Savannah soon.

The check came, Jake picked it up for the table and then after hugs and phone number exchanges that were forgotten last night, Jake and Savannah climbed in the Oldsmobile and headed to I465 first and then to I70 after which would take them the rest of the way to Colorado. Jake was able to find an AM sports radio station on the stock AM/FM stereo that had no tape or CD player and Savannah, who had downed several drinks with Lee and Kathy, fell asleep with her head on his shoulder. For about a hundred miles, this was how they rode, and Jake was simply happy to have her near him. Unfortunately, he also had to take a piss, so after he held it as long as he could, he finally had to stop at a Stuckey's in rural Illinois. They both used the restroom and when they returned to the car, Savannah had the look of a person with something on her mind. As he got back on the road, Jake decided to find out what that was.

"You OK?" Asked Jake. "It looks like something's bothering you."

"Is it that obvious?"

"It is indeed. What's up?"

"Jake, began Savannah tentatively, "since we met, you've been wonderful. No, more than wonderful, you've been amazing. In fact, you're the first man in a long time that I feel that I can trust, and I'd really like a relationship with you. Unfortunately, if it's going to go any further, you need to know that I'm damaged from an emotional perspective, and it may take me some time to be completely open with you... Does that make sense?"

"It does Savannah, and all I can say to you is that you can tell me as much or as little as you want about your past," said Jake sincerely. "You should also know that I will never judge you for whatever you have to say and will keep it in confidence. I'm glad that you think you can trust me, so let me put you at ease by letting you know that whatever you tell me won't change how I feel about you."

Savannah kissed him on the cheek and then said,

"Thanks Jake, I knew I could count on you... and now I must tell you something that is difficult for me to even think about. I need to get this off my chest, OK?"

"Go for it, Savannah, I'm listening," said Jake who felt a very concerned look bond itself to his face.

"OK, so I told you that my ex-boyfriend was an asshole, but I never revealed why. The truth is that I was abused, and this abuse has unfortunately changed my perspective on relationships. Jake, Chad made me feel like a queen at first, and then after he lifted me to a pedestal where I felt very good about myself, he tore me down. Sadly, this didn't happen quickly, as it began with comments that he was 'disappointed' with me about something small or that I'd 'let him down.' Being the perfectionist that I am, this made me feel bad and created an internal desire to do better... to please him. Once this groundwork was laid, he then took it even further by inserting negative comments when I ate something that was fattening or making fun of me in front of his friends if I didn't know some arcane showbiz history that he considered to be common knowledge. When we hit that stage, my self-esteem hit the floor, and I woke up every day with the goal of pleasing him as my first priority. At that point he had me and when he did, I wanted to do anything to make him happy which included giving him all my money to make things better. For a few seconds it was... until it got much worse."

Savannah paused at this point, and it was clear to Jake that what she would tell him next was even more difficult for her than what she'd already revealed. He could see the pain in her eyes and feel the hurt and injury that she had suffered from this relationship in her words. He grabbed her hand and gave it a squeeze. He needed to let her proceed at her own pace.

"Sorry," said Savannah after a few minutes. Her nose was stuffy, her eyes were moist now, and she pulled a tissue from her pocket, wiping her nose before continuing. "At that point, all I wanted to do was please him so I agreed to let him weigh me on a regular basis, and when he did, he would also make me undress and then circle areas on my body where I needed to tone up with a permanent marker. He said that it was for my own good because no one wanted a 'fat chick' in their productions, but I think it was just another way for him to control me. I remember wanting to do anything to live up to his standards... even in the bedroom. Jake, when we first met, lovemaking with him was passionate, romantic, and even very affectionate on occasion but at this stage in his grooming of me, it transformed into something far different. I was no longer someone to make love to, and instead I became an object to be dominated and even humiliated from time to time. He would talk dirty to me and call me all sorts of horrible things. He would make me wear things that I felt uncomfortable wearing, and make me do things that I didn't want to do... and I... and I... just let it happen..."

Savannah then broke down fully and tears were now literally gushing from her eyes as she cried. Jake pulled her close to him on the bench seat, and she laid her head on his shoulder and let go. He figured that she needed to do this for a long time, and he was glad to be there for her now. He just felt so bad for her, and wanted to make her feel better if he could. However, he also needed to remember that she needed to be heard because although most men would love to be the eternal handymen and "fix" a woman's problems, what most women really need is that shoulder to cry on and a sympathetic ear from someone who cares. Suddenly Jake wondered if that was a thought from this reality or possibly something that he'd learned later in life. Either way, he let her cry, hoping that she had told the worst of the tale. The bad news was that she wasn't there yet, and the worst was still yet to come. After several minutes she composed herself and the story continued.

"Jake, thanks so much for listening. It really means a lot. Unfortunately, things got even worse from there. Once my money ran out, and my credit cards were maxed, the financial situation turned dire because he wasn't bringing in any steady income at all and when he did make money, he drank it away almost immediately. I took a job at a coffee shop to help make ends meet, but we just went backwards, and his drinking got worse every day. As time progressed his anger began to spike more frequently when he was good and drunk, and then he began to take it out on me by treating me as his personal punching bag. Sometimes he would hit me so hard I saw stars. But the worst thing was that after he hit me, he would launch into a chorus of 'I'm sorrys' which was quickly followed by retrieving something cold out of the freezer for my injury. He'd then promise to change and tell me he loved me before launching into the forced version of makeup sex that would usually take place afterwards. Jake, when I finally got the courage to leave, he wouldn't let me go and even tracked me down in Georgetown almost two months later because I made a mistake and left my address book in his apartment. When he found me, he tried to take the only thing that I have left, which is my grandfather's watch, but I had some pepper spray, so I escaped and was ultimately able to board the bus and find you. And I'm so glad I did."

"Savannah, I know that took a lot of courage to tell and I'm very happy you trusted me enough to share it," said Jake. "Please don't think that anything that you've told me makes me think any less of you, and most importantly, never think less of yourself. You've had a rough time to be sure, but you're not 'damaged goods.' Don't focus on the girl that was abused… she's gone now and has been replaced by a strong, confident human that has picked herself up off the ground and decided to keep going. And keeping going is most of the battle."

Savannah snuggled close to him and gave him a kiss on his cheek. When he looked at her face, she managed a weak smile. "Wow Jake, you really know how to make a girl fall in love with you, don't you?"

"I'm not sure about that," said Jake with a small chuckle. "But I do know how to remind a friend that she's awesome and that she needs to remember that. The falling in love part is just an extra benefit."

"So, are you saying you are falling in love?"

"I'm saying anything's possible."

Savannah smiled and then fell asleep against his shoulder again and slept until they were crossing the Mississippi River when she awoke and looked around groggily. It was just after six, so there was quite a bit of rush hour traffic and because of this, Jake exited downtown. As they were driving past the convention center, Jake noticed that there was a Holiday Inn attached to the center itself.

"Perfect, another Holiday Inn for the night," said Jake. "Does that work for you?"

"Yeah, that works fine, but I feel bad, I don't have much money to contribute, and this hotel is probably expensive since it's downtown," replied Savannah. "Are you sure you don't want to get a quick bite to eat and then head out of the city to a cheaper place to stay?"

"Savannah, I saved up some cash for the weekend with Angela so now I'm spending it on us instead and for me, it's been worth every penny so far. You don't need to contribute anything, I want to do this, OK?"

"OK, Jake. But please let me get a round of drinks again, that will at least make me feel like I'm helping."

"You got it Savannah."

Savannah and Jake checked into the Holiday Inn, and after settling in a bit and freshening up, they headed out to dinner. They went to an Italian place that the concierge recommended which was about fifteen minutes away and once there, the couple were able to get seated quickly which was a surprise to both as it was Friday night. The food was excellent, and Jake slipped the accordion player $20 to come to the table and serenade them. When the musician came over and began to play, Savannah snuggled close to Jake in the booth the entire time and held his hand as the accordion wheezed out the tune to *O Sole Mio* while the accordion player sang along with a beautiful tenor voice. It was a very romantic evening and after sharing a bottle of Chianti, they were soon ready to go back to the hotel.

When they arrived back at the room, they both changed and jumped into bed, with Jake turning on the TV as he laid down. After a few minutes of old TV shows, Savannah began kissing his neck, which let to kissing his lips, which led to both sets of hands exploring many private areas of each other's body. Suddenly and unexpectedly (even to himself), Jake put on the brakes.

"Savannah, I love where this is going, but we've had quite a bit of wine, and you also had a martini to start the meal. I don't want our first truly intimate experience to be dulled by alcohol. Plus, you unloaded a lot to me today and I think that you may want to let those emotions clear your mind before we take the next step. Don't you?"

"So, you're turning me down?"

"Not at all sweety, just deferring until we're sober and you've at a few moments to process all the feelings that came out today. I'd love nothing more than to keep going right now, but I don't want you to regret anything, and since I'm sort of a romantic, I want it to be special as well. Do you understand where I'm coming from?"

"OK, Jake, you win. I should have known you'd say something wonderful like that. Sheesh, you are just too good to be true."

"My pleasure," said Jake as he turned off the TV and at that moment, she proceeded to snuggle in next to him and laid her head on his chest as he relaxed on his back. The fact was that she was right, because he *was* too good to be true unless he decided to stay. However, the good news for her was that at present, staying seemed to him to be more akin to a probability than a possibility. He still remembered that he had children and could still feel their connection to his soul. But as he fell for Savannah more, this connection became harder to touch and as he fell asleep, he wondered if seeing his kids again was already beyond his reach and that he had already subconsciously made his decision.

CHAPTER 23: NIGHTS ON BROADWAY

Friday, December 1st, 2000

Savannah awakened first and this time, she was the one watching while Jake was the one sleeping. If she didn't know him at all, she would have still found him to be extraordinarily attractive, and the main reason for this was that he was just her type; tall, dark-haired, well-tanned, and very handsome. But the compassion he demonstrated to her when she told him her tale of woe proved him to be the total package and beyond his looks, she was already in love with his mind, his personality, and how he smiled at her. Of course, that last thing was what lit the bonfire for her in the first place. She thought to herself that it was all like some silly episode of *The Love Boat* in the late Seventies because she had fallen in love with Jake in less than three days. How crazy.

Savannah kissed Jake on the forehead, which prompted him to roll over away from her, so she got out of bed and went to the bathroom. After she finished using the toilet, she noticed that it was only 8:31 on the digital hotel clock, so she decided to let Jake sleep for a bit longer while she made coffee. She had originally wanted to be home by now, but all the travel delays enabled their relationship to sprout and grow, and her love for Jake had now taken root in her soul. She couldn't have asked for a better boyfriend and since he had already said he considered himself to be that to her, she figured that they were indeed a real couple at this point and that made her happy. She smiled and sipped her coffee as she thought of a future with him.

Savannah was also shocked at how her outlook on life had changed. No longer was she wallowing in the ocean of self-pity that she had created during the time with Chad, and all the bad things that had happened since she left him seemed to be in the rear-view mirror as well. She now felt optimistic, lighter, and less burdened in mind, body, and spirit. She couldn't believe her good fortune in finding him and couldn't wait to introduce him to her parents when they got to Boulder. She knew that they might balk at the notion of her jumping into another relationship at this point, especially considering the circumstances surrounding her return home. However, she also had confidence that Jake would be able to convince them that his head was in the right place when it came to her future and that he was supportive of her decision to return to school. So, with luck that should eventually lead to their acceptance, although it may take time for that acceptance to occur.

The other thing on her mind was that he seemed to have changed somehow from the time that she met him on the bus in Pennsylvania to now. She couldn't put her finger on the exact nature of the change and really couldn't cite a specific example that supported why she felt this way. However, since he returned to her after initially getting off the bus to meet Angela, he seemed wiser and more thoughtful than he did at first; like a much older man who had learned how to properly treat a woman. While she didn't mind the change at all, she still found it curious and thought that she may even ask him how a few minutes in a bus stop made him more mature. It was a conundrum for her, but in the end, she figured that perhaps he was always the way he was now and that maybe he was just nervous with her at first which made him seem more immature. Whatever the case, she liked the change, so she resolved to just go with it, and not question the reason why it happened.

She showered, put on her makeup, got dressed in jeans, a white turtleneck, and a long blue cardigan, and then dried her hair before Jake finally rolled out of bed. She kissed him on the cheek as he walked past her on the way to the bathroom, and he gave her a huge hug when she did. He then rushed into the bathroom with some urgency as his bladder was probably quite full as it had not been emptied for several hours. Savannah then packed things up while Jake took a shower, shaved, and made himself even more attractive to her. After he finished, he came out of the bathroom dressed in jeans and a UVA hoodie, packed his stuff, and they checked out at about 9:45. Savannah had never been to St. Louis before and asked Jake if he wanted to see a few sights before they continued to Boulder. He enthusiastically agreed.

The first St. Louis landmark that they visited was the iconic Jefferson National Expansion Memorial or as it is better known, the Gateway Arch. Jake and Savannah parked the car that she had recently named "Beastmobile" nearby, and walked to the huge metal structure so they could take an elevator to the top. There was a decent-sized line of people waiting their turns to go up, so the couple had to wait about thirty minutes before their turn came and they were able to take their seats in the weird little elevator pods that looked to be out of a sci fi movie from the Fifties. When they got to the top, the view out of the windows was breathtaking, and because it was a bit windy that day, they could feel the structure sway back and forth as it was designed to do. It was a weird sensation so because of that and because there wasn't much to do up there, after only ten minutes they were ready to go back down. At the bottom, Jake bought Savannah a miniature model of the arch as a souvenir, and she thought that to be very sweet of him. Of course, she rewarded him with a kiss and then they walked back to Beastmobile and went to the next landmark.

The next destination was the Anheuser-Busch brewery which looked more like the chocolate factory that was owned by Willy Wonka than a place that made beer. As it turned out, the tour was unexpectedly awesome. The scale of the operation was impressive and while this was the company's flagship location (as it was the original) it was only one of thirteen breweries that Anheuser-Busch had in the United States. The tour took about an hour and at the end, each had to have a beer. Budweiser was never Savannah's favorite libation, and she rarely drank it. However, for some reason it tasted good after the tour and was very refreshing. So, although she wouldn't order it anywhere else, she decided that when at the brewery in St. Louis, it was acceptable.

It was noon and they were now both very hungry, so they drove to the part of the city that was called Laclede's Landing and was located close to the Mississippi River. They parked and went to an awesome little hamburger joint called Sundecker's and both had cheeseburgers and fries. The food seemed otherworldly tasty, but that could have been because she was hungry. Either way, when they hit I-70 again after they were finished, both felt very satisfied.

After about two hours of driving, they stopped at a place called Kingdom City to get gas and decided to take a small detour to Fulton, so they could visit the Winston Churchill Memorial and Library at Westminster College. After World War

II, Churchill was invited to speak at the college and on March 5, 1946, he gave his famous *Sinews of Peace* address which is where he coined the term "Iron Curtain" to refer to the Soviet Union. It was a fascinating little detour for them, but they only stayed for a half an hour or so, because Jake wanted to make it past Kansas City before they found a place to stay for the night. Plus, the weather was cold and a bit blustery, so a seat in a nice, warm car was welcome and they were on their way west again before 4:00.

The sun fell below the horizon as they drove, and they made it through Kansas City at just before seven, as they missed most of the heavy Friday night traffic. They drove for another hour and decided to stop for the night in Topeka which was the last decent-sized city in Kansas that was on I-70. To keep with the theme of the adventure so far, they got a room at a Holiday Inn that had a restaurant, a small nightclub, and a "Holidome" that housed an indoor pool. They checked in at about 7:45 and went to their room. As they opened the door, Savannah had an idea.

"Jake, it looks like there will be live music tonight," she said while throwing her arms around his neck and looking into his eyes which were the same color as her own. "Since we grabbed food at that barbecue place in Kansas City, I'm not really hungry, and I really want to dance. Will you take me dancing?"

"Absolutely Savannah, let's go!" Said Jake enthusiastically. "I just need to change my shirt and wash my face, and I'll be ready."

"Awesome," she replied and then gave him a kiss. "You change out here, and I'll go into the bathroom because I have a surprise for you. In fact, you can even go and get a table because it may take me more than a few minutes to get ready, OK?"

"No problem, I'll just change and go to the bar to get a drink," said Jake, "and look forward to my surprise."

She went into the bathroom with her backpack and took a quick shower to freshen up. After the shower, she began to get dressed. She really wanted to look her best tonight, and the first step to doing that was by wearing the right underwear. After rustling through the backpack, she found a very lacy strapless bra that had an equally lacy matching thong. She donned the two tiny garments and then admired her own reflection for a minute in the full-length mirror that was on the back of the bathroom door. She decided that she looked pretty damn hot... she just hoped Jake would feel the same. She then pulled out the little black party dress that she last wore when she went out with Kate, but it was a bit wrinkled, and needed a little quick ironing, so she decided to wait until he left to get that done. Fortunately, in the next minute she heard him say goodbye and walk out the door. As soon as he was gone, she left the small bathroom, located the iron and ironing board, and then did her makeup and hair while the iron was warming up. She then ironed the dress, put in on, and finished off the look with the one pair of heels that she still owned, because she really liked them and had spent a good chunk of change on them when she bought them last year. Savannah was now ready to dance and because she had taken ballet lessons for several years and had been in show choir in high school, she also considered herself to be pretty good at it. She couldn't wait to show Jake her outfit and then wow him on the dance floor.

She left the room at just about 8:30, and walked down to the small nightclub that was attached to the hotel and went in. When she did, she felt that she had gone back in time to the Seventies as the nightclub was just one large room that was quite dark with all sorts of funky light fixtures scattered here and there and giving off dim light. In fact, they looked like they could have come from a thrift store's basement. The bar itself was quite small, there were several tables scattered throughout the room as well. But the star of the entire show as far as the nightclub was concerned was the lighted dance floor complete with a disco ball and stage lights overhead. The whole setup could have been purchased from a Studio 54 liquidation auction and was a pretty rare sight in what was now the newly minted 21st Century. Nevertheless, Savannah loved the whole thing, knew that dancing would definitely happen tonight, and that she'd drag Jake out to the dance floor if she had to.

She walked over to one of the small tables in front of the bar where Jake sat and put her small clutch purse down in front of the chair opposite of him. When he saw her, his jaw dropped, and this made her smile. The look in his eyes told her everything she needed to know.

"Wow Savannah, I'm speechless," said Jake.

"Oh, why is that?" She asked in the flirtiest way possible while also being certain that she knew the answer.

"Because although I've thought you were beautiful since the first moment I saw you, you've certainly taken it up a notch tonight. Savannah, you're stunning."

"Thank you, good sir, you're not too bad yourself."

Just as she was getting ready to sit down, a song began to play. It was *Nights on Broadway* by the Bee Gees, and just as the first notes were played on the surprisingly decent sound system, Jake's face lit up. Suddenly, Savannah realized that she wouldn't have to be the one to ask for a dance.

"Oh, hell yeah!" Exclaimed Jake as he jumped up and grabbed her hand. "Let's go dance! I'm going to show you how it's done!"

Jake literally pulled her up to the lighted dance floor which was currently empty. He then let go of her hand and when the lyrics to the tune began, he began lip-syncing the words to her in a musical theater style as he intermixed a few well executed spins along the way. It was remarkable how he moved, and he flowed his movements into every word in the first verse like he had practiced it a thousand times. It was clear that he also had dancing experience, and that made it even more exciting for her as she had never dated anyone that could dance, and dancing was something that she truly loved to do.

Savannah didn't have time to get too mesmerized because just as the first verse ended and the familiar refrain began, he grabbed her hand and the two then began to dance together and when that happened, her excitement increased even more. He led beautifully, and they spun into and away from each other like they were reading one another's minds; one minute she would spin out and the next second they were close enough to share a heartbeat. It was effortless and amazing, and suddenly she noticed that they had an audience and several people in the night club were now watching. *"OK, Savannah, let's give them a show,"* she thought, and just as the refrain ended and the musical intro to the second verse began, she pushed away from him and let go of his hand. It was now her turn to pantomime the lyrics because she knew the song too, and maybe better than Jake did.

With perhaps the best and most theatrical effort that Savannah had made in a while, she brought the second verse to life in the same way Jake had done with the first one, and she did it with perhaps an extra dose of attitude and flair. There was now a group of people on the dancefloor watching and cheering, and Jake played off her with gestures of his own as if they were doing a dress rehearsal and not improvising the entire thing. She exaggerated every move, made them all dramatic as possible and when the second refrain began, he immediately grabbed her and spun her around like he did before only adding even more flourish and even released her hands a few times for some more spins of his own. It was wonderful, and people were cheering like crazy until the much slower bridge began, and when that happened Jake pulled her in close. They looked into each other's eyes for an endless moment and then, very softly and only for her ears, Jake spoke.

"Savannah, I love you. I wanted to make sure you knew that."

"Jake, the feeling is completely mutual. I love you too and after only three days, I know that I'll never love anyone else."

Jake began to move in for the kiss, but the bridge was now over and as the song moved again to the much faster refrain, she smiled at him playfully, pushed away from him hard and then spun once, twice, and a third time before she put out her hand for him to catch it... and he did, right on cue. After this move, there was wild applause from the audience that now included almost everyone in the nightclub. Jake and Savannah kept dancing as if everything in their lives had led them to the amazing moment and when the song ended, he embraced Savannah in a beautiful kiss while she was vaguely aware of cheers from all around. It was magical.

The couple kept dancing through the next song because it was a slow one and then left the dancefloor for a drink before dancing again for a few more songs afterwards. They still moved as if they had been dancing together for their entire lives but didn't put on anywhere near the same show as they did with *Nights on Broadway*. They were there for about an hour and a half when they ordered what would be their final drink at the small table. Savannah moved in for another kiss which was just as wonderful as all the others they had together.

"Jake," said Savannah after the kiss "That was wonderful, but I don't want to dance anymore... I want to go back to the room. You OK with that?"

"Absolutely babe, let's go," said Jake grabbing her hand, and with that they walked out followed by cheers and applause from the remaining crowd still in the bar.

Savannah pulled him back to the room, and they were both giggling like giddy kids the entire way. They got to the room, opened the door, and she dropped her clutch purse on the floor as he took her into his arms. They began to kiss again, but after three nights of sleeping together and only kissing, Savannah was now ready for more and decided to unbutton his shirt. As she started this, he unzipped her dress, and she let it fall off her shoulders to the floor as she finished pulling off his shirt. She then went to his belt as he undid her bra that snapped in the back, and it fell off her and hit the floor at the same time that his pants did. Her libido was on overdrive now and they needed to get to the bed soon because the anticipation was killing her. It was time for her to fully trust a man again… it was time to finally make love to someone for real and to share herself completely with another soul… it was time to finish falling in love.

She had her back to the bed as they got there, and right before she sat down, she felt his fingers pull the thong off her hips where it too, dropped to the floor like all the rest of her clothing. She sat on the bed now completely naked, pulled his boxer shorts, and then scootched back a bit as he laid on top of her while they continued to kiss each other. Then all at once it happened and they were connected physically as well as emotionally where she peaked almost immediately as he moved with her in the blissful rhythm of human passion. She hit the summit several times during what seemed like an eternity before he finally let go and joined her there so they could plant their metaphorical flags together and after that they both collapsed breathing hard.

"Jake, the deal is sealed, you're mine forever now," said Savannah as she put her head on his chest.

"I know, and I wouldn't want it any other way," said Jake with what could have been a hint of sadness in his voice. However, that could've just been her imagination. After all, what could go wrong now?

CHAPTER 24: A CRUEL CHOICE

Saturday, December 2nd, 2000

Jake awakened early, just after 6:00. The adrenaline surge that he experienced after a night of lovemaking with Savannah had finally dissipated at about 2:00, so he was only working on about four hours of sleep. However, it was worth every second and he was still amazed by the gravity that the experience held for him even now, hours later.

The first time they made love, it took him to a place that he had never been with anyone, and for some reason, he felt that included future sexual experiences as well. The second time came after some wonderful conversation with her that always flowed freely whenever they talked and was as good as the first time and much longer as well. The third time came after they had both fallen asleep for an hour or so and seemed to slake the carnal thirsts of both and when it ended, he was absolutely buzzing with excitement for quite some time even though Savannah seemed able to fall asleep easily. It was a marathon for sure, but he truly cherished every moment, every touch, and every kiss each time they made love.

What made this experience unique for him was that for almost the entire time they kissed each other, and the actual sex itself only served to augment these kisses, and caresses, and looks that they shared with each other as they were holding hands while taking each other to the pinnacle of sensory pleasure. While his experience with other women wasn't vast, he certainly was far from inexperienced and while some of his partners were into kissing to light the fire for the main event, and others dispensed with kissing altogether, he had never been with someone who never stopped kissing him while they were making love. While most guys his age would probably give him crap if he told them about the tenderness of the experience, he didn't care because ultimately, even the biggest toughest dude wants to feel truly loved, and love he felt in bunches.

Jake got out of bed and made some coffee while he picked up various pieces of clothing that were strewn from the door to the bed in the same way the debris field from the wreck of the *Titanic* had stretched across the floor of the Atlantic. Except this time, the shipwreck had not yet happened but unfortunately was on the horizon with the cruel decision that he would have to make in just a few hours now and as he took a sip of coffee, he remembered Calliope's deal and cringed. He knew that *Nights on Broadway* was the warning song so he took note of what time it was when the song began and at 8:42 this evening, he knew that he would have to decide to stay... or go.

On one hand, he was now more in love with Savannah than he had ever been with any other woman. Due to the short amount of time that they had spent with each other, most people would probably scoff at him if he admitted that publicly and most of his friends would chalk it up to infatuation. However, Jake was convinced that his feelings for Savannah were indeed true love, and that she was his soulmate if such a thing really existed. It was brutal to think of leaving her behind and knowing how sad it would make her, even if her sorrow was constrained to an alternate reality that he could never visit again.

On the other hand, he also knew that he had children in the future, and while his memory of them was so distant and fuzzy that he may not be able to recognize them if they were standing in front of him, he still felt their love as two points of bright energy that served as beacons of their love from across time and in another reality. Strangely, he now felt a third point of energy from that dimension that beckoned him to return as well. This last point wasn't as bright, and he had no idea who it belonged to, but the love he felt from it was there, although distant. So, if he decided to stay, he had at least three people who truly loved him in the future that he would be leaving behind forever, never to exist again in his life, and he didn't know if he could let that happen, either.

He looked at Savannah sleeping beautifully on the bed and finished his coffee with a head full of thoughts. He knew that whatever he chose to do, that the choice would likely come at the last possible minute, and that irrespective of his decision, at least one person would likely suffer greatly from the choice he didn't make. He just didn't know how he couldn't choose either one, and yet the choice that he did make would probably yield happiness for him in the future and this happiness would dull the sting over time. The whole thing was a leviathan, and he wished that he could do both, even if that was completely impossible.

At 7:30, he woke Savannah and told her that he wanted to get on the road early so they could get to Boulder while it was still light out. It was over eight hours to her hometown and potty breaks and coffee stops were likely to add more than an hour to the journey. Bad weather could add even more time and this last factor loomed as a likely issue because flurries of snow began to fall lightly outside the window of the hotel room as Savannah jumped in the shower. He would have jumped in with her, but time was now of the essence, and he didn't want to leave her stranded alone in the middle of rural Colorado at night if he did decide to depart this world and go back to his original reality. If that was the eventuality, he wanted her to be close to home when it happened.

Jake took a shower after Savannah was finished with hers and then they both packed everything up and loaded up the car that she had now dubbed Beastmobile. He thought that to be a great name although the driving experience was more akin to driving a couch down the road than riding a beast. Either way, he was still very thankful to Lee for giving it to them. They would've never been able to do the things that they'd done together if they'd stayed on the bus.

They both grabbed a coffee and pastry to go as they left the hotel, and then they hit I-70 and the long stretch of open road that would be largely unpopulated until they reached Colorado. Savannah sat close to him as usual and for the first hour they said little and enjoyed listening to a sports talk show that they found on AM radio. Jake now had either twelve hours left with her or the rest of his life, and the weight of the decision that he had to make later became heavier with each mile they drove. Savannah must have felt his uneasiness and decided to break the silence.

"Jake, are you OK? You aren't having any regrets about last night, are you?"

"Sorry Savannah, I'm OK, just maybe a little apprehensive about meeting your parents," said Jake. "As for last night, it was truly the most wonderful experience of my life. I love you completely, babe. Please understand that."

"And I love you too, you looked concerned, so I just wanted to make sure," said Savannah. "It was a wonderful experience last night beginning with the *Nights on Broadway*. By the way, where did you learn to dance like that? I've never danced with a partner who had even half your skills."

"I did competitive dance until I was fourteen or so. Then sports took over. You're not too shabby yourself, I think we made a great team and that we flowed together perfectly."

"Yes, and perfectly in bed, also. You know, I've never had a partner with your skill there, either," said Savannah as she kissed his cheek. "Jake, I'm nervous about my parents also... it's been a long time, and I was an immature little shit when I left. It's going to be weird with them for a while I think, but I know they love me, and I love them so I have no doubt that it will be OK eventually."

"I agree Savannah, don't worry. I'm sure that they're very happy that you're moving back even if they don't tell you that," said Jake. "All parents are happy when their kids return to the nest, we just want them to stay forever even though that's not practical in today's world."

"We? Is there some son or daughter that you haven't told me about?"

"No, I was just referring to 'we' in the general sense, as humans," said Jake recovering quickly. In truth, he had no children in that reality, so he wasn't technically lying. However, the fact was that he *did* have children somewhere... just not anywhere currently accessible to him.

"OK, that's a relief," said Savannah. "I mean, it wouldn't change anything about how I feel about you, but at this point in our lives I guess I'm relieved that you don't have kids, just the same. Anyway, let's change the subject. Jake, tell me one place in the world that you've always wanted to visit."

"Wow, that's a hard one because there are many. I've always wanted to visit the pyramids in Egypt and the Great Wall of China, but I would also like to bask in the sun in Bali. However, at the end of the day, I'd have to say if there was one place that it would be New Zealand. Pictures that I've seen of that place are gorgeous, I'd really like to go there. How about you?"

"Well, let me say that all the places that you mentioned are on my list too, so we should have some great adventures someday! Anyway, I have much more modest travel goals myself. If I could go anywhere, I think that it would be Key West. I want to visit Hemingway's house and hit all the bars on the famous Duval Street. I want to watch the sunset in Mallory Square and take in all the history there. Most of all, I'd love to be there with you."

"Savannah, Key West is an attainable goal. Let's try to do that once we get our lives together and you finish school," said Jake.

"How about this. Let's set a date now that's far enough in the future that we'll both be at a point in our careers that will allow us to do this trip right. If it happens earlier, then that's great too but no matter what, we'll stick to this date, OK?"

"Sounds good to me! What day do you have in mind?"

"I've always loved Christmas, so let's have Christmas there," said Savannah. "And as far as a year is concerned, let's choose… 2016, OK?"

"Perfect," Jake began, "December 25th, 2016, it is! We'll meet no matter what!"

"And Jake," she said in a more serious tone, "No matter what means exactly that, as long as we are both still single. I hope that we're a couple forever, but I know that sometimes relationships take weird turns so the possibility exists that we may not be a couple then. So, if we do break up for some reason and we are not married to other people in 2016, we still need to keep this date, OK?"

"Agreed," said Jake knowing that the possibility of them not being together as soon as what was tomorrow for her was a real one and that he may be gone very soon. He still didn't know what he would do at that point, but if he could connect with her later in life in his main reality, then maybe that was the solution to his problem. However, he then remembered that in his main reality he left the bus and met Angela and this conversation and everything that had occurred since he came back to Savannah never happened. So, in the end, setting a future meeting may not be remembered by her so this didn't make his decision any easier.

"Yay, I'm so excited! I can't wait to go there with you Jake, whether it be on that day or earlier. Thanks in advance for sharing my dream." She kissed him on the cheek after she said this and then grabbed his hand tightly. Her touch always felt good to him, no matter what it was or when it happened.

For several hours after they drove on and talked about the things that they normally did, and she kept trying to get him to admit that John Elway was the greatest quarterback ever which was impossible for him because the answer was obviously Joe Montana. She also told him about her play, *A Dollar at the* Ritz, and he was very impressed. In fact, he thought that she had a winner and encouraged her to finish it soon. They stopped a few times for normal restroom breaks and snacks, and the going was slow due to the weather that included light snow and freezing rain. By the time that they hit the Colorado line it was about 3:30 which meant that they were two hours behind schedule. If they could have kept a 70 mile-an-hour pace for the rest of the way and made no more stops, they might have made it to Boulder by 7:00 or so, but the weather was not getting any better and they would have to stop again at least once for food as they were both starving. Ultimately, Jake decided to stop somewhere close to Denver because after thinking about whether to leave this reality for hours now, he had finally made the choice to return to his children.

This choice was the toughest one that he'd ever made but in the end the love of his kids and the need to be there for them was more important than his happiness alone. It's not that he wouldn't be happy living in their reality because he knew that his love for them was as foundational for him as his love was for Savannah. But the tiebreaker for him was that as a parent, he needed to prioritize what was in their best interest over what was in his or Savannah's best interest and because of that he figured that he would probably never see or speak with her again. For him, not seeing or talking to her again was one of the saddest things that he could ever imagine and not touching her again was even worse. Even more problematic for him was that he had no idea how to tell her why he had to leave, and the story was so unbelievable that he didn't know if she would believe him when he told it. So, the only thing to do was to wait until as close to 8:42 as possible to tell her and when the Bee Gees song came on when he said it would, perhaps she would believe him then. However, in the end whether or not she believed him really didn't matter as she would know the truth the moment that he faded away.

The couple finally reached the outskirts of Denver at 8:07 and pulled off the highway at the exit to the little town of Bennett. They had eaten some sandwiches from a convenience store several hours ago so now they were both completely famished. They stopped at the first little diner that they found, went in, and sat at a booth. A waitress who appeared to be on the far side of fifty and wearing the standard pink diner waitress uniform came and took their orders and brought them both a cup of coffee while they waited for their food. He knew that his face showed that he was obviously troubled by something, so Savannah asked again if he was OK, and he lied again for the moment saying that the anxiety of meeting her parents was intensifying as they got closer. Their food came at 8:35, but before he even took a bite, he looked her in the eyes and decided that the time had come to let her know what he had to do.

"Savannah, you were right. There is something else bothering me, and I must tell you about it. You probably won't believe me when I tell you, but please hear me out OK?"

"Sure Jake," said Savannah with a very concerned look on her face while she grabbed his hand. "I love you; you can tell me anything."

"OK, here goes, please let me finish before you say anything," said Jake. He had to move fast because his time was running out. "Savannah, I'm not the person you met when I got on the bus in Pennsylvania. I mean, I am that person, just not the same version that you initially met. Instead, I'm a version of myself from a later time in my own life. You see, I was given a supernatural gift, and that gift was that I could travel back in time to what is known as a critical juncture in my life. When I got to that juncture, I could make the choice that I regretted not making the first time around and follow another path. With you, this critical juncture was getting back on the bus in Indianapolis to tell you I'd changed my mind, and believe me after this last three days, I know now that it was the best decision that I've ever made. The sad part is that I only have three days to decide whether I want to stay in this new reality or return to my old one, and the thing is that I sort of lied to you earlier because back in my main reality in the future, I have two children. Although I can barely remember them in here because they haven't technically been born yet, I know that they love me." Jake paused and was having trouble continuing. The tears were beginning to flow from his eyes and down his cheeks and his voice was shaky. He couldn't help it. "I guess that what I'm saying is that if I stay here with you,

I'll lose them forever and they may not even exist at all. As much as it hurts, I need to let you go and return to them and it's the saddest thing that I've ever done."

"Wow, Jake I certainly wasn't expecting... this," said Savannah looking both sad and confused at the same time. "I'm honestly not sure what to say... the only thing is that I know that I love you more than anything or anyone and if you're breaking things off because you don't want to deal with my parents, I'll run away with you right now and explain myself to them later. After all, I've done it before. Jake, please tell me the real reason why you're doing this."

Jake looked at his watch and he had just over one minute left. "Savannah, in one minute a song from the Bee Gees will play and we will both hear it. Bee Gees songs are the signal that I chose to let me know when my three days had begun, when I have one day left, and when my time is at an end. *Nights on Broadway* was the one-day warning, and it was played at 8:42 last night. In a few seconds another Bee Gees song will be played and when it's over, I'll be gone."

Before she could respond it happened, and the familiar first strains of the classic and often covered song *Words* were heard on the Diner's sound system. When that occurred, Savannah gasped, and by the look on her face, her sorrow and confusion had turned to shock. Jake knew that she now believed him.

"I know that song, it's one of my favorites but I used to listen to the version by Boyzone. I forgot that the Bee Gees did it first," said Savannah who was suddenly beginning to panic. "Oh no, this is really happening, isn't it? Jake, please don't go, I love you, I NEED you!!! Please!!!"

"Savannah, there's no time for that now," said Jake choking down his emotions as he let go of her hand and stood up. "I left all my remaining cash in the glovebox, and the title is in there as well, all you need to do is fill out your name and the car is yours. Please go back home and get your life in order but most importantly, finish your play. The story that you told me about on the road is great, you just need to finish, and you can do it; I believe in you. Babe, please stand up and give me one more kiss, the song will be over quickly."

Savannah reached into her backpack and grabbed something and then stood up and hugged him for an endless moment and then kissed him with all her might. She then thrust something into his hand. It was her grandfather's pocket watch.

"Jake, take this back with you. If you can do that, you can find me again and return it to me when you do. I'll wait for you my love, and you must remember that you made a promise that you'll meet me in Key West in 2016. Don't let me down, Jake... I love you and I'll love you forever."

"And I will always love you too, please never doubt that, Savannah," said Jake and those would turn out to be the last words that he would say to her because at that moment the song ended and he was again blinded by searing light and the feeling of disorientation that always accompanied the trip back to his own reality. He suddenly found himself on the toilet in the hotel room at the Grand Floridian and at that moment, everything hit him like a sledgehammer. All the memories of his children as well as Geneva returned all at once which was almost overwhelming. And then it occurred to him that there was something in his hand. It was Savannah's beautiful pocket watch; her most prized possession. The only problem was that he also remembered that he couldn't return it to her as planned and would never be able to do so, either. And the simple reason for that was because he also remembered that she was no longer living.

CHAPTER 25: WHEN THE DREAM ENDS

Sunday, December 18th, 2016

Geneva had just about given up hope. Then, like the magic that it was, light spread its fingers out all around the door to the bathroom, and she knew that Jake had returned. Her excitement drove her up off the bed and to the door in a flash. She couldn't believe he was back but was happier than ever for his return. Perhaps they could now move forward with the rest of their lives together. Perhaps now he was free of his regrets and could love her like she knew he could. Unfortunately, after what she'd learned a few minutes ago, she didn't think that would happen.

"Jake," said Geneva. "Are you OK? I really didn't think you were coming back this time."

"I'm OK Geneva," said Jake after a noticeable pause. "I'll be out in a second, I'm still very disoriented and trying to get my bearings."

"Was this time more difficult than the last two trips?"

"Yes. Give me a second and I'll be out."

Jake's voice sounded weird. She detected some sadness, but there was something else there too. This trip was definitely different from the other two visits. Geneva went and sat on the bed and waited for him. In a few minutes, he emerged from the bathroom wearing his boxer briefs and looking very forlorn. He also appeared to be holding something in his hand. She stood up and embraced him and the hug lasted for a long time. She pulled back to look him in the face and tears had leaked out of the corners of his eyes and made glistening tracks down each cheek. He tried to smile at her, but the smile was quenched by the sadness that was emanating from him like perfume from an old lady on bingo night. The two sat down on the bed and she grabbed his hand.

"Geneva, it's done," said Jake. "This is hard to say to you considering my feelings for you, but I fell in love with Savannah while I was gone. Now that I'm back and see your face again, I realize that I love you both and I feel guilty as hell about that because I have always been a one-woman guy. I'm so sorry, and I appreciate you waiting for me more than I can say."

"Jake, I'm at a loss for words," said Geneva. "I love you too and was in an absolute tizzy when you hit the three-hour mark. I should be angry with you, I suppose, but that's not fair to you. After all, you didn't ask for any of this. Most of all I'm just happy you're back."

"Geneva, I almost stayed. I was even ready to say the words that Calliope taught me up until the last hour or so. Then, for some reason I could feel my children's love from across time and space, and I also felt love from another source as well which I'm pretty sure was you. So, even though I wanted to stay, my ties here were stronger, so I came back. Unfortunately, this trip did not alleviate my regret from the decision not to stay with Savannah all those years ago. Instead, it intensified it ten-fold. I truly wish that I had left well enough alone and most of all, I wish that I never met Calliope." Jake paused, gathering his thoughts. "But all that is past now, Savannah is gone forever, and it's time to move on. Geneva, I can't think of anyone that I'd rather move on with than you."

Geneva wanted nothing more than to embrace him, tell him that they were going to have a wonderful life together, and go back to how things were last night. She loved him more than she could remember loving any man and wanted nothing more than to continue the dream with him for as long as possible. The saddest part however is that she would be living a lie if she didn't share the new information that she had with him now.

"Jake," said Geneva who felt tears sprout in her own eyes, "I would love to move on with you as well, but I need to let you know about something that happened here while you were gone. Trust me, it will make a difference."

"OK, what's up?" Asked Jake.

"When you had been gone about two hours, I suddenly felt an invisible wave of... energy or something pass through me. It was sort of like a shockwave, but unlike a shockwave it made no sound and washed over me rather than knocking me down. It was the weirdest experience of my life and after it happened, I felt and still feel different than I did before, but not in any way that I can describe... just different."

"Wow, that's crazy. Do you think it had something to do with what I did in the alternate reality with Savannah?"

"Yes Jake, I do," said Geneva. "And the worst thing is that I know I'm right." After she said this, she got up, grabbed her phone, and went to the page that was still up on her browser. She then handed the phone to Jake. "You see Jake, Savannah Scott isn't dead, she's very much alive."

Jake looked at the phone and shock was written all over his face. His expression was completely unreadable, but when he saw Savannah's face, his eyes betrayed the depth of love that he had for her, and when that happened Geneva knew that she had done the right thing, even if it tore her apart to do it. Jake was mesmerized with the phone for several minutes, and Geneva understood why because there were lots of pictures of Savannah available all over the Internet. Additionally, it was also clear that he was having trouble believing what he was seeing. After all, it's not every day that a man finds out that someone he was in love with has come back from the dead. He handed the phone back to her and finally spoke.

"Geneva, she's a famous playwright just like she always wanted to be. I must've done something there to change her stars and that makes me feel happy. But I wonder if anything else has changed. I still remember Kira and Jake so they must exist, right?"

"They do, Jake," said Geneva while handing him his own phone. "Your phone has no password so I looked at your contacts. I'm sorry."

"Yeah, I know, new phone," said Jake, "Wow, so even though I obviously ended up with Angela after all, at least I was able to save Savannah's life. However, the reality is that Savannah Scott won't be looking for me because although she may be alive, the only thing that she might remember about me is that I was a nice guy who shared a moment with her when she was young. She won't remember anything that happened on my trip back to see her last night because it never happened in this reality, and there's little chance that she has no one in her life now either. Geneva, like I told you before I love both you and Savannah, and I will probably always have a warm memory of the time I spent with her. But I'm here with *you* now; you're the one who waited for me to come back not once but twice. Geneva, knowing that Savannah is alive is great, but I love you. I'm not going to let you get away."

He went to embrace her, but she stopped him short. It was time to reveal the last piece of information to him. The piece that would likely change how he felt about her for the rest of their lives. Tears were now gushing from her eyes, and her nose was getting stuffy. But she had to tell him, and she wanted to do so because she truly loved him.

"Jake, I hate to say it but you're wrong. Savannah has never married and is not currently seeing anyone according to the gossip websites. But there is no doubt that she remembers everything about you. Look for yourself."

She handed him her phone again, and on it was a tweet from this morning that said the following:

> *@SavannahSmiles75 is feeling very excited about her visit to a tropical paradise on Christmas day. It won't be long before I see you again. I just can't wait!!! #secretlove #worththewait*

"Social media has gone crazy about that tweet, and everyone in the world wants to know who the secret lover is. Jake, I know it's you. She does remember you."

"You may be right and if so, I think I know why," said Jake and then he showed her what had been in his hand the entire time. It was a beautiful pocket watch that looked to be an antique. "She gave this to me before I faded away. I was shocked that it made the trip back, but maybe it tied me to her somehow. Still, she could be talking about someone else."

Geneva met his eyes and although the tears were still flowing from hers in bunches, she still managed to hold it together somehow. "So now both of your loves are alive in the same reality, and you have a decision to make. Sadly, I know what that means for me."

"Geneva, I said that I wanted to move forward with you, and that's what I plan to do. I made my choice years ago, and no one has touched me the way you have since..."

"Since Savannah," said Geneva cutting him off. "Jake, you're an honorable man, and I know you'd stay with me if I asked you to and that's one reason that I love you. But knowing that she's out there and possibly waiting for you will always be in the back of your mind, and I will always be looking over my shoulder for her to appear and take you away. I could've kept all this information to myself, but eventually you would Google her obituary to see her face and when you did, you'd have second thoughts about us that would last forever. It would create another large regret for you and eventually it would destroy us and anything we're able to build together. I saw it in your eyes when you saw her picture on my phone just now; you may love me, but I'm not your soulmate, she is. So, for that reason, I'm letting you go. It's the greatest gift of love that I can give you even if it hurts like hell to do so."

"Geneva, I'm so sorry that you got in..."

"Jake shush," said Geneva putting a finger to his lips and trying to manage a smile through her tears. "Every moment I spent with you was sublime, and like I told you before, I don't regret a thing. Hopefully, I'll find *my* soulmate someday, but to do so I need to find myself first, and that's exactly what I plan to do."

Jake pulled Geneva close, and they embraced for quite some time. Afterwards, she pulled back to look at him one more time through very teary eyes and then kissed him one last time before hugging him once more. She then got off the bed and grabbed her things while Jake jumped up to help her. Once she had everything together, he walked her to the door.

"I'll never forget you Geneva," said Jake. "I also have no regrets about the time we spent together and loved each and every second. I hope you know that I was sincere when I said I loved you... because I do, and I want the best for you always."

"Jake, you're a wonderful man who will always be in my heart. I will love you as long as I live. Maybe our paths will cross again. Take care, lover."

Geneva walked out the door and nearly ran to her room. For one thing, she was still wearing her pajamas and didn't want to be seen but more importantly she was still working hard to constrain the tears that she felt welling up in her like a geyser. She made it to her room just as the floodgates opened and cried for an hour straight. After her emotional release, she then took a shower and packed up. The bride and groom had already departed for the honeymoon, and she figured that when this honeymoon was over, she'd make sure to tell Layla that the time with Jake was great, but she decided to get her life in order and dump Joe before embarking on another relationship. That way, Jake wouldn't look like a jerk and that was important to her because what happened was beyond his control. However, she did decide to keep the specifics about everything that happened those four days to herself forever. After all, who else but Jake or Savannah would believe her?

Geneva packed quickly and made her escape from the resort easily because the rest of the wedding party (sans bride and groom) had gone to O'hana at the Polynesian Resort for brunch before everyone went their separate ways. Geneva texted all the bridesmaids and said that she had to leave early to address a case that required immediate attention. She grabbed an Uber ten minutes after she called it and was soon on the way to Orlando International Airport to see if she could get on an earlier flight. As she rode to the airport she thought about the weird and wonderful wedding week and smiled to herself for the first time in several hours because she finally made peace with what happened. After all, life is nothing more than a series of moments strung together like beads on a child's necklace with all beads being completely different from each other in shape, size, and symmetry. Nothing lasts forever whether it be good or bad, and every great moment must be savored like a fine wine while it lasts and then remembered fondly for how it shaped the entire journey to our ultimate demise and hope for renewal. Geneva looked out the window and remembered some words that she heard from a cruise director on the last night of a cruise. These words were, "don't be sad because the moment is over, be happy that it happened at all." For Geneva, the memory of the time spent with Jake would make her happy for the rest of her life, so she put her sadness away and moved on to her next adventure with light in her heart, and hope in her soul. The dream of being in Jake's arms for the rest of her life may have ended, but the rest of her life was just beginning again, and the ever-resilient Geneva decided to change her future by focusing on happiness first and in doing so, let everything else fall in place around her.

CHAPTER 26: THE PLEDGE

Saturday, December 2nd, 2000

As the blinding light faded away, Savannah realized that Jake was now gone. Everything that he told her was true and he was now somewhere else in time and space and likely inaccessible to her forever. She collapsed to her knees and sobbed like a little girl who just lost her puppy, except that losing Jake was far worse than losing a pet because he was the love of her life. The café wasn't full, but there were about twenty people eating there, so she figured that any moment, someone would come over and see if they could help her. However, after letting loose for several minutes, no one came. She finally looked up to see if everyone had vacated the building for some reason and when she did, a waitress was standing right in front of her. This waitress wasn't the older lady who served them before with a bad attitude and a permanent scowl on her face. Instead, this girl was young and beautiful and had a smile as bright as the light was when Jake faded away several minutes ago.

"Hello Savannah," said the waitress. "My name is Calliope, and I need to talk to you, could you join me in the booth?"

Just then, Savannah noticed that everyone in the diner, the customers, the short order cook in the kitchen, and even the grouchy old waitress, were now frozen in place doing whatever it was they were doing when the world was frozen. It was like she was looking at a three-dimensional snapshot of the scene and it was one of the weirdest things that she had seen in her life with the exception of Jake disappearing of course, that topped everything. She had no idea what to do next.

"What happened to everyone? Why are they frozen?"

"They're not frozen, it's just that we're now interacting at a frequency that is so fast that they seem to be standing still. Could you please stand up and join me in the booth? I have something to tell you that will likely brighten your day."

"Unless you can bring Jake back, nothing you can say will brighten my day," said Savannah still shattered from her loss.

"Savannah, getting you back together with Jake is exactly what I want to talk about," said Calliope with a big smile on her face. With that Savannah stood up, went to the booth where Calliope sat, and took the seat across from her. For some reason she felt super nervous because not only was Calliope a stunningly beautiful girl, she also exuded a certain confidence that is usually associated with famous world leaders or even royalty.

"Calliope... you're a muse, right? Are you the one that sent Jake back in time?"

"The answer to both your questions is yes," said the muse. "I'm impressed that you knew that I was a muse, not many people even remember us at all these days. Bravo!"

"I love the theater, especially plays written in ancient Greece… and your voice is as beautiful as they say. So, Calliope, how do I get him back?" Asked Savannah. "I'll do anything and pay whatever price that is required. Just bring him back to me, OK?"

"Before I tell you how you can be with him again, let me first ask what Jake told you about his trip back in time. How much do you know?"

"He told me that he came from the future and that he was a future version of himself. He also told me about the critical juncture and how he had made a different decision this time. Last, he told me that he couldn't stay and had to return because he had children that he loved in what he called his main reality. And then he just… disappeared in a flash of light. Is this really happening? Am I in a dream?"

"All life is a dream, really," said Calliope. "But if you're asking if you're having the type of dream that happens while sleeping, I can assure you that's not the case. Savannah, in the future Jake becomes a very successful screenwriter. Unfortunately, he loses his creative voice and when that happens, he also loses his ability to produce the beautiful work that he's capable of creating. He becomes blocked from his talent and this block ultimately destroys his marriage and most of his self-worth as well. After watching him suffer, I had to help him."

"So, you sent him back in time to see me, and he made the choice to stay with me in Indianapolis instead of meeting Angela this time. That was the critical juncture, right?"

"Yes, but that's not the only trip back that he made." Said Calliope. "Jake was so burdened by regret that I sent him back to two other critical junctures as well with two other women. Those relationships would have never worked for several different reasons, but I had to show him why and the only way to do that was to send him back to see for himself. This worked perfectly, and after both of these trips, he was finally learning how heavy regret could be and how much better he felt when he let it go. In the end, he realized that neither of these situations would have worked anyway, irrespective of his role in them and that there's no reason to regret something he couldn't control. But you're different Savannah, you're his soul mate. I didn't know for sure when I sent him back to see you, but had a suspicion that was the case, and because of that both your and his realities have now changed completely. Not surprisingly, you need guidance on how to move forward that you didn't require before. So, I'm here to help, and that's what I plan to do."

"OK, then tell me where he is now, I'll go right to him, and we can start again. Please Calliope, it's all I want in the world."

"Savannah, if I could, I would," said the muse sadly. "But it's more complicated than it might appear and if you went to see him now, it would create even more problems. You see, when I sent him back in time, I didn't send him back to an earlier point on his main reality, I sent him to an alternate reality that had nothing to do with his future because in his main life, it never happened. However, when you made love with Jake the other night, the universe reacted by binding your reality with his main reality. In my lifetime, which extends over several thousand years, I've only seen this happen a handful of times and there are only a few things that can trigger this type of merger at all. One of these things is that the universe always seeks balance and when one soul finds its match with another, that balance is achieved, and chaos is kept at bay. So, in essence, the universe wants you and Jake to be together and has bent itself around you to allow that to happen. Your situation is even more unique, because in Jake's main reality, the one that you have become a part of now, you didn't live past 2010. In fact, in most of the alternate realities associated with you, you die young and alone. "

"So, Jake essentially saved me then, right?" Asked Savannah.

"Yes, he did, and in doing so he also changed your future. Even if you never see him again, since he made you feel truly loved, you'll now become the playwright you always wanted to be. Savannah, you will change the world with what you create, and it will definitely be for the better," replied Calliope.

"Wow, that's awesome I guess, but you still haven't told me how I can be with Jake."

"I was getting to that, but you needed to know the impact of what's been done before I move forward. You see, the version of Jake that exists at this moment didn't stay with you. Instead, he remembers changing his mind after you two spent the night with Jake's friends in Indianapolis, with you dropping him off at a hotel where Angela was staying so he could go to Chicago with her instead."

"But Calliope, why does it have to be that way? Why can't I just go back and find him now?"

"Savannah, certainly Jake told you of his children, because without them I'm one hundred percent certain he would have chosen the alternate reality with you. Unfortunately, Angela is the mother of his children."

"And if he doesn't go back to her, then they don't exist, right?" Calliope simply nodded when Savannah said that, and she was becoming more discouraged and less hopeful with each passing moment. She had no idea how Calliope would get her back to him if he was with another woman, especially if they were tied together by children. "So, is he still with Angela in the future? I don't think he'd want me as a love interest if he was."

"The good news for you Savannah is that he isn't with her anymore in the future and is very much unmarried and alone. But even though his critical junction has changed, he won't know about the love that you forged together after the night in Indianapolis until he makes the trip back to you in 2016. So, if you want to be with him again, you'll have to wait until that point in time, but if you do that both you and Jake will finally be able to be together."

Savannah thought to herself for a moment. While she didn't want to wait, it appeared as if she had no choice. Sixteen years alone was a long time, and she knew that she would miss him terribly. In fact, it would be brutal. In the end, she decided he was worth it. She never felt the kind of love that she did when she was with Jake and didn't think she ever would again with anyone else. She would wait.

"OK Calliope, I'll wait," said Savannah. "But how do I know when the time's right to contact him again? More importantly, what do I do if he tries to contact me first? After all, you said I'd be a famous playwright, correct?"

"Savannah, please listen to me carefully. Do not contact him again until December 18th, 2016. If you do, then he may not fall in love with you on his trip to your former reality and may choose another woman instead. Please know that there's someone else who he will develop strong feelings for in late 2016, so it's important that no contact is made prematurely. Otherwise, he may choose her instead and you'll end up alone, despite the efforts of the universe to bring you two together. For this all to work, you need to wait until he falls in love with you completely like he just did. If you have nothing to do with him until then, that's guaranteed, but only if you follow that cardinal rule. As for him finding you first, I'll take precautions to ensure that doesn't happen. Savannah, you agreed to meet him on a specific date and place in the future did you not? Maybe that's the perfect time for this reunion."

"Yes, Christmas Day 2016 in Key West. That's perfect Calliope, I'll mark my calendar, and I'll also make a pledge to not see him again until then. His love is too important to me."

"That sounds like a wonderful plan," said Calliope. "It won't be easy Savannah, and I know you'll have a long wait to see him again, but I promise that it will be worth it. For both of you."

"Thanks Calliope, I think my path is clear from here forward," said Savannah. "I've got a date set and sixteen years to make it as special as possible. I can't wait to see him again."

With that, Calliope stood up and began to walk back to the kitchen. Then, she stopped and turned back to say something else. "You know Savannah, even though you two are soul mates, none of this would've happened had you not given your pocket watch to him when he left you. Even though he changed your path by saving you from dying young, you wouldn't remember your time together at all right now had you not given him something so precious and personal to you. Like everyone else, you would've remembered him leaving you after the night in Indianapolis. Instead, that item bound you to him forever. Savannah, I wish you the best of luck always and I can't wait to partake of the art that you'll create for all of us in the future. Take care."

With that Calliope went into the kitchen and at that point, everyone unfroze and began doing whatever it was they were doing before the freeze. Strangely, none of them came over to ask her if she was OK, so Calliope must've wiped their memories somehow, and they all carried on as if it was a completely normal Saturday night. She got up, dropped $30 on the table, and left. It was time for her to start over with everything and in doing so look towards a future where she could be with her true love again.

* * *

Sunday, December 18th, 2016

As the alarm on her phone went off, Savannah jumped out of bed like an excited child on Christmas morning. She did this because finally, after sixteen years, the time had come to let Jake know that she wanted to keep the date that they set many years ago for her, but only recently for him. It was time to finally begin to think about his arms around her again because up to today, it was too painful to have those thoughts. But today was different, and the sun was a little brighter than ever before and the air was sweeter to breathe. In a few days, she would see her soul mate again and it was now time to show him that she still remembered him and the beautiful moments that they shared during their trip across the Midwest. Beautiful moments that she yearned to experience again.

After she promised Calliope that she would wait for Jake to come back to her in the future, she went home as planned, finished her bachelor's degree in eighteen months, and then got her Master of Fine Arts from Indiana University in another two years. During her time in grad school, she wrote and produced several short one-act plays that were all lauded by critics as well as virtually everyone else that saw them. At the urging of several of her professors, she wrote and produced her first three-act play and although it started on campus in Bloomington, it was an absolute smash that catapulted her back to New York where she'd once been a failure. This time, things were vastly different.

From 2004 to 2014, Savannah wrote and had a hand in producing five three-act plays, and her work was so significant she was now considered in the same breath as luminaries like Arthur Miller and Tennessee Williams by several national critics. Everyone wanted to act in her plays and everything she did turned to gold. Even that bastard Tom reached out to her, and although she agreed to a dinner to gloat a bit, all he really wanted was to take her to bed again... even though he was still with the wife he was supposed to leave for her years ago. This time, Savannah didn't buy into his bullshit although he was still good looking and charming as hell. This time, she had way too much self-love and self-respect. Most importantly however, she also remembered her pledge. She would wait for Jake.

As expected, the media was baffled by the fact that she never dated anyone because Savannah was considered by many to be one of the most beautiful and interesting women in showbiz. She had grown her hair long and had also adopted a rigorous fitness regimen to keep her body toned. Additionally, she read voraciously and had become an accomplished pianist as well, so it was not a surprise many considered her to be the most eligible bachelorette in town. And it drove them crazy that she never seemed to be with anyone anywhere who appeared to be more than a friend. Naturally, there was much speculation about what her preferences were and whether she liked women, men, or possibly both. But in the end, Savannah just found it hilarious that her love life was so interesting to them and just laughed anytime she read the latest rumors on the web. It just wasn't worth getting upset about.

This morning, she planned to send out a tweet that would be understood by one person only, and that person was Jake. So, she typed it up in the way that she'd planned for several days now and sent it off. She then walked into the living room of her gorgeous apartment overlooking Central Park and sat down at the baby grand to practice the song she'd prepared so long ago for the reunion with Jake. She knew every aspect of that song by heart and learning to play and sing it for him was the reason that she took up the piano in the first place fifteen years ago. In seven days, she would see him again, and when she did, she planned on singing more beautifully than

Calliope herself, so she needed one good practice session before she headed south tomorrow to the Florida Keys. She knew that Jake would be there but also planned on sending a few more hints via Twitter in the next few days to make sure. After all, men could be thick, even a good one like Jake.

Savannah began to play and as she did, the words made her smile. Her wait was almost over, and in an eyeblink of time she'd be with him again. Sixteen years ago, Savannah promised a mythical being that she'd wait for Jake and not contact him until today, and she'd made good on her commitment. Soon she'd make another pledge to Jake to never leave him again, and then the paparazzi will finally get what they have been looking for so long and this time she was happy to give it to them. Savannah's love for Jake had not faded one iota in all these years, and she couldn't wait to share it with everyone. She had been a fighter all her life, but it was now time to reap the fruits of her struggle, and no one deserved it more than her.

CHAPTER 27: THE END OF THE RAINBOW

Sunday, December 18th, 2016

After Geneva left his room, Jake just sat there on the bed for a while trying to process all that had happened to him. In real time, it was only four days but considering his "extra temporal activities," he'd actually spent an additional six and a half days in alternate realities during that stretch which made it seem much longer. Additionally, during this timeframe he spent time with four different women and fell in love with two of them so not surprisingly, he was emotionally and physically exhausted.

After staring at a wall for the better part of thirty minutes, Jake finally got up, showered, dressed, and packed up.

He then left the room and went to the lobby to catch an Uber to the airport. Although everyone from the wedding party was invited to a brunch at the O'hana restaurant located in Disney's Polynesian Resort and only a monorail ride away, Jake decided not to go. The bride and groom had already departed for their honeymoon last night, and he said his goodbyes to them before they left. He also decided to text everyone else later and explain that he needed to get home but that he had a great time and hoped to see them all again soon. The fact was that it would be painful to see Geneva. He figured that she wouldn't go either, but he didn't want to chance it, so he slipped out quietly and quickly. His head was an absolute mess right now, and he just wanted to be alone for a while.

Fortune smiled on him because he was able to get on an earlier flight home. Since the holiday travel season was still a day or two away, travel was quite light and even the horrible security setup at the Orlando Airport (which he had also experienced several years ago during a trip to Disney World with Angela and the kids) was very efficient today, and he was through the screening in ten minutes. His flight took off at 2:10 and as soon as the wheels were up, he fell asleep and didn't wake up until they were on final approach to Dulles. He got off the plane quickly, ordered an Uber on the way to the airport exit and was back in his apartment in just over thirty minutes. Jake then ate an early dinner of take-out Chinese food and crashed at 7:00, right after he called Kira and Jake to tell them he was home safe and that he loved them and couldn't wait to see them later this week. He was simply too exhausted to do anything else and his body and mind simply shut down.

The next day he called in and told Cheryl, his boss, that he couldn't come in for personal reasons. He and Cheryl had a great relationship and since she was a compassionate person, she was immediately able to detect that something was wrong with him. When he hung up his phone, Cheryl had approved time off for him until January 2nd, even though he had just taken time off for the wedding. The fact was that Jake was a workaholic, and he knew that Cheryl never doubted for a second that he would more than make up for his time off later. Plus, it was the holiday season, so goodwill was in the air. But in the end, Cheryl was a good leader who could recognize burnout when she saw it, and even though Jake's primary source of exhaustion came from another source, he knew that additional time off was necessary because he certainly felt more than a little crispy.

After calling Cheryl, Jake fell back asleep and slept until noon. He then got up, threw on some sweatpants and a hoodie, watched TV for a while, and ordered a pizza. He had purchased a bottle of wine and a four pack of Pabst Blue Ribbon from the corner store last night but was too tired to drink anything. So, he decided to enjoy the wine with the pizza instead. Sadly for him, even though the food and wine were good, he just couldn't stop thinking about everything that happened over the last several days. He was having trouble processing all the emotions that had assaulted him recently and how much his frame of reference on the nature of reality itself had been altered. The fact that he was in love with two women at the same time also bothered him greatly. He would never have thought himself capable of such a thing, but then again, his recent circumstances were far from normal. Nevertheless, this was still a major issue, so to clear his mind he watched old movies for the rest of the day, drank the PBRs, and crashed at about 7:30.

The next morning, he awakened with newfound clarity after a night full of dreams that he didn't remember very well. He did recall that both Geneva and Savannah were in these dreams, but that was about it as the images were disjointed and told no coherent story that he could remember. However, he figured that it was just part of the mental processing that was required and today, he had finally come to terms with everything that took place over the last week.

The first thing that he decided was that although he did love two women, he was *in love* with only one of them. Although Geneva is a wonderful woman, he realized that there was something different about his connection with her and his connection with Savannah and while he couldn't put his finger on what that difference was, when Geneva told him that Savannah was still alive and then showed him her tweet, his heart skipped a beat. He knew that Geneva picked that up immediately and at that moment, she realized that Jake's connection to Savannah was stronger. Geneva could have dug in and tried to change his mind, and she could've even hidden any information about Savannah from him, but she knew that doing so would never work in the long run. It was like she had already played out every possible relationship scenario with him in her mind already, and that whether Jake reconnected with Savannah in a week, or a month, or a year, that it was inevitable and once they did find each other again, his relationship with Geneva would likely be over. While he didn't know how she knew that would happen, he figured that she saw it in his eyes as they always reveal our true intentions, and women are so much more adept at reading them than men. Geneva did him the ultimate favor by letting him go, and he loved her for that and hoped that the pain that she felt by making that choice would get better soon but knew that it wouldn't because he knew that she loved him, also. She would always occupy a special place in his heart, and he hoped that she would find her soulmate soon because she deserved nothing less.

The other thing that bothered him with the entire situation was whether both he and Geneva had interpreted Savannah's tweet correctly. Although Geneva didn't know it, the part about the tropical paradise did fit, because when he was in the alternate past reality with Savannah, they'd made a deal to meet in Key West on Christmas Day of this year. However, the reality is that lots of people like to go somewhere warm for the holidays, so that in and of itself didn't prove anything. Additionally, the rest of the tweet could've applied to anyone, as Savannah mentioned no name. What made Jake think that something was different this time, were the two hash tags, "#worththewait" and "#secretlove." Those and the fact that she apparently hadn't dated anyone for years led him and probably Geneva as well to the same conclusion; that the message was intended for Jake. However, since he had no proof that Savannah was referring to him and because her personal phone number was likely a carefully guarded secret, he couldn't just call and ask, either. Because of this, he still didn't know if he should make the trip to Key West in a few days because it might be a complete waste of time, and he had to get ready for the visit from his kids that began on the 26th. He just didn't know what to do and he figured that if he didn't go, then maybe he would reach out to Geneva because he still loved her whether she was his soulmate or not.

Jake got out of bed, showered, shaved, and dressed, and then for the first time in days, checked his e-mail. As expected, there were a ton of messages to sift through with most of them being junk mail. However, as he was going through the inbox, one stopped him cold, and he almost didn't want to open it as he was terrified by what the message may contain. After more than two years, Tara Raines had finally sent him a message about doing the adaptation of her book. He finally worked up the courage to click on the message and when he did, it blew him away. The message was short and to the point and said the following:

Dear Jake,

I hope this message finds you well. I know it's been over two years, but I've finally decided that you're the one to do the adaptation of Little Tears. *Please let me know if you're still interested in this project by the 23rd. If it's a go, we can get together after the holidays to work on specifics.*

I really hope you take the job. I want you to be the one that takes this story to the silver screen.

Sincerely,

Tara

Jake was both overjoyed and depressed by this message. On one hand, it was the opportunity of a lifetime because *Little Tears* was still a bestseller today, even though it had been released almost three years ago. It would take him right back to the big leagues and possibly away from formula-driven stories forever. On the other hand, he still hadn't written anything good since 2010 and wasn't sure if Calliope's trips back in time were successful at restoring his creative voice. The only thing to do was to try and see if things were different now. He decided it was time to sit down and write again because if his creativity was still on strike, then there was no reason to go any further with Ms. Raines.

Jake went into the other room and grabbed *Little Tears* from the bookcase and re-read the first five chapters. He had read the book two years ago and loved the story but wanted to refresh his memory on the details. As soon as he was done, he sat down at the computer and made a silent prayer that his creative voice had returned. Unfortunately, that prayer went unanswered because for the next four hours he tried to write the opening scenes five times. In one draft, he overused narration to account for internal monologues that the main character had with herself. In another draft, he tried to use a dream sequence to depict the main character's internal struggle instead of using narration, but the whole thing sounded stupid and trite shortly after he began writing it. The other three drafts were just as bad if not worse, and after he trashed the fifth re-write, he shut the lid on the laptop, grabbed his coat and headed out to clear his head. It seemed that everything that he went through over the last week did nothing to restore access to his talent. He felt like he was at a dead end and after walking for thirty minutes or so, he decided to stop at a sports bar that was a few blocks from where he lived. He went to the bar and as soon as he went to order a beer, time stopped again just like it had done in the gentlemen's club last week as a very familiar bartender walked up to take his order.

"Hello there Jake, what'll it be today?" Asked Calliope in a cheerful tone of voice. "Hemlock maybe? You look awful."

"How would you expect me to look?" Asked Jake in a tone of voice that betrayed his annoyance. "I mean, I was able to clear two large regrets with both Elsa and Penny, but the situation with Savannah was crushing, and the fact that she's alive now ended any hope of a relationship with Geneva. Worst of all, even though I got picked for the job of my life, I still can't write. So, in the end, I wish that I'd never met you at all. In fact, if you could just leave and let me wallow in my own misery for a while, that'd be great. I've had enough. You've failed me Calliope, please just go away."

"I'll be gone soon Jake, but not before you hear what I have to say. First off, if you're honest with yourself, you've learned a lot from the trips back and like you said, two of your largest regrets have been eliminated from your life. You are free from them and whether you realize it or not, that *has* helped you. However, most importantly, you've realized who your true soulmate is and she's now alive and better than ever in this reality. She's within your reach."

"That may be, but I'm having a hard time believing that she'll still be waiting for me sixteen years later, especially considering her level of fame and success. Calliope, even if she does remember what happened with us years ago, she'll only remember it up to the critical juncture where she drops me off at Angela's hotel after our night with Lee and Kathy. Why would she want a washed-up writer? I'm sure she has a better option at this point and that her tweet was meant for someone else."

"Jake, I'm not going to tell you what to do about Savannah," said Calliope. "All I can say is that you made a deal to meet her on Christmas long ago, so maybe you should head to where you two agreed to meet to see if she's remembered more than you think. And about your writing, it's no longer your regrets that are keeping you from becoming the artist that you've always wanted to be."

"OK, so then what is? Why can't I do what used to come so easily?" Asked Jake after a pause. He had no idea where she was going with this.

"Jake, while your regrets have been cleared, you still harbor hatred for someone that you can never fully get away from because she's the mother of your children. For you to move forward you need to forgive Angela for what she did. This will not only make your children happy, it will also finally set you free from the pain of your past. If you do this Jake, you *will* be able to move forward, and I promise that letting go of your hatred for Angela will finally enable you to write again."

Jake sat there for a moment and realized that she was right. What this adventure showed him was that in the end, his love for his children outweighed everything, even a chance to be with his soulmate. Since a part of both children included a part of Angela, if he didn't let go of his anger for her, it would eventually affect his relationship with them, and not in a positive way. He needed to make the call. He needed to be free of his hatred. Most of all, he needed to move on with his life and be happy again.

"I don't know what to say," said Jake, "other than you're

right."

"Of course I am!" Said Calliope. "Jake, I must go, there are others out there that need me, and as you know muses gotta muse!"

"Goodbye Calliope. Will I ever see you again?"

"All I can say, is that the next time that you hold hands with an exotic dancer, you never know what might happen. Go out there and be reborn as an artist. What happens for the rest of your life begins now."

As soon as Calliope said that everyone in the bar unfroze and continued whatever they were doing when he walked in. However, Calliope was gone, and he figured that he'd never see her again. Suddenly Jake realized he never actually ordered a beer, and after thinking about it for a minute or two he decided he didn't want one after all, so he walked back home.

Once back in his apartment, Jake picked up his phone and made the call that Calliope said he needed to make. Angela answered on the second ring, and as expected was shocked to be hearing from him. They talked for almost an hour and in that time, both became emotional. Most importantly, she gave him an apology that he could accept because he knew it was from her heart, and he not only forgave her for what she did but also apologized for pushing her away in the first place. He finally accepted the fact that what happened was not her fault alone. In the end, they agreed to work together moving forward as both wanted the best for their children. They were not yet friends again, but Jake thought that with some work that friendship would be a possibility again in the future and that alone seemed impossible to him only a week ago. Calliope was right, he felt lighter and better than he had in quite some time and when he returned to the laptop after the call was over his writing finally flowed again.

Jake wrote for hours that day, and by the time he

stopped at 3:30 am on the 21st, he had already finished the adaptation for the first ten chapters of Tara's book. Before he crashed, he sent her a message that he would be honored to take the job and then fell asleep feeling better than he had in years. When he finally awakened at about 11:00, he was starving as he had only eaten a frozen meal last night that he found tucked under a bag of ice in the fridge. Tara had already responded to him, and they would be meeting at her home in Texas over the weekend of January 7th. Now he had only one thing left to do, and that one thing was to get to Key West by Christmas.

He initially tried to book a flight, but the prices were sky high, and the flights available had multiple stops, so he decided to drive instead. Initially, he was going to rent a car, but the weather was surprisingly mild for that time of year, so he decided to take the Jaguar instead. Since he'd taken the car to several shows and car events over the summer, it was in good running condition and ready to go. He went to retrieve it, aired up the tires, checked all the fluids, topped off the gas tank, and parked it in his designated spot in front of his apartment. He packed his bag and made sure to grab Savannah's watch because he hoped to return it to her. He walked back to the sports bar where Calliope met him yesterday and had the first decent dinner since returning from Florida and then went to bed early as he was still exhausted from staying up so late the night before. As expected, Calliope wasn't there.

He left home the next morning at 6:00 because he wanted to avoid the traffic in Northern Virginia as it was always bad. He made a clean getaway and passed through Richmond at about 8:00 as the old Jaguar purred along like it was new and not 48 years old. The one modification that Jake had done to the car was to add a modern sound system that looked like it could have been stock. He did keep the old radio if he ever wanted to restore it to original condition, but he needed his music to get him down the road and was happy that he made the change as the miles passed under his tires and the weather stayed nice. He was thoroughly enjoying the ride.

As fate would have it, the halfway point on this sojourn was Savannah, Georgia and for obvious reasons he thought that was a perfect place to stay. He stopped at a Hampton Inn for the night when he got there, had dinner nearby, and then wrote for an hour or so before falling asleep. He didn't leave as early the next morning as he did yesterday, but was still on his way by 8:00 on the 23rd, and as he drove out of town, he played *Savannah* by Relient K. which is more about the city than the girl, but today it was about both. So, as he was leaving Savannah, he was also listening to *Savannah* and thinking about Savannah all at the same time. He just hoped that his hunch about her was correct.

He stopped to have a quick lunch in Port Canaveral, and then he continued to Key West finally pulling into the Westin Key West Resort at 6:35. He checked in to the hotel, unpacked and then went to Irish Kevin's for a Reuben and a couple of pints of Guinness. He then crashed at about 9:00, exhausted from the ride. The next morning, he awakened at about 10:00, and when he looked at Savannah's twitter account as he had done every morning since last Sunday, the following tweet was there:

> *@SavannahSmiles75 says **Words** alone can't explain how much I want to see you again. Seeing your face will be better than any **Nights on Broadway!** So, ask yourself this: **How Deep is Your Love**? #youknowwhoyouare #secretlove #gogreyhound #holidayinn #beastmobile*

Once Jake read these words he knew for sure; Savannah remembered him. He suddenly felt his spirits soar and was filled with more hope for the future than he had felt in a very, very long time. The only thing that he still didn't know was where to find her, but he also knew that she would provide a clue soon as it was obvious to him that she wanted to see him as much as he wanted to see her. This was surprising because how he left must have shocked her as much as she's ever been shocked in her life. But the fact remained that she'd waited for him, and with her looks, Jake was sure that she had no lack of suitors.

Jake got out of bed, put on his clothes quickly, and then set about doing errands. The first thing that he did was to change Kira and Jake's flights from Dulles to Key West. It cost him a fortune, but he didn't care. If things went the way he hoped they would, he'd be able to spend the holidays with the three people he loved the most.

He then went out and did Christmas shopping for his kids and Savannah as well. Key West has no shortage of cool little shops and stores, and he was able to find something nice for all of them. He even remembered to decorate his room because he also felt more holiday spirit than he had in years.

Finally, he went out for a "Cheeseburger in Paradise" at Jimmy Buffett's before returning to the hotel, working out in the gym for an hour or so and then showering and going to bed. Like a child, he laid there, unable to sleep. However, Santa Claus for him was a beautiful blonde who also happened to be his soulmate. He finally fell asleep after watching *How the Grinch Stole Christmas* followed by *Love Actually*. After the second movie, he finally felt sleepy and fell asleep but for some reason, that night he didn't dream.

He left the bathroom window in his room open and was awakened early on Christmas day by the roosters that are plentiful in Key West. He tried to get back to sleep for quite a while, but it didn't work, so he got out of bed and was dressed and ready for the day just as the sun cleared the horizon. He didn't know what to wear, so he just put on khakis with Topsiders and a fitted white t-shirt. He figured he'd go Key West style all the way. He found himself pacing in his room, so he took a long walk and grabbed breakfast, but by 9:30, he still hadn't heard a thing from Savannah so he walked to the Hemingway House thinking she might be there. Surprisingly, it's open 365 days a year, so he took a tour and bought a copy of *The Sun Also Rises* on his way out. And then, just as he was just about to lose his mind with anticipation, he got the tweet that he had been waiting for:

> *@SavannahSmiles75 says Merry Christmas to all!!! Jake, if you're here* ***Run to Me****. If you know where to throw a coin into the grouper's mouth, then you'll know where I'll be.*

Jake knew that he had to figure this out quickly, so he asked a few people who told him that it was Captain Tony's Bar which was otherwise known as the original Sloppy Joe's. He got directions from the person who told him the name of the bar and then ran, just as she asked him to, to the famous Key West landmark. When he got there, the bar was closed, so he began banging on the door like a madman. He wouldn't be denied. The door opened and an enormous bouncer poked his bald head out.

"We're closed for a private Christmas Party," said the large man. "Come back tomorrow."

"No," said Jake, "I'm supposed to be here! My name is Jake DiVincenzo, please tell…"

"Jake, you say?" Asked the man, cutting him off. "If you're really Jake, then what kind of car is called the Beast-mobile?"

"It's a 1972 Oldsmobile Delta 88," said Jake, "with the longest doors ever put on a car."

"Why didn't you just say that earlier?" said the big guy who now wore a smile on his face. "She's on the stage waiting at the piano."

Jake walked into the building which was empty except

for the bouncer at the door, the bartender, and most importantly, a smiling Savannah who was sitting at the piano just like the bouncer said. She looked radiant with hair that was much longer now and wearing a form-fitting red dress that was strapless and a Santa hat on her head. While he knew that he had aged over the last sixteen years, she hadn't at all, and her smile made him weak in the knees like a seventh grader who was slow dancing for the first time. He never thought he'd ever see her again and there she was, more beautiful than ever.

"Merry Christmas, Jake," said Savannah. "I've spent fifteen years learning this song. It's now my gift to you."

After she said that, she began to sing the classic Bee Gees song, *Run to Me* and not only did it fit the situation perfectly, out of the entire Bee Gees catalog, it was Jake's favorite song. She played the piano like she'd been playing all her life, and she sang so beautifully that Jake didn't think that Calliope or even Barry Gibb himself could have sung it better. The notes flooded his ears and floated around his head until the tears began flowing out of his eyes in buckets. The bartender brought him a napkin and smiled at him as she finished the song. It was truly the best Bee Gees song that he had ever heard. She got up from the piano, walked over to him and then kissed him. He had never felt happier in his life. After the kiss she pulled back to look at him and her eyes were wet, also.

"You kept your promise," said Savannah. "So, what do you say Jake, are you ready for more adventures with me?"

"I couldn't think of anything that I'd want more. I do have one question, why did you wait for me? How'd you know I'd come back to you?"

"Let's just say that a certain muse may have told me right after you disappeared sixteen years ago. She also said that I was your soulmate, so I pledged to wait for you, and you certainly didn't disappoint. We are finally at the end of the rainbow Jake, and you're my pot of gold."

"Savannah, I have something for you," said Jake who then reached in his pocket, pulled out her watch, and put in in her hand. "I'm so happy to be able to return it. I love you; you know."

"Jake, having this back means the world to me, thanks for keeping it safe," said Savannah who hugged and kissed him again. "And I love you more than I can say."

"So where do we go from here?" Asked Jake.

"Anywhere you want to, my love. After all, it's Christmas."

And with that, their two souls became one once more as they found each other again as they had in ages before, and the sun smiled on both as they walked out of Captain Tony's and down to Mallory Square. When they got there, Jake took Savannah into his arms as they looked out on the seemingly endless expanse of water that stretched out in front of them, and as they stood there basking in the glory of the reunion that Jake never thought he would have, three dolphins surfaced nearby as if Poseidon himself had sent them. And somewhere not far away a muse who sometimes posed as an exotic dancer watched them together and smiled to herself at the satisfaction of a job well done. She knew that the light that Jake could put out into the world was no longer blocked by hate and regret, and for today at least, darkness was kept at bay.

The End

EPILOGUE

Monday, December 18th, 2022

Geneva awakened early to a chilly New Mexico morning with an overcast sky. While there was no precipitation falling at that moment, rain, sleet and/or snow was forecasted later in the day. Because of this, she figured that it was probably a good idea to take Socrates, her Border Collie, on a hike with her this morning as she certainly didn't want to have to deal with a wet dog if they went later. Geneva purchased a cozy cabin in Ruidoso five years ago last August, after she quit her job at the law firm that she was with in Philly and decided to make a radical job change. Instead of litigating, writing briefs, and negotiating contracts, she now used a brush and canvas to make her living as she had decided to pursue her dream of being an artist full-time, and fortunately for her, this career change had worked out well so far and was only getting better.

Geneva put a leash on Socrates and then jumped into

her Jaguar SUV for the twenty-minute drive to her favorite trail. It was a loop of just under eight miles, and Socrates loved to walk with her there whenever they went which was usually at least once a week. When they got to the trail, Socrates eagerly left the car and ran to the trailhead while Geneva grabbed her Patagonia jacket, locked up the vehicle, and then walked to where the dog was waiting while eating a protein bar. It was chilly, so she set a strong pace, not even waiting for Socrates when he marked a tree. Of course, he was well trained and caught up to her quickly each time and was never too far away. He was a great dog, and she was happy to have him in her life. Especially on this day, because it was the last day that she ever saw Jake, and she still felt sad about it each year. Even though their time together only comprised four days in her life, she still thought of him often, and on December 18th, she thought of him the most of all.

After she'd returned from Layla and Lawrence's wedding six years ago, she did what she said she would do and broke up with Joe. He begged and pleaded with her to give their relationship another chance, but after her time with Jake, she knew that they weren't right for each other and that they never would be. So, she moved out when their lease was up and decided to put him in her rear-view mirror for good. Fortunately, he stopped calling after a few weeks and finally seemed to accept that they were finished as a couple. The last thing that she knew about Joe was that he found another flight attendant a year or so later and that they were married six months after that. Even though she didn't want to be with him, she was glad that he found happiness with someone because since her time with Jake, she certainly hadn't.

As she and Socrates moved along the trail, she asked herself the same question that she had asked herself every year on this date: did she do the right thing by letting Jake go? On one hand, she was angry with herself for not fighting harder to convince him that she was the one he should be with and not Savannah Scott. After all, they were compatible in so many ways and their attraction to each other was off the charts as well. Unfortunately, when a man goes back in time and brings a former love back to life, convincing him that you're the one for him is a tall order. And when she saw the look on his face after she showed him Savannah's tweet that morning, she knew that for her, the game was over. So, just like she did in each of the last five years, Geneva decided that she'd done the only thing that she could do, and even though her rational self was always satisfied each time she went through this annual mental exercise, it still didn't make her feel better from an emotional perspective.

Since that day six years ago, Geneva hadn't seen or even communicated with Jake again. Since Savannah was a public figure, she knew that they had gotten married, and as strange as it seemed to her, she found herself happy for them. However, at least for now, Socrates was the only "man" in Geneva's life although before she moved to New Mexico, she did date a junior partner in her old firm for a while before she decided to leave the East Coast and pursue what she'd always wanted to do. The relationship lasted three months, but her passion for painting only grew, and not unexpectedly to anyone who knew her, she'd excelled with that endeavor.

Geneva had always been good at drawing, so after she hung up her barrister robes, she took the money that she'd saved for several years and decided to move somewhere where she could immerse herself in her artwork and although she'd initially targeted Santa Fe, when she visited Ruidoso, she fell in love with that place immediately. She loved to sit outside and have her coffee each morning while breathing in the cool air that was filled with the scent of evergreens. Of course, the best news was that she was close enough to Santa Fe to be able to take advantage of the artist community there and the copious amount of wealthy Californians that regularly visited to buy what she was offering. So, the volume of her sales had increased with each passing year. In fact, she was even able to sell quite a few of her paintings during the COVID-19 pandemic which was better than many could say during that awful time in world history. As a result, Geneva was mostly happy with her life now, even though her loneliness seemed to be getting worse all the time. She truly hoped that would change.

Geneva and Socrates finished the trail loop, and she headed home. On the way, she remembered that the dog was low on kibble, so she diverted her trip to the grocery store to retrieve a bag of dog food and a few other odds and ends. They went into the store and for some reason, Socrates seemed very anxious to get to the pet food aisle. When they got to that aisle, she saw why because there was a beautiful Australian Shepherd there, and that pretty doggie seemed equally enthusiastic about meeting him as well.

"Matilda, heel!" Said the very attractive dark-haired gent that appeared to be the other dog's owner. "I'm so sorry, she's been cooped up in her carrier for a few days and has been brutal to deal with today."

"Not a problem, Socrates always seems to know where the ladies are," said Geneva. "You look lost, do you need a hand?"

"Bloody hell, is it that obvious?" He asked with a chuckle as he finally was able to control his dog. "Are you South African?"

"Guilty as charged," said Geneva. "And you're an Aussie... from Brisbane I think, right?"

"You hit it on the nose! I'm Liam, and this is..."

"Matilda, yes, I know," said Geneva cutting him off. He had the most beautiful blue eyes and a wonderful smile also. "Are you visiting my little mountain hideaway on business or pleasure?"

"Actually, I'm here on business for the just this evening," said Liam. "I'll be moving on in the morning. Listen, if you could help me figure out what kind of food to get for Matilda, I'd be more than happy to repay you with dinner tonight. You can even bring your husband; I'd just love some company as I'm traveling alone."

"I'm not married."

"Brilliant! It's a date, then! Do you know a place where a bloke can get a good steak?"

"The Texas Club at the Innsbrook Resort is good, I'd go there if I was looking for a steak. Unfortunately, I'm meeting a potential client at five, so I'll likely be busy for dinner," said Geneva who then pointed to a bag on the lower shelf. "Oh, and this is the kibble that Socrates loves, so you should get it for Matilda. Best thing is that it's organic."

"My meeting is at five as well, are you sure you don't want to meet after?" Asked Liam. "I'm damned fine company, you know."

"Best not," said Geneva. "My clients usually like to take their time when they come. I wouldn't want to leave a hungry Aussie waiting."

What a pity," said Liam. "Oh well, Matilda will keep me company. But if you change your mind, my last name is Manchester, and I'm staying at the Ruidoso River Resort."

"You never know, let's just see what fate has in store. It was very nice to meet you Liam, maybe we'll see each other again. Have a great visit in Ruidoso."

"I really hope so, and thanks for the help with food for both me and my girl Matilda. By the way, what did you say your name was?"

"I didn't," said Geneva who then smiled and turned to walk away from him after she grabbed her own bag of dog food. She stopped to look back once more. "Take care, blue eyes."

She paid for the kibble, loaded it and Socrates into the SUV, and on the way home she thought that perhaps she should have taken Liam up on his offer. After all, she hadn't had any sort of date in over a year and had no important relationships since her four days with Jake. Additionally, she was very attracted to him physically and he seemed to have a good energy about him as well. But it was still December 18th, and because of that she chose to wallow in her own misery instead.

Geneva walked into her house at about 2:30, fed and watered the dog, and decided to lay down for an hour or so before she got ready for her meeting at 5:00. She had no idea who was coming to meet her and didn't even know if it was a woman or a man. Apparently, Angie, the manager at the gallery where she displays and sells her works in Santa Fe, had been contacted by the personal assistant of a "prominent art collector that preferred to remain anonymous until mutual interest was established." Initially, Geneva refused the meeting because of this anonymity, but after Angie told her that $30,000 had already been wired to the gallery for a triptych that Geneva recently had displayed there, she decided to meet this mystery person. To be safe, she also told Luther, the neighbor across the street, to keep an eye on her place while the visitor was there. He was a retired New Mexico state trooper, so he told her he'd clean his revolvers on his front porch until she texted him that everything was OK.

Geneva napped for just over an hour, and then showered, did her hair and makeup, and got dressed in jeans with a while cable knit sweater. She also threw on her Merrell hiking boots and poured herself a glass of Cakebread chardonnay. Her mystery buyer would be arriving in five minutes if he or she was on time, so she decided to start the gas fireplace as it was getting colder as night fell. Right on cue, the knock on the door came, and when she opened it, she was looking into a familiar set of eyes.

"Well... hello there!" Said an excited looking Liam. "So, you're Geneva DeHaan? There are no pictures on the internet, so I expected a ghastly hag... but you're definitely not..."

"Not a hag?" she asked rhetorically and cutting him off with a smile. "Wow, what a silver tongue you have Mr. Manchester. Oh, and I like my privacy and would rather have my buyers focus on the art first and the artist second, so I don't post pictures of myself. Would you like to come in?"

"Drat, that didn't go well, did it?" Said Liam as he walked into her house and stood there awkwardly. "I'm sorry, I really need sleep, as there was too much travel last week. How about this instead: Hello, my name is Liam Manchester, and I collect art because I've nothing better to do right now. I absolutely love your paintings and would like to buy them all. But as beautiful as they are, I simply cannot put the art before the artist, because Geneva, you are certainly one of the most gorgeous creatures that I've ever seen, and I really think you should let me take you to dinner, so we can discuss fair compensation."

"For my art, or for me?" Asked Geneva playfully. She loved how he stumbled on his words... it betrayed a sweetness in him that she'd only seen in Jake. She was also very attracted to him.

"Both, really, if possible," he said. "Geneva, my fiancé left me at the alter six months ago and shortly thereafter my Da passed unexpectedly. The good news for me is that I've just inherited more money than I could've ever imagined, but I don't know what to do with myself, so I fly all over the world buying art. Initially, Matilda and I were going to stop here for two days only and then go to Napa Valley for six months or so until my visa expires. But I think that my plans could easily be diverted to New Mexico instead."

"Where is Matilda, by the way?"

"She's back at the hotel with a dog sitter," said Liam. "Had I known it was you I was meeting, I would have brought her along. But maybe it's better she's not here so our dinner will be quieter."

"Liam, if I'm going to go to dinner with you this evening, I need to ask you a question and you need to answer honestly, OK?"

"Sure, what would you like to know?"

"How many times have you thought about having sex with me since you met me in the store?" Geneva saw him blush a bit after she asked this and thought that was adorable as well. She just smiled wider.

"Wow, that's quite a question, why would you want to know that?" Replied a very shocked Liam. She knew she had thrown him off-guard.

"I'm just trying to gauge your level of attraction for me. So, what's your answer?"

"Bollocks, I know I'll booger this up. Bloody hell woman, you sure know how to throw a man off his game. Anyway, if I'm being honest, and you really want to know, I already envisioned us in my bed back at the resort. You should answer the question as well, it's only fair."

"Maybe I'll tell you at dinner... or maybe you'll find out after dinner, it all depends how you play your hand... as they say. I'll get my coat."

"Perfect, you're quite a girl, you know," said Liam who seemed as excited as a little boy on his name day. "How are you still single?"

"Maybe when we get to know each other better, I'll tell you that story as well," said Geneva who walked over to Liam after donning her coat and kissed him with all her might. It was wonderful and all at once Geneva realized that she may have finally found who she was looking for in this life because the kiss felt even better than the first one did with Jake. Maybe this is what true soulmates felt.

"You're just full of surprises, aren't you? Why did you do that?"

"I had to be sure you were the one."

"And?"

"I'm sure."

Geneva and Liam jumped into the rental SUV that he was currently driving, and he selected the first song for their ride to dinner which was *Empress* by Snow Patrol. She grabbed his hand, and he smiled at her as they pulled out of her driveway. Just as she had lost hope that she would ever meet anyone who could touch her heart the way Jake did, someone had come into her life that seemed to have the potential to complete her. Although they had just met, there was a certain way about how he looked at her that made her feel as if they would never be apart again.

Yes, it was December 18th, the day that she'd reserved for sad movies and ice cream for the last five years. However, on this particular December 18th, she finally felt as if her desire to love another person had been reborn. And in this resurrection, the universe smiled and laughed and raised its metaphorical glass to the one axiom that was constant in all realities for all time. And that is that everything does indeed happen for a reason.

SONG LIST

(In order of appearance)

The Frog Prince by Keane
I Know About You by Dashboard Confessional
Iris by The Goo Goo Dolls
Words by Boyzone
Love You Inside Out by The Bee Gees
*I Started a Jok*e by The Bee Gees
Night Fever by The Bee Gees
Closer by Travis
To Love Somebody by The Bee Gees
Afternoon Delight by The Starland Vocal Band
Massachusetts by The Bee Gees
A Bad Dream by Keane
Why Does It Always Rain on Me by Travis
Shiny Happy People by R.E.M.
(You Want To) Make a Memory by Bon Jovi
Only Time by Enya
Come to Me by The Goo Goo Dolls
All You Need Is Love by The Beatles
Is This Love? by Bob Marley and the Wailers
How Deep is Your Love? by Bee Gees

Words by The Bee Gees
Savannah by Relient K
Run to Me by The Bee Gees
Empress by Snow Patrol

PRAISE FOR AUTHOR

"Refreshingly witty, and well written. An excellent read, creatively written to keep you wanting to read more. I highly recommend this book."

"Fun read and difficult to put down at times. The author did a great job of making me turn the page."

"A once in a lifetime novel reminding us to cherish very second of every moment...a true must read"

"How could you go through life without reading 'Last Exit to Fate' by K. Turk Osman. A deeply well written classic in the making connecting the reality of life with the true belief that all should cherish and capture lifes moments no matter how small. This wonderful author created a true to life classic driven by the human nature to find the "one" while learning to cope with the apparent loss. A true must for all!!"

"Amazing!"

- LAST EXIT TO FATE

BOOKS BY THIS AUTHOR

Last Exit To Fate

Join Drew Phillips and Emmy Lee as they explore many beautiful locations in Western Europe as they fall in love despite challenging circumstances. Follow Drew to both the pinnacle of happiness, and the depths of sorrow as he tries to do the one thing in life that makes it worth living. That is finding his soulmate again once she is lost to him, where finding her is nothing that he would ever expect.

HOLDING HANDS WITH AN EXOTIC DANCER

www.ingramcontent.com/pod-product-compliance
Lightning Source LLC
LaVergne TN
LVHW010637110826
845149LV00014B/2864